MIDNIGHT INTERLUDE

Rosaleen's masked rescuer tightened his hold on her and began walking toward the cottage. Truly uneasy now, Rosaleen began to struggle hard. However, he just kicked open the cottage door with his booted foot and strode in with her still in his arms.

When he set her on her feet, he held her wrists above her head with one hand, then reached into the folds of his cape and pulled out the sword from the scabbard on his hip. He cut the rope binding her hands while blocking her way to the door.

Rosaleen swallowed. "My father will pay you a great deal if you return me to him unharmed."

Close to her now, he whispered, "Wouldn't your *husband* pay more to get his wife back?"

Instantly Rosaleen became more alert. She inhaled the scent of sandalwood. It was him!

Stunned by her discovery, she tried to think. Why would he be keeping his identity from her. Was it to punish her for breaking her word? She fumed, stamping her booted foot. "Kill me then and have done. Finish what you came for."

"That I will," he said in a gruff voice. He stepped back and raised his foil threateningly.

"Strip," he ordered.

LET ARCHER AND CLEARY
AWAKEN AND CAPTURE YOUR HEART!

CAPTIVE DESIRE (2612, $3.75)
by Jane Archer

Victoria Malone fancied herself a great adventuress and student of life, but being kidnapped by handsome Cord Cordova was too much excitement for even her! Convincing her kidnapper that she had been an innocent bystander when the stagecoach was robbed was futile when he was kissing her until she was senseless!

REBEL SEDUCTION (3249, $4.25)
by Jane Archer

"Stop that train!" came Lacey Whitmore's terrified warning as she rushed toward the locomotive that carried wounded Confederates and her own beloved father. But no one paid heed, least of all the Union spy Clint McCullough, who pinned her to the ground as the train suddenly exploded into flames.

DREAM'S DESIRE (3093, $4.50)
by Gwen Cleary

Desperate to escape an arranged marriage, Antonia Winston y Ortega fled her father's hacienda to the arms of the arrogant Captain Domino. She would spend the night with him and would be free for no gentleman wants a ruined bride. And ruined she would be, for Tonia would never forget his searing kisses!

VICTORIA'S ECSTASY (2906, $4.25)
by Gwen Cleary

Proud Victoria Torrington was short of cash to run her shipping empire, so she traveled to America to meet her partner for the first time. Expecting a withered, ancient cowhand, Victoria didn't know what to do when she met virile, muscular Judge Colston and her body budded with desire.

Available wherever paperbacks are sold, or order direct from the Publisher. Send cover price plus 50¢ per copy for mailing and handling to Zebra Books, Dept. 3588, 475 Park Avenue South, New York, N.Y. 10016. Residents of New York, New Jersey and Pennsylvania must include sales tax. DO NOT SEND CASH.

MARY BURKHARDT
MIDNIGHT HEAT

ZEBRA BOOKS
KENSINGTON PUBLISHING CORP.

To the memories of my dear aunts, Margaret and Mary Donovan of Oswego, New York. May they now experience the joy they gave so readily to others, even through all the difficult times in this life.

ZEBRA BOOKS

are published by

Kensington Publishing Corp.
475 Park Avenue South
New York, NY 10016

First printing: November, 1991

Printed in the United States of America

Chapter One

Kinsale, Ireland, July 1762

Rosaleen O'Rahilly saw her mother stop speaking with Vicar Nigel Somerset and motion her over.

Millicent's smile faded upon noticing the puffy bluish mark on the creamy smoothness of the ten-year-old's jaw. "Not another scuffle with your brothers and Fitzroy cousins, Ross."

"It was an accident, Mama. I was the admiral, and my ship was attacked by bilge rats. Had to carve their gizzards." She made a slicing motion with her right hand along her slender throat. "Then I had them drawn and quartered before we could put them in irons," she rattled on, puffing out her flat chest. "My cousins, I mean my men, caused a little mutiny, but I put that down quick enough with a cannonball in their grimy guts."

The vicar appeared shocked by the child's colorful language. The full-bottomed, powdered wig and two white tabs at Nigel's throat contrasted sharply with his black coat and knee breeches. "Bless my s-s-soul if she doesn't take after her father. Fergus Mulcahy

5

was always patching Taggart up after a s-scrape . . . when he wasn't . . . ah, indisposed," Nigel stuttered. "Hear the old Fitzroy retainer s-still finds excuses to visit the barn to soak his tonsils in whiskey."

Appearing ready to bestow a pearl of wisdom, the middle-aged man continued. "You should, my lady, encourage your daughter to take up cataloging mushrooms. Nothing like getting out in the open air, communing with God's earth—it keeps one out of mischief. My nephew, Lucien, is bright, studies science, treks about with me, and the lad knows more than I do about herbs and plants. Why, I lose track of time and all the troubles of this world when I dig fungus from the dirt. Mushrooms have a restorative power. I've even s-sent some over this month to get Calvert on his feet. With the practical care of Dr. Liam Collins and my mushrooms in that lamb stew he likes, my brother-in-law's stomach pains will soon depart; Calvert will be a new man in two weeks, mark my words."

Nigel peered down at the Irish girl. "My dear child, you should be with the other little girls near the earl's rose garden. Boy's rough play is no place for the niece of Dunstan Fitzroy."

"Yes, sir." For her mother's sake, Rosaleen attempted to stifle her true nature in the face of another bout of adult criticism against her behavior. "But, Vicar," she tried, "all the girls wish to do is dress their dolls and fuss over their samplers. I do not like embroidery. Pirating is more fun."

"Dear me . . . upon my soul." The flustered Englishman gave the child's mother a look of sympathy. "The girl must be a trial for you, my lady. She is so . . . so unusual." Then his features brightened. "Yes,

6

get young Rosaleen out digging mushrooms, and she'll never be in a fracas again. Hey, what?"

"I dare say," was all Millicent added. "Pray excuse me, Vicar. I shall put a cold cloth on Ross's bruised face. That should make it hurt less. Come along, dear."

Rosaleen pulled back after the two of them were away from the Anglican clergyman. "Not needed, Mother. It doesn't hurt."

"As you wish," Millicent conceded with a long sigh.

Half an hour later, Rosaleen noticed the tall, handsome teenage lad again as he stood near a boxwood hedge. The boy reminded her of a golden Apollo from her storybooks. When he'd arrived earlier with his mismatched parents, she'd missed being introduced to him. His elderly father, Calvert, dressed in a longer waistcoat and fuller outer coat no longer in fashion, returned Taggart and Millicent O'Rahilly's warm greeting. However, never had Rosaleen seen her father and mother so coolly formal as when they addressed Calvert's much younger wife, Garnet Huntington. It still confused her because the duchess appeared enchanting—blond, cornflower-blue eyes, dainty features outlined with delicate ruffles of her aqua gown. When Garnet had taken Rosaleen to play with the other children, the colonial girl had been whisked away on a delightful cloud of blue silk, lace, and the intoxicating scent of white roses. Now, among the playing children, Rosaleen noticed this English couple's son appeared unsure of how to act with her and her brothers. Always one to tackle problems head-on, she went over first and motioned him to the side, away from the others. When the lad did not follow her into an empty area behind two taller yews, she whispered, "Over here, come on." The dimple at the right corner of her mouth softened her directive.

Shrugging his shoulders, Lucien followed. What strange creatures these American colonials were, he thought.

"My name is Rosaleen O'Rahilly. My parents grew up here, though this is my first visit to Ireland." She gave the boy a friendly smile, then curtsied gracefully as her mama had taught her. "Now it is your turn."

With the reserve his mother had drummed into him, Lucien looked down at the short girl with the impudent dark eyes. "Hasn't your mother instructed you that proper young ladies do not invite gentlemen to meet them behind secluded shrubbery?"

"But there are hordes of people all around us. Why wouldn't it be proper?"

He peered down his slender nose at her once more. "As a gentleman, I cannot explain it to you," he added loftily, not wishing to confess he wasn't sure of all the details himself.

Rosaleen appeared perplexed. "You're not a gentleman; you are a boy like my brothers."

"I am a marquis."

"Is that higher than a sea captain?"

A disdainful snort came from the marquis' direction.

Used to being the center of attention in Williamsburg, Rosaleen did not understand why this young man was making her feel uncharacteristically gauche. She looked down at the grass stain on the bottom of her pink and white striped gown. Did he notice it, too? He was staring at her as if she were something a groom had mucked out from one of the horse barns at home.

Her dark head snapped up. "I was only trying to be nice to you, to introduce you to my family. My mama says kindnesses are always more important than . . . than prac . . . prattlecall." Her small chin jutted up at a slight angle. "But I dare say she never met you."

"The word is 'protocol,' " corrected Lucien, but he smiled despite himself.

"Harumph." She turned to leave.

"Miss O'Rahilly. Wait. Please." This open offer of friendship was difficult for him. Lucien suddenly felt chagrined by the girl's set-down. Not understanding why, he wanted the black-haired girl to stay.

Rosaleen turned about to face him, but her gaze was wary.

Lucien removed his right glove and doffed his tricorn hat. Holding both items in front of him, he bent from the waist and executed a perfect bow. "My name is Lucien Huntington, Marquis of Raythorn. Your servant, Miss O'Rahilly."

"Pleased to meet you. I accept your apology for your earlier rudeness."

The blond head snapped up with the return of his military posture. "I made no such apology."

"You regret the words, don't you?"

It was disconcerting to meet someone who could read his feelings so accurately. "Well, yes, but I never said—"

"What does your father do?" she interrupted.

The marquis blinked. Her question had no meaning for him. "My father is a duke."

9

"Well," she pressed, "what does a duke do?"

No one had ever confronted him with such a question. It took the English boy a moment to reply. "We live in London part of the year and Paris, with summers spent in Ireland. I enjoy chemistry," he went on, amazed he was opening to anyone in this manner. "I have a small laboratory here that my father helped me furnish because Mother will not allow it in our other homes. There is a microscope on the table and glass bottles. My uncle Nigel, I mean Reverend Somerset, is a smashing help with collecting me leaves and plants to study, though he prefers mushrooms. Father says our cook's lamb stew with Nigel's mushrooms before bed is the only thing he can digest these days. Father has arranged for me to go to Cambridge in a few years." He stopped. Never had he chatted on so about himself at one time. He felt the light features of his face warm. Would this girl think him an idiot to go on so?

Having listened with interest, Rosaleen's dark eyes still mirrored her confusion. "But how does your papa earn the money to take such good care of you?"

"He does not earn money; we just have it."

"Sounds dishonest. My papa works hard in a big office behind our house above the James River in Williamsburg. He has a bunch of ships that sail all over the world, buying silks, molasses, sugar, tea, coffee. He runs a huge plantation where we grow tobacco, along with cotton. The tobacco pays for our clothes and food. My mama takes care of us, sees to the black people when they get sick, and helps with the old people in town. I've been to Governor Fauquier's palace, and Papa and Mama have gone to balls there."

"With all their activities, it is a miracle your parents find the time to raise four children," Lucien commented with unveiled sarcasm. "I am an only child."

"Oh, I'm truly sorry."

"I do not have to share with anyone," he countered, feeling defensive but not knowing why this forward little girl could be the cause.

"That's probably why you're so unfriendly."

"Will you kindly stop calling me names. God's teeth," he grated with unusual lack of formality. "Are they raising you like a savage in the colonies?"

"I am not a savage. Take it back," she ordered, her cheeks puffing out with the first sign of anger. "You're the meanest, coldest boy I've ever met. If all English aristocrats are like you, no wonder the Irish here hate you. My papa says I can visit Uncle Dunstan any summer I want. Why, I'll come back to Kinsale and get all the Irishmen together, and we'll chase the lot of you toffee-nosed English right into the Irish Sea, just like when St. Patrick drove the snakes out."

"That is treasonous," her companion whispered, horrified at the girl's remarks.

"Go call the magistrate, then. I wouldn't be surprised if you had them hang me by the neck here in Uncle Dunstan's flower garden, right over the punch bowl. I've heard about your English laws against Catholics. You won't allow them to go to school, and you're horrid to their priests."

"But the earl of Holingbrook and his family are Anglican. You . . . you are a Catholic?"

He might have been calling her a vile name the way he'd said it. Dark brown eyes challenged blue. "I am,

11

and so's my family; even my English mother goes to Mass with us at our private chapel at home."

Lucien knew his own mother would not approve at all if she saw him speaking to a Catholic. Anglican, she always said, was the only proper church for an Englishman. Catholics were not to be trusted. He made a motion to leave, though he did not like himself for going in this manner.

"That's right, run away, English boy. And I stand by what I said. You're rude and a pansy-dressed coward to boot."

At these last words, Lucien's black leather pumps almost skidded on the moist grass when he abruptly halted his retreat. Never could the marquis remember experiencing such strong emotions. During these last few moments, this slip of a girl had managed to insult him and his family, questioning everything he stood for.

He bounded back at her.

When she saw the look in Lucien's blue eyes, Rosaleen stepped back a pace, then chided herself for showing such temerity. "Well, Lucifer, perhaps 'coward' was a bit hasty."

His jaw hurt from grinding hard on his back teeth. "The name is Lucien." His cultured speech became more clipped. "It is a French name my mother chose."

At the moment, he did appear like a golden, formidable devil to Rosaleen. However, fear always made her more determined to stand her ground. "You live off the work of others. Why, a gin-soaked rummy probably isn't as idle as you." Vaguely, she wondered if a marquis could have her tried for treason. She swallowed.

12

"You, Miss O'Rahilly, are the . . . the most irritating girl I have ever had the misfortune to meet." The hands below the ruffles at his wrists clenched and unclenched. "Gypsy," he said in a higher octave, before turning on his heel to exit with what little dignity remained. He pulled on his leather gloves, then shoved the three-cornered hat back on his blond head. "Rag-mannered savage," he muttered.

There, he called her "savage" again after she'd ordered him not to. With a reflex action born from unleashed temper, Rosaleen crouched down and grabbed two huge handfuls of grass and mud. She hurled the muck at the marquis' back.

The wad hit him squarely in the center of his gold silk coat. At first Lucien could not believe the chit had dared this new outrage.

When Rosaleen saw the pair of black shoes and white hose stalking back to her, she was prepared for a second attack. With practiced skill, the girl tossed the mud ball at her opponent. A smirk lit her small face when her ammunition landed right on target.

Feeling a complete ass, the duke's son almost keeled over when he lost his balance after this last barrage. Sputtering, he was forced to fumble in his right coat pocket for a lace handkerchief to wipe his face. Niceties hurled aside, with a bellow of rage, he bounded after Rosaleen.

"Stay away from me, Lucifer!" she shrieked, then raced for protection to the hedges behind her.

Oblivious to the other children and adults eating about the carefully prepared tables, the marquis of Raythorn jumped after her, shouting for her to halt. "At once I say!" With his long legs, he caught the

13

source of his torment by her shoulders and spun her around to face him.

The boy was strong for someone Rosaleen assumed only sat on his rump all day. In any other circumstance, she might have smiled at the golden-featured boy with smudges of mud all over his face. However, the ice-blue of his eyes made her gulp with the first twinge of genuine fear. Rosaleen had cajoled her older brothers into teaching her in secret all they knew of pistols and swords. How she wished she had a weapon of defense in her hands right now.

A menacing smile curled the marquis' lips as he easily held her squirming form. Yet, his father's teachings were strong in him, too. "Blast it," he grated, knowing he could never strike a girl. But after glancing about quickly to be sure the irksome brat wouldn't come to any real harm, he gave her a calculated push.

With a cry of outraged surprise, Rosaleen landed on her gown-covered bottom in a soft bed of yellow flowers. She wasn't hurt, but it did nothing to assuage her O'Rahilly pride. She said a word aloud.

Lucien's blond eyebrows shot upward. The word would be familiar to a cavalryman or farmer, but he'd never heard a girl use the term, and at the earl of Holingbrook's garden party, no less. Taken aback once more by this unusual girl from the colonies, the marquis did not see her come at him until it was too late. Like a spitting black kitten, she hurled herself at him, and before the young man knew what she was about, they were tussling on the ground. She was at him with fists, legs, and sharp teeth, while he was only trying to protect himself from being maimed for life. "Ruddy code," he muttered, knowing full well he couldn't fight back but aware he was taking the worst for it.

"My baby!" Garnet screamed. "Calvert, don't just sit there while your baby son is murdered by that—that O'Rahilly's spawn." Unlike her usual tiny steps, the duchess charged over to the brawlers.

Rosaleen's father, Taggart, pulled them apart, then stood protectively near his daughter while Garnet hovered over Lucien. It was clear the boy had suffered the most. Covered with dirt, his obviously expensive clothes were ruined beyond salvage. Blood spewed from his nose where Rosaleen had landed a punch, and there was the beginning of a discoloration on the left side of his jaw. Calvert stood silently behind his wife.

"Oh, my poor boy," Garnet screeched, while holding her perfumed pocket handkerchief to her son's nose. His tricorn hat had fallen off with his quick descent to the hard ground, and the ribbon at his nape had long since disappeared, leaving his shoulder-length, dark-blond hair in disarray. "What has that little monster done to you?" The malevolent stare the duchess gave the small girl would have cowed the most seasoned sailor. "Irish vermin."

Rosaleen swallowed as disapproving adult glances filtered her way. She could hardly believe the change in the beautiful duchess's attitude toward her. The girl's lower lip trembled as she tried not to give way to tears. "I . . . I never meant to hit him on the nose. His face got in the way of my fist." She gulped, her voice shaking. "I feel just terrible about it now," she said with uncomplicated honesty. Rosaleen didn't understand why she heard male chuckles from the crowd. Aware the pins had tumbled from her carefully arranged hair, she could visualize the riot of black curls streaming across her shoulders. Feeling like the savage Lucien had called her, she tried to brush some of the grass and debris from the bottom of her torn gown.

When his mother began clucking over him once more, Lucien pulled back, despite the throbbing pain from his swollen nose and jaw. "Thank you, but it has stopped bleeding. Please do not fluster yourself, Mother."

"The lad's right," the man in his seventies cut in as he slowly came over to his son. "Did you strike the girl?" he demanded in a sterner voice.

"Oh, no . . . Your Grace," Rosaleen defended, even before Lucien could answer. "The marquis never hit me back."

The corners of the older man's mouth seemed to quirk up for a second. "Then, you behaved like a gentleman, Lucien." Calvert put his veined hand on the boy's shoulder. "Come along, let's clean you up." He was just about to lead his son away when Millicent O'Rahilly reached them.

Dunstan Fitzroy was able to disperse most of his guests. The earl directed the sea of powdered-wigged ladies and gentlemen back to the tables of wine and food.

"No, Percy, ah . . . Major Bembridge," Garnet corrected, addressing the scarlet- and gold-coated officer. "I should like you to stay. There may be some English laws broken here. Assaulting a duke's son is no small thing during these difficult times in Ireland."

The black-haired girl shuddered when she saw the military officer come over to the duchess. In his mid-

16

thirties, he was tall and slender, and wore a white powdered wig with the fashionable side curls. His shiny black boots, gleaming medals, and gold braid on his scarlet coat almost hurt Rosaleen's eyes.

"Your most obedient servant, Your Gwace. Pway tell me how I may assist you," the immaculately groomed officer lisped.

When Major Bembridge scowled at Rosaleen, she was forced to look down at the tops of her ruined slippers for fear she'd start to cry and further disgrace herself. Was this British officer going to have her shot? She moved closer to her father.

Taggart appeared uncomfortable, but he gave his beloved little girl a reassuring smile.

"Rosaleen," Millicent commanded, "I want you to apologize to the marquis immediately. By hitting him you took advantage of a gentleman who would never strike you back. You have behaved in a most unladylike way, and I am very displeased with you."

Never had her mother spoken to her in this manner. Rosaleen was unable to stop her cheeks from suffusing with color as she became more aware of the adults' and Lucien's eyes on her. "Papa, do I have to?"

Taggart looked at his wife and read the uncompromising glint in the gray eyes behind her wire spectacles. This time Millie would not be put off. And part of him did see the justification for her directive, for he and his wife had tried without success to reason with Ross about controlling her fearful O'Rahilly temper. Letting go of his daughter's hand, he bent down to talk with her face to face. "*Gleoite,* Papa would like you to apologize. Sure and I know ya didn't mean ta hurt Lucien; but ya did,

17

and I think ya owe him that at least."

Even though Taggart had used his pet Gaelic name for her, Rosaleen sized things up accurately. And it still hurt to remember the names Garnet had called her with such hatred, when just minutes before Rosaleen had been awed by the woman's beauty and warm charm. How could the fairy princess change her feelings so quickly? It had been a terrible day. She couldn't play the way she wanted because she was a girl, the blond-haired boy probably hated her because she'd let her temper get the better of her again, and—she craned her neck to look up at her father. "All right, Papa, since *you* want me to do it, I will." There was a sniffling sound as she brushed some imaginary moisture from the corner of her right eye.

" 'Tis me brave darlin', that ya are." Emotion always made his brogue thicker, and Mr. O'Rahilly almost burst into tears himself at the forlorn expression on his daughter's face. She was only a baby, he told himself, right now irritated by his wife's insistence.

Short for her years, Rosaleen walked slowly over to the taller Lucien, who, despite his bruised face, stood looking reserved between his white-haired father and stylishly dressed mother. It made her feel a little better when she saw the old duke's craggy features wrinkle into a smile. Keeping her eyes on the toes of Lucien's once shiny pumps below his now torn and grass-stained hose, she said, "My lord, I am sorry I punched you on the jaw . . . and on the nose."

His first fight, Lucien thought with humiliation, and it had been with a girl—who'd beaten him soundly. He nodded stiffly and accepted her apology. "I do hope, Miss O'Rahilly, you will not make a habit

18

of fisticuffs. Clouting a chap on the nose is just the sort of thing that can put a fellow off."

Rosaleen looked up quickly. If he was making fun of her, she could not prove it by his appearance. Yet, she thought she saw his face relax with just the hint of a smile as the sky blue of his eyes took on a warmer hue. But then it was gone.

"Lucien," Millicent offered, "if you come with me, I shall tend to your face."

"You will do nothing of the kind," Garnet stated. She turned to her husband with the countenance of one in full command. "Calvert, the marquis and I wish to go home . . . now. Dr. Collins, you will please accompany us. I should like you to check my son. He may have broken bones from being mauled by that little heathen's attack. Major, it appears an arrest will not be necessary."

"Oh, Mother," Lucien complained. "I am all right. Pray do not carry on so."

"Mama knows best, my precious."

Liam Collins appeared enraptured by the blond-haired beauty. "I shall be happy to accompany you if that is your wish, Your Grace."

Garnet gave her latest admirer a beguiling smile. "And you can check poor Calvert again. He is still not eating well, you know."

As Calvert, Garnet, Dr. Collins, and Lucien piled into the duke's coach, Taggart reached down and took his sad-looking daughter into his arms. He hugged her while holding her high against his chest. "I know that was difficult for you, and Papa was very proud of you just now, *Gleoite*."

While the adults in the carriage talked, Lucien peered out the window. He could see Rosaleen's face above her father's shoulder as Taggart carried her. Her black eyes suddenly captured Lucien's. The young Englishman was shocked when she stuck her tongue out at him and mouthed the word "bastard" while no one else was looking.

Lucien quickly popped his head back into the closed carriage. "That O'Rahilly girl is loathsome."

"I'll wager," Calvert said with a chuckle, "you will not feel that way in a few years."

"Well," the duchess commented, patting her son's arm while bestowing a sharp look at her elderly husband. "Her father tells me they will be returning soon to Virginia, and you'll never see her again. Those colonial boys will have to contend with that uncivilized baggage."

"They will need a suit of armor and a battle-ax to survive her fists," murmured the young marquis.

The duchess seemed unable to hide her pleasure at her son's remark. Her childlike laughter filled the coach. "No doubt she takes after her Irish father. The late earl despised Taggart O'Rahilly, former groom of Fitzroy Hall. Called him an upstart. Uncouth man will never be an English gentleman, not like you, my darling boy."

Working on the intricate clasp at the back of her neck, Garnet Huntington glanced up to see her thin husband's sickly reflection in the dressing table mirror. "I should imagine manners are still in fashion even here in Ireland. Kindly knock before entering my rooms." She made no effort to hide her displeasure with this unusual visit to her boudoir. Usually, she had the duke out of the way in his own rooms by this time so that one of her servants could let Percy up the back stairs to her apartments in secret. When Calvert sat down on a wing chair next to her writing desk, the duchess tossed the diamond and sapphire necklace on the table.

The duke informed his wife he'd sent the officer home.

Garnet turned her petite frame on the overstuffed dressing stool. Glaring at her husband, she pointed out, "You had no right to dismiss Major Bembridge in such a manner. I asked him to look in on us merely to be certain we'd arrived home safely. Why, the way Irish highwaymen have been accosting innocent Englishmen on these wretched Kinsale roads, you should be thankful I had the foresight to see to your protection."

"Thirteen years ago, madam, I might have been duped by your wifely concern for my safety." There was a resigned bitterness in his voice. "However, you quickly cured me of my romantic notions. No need to go over that business again, is there?"

The scene in the thick grove of trees on Fitzroy land still tormented Garnet—Calvert coming upon her coach as she waited for her lover to come to her. What grim satisfaction the old fart had gotten out of telling her John Nolan had just been killed in a duel of honor.

"Why have you come here at this hour?" she demanded. The apricot silk of her nightwear billowed about her curvaceous form when she stood.

Calvert got slowly to his feet. "Because of what I saw at the earl's party this afternoon. You are growing careless, Garnet. I pride myself on being open-minded enough to look the other way when a handsome young man, like Liam Collins, pays verbal compliments to my wife." His voice took on a harder edge. "However, I will not stand by mutely while that military peacock, Bembridge, feels my wife's tits in public like some stable hand pawing an overripe milkmaid."

"How dare you insinuate such vile things."

"Insinuate? Dam me, I saw it with my own eyes before you spotted Lucien boxing it out with that O'Rahilly girl." The duke's voice rose. "He may be one of His Majesty's finest officers, but I'm hanged if I'll allow your lover to visit you under my own roof. And I am beginning to suspect this is not the first clandestine visit the major has made to this house."

Unwilling to have Calvert probe this matter further, his wife took the offensive. "I refuse to discuss such an unsuitable topic with a man overwrought from the day's activities." Her eyes turned to blue chips. It was difficult to maintain her composure, for she was livid that Calvert had dared to send Percy away. "It is late, and you should be in bed. Remember what Dr. Wexford told you about getting excited."

"Gad, I'm delighted that idiot went back to London. He'd all but drowned my kidneys with his infernal tar-water. I'll take Liam Collins and his sensible doctoring any day. And do not imagine," he added, giving his wife a determined look, "you'll blubber or faint your way out of it this time, Garnet. I've warned you before about it. There is Lucien to think of now. The boy's getting older, and he is no fool." Calvert's eyes became menacing. "For months I've been wrestling with what to do. But tonight helped make up my mind. Scandal or not, I am divorcing you. By the end of the week, I want you and your belongings out of this house. You can have the chateau in Paris, for I've always loathed that over-gilded palace you furnished. Lucien and I will live here permanently. You may visit the boy here each summer."

Totally unprepared, the duchess lost much of her composure. "You cannot throw me out. I'll . . . I'll tell my brothers—"

The duke's harsh laugh cut her off. "Your brother Nigel is a good friend of mine. No, the vicar won't give you sanctuary, especially if you force me to tell him about your dalliances. I have dates and places, like the Inn of Three Cranes. Oh, yes, madam, years ago you taught me the usefulness of spies."

Her face drained of color. "But Edwin will be home from Italy soon."

"Bah, your younger brother is too infatuated with his prince to take any interest in his sister's escapades. Besides, I hardly think Edwin's propensity for male lovers makes him the ideal sort to furnish you with a character."

"Son of a pox-ridden whore!" Garnet shrieked, then reached for the nearest object on the tea table to her right. She hurled the Chinese vase at her husband.

Despite his years, the duke managed to step out of the way, just in time. White and blue pieces of expensive pottery shattered against the carved wooden wardrobe behind him. He could not hide his shock at his wife's phraseology. "Your speech is as vile as your manners."

"You won't get away with this," Garnet yelled. "I've stayed with you, endured your feeble attempts at lovemaking, had to look at your old-fashioned

23

clothes, agonized over thirteen summers in this uncivilized part of the world because you love Kinsale." She let him see her hatred. "You think I'd let you steal the wealth and title I've earned, you boring old fool? Just go to Paris quietly, accept divorce and be ostracized by polite society?" Her jeering laugh filled the room.

"I'll not have you carrying on under my roof in front of my son!" the duke thundered.

Her look mocked him. "Your son, old man? Lucien is not your son."

Calvert blinked, then stepped back, unsure. "No, you will not trick me this time. I know your taste for vengeance. I stand by what I said. A week, Garnet," he hurled at his wife, then left her rooms.

Rosaleen O'Rahilly watched the new duke of Montrose. Grief etched across the boy's face as he tied his horse's reins to the branch of a nearby elm. Somberly, he removed his black tricorn and tucked it under his arm, before walking over to her in the hidden grove of trees on her uncle Dunstan's lands.

"Thank you for meeting me here this afternoon, Your Grace."

"Your note said it was urgent."

"Well, you see," Rosaleen began hesitantly. "Papa is taking us back to Virginia. We sail in the morning. But I . . . I had to tell you how truly sorry I am about your loss and the . . . difficulties that followed."

"Scandal would be a more accurate term," the young man corrected. He found he had to close his eyes as the pain buffeted him once more. Unknown to anyone, it had become Lucien's recent habit to check on his ailing father during the night. He was still haunted by the expression of horror on his dead father's face as his lifeless eyes stared at the half-eaten plate of mushroom stew. Had his father tried to tell him something? The scientist in him had prompted the boy to stuff a handful of the abominable muck in a pocket handkerchief before racing to tell his mother the dreadful news. Everyone but Lucien assumed elderly Calvert had died in his sleep until the chief magistrate, Sir Jeremy Cartgrove, charged to the graveside among the English and Irish mourners to arrest Dr. Liam Collins for the murder of Calvert Huntington.

Thinking to expedite English justice, Lucien had analyzed the mushrooms under his microscope and used his plant books to confirm it. He had openly presented his findings at the trial. Amanita phalloides, he'd told the judge and jury. Often called death cap, they were poisonous and grew alongside the innocuous mushrooms. It was the color of the spores that differentiated them, and the cook would never have been able to tell the difference. They tasted the same as nonpoisonous ones.

Liam Collins had brought him into the world; however, Lucien believed the Irish physician deserved punishment if he'd murdered his beloved father. Yet, no one could have foreseen Uncle Nigel's role in this tragedy. Ashen-faced, the vicar had stood up after asking Lucien some pointed questions, then declared he had obviously murdered his own brother-in-law through a mishap with separating the poisonous mushrooms he studied from the harmless ones he'd lately been supplying to Montrose Hall. The court

25

had gone into an uproar; his mother, Garnet, had fainted. Everyone knew poor, befuddled Nigel incapable of deliberate manslaughter. Finally, the court had ruled Calvert Huntington had died from accidentally ingesting poisonous mushrooms.

Lucien blinked when he heard Rosaleen's lilting voice once more. He looked down at the Irish girl. For the first time he noticed her flowered gown and the attractive way her black curls were tied back with a lilac ribbon.

"I said, how is the vicar?"

Sadness tinged his reply. "Uncle Nigel still attends the duties of his small parish, but he is a broken man. Aunt Abigail tells me her husband has locked all his notes on mushrooms away, and he refuses to engage in anything connected with the hobby he has enjoyed since boyhood. My mother is brave and does not mention it. She is starting to see some of her old friends again, though she insists she is merely passing the time until she can join my deceased father."

Rosaleen appeared perplexed. "But I still do not understand why Dr. Collins must leave. He was cleared of all those false charges."

Sighing, the duke tried to explain it to her. "The scandal, the result of the chief magistrate's formal accusation and servant gossip, has ruined the Irishman's practice in Kinsale. No patient would even take the most innocuous powders from him now for fear he might be poisoning them. I spoke with Liam a few weeks ago, and he told me he was going back to the University of Padua to teach medicine. Having been a close friend of my father's, he says he will write me often from Italy. It was all such a terrible business."

Then Lucien noticed the moisture in his companion's dark eyes. "But you did not know my father well" slipped out in his puzzlement.

"That is true." Rosaleen brushed at her eyes. "But I know how I'd feel if my papa died, and I hurt for you."

Touched by her honesty, Lucien patted her shoulder, not really understanding why he suddenly regretted seeing this unusual, irksome, yet somehow endearing girl leave Ireland. He was tempted to tell her he'd be certain to pay a visit to the colonies. Then he remembered he had many responsibilities now. He was not so free to do what he pleased, and somehow he realized his life would never be the same.

Impulsively, Rosaleen asked, "May I kiss you good-bye?"

He was not used to being touched. His parents always showed a coldly formal attitude toward each other. But when he saw the hopeful look in Rosaleen's large brown eyes, he could not refuse her. "Well . . . if you really feel you must, I suppose I can stand it."

She stood on tiptoes and kissed Lucien on his smooth left cheek when he bent closer to her. "If you write me, I shall be pleased to answer. God watch over you always, Your Grace. I shall never forget you." Then she gave him a quick hug, but the dampness started in her eyes once more. She turned away and began running back toward Fitzroy Hall.

Lucien stood watching her until she was out of sight.

Chapter Two

April, 1771

"Faster, Bradai, faster." Rosaleen O'Rahilly hunched her upper body over the stallion's neck. Laughter bubbled up inside her as she charged across the damp earth, oblivious to the spattering of mud on the hem of her riding skirt. How wonderful it felt to have a reprieve from those chattering English matrons taking tea with her aunt Edna. When the word "marriage" had surfaced, accompanied by disapproving looks in her direction, the young woman knew it was time to make a polite but hasty exit. On a day like today she could almost forget why she'd been sent here in disgrace, months ahead of the rest of her family.

She tightened her hands on the reins, slowing Bradai's pace to a trot. Her features became more serious. England appeared to value the people of Ireland even less than their American colonies, she mused, as they came upon Montrose lands. Ill-clothed and badly fed on a monotonous diet of milk and potatoes, the Montrose tenants were far worse off than any slave she'd seen on her father's plantation in Virginia. She knew also that her uncle Dunstan's tenants fared much better than these wretches. Why was the duke of Montrose ignoring his estates here in Ireland?

Though her aunt and uncle told her Tom Bennet did his best to keep up the stables, it was clear to Rosaleen all the servants realized no Montrose owner would be here again this year. Many of the red bricks had deteriorated and not been replaced on the mansion house. The barn needed repairing. Stray cows and sheep wandered about the grass-covered hills. Even Calvert Huntington's beloved flower garden was strewn with weeds.

Did Lucien, the current duke of Montrose, ever think of her? Rosaleen couldn't help wondering once more, as she breathed in the earthy smell of nature's begging warmth. Often she'd thought of the tall, blond-haired Englishman. However, knowing a lady could never initiate a correspondence, she was saddened that he never wrote her in Virginia or came back to Kinsale. She had looked for him here each summer when her family visited—only to be disappointed. Well, she mused with a toss of her dark head, it was too lovely a day to dwell on unhappy thoughts.

She pulled up abruptly on her stallion's reins when she heard the sound of a fist connecting with someone's flesh. The man's painful outcry tore at her. Instantly, she was off her horse, heading for the open door.

When she peered inside the barn, Rosaleen saw Tom Bennet, the Montrose head groom. He was punching a smaller, older man Rosaleen did not recognize. The poor man's face was covered with blood. His thin arms came up to his head to ward off another blow.

"You're a lazy good-for-nothing, Kelly. This barn is a pigsty. You haven't done a lick of work all week."

Sickened by Tom's bullying manner to someone unable to defend himself, Rosaleen called Tom's name in the hope her interruption would stop his cruelty. But the young Englishman seemed oblivious to her presence, for he reached back a meaty fist intent on striking the Irishman once more.

"Tom Bennet," she yelled in a sharper tone. "Stop hitting that man at once!"

Tom looked toward the voice. He kept his hold on the old man, who started begging to be let go in a louder whine. Bennet scowled down at the petite nineteen-year-old woman in the dove-gray riding habit and matching tricorn hat. "This is no place for you, Miss Rosaleen," said the dour-faced servant. "You best be getting back to Fitzroy Hall. This don't concern you."

Miss O'Rahilly moved her booted feet closer into the dim light of the barn. Her nose told her the place did need a good cleaning, but she could not leave when she saw the pleading in the small man's eyes. "My father in Virginia and Uncle Dunstan at Fitzroy Hall taught me to command respect from servants without beating them senseless."

Tom's features become more unfriendly. He shook his quarry like a distasteful rat he'd just captured. "A few knocks to the side of the head is all Sean Kelly understands. He's just a lazy, freckle-faced weasel. And this ain't the first time I've caught him stealing one of His Grace's sheep."

"I was hungry," cried Kelly. He recognized Rosaleen O'Rahilly right away. "Me brother's widow and her kids are starvin'," he cried, wiping his bloodied face on his tattered sleeve. "But there ain't no man ta care for 'um. Sure and 'tis himself thinks we're just scum under his big English boots. Go ahead kill me, Bennet. Ya'd be doin' me a favor."

Tears stung the corners of Rosaleen's eyes at the Irishman's words. "Please, Tom, have done. You've hurt the poor fellow enough."

"He's got you fooled, Miss Rosaleen. You go along back to your embroidery or whatever you rich females do. Leave the running of estates to the men."

His complacent dismissal sparked something in the colonial girl. "I am sure His Grace would not like to hear that his overseer treats his servants so barbarically. I shall write the duke this very day and tell him how you are abusing your office. No doubt a more suitable overseer could be found quickly." Though she knew Lucien Huntington was in London right now, she had no idea how to contact him. Hopefully, her show of bravado would cause Bennet to back down. Her chin jutted out, and her dark eyes challenged the towering Englishman.

She sighed with relief when Bennet shoved Kelly away, then winced when the old fellow landed in a heap on the dirt floor.

"Bah, Kelly, you ain't worth my time, for I've got to see to the ailing mare next door. But you have this barn cleaned by tonight or I'll—" He looked at Rosaleen, then at the sniveling Irishman, appearing frustrated as to what he could do in front of this outspoken girl. "I'll write to His Grace myself to tell him about his slovenly Irish servant, and the nosy chit from the nearby Fitzroy estate." Tom turned and stalked out of the barn, slamming the rickety wooden door behind him.

"As if that clod could tie his own shoes, let alone be writtin' his name on a letter," muttered Sean, still squatting on the dirt- and straw-covered floor. "I don't think I caught yer name, but I thank ya for comin' ta me aid. 'Tis certain Bennet would have killed me had ya not stood up for me."

Rosaleen helped Sean rise. After assisting him in walking the few steps to a bench on the side of the barn, she raced for the leather satchel tied across the pommel of her saddle. Her mother, Millicent, had taught her how to tend to injured slaves on their estate, and she knew what to do. Wash, then salve for the cuts and bruises.

Sean Kelly had never had such gentle treatment. He could tell Rosaleen was moved by his plight. Hadn't he seen her riding over here often. But this time her parents weren't around, for he knew how important it was to stay out of sight when Taggart, her father, was about. Sean accepted the brandy the girl offered him from a metal flask. He could have drunk it all in one swallow but stopped after a short swig. "Oh, 'tis too strong, me lady." He imitated a cough and wheeze. "Unaccustomed to spirits as I am."

"It does take getting used to, so my father says. There, I shall leave you the rest of this salve to put on your cuts again tomorrow. You must keep them clean, else they will fester."

"Ya have a gentle touch, me lady. You're the first person who's ever shown me the least bit a kindness in me whole life."

Rosaleen felt embarrassed by his words. "Please, just Rosaleen or Ross. That's what my family calls me. Do you have any family, Sean?"

"Just me widowed sister-in-law, Annie, and her children." A few more tales of English cruelty and she would be his, he thought, forcing a sad mewl into his voice. Weakly, he tried to get to his feet, but a feminine hand stopped him.

"No, Sean, you must stay abed today and rest." She studied him more closely. "When was the last time you ate?"

"Oh," he answered with hesitation, "I might have had some mush yesterday . . . or was it the day before?" He hoped she couldn't smell the lamb pies on his breath that he'd stolen earlier from the main kitchen when the old cook was talking with Brian Fogarty.

"This is intolerable." A frown marred the smooth skin of Rosaleen's face. "I have never seen such deplorable conditions. Montrose tenants are starving, and the poor Catholic folk are treated worse than these English aristocrats handle their livestock," she fumed, then eyed the recipient of her rescue once more. Gray at the temples of his spiky red hair, he was clearly not dressed warmly enough. She would be sure to give him one of the discarded coats her male cousins had outgrown. Her aunt Edna would certainly not mind if she gave this starving wretch some of the food they usually doled out to Fitzroy tenants. "Something should be done about the horrible English treatment of their Irish tenants," she muttered to herself.

Sean saw his opening. "Well, Rosaleen, there is a small group of four Irishmen who try to bring about

33

a more even distribution of English wealth. But I can say no more." Sean clutched his arms to his chest, shivering against the morning air. "I wish that ox had killed me, for I mind the cold so much, and me body pains me more than a hundred stab wounds. I want ta die."

"Sean, please do not despair. Here, take the rest of the brandy with you." She put the silver bottle in his hands. "It will help ease the pain from those bruises." Sitting next to him, the colonial dug further into the leather satchel, before putting away the bandages and scissors. "Here, I want you to have these. Please purchase a blanket and some food with it."

Sean looked down at the coins. " 'Tis too much, me lady . . . I mean, Ross."

"I insist you take them. Please, you will be doing me a favor, for I cannot leave without assurance you will be all right. I do hope Tom does not put you off the estate."

Sean stifled a roar of laughter. With Garnet Huntington relying on Sean for all the information he got from spying for her, Sean and Tom both knew the Irishman's post was secure, one reason Bennet was so riled by his insolence. "Well, perhaps with the good Lord's mercy, Tom will give me another chance," said Sean, with the right touch of humility. He felt the girl pat his gnarled hand as she clucked over him. "If there is anything I can ever do for ya, Rosaleen, ya only have ta ask Sean Kelly."

Rosaleen watched the little man. His battered and lined face was no longer bleeding, but the discoloration at his left eye and cheek tore at her. "You could tell me more about that small group of Irish patriots."

A look of horror crossed the older Irishman's face. " 'Tis dangerous even ta tell you, for me and the lads would be hung on the spot if Sir Jeremy Cartgrove ever found out our identity. And word's about the chief magistrate has sent for Colonel Percy Bembridge ta come back ta Kinsale ta snuff us out."

"So, you are a member," she stated, admiration showing from her brown eyes.

"Oh, me lady, sure and yer charmin' ways led me to give meself away." He looked at her, appearing ready to burst into tears. "I'm a dead man."

"Nonsense," she countered, patting his arm once more. "I would rather die than betray a friend."

"Friend, am I now?" Sean feigned astonishment. "Sure and no one ever called Sean Kelly friend before." This part was true, for his dearest companion was himself, the man he put before all others. He attempted an expression he assumed a sweet-natured codger might bestow on an innocent girl.

But the expression had a different effect. "Is your stomach troubling you?" Rosaleen asked solicitously.

Kelly concluded he was not the benevolent old duffer type and resumed his normal morose expression. The usual whine returned to his voice. "The English are murderin' us with their taxes and cruel laws. We can't even own the dirt we live on, nor send our children ta school ta make a better life here. Oh, 'tis killin' me poor heart ta dwell on it. Nobody cares, and nobody does nothin' about it. I want ta die, I tell ya. I can hear the wail of the banshee, for she's welcomin' me with open arms."

While the unfortunate creature moaned on, Rosaleen began feeling more determined to add her skills to assist the Irish people of Kinsale. In Williamsburg, she did not fit in, for she'd been raised with her brothers' tutors and was used to asking questions and speaking her own mind. While she might possess her mother's gentle voice and interest in caring for the less fortunate, Ross did not enjoy dabbling in watercolors or many of the other "acceptable young lady" pursuits. For the first time, she felt free to make her own choice. Unlike her mother, Rosaleen believed in a forceful response to injustice. "Sean, please," she blurted, "let me join your group."

Sean answered quickly. "Absolutely not, Miss O'Rahilly. We go out after midnight, masked, and we work when news gets about of a party or gathering where rich Englishmen will be out on the road. 'Tis no proper place for a young lady."

"Proper place?" Rosaleen echoed. The familiar phrase burned her tongue. "Why can't I choose my place, as men do?"

Sean still looked unconvinced. "No, ya ought ta be thinkin' about a husband, not helpin' starvin' folks without hope."

"A husband is the last thing I want." Her voice became coaxing. "Besides, I can fence and use a pistol—I dare say, perhaps better than my brothers." Hadn't she badgered them since childhood into secretly teaching her to use the weapons? Her heart sank when she saw Sean stand up and shake his head. About the same height as Kelly, Rosaleen went over to stand in front of him. She would not be defeated. "But. . . ." She thought for a moment. "Could you not at least once allow me to accompany you and your men? If I slow you down or prove incompetent, you have my word I'll never mention it again. Your men will be masked, so I shall not be

36

able to identify them; and I've already given my word never to tell anyone about this. Please," she added, earnest entreaty in her dark eyes as she looked across at the pug-faced Irishman.

He was not a sheep like so many she had seen. He did something about injustices. Her mother and Aunt Edna helped the tenants through their charity work and pleaded with their husbands to try to change things in their voting and petitions to those in authority, but Rosaleen suddenly saw joining Sean's group of patriots as an important opportunity to take a more active role in bringing about change. Besides, this was just the sort of adventure the bored young woman had prayed for.

Kelly ran a hand across his nose. "How would ya get out of the house after midnight with no one seein' ya?"

Rosaleen looked smug, her quick mind already ahead of him. "My small bedroom used to be my mother's old room. It is in the back of the house, secluded. I would climb down the elm tree outside my window after midnight, dressed in my brother's old breeches and shirt that I've worn to ride on our lands at home. You could be waiting in the grove of trees behind the house with a horse for me. I'll pay you for the service," she added, realizing this battered old darling had no money to get her a horse. "Taking Bradai out of the stables might waken the groom. I brought my own pistol and sword with me from the colonies." She giggled in remembrance. "I placed them in a trunk with my shirt and breeches that Mama thought contained only my intimate apparel. My family is used to my preference for going my own way. And Papa wrote Uncle Dunstan and Aunt Edna that I'm to be allowed to see to myself. Papa's always understood my need for freedom. Mama says Papa is my kindred spirit."

Sean admired the girl's backbone and ingenuity. "Well," he said with grim finality. "I guess one time I could take a chance, but I don't like it. 'Tis no place for a girl ta be," he repeated.

"I realize you will have to ask your leader if it is all right to take me, and—"

"I'm the leader." Sean puffed out his chest.

"Oh, that is smashing," Rosaleen gushed happily. "Then, it is settled?"

Sean held up a dirty hand. "Easy now. Sure and ya'll have us all swingin' from a rope if ya go openin' yer gob about how happy ya are ta be takin' up with a group of highwa—Irish patriots," he amended. "That dimple at the corner of your mouth almost shouts yer up ta some mischief."

"Sorry." Rosaleen looked subdued, for she did understand the seriousness of this venture.

" 'Tis better I'm thinkin'. Now, me and the lads are plannin' an evenin' out this Saturday. Be outside near the grove of trees on Fitzroy property just after midnight. If ya ain't there, we leave without ya."

"I'll be there." Rosaleen was so overjoyed finally to be doing something more useful and exciting, she reached across and hugged Sean. "Oh," she said, looking contrite. "I'm truly sorry. Have I hurt you more? Tom Bennet did beat you savagely."

"Get along with ya now," Sean said gruffly, uncomfortable with the lady's concern right now. He watched Rosaleen mount her horse, wave and then ride off. For the first time in years, Sean Kelly felt the hint of a smile on his sullen features. He could hardly believe his long-awaited desire for revenge against the O'Rahillys had come to him, like a present from heaven. His brother, Patrick, was dead because of this girl's father and mother. And now, here was their only daughter—this small young woman would be the powerful means to ruin the O'Rahillys forever.

By the next month, Sean Kelly had to confess Miss O'Rahilly might be inept at embroidery and a deplorable cook, but she was a natural at highway robbery. She had cool nerves, a sharp mind, even seemed to enjoy the danger. In truth, the three other men with them were starting to look to Ross as their leader; for she was quick in planning their raids, and the take was higher than when he'd been spying to find out which road they should choose.

Rosaleen was unusually silent as the two of them rode back toward Fitzroy Hall near three in the morning. In black breeches, shirt, old wool coat, and felt hat pulled low over her head, Rosaleen rode astride with practiced ease.

"Any trouble gettin' away tonight?"

"No." She spoke again after a few moments. "Sean, you did say the coins and jewelry are going to the tenants, are they not?"

"Oh, I give ya me word, Ross, every bit of the bounty we take goes ta the tenants. Course, I feel the three lads should get a few coppers for the risks they take."

"Yes, but we must remember never to harm any of the passengers. I mean, I thought Morgan was just a little too ready to strike that old man when he refused at first to hand over his gold stickpin." Rosaleen had never seen the other men's faces, and she had requested it to remain so, for all their sakes. Only Sean knew her real identity. He'd introduced her to his three partners as Black Ned from Cork, a trustworthy orphan lad who wished to join them.

"Morgan did say afterward he wasn't going to strike that frail Englishman," she added. "However, I thought at the time he was ready to hit him. I hope Morgan will not hold it against me that I shouted for him to stop."

"As long as ya don't try ta make us any more victuals on the open fire, I think Morgan will overlook it."

"Well, I guess my stew was a bit gamy."

Stew? Sean thought, looking straight ahead as they continued riding next to each other. This chit couldn't boil a potato without burning it and ruined precious meat by mixing the wrong ingredients. "Best leave the cookin' ta Morgan."

Not taking offense, Rosaleen nodded. "I dare say, culinary endeavors were never my strong point. Mama despairs at my lack of domestic skills." As they rode past Montrose Hall in the distance, thoughts of Lucien came unbidden to her. It was a shame the duke allowed Calvert's beloved estate to go to such ruin.

"I saw a poster in town today," Sean commented. "Sir Jeremy put it up near the courthouse. 'Tis a reward notice for the capture of Black Ned, dead or alive."

"Is it a good likeness of me?" Rosaleen asked in a saucy manner.

"Covered in black from head ta toe, eyes peekin'

out from a black mask—a menacin' lookin' fellow if ever I saw one." Even the usually dour Sean grinned. "No resemblance ta ya a'tall, Ross. And the reward is less than they offered last year for that dead bandit, John O'Mara."

"The idea," Rosaleen scoffed. "Black Ned is worth three O'Maras any day. No matter. In a few months time, I am certain the reward will increase."

"You're a game one, Rosaleen O'Rahilly." Sean could not hide the hint of admiration in his voice.

"Sure and I do me best," answered Black Ned, then laughed, waving to Sean as she left him with her horse in the grove of trees. Used to the dark now, Rosaleen raced for the elm tree, glanced to the right and left, then expertly climbed up the tree to slide her coltish legs across the open widow ledge outside her room.

Lucien Huntington, Duke of Montrose, scanned the contents of Liam Collins' letter once more. A frown etched across his blond features. He placed the missive atop his most recent letter from Antoine Lavoisier, in which they'd been discussing their mutual interest in liquid vapor experiments.

Lucien stood up and walked over to the window to peer out at the elaborate gardens of his estate just outside London. His mother had arranged for him to take a Grand Tour. However, right now the man in his mid-twenties did not wish to go gallivanting about France, Switzerland, or Italy.

Unknown to Garnet, the duke's mother, Dr. Collins' letters during these last nine years had sustained his interest and affection for Ireland. The duke valued the opportunities for their shared interests in politics and learning. Lucien had opened to this Irish physician in a way he'd never done to anyone except his late father. Liam wrote that his brother, Father Michael Collins of Kinsale, had just told him Lucien's estate and her tenants were in a miserable condition.

The duchess of Montrose made little effort to hide her loathing of Ireland and all Irish Catholics. Yet, as her son watched the swans glide on the pond, he began visualizing the green rolling hills, and dark and light stones along Kinsale's harbor, along the estuary of the river Bandon. Calvert, his father, had loved Ireland.

Why, Lucien wondered, had Brian Fogarty, his trusted servant, never told him how run-down Montrose estate had become? During the last nine years, the duke had allowed Brian to return alone a few times to his beloved homeland for a visit. Garnet had made Lucien promise never to set foot in that "horrible country" again after his father had died. But right now the duke felt he could no longer keep that promise, for he suddenly realized her childlike trust in others had made her less than prudent in dealing with his father's Irish estate.

Coming to a decision, Lucien went back to his cherry-wood writing desk and reached for paper and quill pen. With his mother enjoying another summer outside Paris, he could easily slip out and sail to Kinsale instead of taking that Grand Tour. He now felt Montrose Hall needed him, and in truth, he looked forward to returning to Ireland.

The water felt refreshing against Rosaleen's skin.

The July afternoon was as warm as the most humid day in Williamsburg. Floating on her back, she closed her eyes, enjoying again her secret place on Montrose land. This was the one spot where she was not a colonial heiress visiting her uncle and aunt, nor Black Ned, Irish patriot — or notorious highwayman, according to Kinsale's chief magistrate. This was her time where she could be herself, free to languish in the tranquil water, and —

The sudden sound of a horse approaching startled her. Never had she been troubled by intruders during these private times at the absent duke's pond.

Quickly, she rolled on her stomach, then began swimming toward the shore, where she had folded her clothes on a nearby rock. However, a quick peer over her shoulder caused Rosaleen to bite her lower lip when she saw the outline of a rider. He was too close for her to make a dash for the bank. To stay hidden, she would have to remain in the deeper water. Spotting one of the larger boulders jutting out from the middle of the pond, Rosaleen swam to the side of it to hide until the fellow left. She used her hands for leverage and pushed herself higher out of the water to take a peek around the large rock.

The rider stopped and leisurely moved his horse closer to the edge of the water, allowing the animal to have a drink. Ross sighed with relief. He hadn't seen her. However, her breath caught in her throat when the gentleman took off his tricorn to wipe his face with a pocket handkerchief — it was Lucien Huntington, Duke of Montrose!

Chapter Three

Even after nine years, Rosaleen knew him immediately. He was taller, his shoulders had broadened under the brown linen coat, but the Irish colonial knew the blond head and handsome features. Hadn't she dreamed of meeting him again? Yet, she'd envisioned herself dressed in a lovely ball gown at a party, not like this, dripping wet, and— Rosaleen's foot slipped suddenly on the moss-covered rock she'd been standing on. In a reflexive motion, her hands pushed forward, and her body made a loud splash as she came up sputtering in an attempt to right herself in the water.

Instantly, Lucien knew he was not alone. No fish in the pond made that much noise, and he hadn't missed the human cry of surprise before the splash. On his first day out inspecting his estate, the duke was appalled at the conditions on his property. For years his mother had assured him Tom Bennet had everything in hand. How little his too trusting mother knew. And Brian Fogarty had been oddly evasive when Lucien had demanded to know why

44

the older Irishman had refrained from telling him how bad things had become on Montrose lands.

When Lucien spotted just the top of a dark head popping up like a cork in the water, he smiled for the first time in months. Probably some Irish urchin playing in his pond. Well, he might at least make a friend of the little nipper. "Don't be afraid, lad," the duke called in a pleasant manner. "You can come out, for I'll not harm you."

"Go away," Rosaleen shouted, alarmed that the horse and rider were now so close. Embarrassed, she thought frantically for a way to get him to leave. "Me and me friends," she tried, mimicking an Irish brogue, "don't like strangers. Sure and this is our pond," she added, inflecting a lower pitch to her voice. "Now, shove off before I . . . I come out and slice yer gizzard."

Blond eyebrows arched in surprise. This Irish boy had certainly never been instructed about respect for his elders. Though at first Lucien planned to go his own way, something in this Irish lad's tone pricked the hairs at the back of his neatly tied queue. "I am Lucien Huntington, Duke of Montrose, and I own this property, young man. While I do not mind you boys swimming here, I will not be spoken to in that surly manner. Now, come out of that water at once, I say," ordered the Englishman from atop his chestnut horse.

Her initial irritation at being caught at such a disadvantage changed to a more heated emotion when the blackguard got off his mount, planted his shiny boots slightly apart on the bank, and stood with hands at the waist of his well-tailored coat and breeches. She saw him scowl in the direction of her hiding place behind the rock. The picture of all the starving tenants on Montrose land buffeted her. He had no right to take that authoritative tone with her. Deciding to take advantage that he thought she was some inconsequential Irish boy, she shouted, "Bugger off, Montrose. Go back ta your doxies in London. We don't need no foppish knave tellin' us what ta do."

His lips compressed to a firm line. "You need a lesson in manners, jackanapes." In an instant he had his outer coat and black boots tossed to the ground. Without hesitation, he stepped into the shallow end of his pond.

"Wait!" Rosaleen screamed, forgetting to lower her voice. "Please, don't come over here. I . . . I'm not a boy," she shouted in desperation.

Lucien halted at her confession. The code, he reminded himself, thinking of what Calvert had taught him. He turned about and sloshed back up the bank. Ignoring his mud-covered stockings, he quickly put on his boots and frock coat. "Well, child, then I will wait here for you to come out." He sat down on a nearby rock and stretched his long legs out in front of him, giving the impression of a man in no hurry.

Heat suffused Rosaleen's face. Never had she expected this turn of events. The water suddenly felt cold against her skin. "Sir, I demand—ahem, I mean, I request you leave here so that I can come out."

"I am used to seeing the ladies at Bath in their mobcaps and brown head-to-toe bathing costumes.

Come along, now. Be quick about it, else I'll haul you out of there myself."

Oh, this was monstrous. "But, Your Grace, I am not wearing. . . ." The warmth in her cheeks increased, despite the bumps on her arms now making her teeth chatter. "That is, I am not wearing any bathing costume."

"Oh." Blond brows rose to his hairline; then a roguish grin split the duke's handsome face. Faith, this had to be some Irish tenant, for no English lady of his acquaintance would ever come to a pond alone to bathe in the nude. Suddenly, he felt wickedly intrigued to know more, especially when he remembered how this impertinent girl had addressed him. "You must be getting rather chilly behind that rock, treading cold water."

"A gentleman would never spy on a lady in this manner, especially when she requested him to leave."

The corners of his mouth shifted northward. "Ah, yes, but as you have already pointed out, I am a foppish knave, therefore, I suppose my true nature has come to the surface."

"Knave was too kind," Rosaleen muttered under her breath. She looked about for another exit. Her clothes were to her right, clearly out of range of the duke. "All right, Your Grace, I will come out, but will you please close your eyes?"

Drawing out this impudent child's punishment a bit, the duke pretended to hesitate. "Dash it all, you know a knave finds it difficult to do the honorable thing."

"I am sorry I called you a knave. Please, Your

Grace, I am shivering in this water," she added truthfully.

"All right." He closed his eyes. Instantly, Lucien heard the sound of splashing water as the unknown child moved closer to the bank.

Rosaleen raced to the right shore for her clothes. So in a hurry to be on Bradai's back in the distance and far away from Lucien before he opened his eyes, she didn't pay her usual attention to the sharp rocks along the embankment. Instantly, she realized her mistake when excruciating agony shot up her right foot after she stepped hard against the jagged point of one of the gray stones. She toppled over in a heap on the ground, her knees scraping against the round, large rocks along the bank. Blood began pouring out of the cut across the ball of her foot. Tears stung her eyes as white-hot pain, embarrassment, then anger with Lucien washed over her.

Hearing the girl's outcry, the duke bounded automatically to his feet and rushed toward the sound. All humor left his features when he looked down at the girl before him. At first he thought she was a child, her long, wet hair cascading down her back. However, when she turned around, he saw the tear-stained face, dark brown eyes, pale skin, and pair of firm, voluptuous breasts that she quickly sought to hide with her curly, raven locks. When he viewed the amount of blood spurting from her injured foot, he knelt down beside her quickly. He felt ashamed for having teased her, now blaming himself for this mishap.

Mortified by his proximity, Rosaleen tried to wiggle away, for no man had ever seen her naked before. Tears of humiliation coursed down her face. "Please, go away. I am not dressed."

Comprehending that part of her distress had nothing to do with her injured foot, Lucien shrugged out of his outer coat. She appeared so small, he enveloped her in the brown coat in seconds. Without hesitation, he lifted the protesting bundle in his arms.

"No, please put me down. Let me go."

"Shh," he tried to soothe. "I will not harm you. I just want to tend to your foot."

Wiping a thick strand of wet hair from her face, Rosaleen looked across into a pair of concerned eyes the color of the cloudless blue sky. She stopped struggling. "My clothes are over there." She pointed to a flatter rock behind a clump of green foliage.

"First, let's see to that foot; then I'll come back for your clothes."

"No. I want my clothes now."

"My coat will protect your modesty, and it is more logical to stop that bleeding first." Then, ignoring her continued protests, he placed her gently on the bank and went back to his saddlebags. All business now, he washed the cut, then applied a measure of pressure to it with a pristine square of cotton to stop the bleeding.

Lucien tired to keep his mind on his work. But he could not help looking down into her face once more to be certain he had not frightened her. She was the most beautiful woman he'd ever seen—hair the color of a raven's wing, smooth pale skin. He'd felt her curves when he carried her. Not just for her sake but his own, the duke decided it would be better to get this girl clothed now that the bleeding had stopped. "Hold that against your foot, and I will go back to retrieve your garments."

He returned minutes later carrying the simple clothes and scuffed boots. She was probably one of the tenants, he mused. The garments were serviceable but well-used. He placed her meager belongings next to her. "I will keep my eyes averted as much as possible, but you will need assistance getting into these."

"I can dress meself," she countered, this time remembering to sound like an Irish peasant. At first Rosaleen attempted to dress while keeping his brown coat about her as a kind of shield. Awkwardly, she got back into her shift, petticoat, and worn blouse. No time to get the combs to tie back her hair. However, when she put the paisley skirt over her head, she gave a squeak of protest as Lucien lifted her up so that she could tuck the skirt under her. A quick glance up made her relax after she saw he was looking away from her while he helped. She cleared her throat. "Sure and I'm thankin' ya fer the use of yer fine coat. I'm afraid I got a spot of blood on the pocket from me foot."

"No matter," he replied. He took the coat from her small hands and placed it behind him on the ground. It was then he glanced down to see the two diamond-studded hair combs that must have fallen out of her skirt pocket when he'd lifted her.

Rosaleen followed the direction of his displeased expression. Determined not to confess these expensive items were hers, she realized they added another suspicion against her character. Though he said nothing, she decided he must be thinking she stole them. "Don't forget ta check yer pockets in case I fleeced ya." That should speed him on his way, she thought with satisfaction.

Automatically, the duke's right hand went back to the leather purse inside his coat on the ground. His coins were safe. He turned back to the smirking girl. "It is a good thing you did not rob me, young lady," Lucien warned, purposely making his voice stern. A little scare might do this errant brat good. "Sir Jeremy Cartgrove was a good friend of my late father's. No doubt the chief magistrate of Kinsale would know how to deal with you."

Her look was scathing. "More criminal in me own mind is a duke who lets his land and his tenants go ta hell in a handbasket while he sees only ta his own pleasures in London, or is it Paris where most of ya English parasites with more money than brains go this season?"

"You . . . rag-mannered hoyden, how dare you use that tone with me." Though he'd already berated himself for neglecting his responsibilities here, this peasant girl was—despite his usual quiet manner, Lucien felt his face flush with the first vestige of strong emotion. He forced himself to gulp in a few breaths of air. His expression was unreadable when he went back to tending her foot.

"The bleeding has stopped, thank God." His voice was strained. "You gave me quite a fright, Miss . . . ?"

She clamped her lips together.

"Will you not tell me your name, at least?"

"No."

"Are you one of my tenants?"

"In a pig's eye."

"I see. Still not forgiven, so I am not to know your name."

"If ya hadn't charged inta the pond ta run me down like a dog, I wouldn't have felt the need ta rush away from here ta save me life."

As she continued to berate him, Lucien methodically patted some green salve into the cut on her foot.

She wrinkled her nose. "Blessed saints, what's that evil-smellin' slime?"

He tried to hide his displeasure at the girl's phraseology. "Hold still. It is a mixture of herbs that promotes healing."

The cut did feel better. "How does a fancy English duke know about such things? I thought most of ya aristocratic nincompoops only knew how ta ride ta the hounds, eat and drink yourselves ta gout, and mount loose women."

His late father's gentleness came to the duke's rescue once more, and he managed to keep a grip on his emotions. "I enjoy studying plants and conducting experiments. Not all Englishmen are village idiots," he explained in a patient tone.

"Harumph. Ya best be havin' a care about goin' about practicin' healin'. Next ya'll be changin' peat inta gold. Yer probably a warlock, a practitioner of black arts."

Laughter escaped his sensuous lips. "Then, you had better improve your manners, lest I conjure a spell to turn you into a silent, lop-eared rabbit."

Despite herself, Rosaleen chuckled at his quick

rejoinder. "Well, at least I would have four feet ta scamper home on; then one injured one wouldn't make such a difference."

His expression became more serious. "In truth, young woman, I do blame myself for your unfortunate accident. Your earlier rudeness in the water caused me to do something I have not done since I was a young boy visiting Kinsale—I lost my temper. For that, I do apologize. I own I am partly to blame for your injury."

Rosaleen brushed another stand of wet, black hair away from her face. His concern touched something deep within her.

Lucien's breath caught in his throat as he looked down into her fathomless dark eyes once more. What did he read there? Mischief? Mystery? "Who are you?" he asked.

She watched him from beneath lowered lashes. "It does not matter."

"Are you some Irish elf, like the ones my father used to tell me about?" Lucien teased. "More likely one of my tenant's children, stealing an afternoon away from her kitchen duties to play truant." He smiled when her willful eyes challenged him once more. Yet she said nothing.

Rosaleen watched him skillfully bandage her foot in silence. Of course, she tried telling herself she should be glad he did not recognize her, for this was not the way she'd envisioned their reunion.

"Has the pain lessened?" her companion asked when he looked down at her.

She felt the warmth of his hands as they cradled her right foot. She nodded her head, not trusting her voice. The physical pain had lessened, but suddenly she had to fight the moisture at the corners of her eyes. Lucien did not know her. All they had been through nine years ago, and he didn't even remember her.

"I am sorry. Did I hurt you?" Lucien's strong, yet graceful hands placed her foot back down on the grass-covered bank. "I have finished bandaging it."

Inhaling the faint scent of sandalwood from the duke's close proximity, Rosaleen closed her eyes. No, he did not remember her, she thought once more. She was merely an unknown Irish peasant to him. "I must leave." Pulling on her worn boots, the nineteen-year-old forced herself to stand on her injured foot. "Again, thank you for your kindness." She remembered to mimic a brogue this time. "Sure and they'll be the devil ta pay if I'm not back ta the kitchen."

Lucien was suddenly surprised to see how late it had become He stood up and looked about him. "I can almost believe Ireland is bewitched the way the mist engulfs the land so quickly."

" 'Tis gettin' dark, and the fog has rolled in."

After putting his coat back on, he reached into his leather purse and pulled out a handful of coins. "Those hard boots are not the thing to wear with your injured foot." He thrust the coins into the front pocket of her skirt. "I shall take it as a favor if you'll buy yourself a soft pair of slippers that will not hurt your foot while it heals." He saw her open her mouth to protest. "Not another word; I want you to have them. Come, I will see you safely home

54

on Jasper's back. I shall explain everything to your employer so that you will not be punished." He offered his hand to her.

What now? She had to get back to Bradai and be gone from here alone. Not taking his hand, Rosaleen forced a look of discomfort, then peered down at the toes of her boots. "Before ya see me home, Your Grace, I need. . . . I mean, I require a moment of privacy. Must be all the water I swallowed earlier when ya gave me such a fright by stalkin' after me in the pond."

Amused to see the lass had a bulldog's determination to point out again she was the wronged party, nevertheless, Lucien sought to ease her embarrassment over her request. "Of course. I will walk over to that clump of trees ahead with my back to you. Please call me when you are . . . ready to leave, and I will return with Jasper to spare you the distress of walking over to us."

When she saw him pick up his things and walk toward his reddish-brown horse, Rosaleen was touched by his gallantry. However, she forced herself to move quickly back where the trees thickened to the spot where she'd tied Bradai in the distance. Jumping on the black stallion's back, Rosaleen sat astride and touched her knees to the horse's flanks. They went galloping off through the thick mist.

At the muffled sound of a horse's hooves on moist earth, Lucien raced back to the spot where he'd left the unknown Irish girl. "Wait!" he shouted. He squinted about him in all directions, but the dense fog forced him to realize she was far away by now. He shook his head, then walked slowly back to swing his long legs up on Jasper's back. God, he hoped she hadn't stolen a horse, too, he thought, fretting about any harsh consequences the rambunctious girl might receive from her employer. The evening scents of damp grass and the clear pond assailed him. Was she a dark-haired elf that had appeared to enchant him? he wondered, then chuckled at his decidedly illogical thoughts about Irish leprechauns and fairy stories. He did not know her name or where she lived. But something inside him wanted to find this intriguing lass again. He would ask Brian Fogarty and some of his tenants. Surely, they would know where this captivating Irish girl lived.

"Lucien, you mean you have not heard of Black Ned?" Lady Prudence Lorens smiled at the handsome duke sitting on the leather carriage seat next to her. "Kinsale has talked of little else for the last three months."

Across from them, Henry smiled indulgently at his younger sister. "Lucien had nerves of steel even in our Cambridge days, Pru. I doubt the duke would be impressed by a band of scruffy Irish peasants. Besides, I've never seen this Ned fellow. All just humbug."

Prudence reached across and rapped her brother on the knuckles with her pink fan. "For shame, Brother, I believe Black Ned is a romantic rogue. Elizabeth Fitzroy says she heard the bold fellow kisses all the ladies in the coach after he robs them."

"He'd best not try anything with us," said Henry, tapping the sword that rested on his left hip. "Or the rascal will get a taste of steel through his liver, eh, Montrose?"

Lucien appeared disinterested. "On the whole, I'd rather have an uneventful ride home, if it is all the same to you."

"Where is your sense of adventure, Lucien? I hope we do meet Black Ned," the blond-haired beauty rattled on. "It would be too divine for words. They say he is tall, voice as low as thunder, with a gypsy's swarthy complexion."

"Thought he always wears a mask."

"Really, Henry, you never listen. I told you yesterday Elizabeth Fitzroy heard that Colonel Percy Bembridge's aunt was in a coach Black Ned robbed last month. When the old darling fainted, Black Ned picked her up in his enormous arms and placed her tenderly back in her coach without taking so much as a farthing from her. The elderly Miss Bembridge says she got a glimpse of his jaw when his masked slipped."

"Black Ned's mask isn't the only thing that's slipped, if you ask me."

"Upon my soul, Henry, you've all the romantic soul of a turnip." Nose in the air, Lady Prudence turned back to the man sitting next to her. "Just the same, I do hope we meet Black Ned. It would be so much fun to be able to tell Elizabeth I met him in person."

Lucien did not share the lady's enthusiasm. They should have left sooner. Invited by his childhood friends to attend a soiree at their distant cousin's home outside Kinsale, Lucien had agreed, but if Henry had known of even the chance of danger on these roads, Lucien felt he'd been remiss not to insist his sister be safely home before dark. Though, looking at Prudence now, Lucien could not suppress a half-smile at the eagerness she exuded at the prospect of being waylaid by the bandit.

The duke inched away once more when he felt one of her gown-covered legs touch the side of his knee. The expensive pink material of her gown fluffed about his silk-covered thigh. He had to admit Prudence possessed the blond, pale beauty and regal bearing so in vogue. However, he began to realize the earl and his sister had plans for his future, and Lucien was not sure he wanted to go down the matrimonial path with Prudence Lorens or anyone else right now. The hint from the lady about Montrose Hall being so large for one person made Lucien quickly change the subject. "You have done some wonderful things with Lorens Hall."

The earl beamed at what he clearly assumed was a compliment to him. "They say the previous owner, the late squire John Nolan, was tightfisted, and it shows. Mother and Father were appalled when we moved in thirteen years ago. The walls needed redoing; even the ballroom floor had boards missing. So glad Father delayed dying so that he could see what I'd done with the place. The old boy was so proud of me."

In a clear pretext of adjusting her gown and hoops, Prudence again moved closer to Lucien. "Papa used to say those Irish Catholics are the laziest workers in the world. I had to get a maid from

58

Paris because none of the local girls could take proper care of me. Lorens Hall is a showplace now with the new furnishings. Henry sent to China for the dining room wallpaper, and . . ."

The duke found it difficult to continue listening to Lady Prudence as she chatted on about her home. His mind kept going back to the previous day when he'd met that black-haired Irish girl. And when he'd asked Brian and a few of his tenants about her this morning, they had all looked at him as if he'd taken leave of his senses. No one knew of any beautiful Irish tenant who swam at the Montrose pond. Who was this feminine mystery? At first she'd been all temper as she'd berated him for neglecting his responsibilities. Then there was something oddly familiar in the smile she'd given him after he'd finished tending her small foot. That dimple in the right corner of her mouth had pricked something in his memory, then it had vanished. Never had he felt such an overwhelming urge to kiss so adorable a mouth. But his father's teachings were strong in him. That unknown Irish lass and he came from totally different worlds. His logical side warned he should forget her, for he'd not come back to Kinsale to take advantage of his Catholic tenants — no matter how intriguing one in particular might be.

Miss Lorens fluttered her lacy fan in front of her pretty face. "Upon my soul, Your Grace, you are as silent as the grave tonight."

"Pru," admonished her brother, "poor Montrose's ears are going to fall off from your uninterrupted banter. Give us a rest, hmmm?"

Prudence's blue eyes lost some of their vacant sweetness. She leaned closer to her companion on the leather cushions, moistened her soft lips, then asked, "Shall I stop talking, Lucien?"

There was no more room for him to move away from this blond temptress, else he'd be on his silk-covered backside in the middle of the muddy road. From the bouncing of the conveyance, he knew they had a long way to go before reaching the better roads close to the Lorens estate. He looked down into Prudence's eyes. "Pray continue speaking, my lady, for your voice reassures me." That part was true, for when she was talking, he didn't have to worry about avoiding her less than subtle advances.

Encouraged by the sparkle in his vivid blue eyes, Prudence settled back against the plush cushions. "As I was saying, it took so many years to get the place up to our standards because these stupid Irish tenants are so unwilling to work. Popery does that to them, you know. Makes them laggards."

Lucien thought it more likely the lack of food and a say in how they were governed; but he said nothing, for suddenly he felt the Lorens coach jerk to a halt. Opening the door on his side, he peered out into the warm evening air. Puzzled, he looked down. No, the wheels were fine. However, when he glanced ahead, he swore under his breath.

Lucien could make out at least five masked riders a few feet in front of the Lorenses' conveyance. Quickly, he popped his head back into the coach. What good were their dress swords when these ruffians had loaded pistols? He had thought this area of Kinsale was the bucolic, quiet place he'd enjoyed as a boy. Now Lucien cursed himself for not bringing his pistol tonight. "Henry, does your driver carry firearms?"

"Of course not," Lady Prudence answered for her brother. "We are in Ireland not London. The most exciting thing that happens here is when a pig gets loose." Apparently she saw something in Lucien's face. "Oh, you mean there are real highwaymen out there? This is too, too divine. Is it Black Ned? Let me get a better look."

"Stay back," Lucien ordered in a tone he'd not used with this Englishwoman before. He was relieved to see the girl sink back and remain silent.

"Stand and deliver!" came a masculine order from the other side of the coach. "Out of the carriage. Be quick about it. Black Ned here ain't one ta be kept waitin'."

Lucien realized they had little choice. "Stay here, Prudence, and do not make a sound. Come on, Henry, and for God's sake don't do anything foolish like drawing your sword. I counted five of them, and all but one has a loaded pistol pointed in our direction."

Dressed in black from head to toe, Rosaleen O'Rahilly's eyes widened behind her full mask when she recognized the taller gentleman climbing out of the coach. Glad to be on her horse, she could not explain why her legs felt weak as she took in his handsome features in evening clothes. The lanterns on either side of the coach gave her a clear view of him: blond hair tied neatly at the back of his neck with a black taffeta ribbon, straight nose, strong jaw, muscular body outlined in dark-blue silk coat and knee breeches, white stockings above black leather pumps with sparkling diamond buckles. He held himself straight as he glared up at them in silence. Then she spotted the shorter gentleman next to him. It was Henry Lorens. She swallowed, for the first time feeling uncomfortable in her role. Never before had they robbed anyone Rosaleen actually knew.

Next to her, Rosaleen heard Sean Kelly whisper almost to himself. "What in hell is Montrose doin' here? Her Grace promised me he'd never come back." Sean knew Garnet would have his guts for garters if she ever found out he'd robbed her son. "We got ta let them go."

"I agree," Black Ned whispered. Relief coursed through her. Usually silent on their raids, she pulled her horse back to the shadows while Morgan and Kelly went closer to the two English aristocrats and their scared coachman.

Henry Lorens spoke before the two highwaymen could order them on their way. "You have made a grave error here. I am Sir Henry Lorens, Earl of Dunsmore." He fingered the hilt of his sword. "You Irish scum better think twice before you attempt to waylay one of His Majesty's closest friends. This gentleman has just returned to his estate in Kinsale," he said, pointing to his taller companion. "He is Lucien Huntington, Duke of Montrose, close friend of George III."

"For God's sake, shut up," growled Lucien from the side of his mouth. Reaching into his coat pocket, the duke pulled out a leather pouch. "Here, take my purse and leave us in peace."

"No, Montrose." Henry grabbed the purse and tossed it into the open widow of the coach. "You'll just encourage them in their criminal ways." Henry turned back to the men on horseback. "You will get nothing from us but cold steel." He drew his sword out of its sheath.

"Don't be a fool, Henry. Put your swo—"

There was the quick sound of pistol fire, then smoke, followed by Henry's outcry. He dropped his sword as if it burned his fingers, then clutched the back of his bleeding hand.

The commotion caused Prudence to stumble out of the conveyance. "Oh, Henry, what have they done to you?" she cried, quickly going to her brother's aid. He leaned against the wheel of the coach while his sister took his pocket handkerchief and began tying it about his wrist. "Oh, careful of my gown, Henry," she admonished.

Henry stepped back from her expanse of hoops and pink silk.

"Bloody hell," Lucien swore. To add to his troubles, the highwaymen now realized there was a pretty young woman with them.

Chapter Four

The duke of Montrose watched as the short man who shot Henry got off his horse and retrieved the fallen sword.

"Lovely evenin' ain't it, Yer Grace?"

Lucien continued his tight-lipped silence.

Sean Kelly was now at ease, for he felt secure in his anonymity. He reminded himself Garnet had no idea of his other life, and she'd never set foot in Ireland again, he was certain. The shorter man addressed Lucien. "Me and the lads ain't had this much drama since we stole a horse and two sheep from yer barn last spring. Another thing, Montrose, ya ought ta sack that Bennet fellow, if ya want me opinion. Yer stables are a stinkin' mess. 'Tis certain me and the lads could a got more for the leather harness and saddle we took two months ago if ya'd kept yer stuff in better repair."

A vein throbbed in Lucien's temple as he bit out, "Words cannot describe my feelings at being taken to task because you sustained a loss on the property you stole from me."

"No need ta get uppity about it. Sure and I feel

64

honored ta be robbin' ya. I'm even lettin' ya keep yer sword. Yer friend's sword I keep for putting me ta the trouble of shootin' him in the hand." He tossed Henry's rapier up to one of his companions.

"Oh, you must let us go," Prudence cried. Leaving her brother propped next to the carriage wheel, Lady Prudence scampered over to the duke's side. She threw herself in his arms, sobbing "Lucien, you won't let them harm me, will you?"

The duke could only hold on to the tall, clutching woman while she leaned even closer against his body, giving the impression a faint was imminent. "There, there, Prudence, Henry and I will protect you. This is just a robbery, not a kidnapping. Please do not carry on so. Now, don't fret, there's a good girl. I won't let anyone hurt you."

Trusting orbs looked upward. "Oh, Lucien, you are so comforting, so brave." She stepped back but continued to stare adoringly at her knight.

The Englishman forced a calmness in his voice he did not feel. Before the squat Irishman could walk back to his horse, Lucien said, "Since you have disarmed the earl of Dunsmore, I would suggest I retrieve the coins from the carriage for you; then we will be on our way."

" 'Tis up ta Black Ned. What do ya say, Ned?"

This was the first time Sean Kelly ever maneuvered her into speaking with a detainee. Slowly, Rosaleen moved her stallion a little closer to the circle of people. Fully intending to let them go, something in the way Lucien comforted Lady Prudence caused Rosaleen to experience an emotion she'd never felt before. She found herself saying in Black

Ned's voice, "Well, the wench might be useful makin' us supper tonight."

Prudence's look of adoration for the duke changed to outrage at Black Ned. "Upon my soul, I am no domestic. Get one of your Irish drabs to act as scullery maid."

Like the others, Rosaleen's mask had holes for eyes, nose and mouth. She smiled behind the black leather. "Well, me lady, do ya have any other skills me and the boys might value?"

Lady Prudence's face turned pink at the barb. However, instead of running to Lucien as before, Prudence raced over to Black Ned's feisty stallion. "Oh, please, Mr. Ned, do not ravish me."

More concerned Prudence was going to scare her horse, Rosaleen tightened her gloved fingers on the reins. "Ravish you?" echoed Black Ned. "Why, I wouldn't touch you —" catching herself, Ned gave a low cough.

Prudence began sobbing, pulling on Black Ned's right boot, all the while whimpering to escape a fate worse than death. "Please, Black Ned, don't hurt me, or my brother, or the duke, and even though the coachman is from Surrey, he should be spared too."

All Rosaleen was attempting to do was get this nitwit to unhand her right foot. In her distraught condition over her imagined danger of immediate ravishment from Black Ned, Prudence slammed down with her fist on Rosaleen's foot. The force from this delicate English flower stunned the Irish girl. Rosaleen's foot was still tender from the cut on that rock. She had to bite down hard on her lower lip to keep from crying out as red flashes of pain shot up her ankle.

Henry tried to rise, but the flesh wound on the back of his hand appeared too much for him. He sobbed and fell back against the carriage wheel. "Oh, monstrous blackguard, if only I were not mortally wounded, I'd thrash you with my bare hands. Kill me instead, but I beg of you with my dying breath, do not touch my chaste little sister."

"Blessed saints," Rosaleen muttered as she tried to wiggle her leg to the right and left in an unsuccessful attempt to dislodge Prudence's death grip on her foot. If only she didn't have her back to her men, they could have seen she needed their help.

Watching poor Pru and Henry plead for their lives and Prudence's honor, Lucien's usual reserve in the face of adversity snapped. "Irish guttersnipe, let that woman go!" he shouted in clear, masculine anger. The tall man stalked over to Prudence and Black Ned. Without hesitation, he grabbed Prudence and shoved her behind his muscular frame. "Cowardly bastard, is a defenseless woman the only target you are able to fight?" His bold eyes took a cursory inventory of the highwayman atop his horse. "For the life of me," he scoffed, "I cannot see why Kinsale is giving a farthing in reward to capture the likes of you. The tales are exaggerated in your favor, Ned. Notorious highwayman?" he hoisted, with a scathing laugh. "I see only a badly dressed runt."

Runt? Though she knew she was peti—all right, short, the duke's jeering comments and Prudence's giggle behind her protector changed Rosaleen's intentions. Fire in her dark eyes, she bounded off her horse. Never could she remember being so outraged. It wasn't only the way he comforted Prudence; it was his arrogance in making a fool of her in front of her men. Without hesitation, she drew her sword out of the scabbard on her left hip. "Sure and I'd love ta see if the English coxcomb is as skilled with his sword as he is with his braggin' tongue," she challenged in her perfect imitation of Black Ned.

"How do I know your men will refrain from putting a ball in my brain if I draw my sword?"

Black Ned turned to his men. "This is to be a fair fight between the duke and me. You are not to fire, lads, understood?"

Sean was at her side instantly. "Ned, let's get out of here."

"No," Rosaleen hissed. Then Black Ned said for the benefit of all, "We'll leave after I teach this English fop some Irish manners."

"Aye, you do that for us, Ned," one of the highwaymen said. He and the others put their pistols away and dismounted to watch the entertainment.

Lucien directed Prudence to go back to her brother. Shrugging out of his blue coat, Lucien rolled up his ruffled sleeves. As he walked over to Ned, standing near the man who had shot Henry, Lucien noted the two were about the same height. Only Ned was thinner. Their leader was no more than a lad, with the voice to match. This young Irishman was the talk of Kinsale?

Peering down his straight nose, the towering Englishman took in his black-clothed opponent—scuffed boots, breeches, bulky outer coat, slits for eyes, nose, and mouth in the leather mask covering his whole face, and a laborer's tattered felt hat squashed down over his head. "Tailor been ill this week, has he?"

Rosaleen knew the Englishman was attempting to goad Ned by ridiculing the outlaw's attire. She ignored the barb and took the on-guard stance. Having practiced in secret with her brothers since childhood, she felt at ease fencing. But this was the first time she had the guard tip off her sword, as did her adversary. She knew her opponent had the advantage of muscle and weight, but if she could keep a cool head, this Englishman might receive a small lesson in humility.

Rosaleen saluted her opponent by raising her sword.

"I refuse to return that fencing courtesy, since it is quite apparent, Black Ned, you are no gentleman."

"And 'tis himself agrees with ya," quipped Rosaleen, barely stifling a feminine chuckle. She waited for him to take the offensive, determined to conserve her energy until she needed it most.

Lucien lunged and thrust his rapier at his opponent.

Rosaleen parried the attack, then added a counter-thrust. The sound of steel hitting steel echoed through the still forest. Her senses became more acute as she took in the scent of trees and moist earth at nightfall. They were on her turf now.

Attack, parry, riposte. She kept her attention focused on her antagonist, trying to ignore the sweat from all the clothes she wore to disguise her identity. But she saw that Lucien's face was also beaded with moisture, and there were wet stains under the arms of his lawn shirt. Once she just missed having Lucien's arm brush the front of her bulky coat. Even the binding about her breasts might not hide her sex from a man as perceptive as the duke.

Lucien could hardly believe this Irish bandit knew how to fence. And the blasted scoundrel had grace and proper form. The duke's scientific curiosity got the better of him. Breathing hard as he kept up the offensive, he demanded, "Who taught you . . . those intricate fencing maneuvers?"

"A better man than yerself, Yer Grace," countered the impudent rogue.

It was time this bloody nonsense ended. The duke ground the back of his even white teeth as he increased the speed and force of his attack.

The wind was knocked out of Rosaleen when Lucien took advantage of an opening and pushed the guard of his sword down to her face. She stifled an outcry of pain when her full weight came down on her tender right foot, but she managed to shove her own sword guard up, even if it was an awkward counter-attack on her part. Aware her sword arm was shaking with fatigue while Lucien's muscled arm remained as strong and straight as ever, Rosaleen knew she had to end this duel soon or she would lose. She used her whole body to increase the pressure of her guard against his. His face was so close, she could smell the sandalwood soap on his perspiring skin and feel the warmth of his hard body as he pressed down upon her. A sudden weakness overcame her, and these new feelings frightened her more than the physical danger. She forced herself to concentrate on a plan of action.

"Give up, lad," Lucien advised. "You've lost, for I outweigh you three times over."

"Then, don't I have St. Patrick's luck all yer poundage is located in that conceit between yer ears?"

The duke's eyes became chips of blue ice. With a growl of lost patience, he gripped the handle of his foil tighter and shoved the guard with all his strength down against Ned's.

With lightning speed, Rosaleen sprang back to the right. As she expected, inertia kept Lucien pitching forward.

"Bloody hell" was all her opponent had time to utter. Completely off guard against this unheard of tactic in the gentlemanly art of fencing, Lucien lost his balance and catapulted against the night air instead of his opponent. To add insult to his lost dignity, the duke felt Ned's small booted foot on the seat of his breeches as he pitched by, which only hastened his hard descent to the muddy ground.

"Sure and do ya like me new fencing salute?" asked Ned. Feet spread apart, she smirked down at her adversary. Rosaleen heard the loud guffaws of her men as they enjoyed the scene before them.

"You're a plucky one, Ned. Me and the lads give ya that," shouted Sean, open admiration in his whiny voice.

Murder in his eyes, Lucien Huntington bounded to his feet, his rapier raised to do serious battle.

The duke hadn't felt this humiliated since his last visit here years ago when that brat from the colonies—what the devil was her name, Rosebud, that chit with the blasted mud ball who'd beaten him to a pulp? It had been the first time he'd completely lost his temper. He slashed the air with his sword in remembrance; then a menacing smile transformed his blond features. He was not under any ruddy code of honor here. This was no obnoxious girl; this was a highwayman. "All right, Irishman, you have won the first round. Let us see how well you fare with the gloves off."

Rosaleen read the signs and quickly pulled her loaded, short-barreled pistol from the folds of her black coat. "Put it down, Montrose. The duel is over." Rosaleen expertly pulled back the jaw-screw and aimed the muzzle at the Englishman's chest.

"No, Ned, don't!" Sean Kelly shouted in alarm.

It was important to give them all the full impression she meant business. Rosaleen had to get Lucien unarmed, for his expression told her clearly he was prepared to push this to the death. He was ready to hand over his bag of coins but not his honor. While she admired him for this, she knew hers was the cooler head right now and sought a less violent solution. "Is yer wounded pride worth dying for, Yer Grace? Surely a man of logic would not toss his life away from mere pique, or would he?"

Lucien closed his eyes and forced deep breaths of sweet night air into his heated lungs. It shocked him to realize he'd let anger rule his head for the third time in his life. First that brat years ago at the earl's

72

party, then the cheeky peasant at his pond, now this. Always here in Ireland when it happened, he mused. He tossed the sword down on the ground in disgust. "It appears you have the slight advantage for today," he said, his clear baritone once more returned to normal.

"Oh," cried Prudence, racing over to her mud-covered hero. "Poor, Lucien, are you all right? Here, you," she directed to Sean Kelly. "Fetch His Grace some water and clean linen so that I may wash the mud from his face."

Sean did not move.

"Oh, infamous villain," hoisted Lady Prudence, "to treat an aristocrat with such callous disregard for his toilet." The Englishwoman appeared ready to fling herself into Lucien's strong arms once more, but a quick glance at the oozy mud covering his formerly immaculate attire caused her to move back a pace. "Perhaps you should recline on the ground, like poor Henry."

"No, I am all right, Pru. Pray do not fuss." Lucien felt irritated right now with Prudence Lorens and her brother. If they'd done as he'd ordered, they would merely have lost a few coins and been on their way home by now.

Rosaleen went over to check Henry. Before he could pull away, she observed the superficial graze on his hand. Thank God Kelly was not the best shot. Now, to get them on their way. "Lads, help the lady and two gentlemen ta their coach. You," she directed to their coachman, "please drive yer charges back on the Teran road. It is safer and in better condition than the one ya were using."

The blond-haired girl flounced by Lucien and Ned to head toward her waiting brother. "I must say this is not what I expected after hearing how highwaymen are supposed to act. Churlish group of unimaginative clods," she grumbled.

"And how would ya expect us ta be actin', me lady?" Sean Kelly looked up at the haughty Englishwoman.

Nose in the air, Prudence appeared bored by the question. "You seem more a bunch of masked buffoons than any romantic highwaymen I have read about. For one thing, you and Black Ned are embarrassingly short."

"For God's sake, Prudence, will you get in the damn carriage," Lucien snapped. He walked over to his two companions, bent on nothing but shoving them into the Lorenses' coach and getting the hell out of here. "They didn't do us any real bodily harm and haven't robbed us. What the deuce more do you want?"

"Oh," Ned pointed out. "How lax. Sure and we did forget a few details, didn't we, lads? Our time and the fencing lesson ta His Grace, 'tis worth somethin'. You men get that purse from the coach and collect anything of value from our guests, all except the coachman. Forced ta work for the earl and his sister is punishment enough, I'm thinkin'."

"How dare—surely, you will not rob a lady?" Prudence demanded.

From behind her mask, Rosaleen looked up at Prudence. "Since me height disappoints ya, at least me and the lads can help ya keep some of yer illusions about highwaymen. That brooch you're wearin' and the earrings—hand them over."

"This is not to be endured. I refuse to part with my jewels. Lucien, Henry, do something."

"Both men are too busy emptying their pockets and removin' their diamond stickpins ta come over here, me lady. Besides," Black Ned added with relish, "I still have me sword and pistol as a kind of inducement, ya might say."

Clearly outraged, Lady Prudence unclasped her sapphire and ruby peacock pin from the front of her silk gown, then came the matching earrings. "There," she said, tossing them at Ned. "Take them, you horrid toad."

Ned turned one of the earrings over in his gloved fingers. "Do you know how many starving Irish children I can feed with just this tiny earring?"

"Certainly not. These Irish Catholics breed like distasteful rabbits. Vermin, all of you, not fit to be in Ireland."

Lady Prudence could only follow when Ned turned his back on her and returned to the duke and earl. Ned tossed the jewels up to one of his men, who placed them with the others in a tattered piece of cloth.

"Isn't . . . isn't there anything else you would rather have instead of my jewelry?"

Rosaleen did not miss the look of shock on Lucien's face at Prudence's bold offer. Even Henry looked appalled. "Well, let's see," Rosaleen said in Black Ned's voice. She walked about Prudence, imitating a man checking over the points of a horse for sale. "Is there anything else I want?" she repeated

Prudence's question, then stepped over to the duke of Montrose. "Sure and I've always fancied a pair of blue silk breeches."

The thought of returning home stripped like a plucked goose caused a crimson stain to spread across Lucien's face. At the moment, he could have choked Prudence with his bare hands.

Her joke on Prudence appeared lost on the duke of Montrose, so Rosaleen quickly sought to reassure him. "Ya can keep yer drawers, Yer Grace, for they're ruined beyond salvage. Take yer friends and go."

Prudence appeared disappointed. "You mean . . . you are not even—you do not intend to kiss me?"

"I'd rather eat a bucket of peat," Black Ned told Henry's sister.

Despite himself, Lucien found the corners of his mouth twitched at the Irishman's rejoinder.

By the time the highwaymen were ready to assist the three English aristocrats back in their coach, Rosaleen's ears were burning from the colorful curses coming from Prudence Lorens's supposedly ladylike lips. As the storm blew on and on, Rosaleen could feel her irritation rise. It was obvious Pru's brother and the duke had given up trying to quiet the harridan's flare-up over losing her jewelry.

"Wait," Black Ned shouted. "Just the coachman will drive home." Raising her gloved hand, she gave the lead horse a forceful swat on the rump. The frightened coachman could do nothing but hold on.

As the rattling sound of the coach and hoofbeats muffled in the distance, Prudence seemed to realize the implication of Ned's actions. "It is over two miles back to Lorens Hall," she screeched, looking up at the five Irishmen atop their horses.

Black Ned appeared unmoved. "The walk will do the three of you good. Perhaps when you meet another Irishman on these roads, me lady, you'll be less apt ta curse him with such foul language. You may keep your sword, Lucien, for Black Ned would never leave a man defenseless. If Lady Prudence gives ya too much lip, ya may have ta use it on her. Take the road ta yer right. It will be safer for ya and is in better repair than the roads on Montrose lands." She turned to the four riders next to her. "Come on, lads, we've wasted too much time here."

Alone with her brother and silent Lucien, Prudence could hardly believe she was going to have to walk at night, in her Paris gown, through the mud and wet grass, and she began spouting her feelings to the two men with her.

"Sir Jeremy Cartgrove will hear of this, I promise you." She had to trudge faster to keep up with Lucien's long-legged stride. Behind her, Henry kept complaining about the "mortal wound" on his hand.

A dull pounding started behind Lucien's eyes. At least Black Ned had given them directions to get home. Only back a few days, he was not that familiar with the roads yet. As Henry and Prudence kept up their diatribe, the throbbing in Lucien's head became worse. Tempted to leave both caterwauling Lorenses in the middle of the road, his lips compressed to a grim line as he led their way home. The duke of Montrose suddenly wished he were riding next to Black Ned and his men—at least those

77

Irishmen did not have to contend with listening to these two pampered English aristocrats.

"Liz, do you think this cape looks better buttoned to the throat?" Sitting on the couch next to her Fitzroy cousin, Rosaleen rebuttoned the top clasp of her purple cloak.

"Either way looks fine, Ross." The girl patted Rosaleen's gloved fingers.

Rosaleen gave Elizabeth a grateful smile, then went back to gazing out the carriage window. Aunt Edna had insisted she accept this invitation to meet "suitable" young people at the Lorenses' party tonight. While the earl of Holingbrook's niece admitted she could not avoid these social functions forever, the prospect of seeing Lucien again filled her with both excitement and dread. Certain Black Ned's identity was safe for the present, Miss O'Rahilly knew the duke would now realize she'd been the mysterious trespasser in his pond. How would he react to this discovery? Would he be appalled at her unconventional behavior? Or could he understand her need for those rare moments of freedom so precious to her? Wouldn't a man as skilled and gentle in tending her injured foot be progressive in his thinking about women? Of course, she reminded herself, the duke had been raised in the best London schools, along with all those stuffy, unbending English aristocrats who probably thought the honor of King and Country depended on women keeping their "proper" place.

That word again set her teeth on edge. She fidgeted with the top clasp of her cape once more. Would the cursed thing look better unbuttoned? she wondered, suddenly wishing she were riding on the roads with Sean Kelly tonight, not on her way to her first ball in Kinsale.

Lucien tried to pay attention as Lady Prudence Lorens went on speaking with her enraptured guests. Apparently, a few days' rest had altered the lady's memory of their encounter with Black Ned.

"Oh, I can tell you Ned is divinely handsome — dark, towering height, with the air of a man used to giving orders. He and his men swooped down on our carriage before we knew what they were about. Henry was savagely shot before he could overpower them."

"Did Black Ned kiss you?" Lucien heard one of the ladies ask her friend.

The blond Englishwoman looked aghast. "Well, he would have, but I defended my good name as best I might; then the duke challenged Black Ned to a duel. Imagine," Miss Lorens went on, her pale eyes shining, "His Grace fought a duel to defend my honor. It was all too, too divine."

"Good show, Montrose. Overpowered the rotter, did you?" James Winthrop asked.

To Lucien, manure wafted in the air from Pru's fabrications. He answered his old schoolmate with the truth. "Alas, Black Ned used a vaulting maneuver not in the code books. I was left feeling a complete ass, facedown in the mud."

"Oh, Your Grace, you are too harsh on yourself."

The stuffed bluebird perched in the center of Prudence's high, powdered wig moved forward with her agitation. "You fought most valiantly. Why, I can still see you—coat off, sleeves rolled up, sword flashing against Black Ned's in the moonlight. It was glorious. Upon my soul, if you were not already a duke, I should write to King George to have you knighted for your courage in defending my honor from those huge, dangerous cutthroats."

Lucien groaned inwardly as Prudence went on with more colorful renditions of the event.

"This quiet gathering tonight must seem rather tame stuff for you after London and Paris, eh, Montrose?"

The duke looked at James and smiled. "Winthrop, I assure you this Lorenses' party could rival many I've attended in London or Paris."

Hardly hearing Lucien's answer, Winthrop looked adoringly at Lady Prudence when the tall, slender beauty consented to dance with him. It was clear to Lucien, the young lawyer was smitten with her.

Lucien glanced about the large ballroom. Henry seemed to spare little expense making this the showplace of Kinsale. Huge crystal chandeliers gleamed with lighted candles, and the walls were covered with hand-painted paper from China of birds and peonies. Men and women in the latest Paris attire and powdered wigs moved slowly toward the next room, where the food tables were piled high with cold ham, beef, and salmon. White-gloved servants in black livery were at their beck and call. An orchestra began playing another piece by Handel. It all reminded the duke of countless other functions he'd attended—and promised to be just as dull. In truth, he would rather have been at Montrose Hall in the basement working at getting his laboratory in order. Furthermore, he had to look for a new overseer to replace Tom Bennet, whom he'd fired this morning. Then there were the tenants' cottages to repair.

He'd dutifully danced with the dowagers and the eligible daughters they eagerly presented to him tonight. It was evident they considered him a "catch." Though he tried to be pleasant, Lucien admitted he would probably never fall in love with any woman. That outrageous Irish hoyden at his pond was the first young woman to intrigue him. He could not help smiling as he remembered her angry little face when she had berated him for his neglect of his Montrose lands here.

With an inward sigh, Lucien decided to make his polite adieus and return home.

On his way to find his hostess, Lucien left the ballroom and headed toward the entrance hall. He stopped in his tracks when he saw the young woman just entering the Lorenses' home.

Henry Lorens assisted the late arrival with her dark purple cloak. A taller young woman accompanied her, but Lucien had eyes only for the petite beauty. Black hair pulled back and up, with adorable ringlets framing a sweet, oval face—it was *her*—the naked Irish elf from his pond!

Astonishment, then delight transformed Lucien's features.

As Henry escorted the two ladies toward him, for

the first time in his life the duke found he could not move or utter a coherent word.

"Leaving us so soon, Your Grace?"

Lucien knew Henry was speaking to him. He tried to get his usually logical thoughts in order, but they tumbled about his mind like lumbering oafs in a china shop. "I—that is I—" All the while, he kept staring at her.

Rosaleen looked up at Lucien. At such a close proximity, the expression in his blue eyes made something flutter within her chest. Golden Lucifer, she called him in her mind, then tried again to get her riotous emotions under control. Perhaps Elizabeth's maid had tied her corset too tightly, Rosaleen thought. Why else would she feel faint in such a large hallway? She could not help taking in his attire. He was dressed impeccably in black coat and knee breeches, his embroidered gold waistcoat matching the dark gold of his hair. "Perhaps," she finally managed, "you should introduce us, Henry."

"Lady Elizabeth Fitzroy, Miss Rosaleen O'Rahilly, I should like to present Lucien Huntington, Duke of Montrose."

Each woman executed a perfect curtsy.

Bow, you idiot! Lucien shouted at himself. First he executed a proper bow to the taller girl. When he came to the source of his captivation, his movements felt uncharacteristically clumsy.

Henry looked surprised at his friend's odd behavior but apparently tried to cover it with conversation. "Miss O'Rahilly is the earl's niece. She is visiting us earlier than usual this year, and we are most grateful."

"We have met before," Lucien blurted.

Rosaleen's eyes darted upward in alarm. Was he going to humiliate her by bringing up that unfortunate meeting at the pond?

As if reading her thoughts, Lucien hastened to add, "The lady was ten but still managed to best me with a barrage of mud balls. I felt the effects of her fists on my jaw and nose for a week."

Henry chuckled. "Now I remember. Elizabeth, we were all at your father's garden party. I say, what a first meeting. Not every day you meet an old sparring partner, Rosaleen."

"Quite so." Rosaleen could not hold back a smile of relief that he was not going to give her indiscretion away. "I fear I made a most unfavorable impression on His Grace." The warm expression in his azure eyes almost took her breath away. "I pray you, sir, please do not judge all Virginians by my deplorable behavior."

Lost when the dimple popped out at the corner of her mouth, Lucien returned the lady's smile. "You were hardly more than a baby at the time, Miss O'Rahilly, and I should have been horsewhipped for my boorish manners. Shall we call a truce, then, for I am loath to think I will never have another opportunity to redeem myself in your beautiful eyes?"

Despite her intent, Rosaleen could not keep the faint pinkness from washing across her smooth face at his words. "I have been told you are a man of science, a gentleman more at home with books and air pumps," she could not help teasing. "Yet, I find you speak like a courtier, quite at ease spouting pretty speeches to charm a roomful of ladies."

Rosaleen saw something glint in Lucien's eyes at her flippancy; then it was gone. Henry and Elizabeth stared at them. Could they feel the sparks between them, too? she wondered. The silence was disconcerting.

"Well," finished Rosaleen, intent on putting distance between her and Lucien, "Elizabeth and I will pay our respects to Prudence."

"Oh, Henry can do that for you later," Lucien said, inwardly amazed at his boldness. "I am certain Lady Elizabeth would like to dance. And that will give Miss O'Rahilly and I a chance to catch up on old times." Blue eyes captured dark brown with just the hint of a challenge.

Chapter Five

Rosaleen realized Lucien had outmaneuvered her. She could not refuse without appearing ungracious. She turned to her auburn-haired cousin. "You go along, Liz. I shall join you presently."

When they were alone, Rosaleen waited for her companion to speak.

"I am not a very good dancer," Lucien admitted. "But I should be honored if you care to accompany me for the next minuet."

Though tempted, Rosaleen forced reason to dominate. "Thank you, but I must decline." Why ever was he looking at her in that way again?

Lucien enjoyed studying her. Unlike so many of the ladies here, Rosaleen's hair was not powdered, nor had she opted for a wig frizzled into one of those towering concoctions. She must know the elaborate wigs favored by Lady Prudence and her friends would look dreadful with her small features. He took in her gown, aware again she did not let the ton dictate her style. None of the pale pastels in satin for her. On such a warm summer evening, this colonial wore a more practical gown—simple, yet elegant. The soft cotton of the ecru background cascaded with lovely lilacs. He noted only the finest Dutch lace appeared at the elbow-length sleeves. An ecru-colored silk ribbon entwined her dark curls.

Dismissing the reserve his mother had insisted from him since childhood, the duke moved closer. He delighted in the faint scent of lilacs that seemed to cling to Rosaleen's soft, pale skin. The top of her lovely dark head just reached his chin. How endearingly petite she was, he mused. Without jewelry, she wore a richly embroidered ribbon about her slender throat.

Rosaleen was more than disconcerted by his unhurried perusal. "Sir, it is not proper for you to stare so. We are being watched. Since there are many more beautiful ladies here who I am certain are eager to dance with you, I will bid you good evening. Pray, be kind enough to escort me to my hostess?"

No answer.

Miss O'Rahilly now wondered if the blond-haired man could even hear her. "Your Grace, is it your intention to keep us standing out here in the entryway until there is a change of season?"

"What—oh, yes, of course. The air is cleaner here than in London." From his companion's expression, it was clear he'd made a slight faux pas. Heat rushed to his face. What the devil was wrong with him? he asked himself. He'd had women before; why was this one so different? Remembering his manners, he offered the lady his arm and began walking with her toward the crowded ballroom.

"Did you embroider those lovely butterflies yourself?"

"No," Rosaleen answered truthfully. "It was a present from my mother." She touched the soft ribbon at her throat. "Gentle and kind, Mother has many wonderful traits, which I lack. I fear I may never master such domestic arts as needlework."

"Enchanting," Lucien murmured. "Adorable angel from heaven."

"For God's sake, Lucien, get a grip on yourself. You are acting like a complete jackass," Rosaleen hissed for his ears alone. Everyone else would think they were sharing some pleasantry.

Catapulted back to earth, Lucien cleared his throat.

"Recognize your name, do you?"

"You mean Lucien or the four-legged creature?" he asked, not able to explain why he did not mind whatever she called him right now.

"I am sorry, Your Grace."

"Call me Lucien. Please."

As two gentlemen approached, Rosaleen was almost overcome by Edwin Somerset's jasmine cologne. Used to seeing Edwin and his younger companion, Prince Rinaldo, in Kinsale each summer when Garnet's brother returned once a year to check on his estate here, Rosaleen was confused to feel the corded muscles of Lucien's arm tighten under her gloved fingertips. He appeared uncomfortable at seeing his uncle.

It was clear the more elaborately dressed man was waiting for His Grace to make a proper greeting.

Lucien did not expect Edwin to be here with his

amour, the darkly handsome Rinaldo. Well, nothing for it but to bold it out. His smile was a bit strained when he turned back to Rosaleen. "Rosaleen O'Rahilly, I should like to present my uncle, Edwin Somerset, and Prince Rinaldo, visiting here from Italy."

Curtsying, Rosaleen looked across at Lucien's uncle. The slender man in his mid-forties wore yellow-and-green-striped coat and breeches. His wig was powdered to match his canary-yellow waistcoat. The black triangular patch on his right cheek stood out against the heavy powder on his face. The man appeared to be wearing rouge.

"Mr. Somerset and I have met before during my summer visits to Kinsale with my parents," Rosaleen explained.

Edwin bowed over her gloved fingers. Peering at the lady through his quizzing glass, he gushed, "Charming, my dear. They tell me this is your first appearance at one of these functions. For shame. You should attend more parties given by the gentry, for you are a breath of fresh air from the colonies."

"Thank you, sir."

"Exquisite. You have your father's eyes, Miss O'Rahilly."

Taken aback that this Englishman did not smile when he made the remark, she was glad when his younger companion bowed to her, for she did not know what to reply to Edwin.

"Madonna, who could imagine such a dark rose would be blooming here in these rough hills of Ireland?"

"I am a transplant, Your Highness." The dimple

popped out at the corner of her mouth. "But I thank you for your kind remark."

About thirty, the prince was dressed similar to Lucien in dark evening clothes with his black hair tied neatly at the back of his neck. Without powder or rouge, his swarthy good looks were not hidden. While she conversed politely with Edwin, Rosaleen noticed Lucien relax as he and Rinaldo exchanged a few pleasantries. Then Lucien excused them, leaving her no choice but to continue walking through the crowd with him.

"I am sorry," Lucien said. "I had no choice but to introduce you."

Rosaleen sensed his discomfort. "Think nothing of it, Your Grace. I am aware of such things. My father told me about your uncle and his . . . inclinations when I asked him one summer years ago after I saw Edwin and Rinaldo out riding together."

Taggart O'Rahilly was certainly an unusual parent, Lucien mused, not sure he approved of the Irishman's openness on such matters with his innocent daughter.

The duke maneuvered them to a more secluded corner at the back of the large room, for he wished to speak to her with as much privacy as decorum allowed. He stopped when satisfied with their location. Standing in front of her, Lucien wanted no one else's eyes on her but his. He desired to learn everything about this captivating lady.

"Pray forgive my earlier unkind remark, Lucien. Patience has never come easily to me." She could not help returning his good-natured smile. "Thank you for not giving me away, about our meeting the other day near your . . . your property."

Something lurched in his chest at the way she blushed so adorably. The candles in the room gave her skin an ethereal glow. He shoved his hands behind his back for fear he might reach out to touch her smooth cheek or fondle one of those midnight curls that draped so alluringly on her bare shoulder. He whispered close to her dainty ear, "You may swim in my pond any day you choose, Rosaleen."

When she stepped two paces back, he saw her take the ivory fan that hung on her gloved wrist and open it. He watched as she fanned her cheeks in a clear attempt to get the rose color to recede. Did she blush all over, he wondered, a roguish smile coming to his sensuous lips once more. This raven-haired temptress was causing him to think the most wickedly erotic thoughts.

"You have bewitched me, sweet elf. Never have I felt or spoken this way before. When you tossed my compliment about your lovely eyes back at me, you knew I was displeased with you. I wonder," he mused aloud at the surprise on Rosaleen's face, "are you a dark-eyed conjurer of spells, for I feel quite lost in the depths of those gypsy eyes. I assure you, enchantress, air pumps and microscopes are not on my mind right now. You have darted in and out of my thoughts since that first afternoon I found you, a most enticing little mermaid. Had it all been in my mind? I thought, for I did not even know your name, or how to find you. Try as I might, I could glean nothing more about you. You disappeared as quickly as you charged into my life. I was close to

90

believing I'd come under some Irish mischief from the little people."

"Please, Lucien, for both our sakes speak no more of these romantic musings. In truth, I regret that afternoon more than you will ever know."

A thought occurred to him, and the amusement left his features. "Your foot, does it still hurt? Would you like to sit down?"

"Oh, no," she hastened to reassure him. "It is almost healed, thanks to your salve and excellent ministrations." How could she tell Lucien she regretted the afternoon at the pond because of the false conclusions it was causing him to believe about her character?

After a few silent moments, he asked, "Why did you keep your true identity from me?"

A sigh escaped her lips. It became clear this man was determined to have his questions answered. "I was embarrassed at being caught at such a disadvantage. Also, I suppose my pride felt bruised because you did not remember knowing me years ago."

"I see." His expression was accepting, with just the hint of amusement. "I hope this will not offend you, but you were a trifle bedraggled when I first spotted you. Then—" he chose his words carefully—"with your lack of attire, I did attempt to look away from you to avoid taking advantage of the situation."

"You did behave with circumspection; for that I thank you. I . . . I now realize from your words tonight you must think me quite . . . quite lacking in decorum for daring to—I mean, it is not the first time I have gone swimming there in that way." She bent her head, unable to watch the shock and censure she believed would enter his eyes. She was confused by the way he had first looked at her this evening. He had watched her with the eyes of a man worshipping a goddess. Yet, it made her feel ashamed. More than anyone, she knew her shortcomings.

"To cure you of your misguided infatuation, I must tell you some truths of my nature." She went on. "I have on occasion what my family despairingly calls 'the devil's own temper.' I do not enjoy such ladylike pursuits as embroidery or playing the harpsichord. I have been visiting Uncle Dunstan and Aunt Edna since April because I got into trouble with the Royal Governor of Virginia when I criticized England's treatment of her colonies. It was at an elaborate ball where dignitaries from England and the colonies were in attendance. My poor parents felt it would be safer for me to come to Kinsale ahead of their usual visit in a few weeks in order for the gossip about my outspokenness in Williamsburg to die down." Rosaleen continued to gaze at the tops of her purple slippers. For an unexpected reason, she felt moisture sting the corners of her eyes. This would end any romantic notions about the duke of Montrose. God, how he would despise her if he knew the whole truth, she thought. "Excuse me, Your Grace. I must find my cousin."

"No, wait." Lucien reached out to stop her, but he was too late. She was gone in a swirl of wispy lilac. Prudence came at him before he could get away from the crush of people. "Blast it," he muttered under his breath.

Quickly, Rosaleen dashed for the next room, looking up only when she was on the far side of the food tables. People stood about eating and chatting. It was just as stifling in here as the heated ballroom, but she congratulated herself on her exit. She had done it, ended it before it could start. And she had to do it, for her work as Black Ned was too important to jeopardize. Hadn't she dreamed of seeing that warmth in his blue eyes? Yet, when the moment actually happened, it frightened her, just like the night they had crossed swords outside Kinsale. Something drew her to him, and tonight she realized Lucien experienced the same magnetic pull. Only, Rosaleen also felt the danger. Too many people depended on her. Though it was amusing the way he'd first been so tongue-tied, she knew Lucien was shrewd. When his faculties returned to normal, he might prove dangerous. Even not meaning to, he could destroy her and harm the people she desperately wanted to help.

For the rest of the evening, Rosaleen made polite conversation with Prudence and her guests, even accepting the requests for dances from at least five young bucks. Forcing herself to appear the picture of gaiety, Rosaleen did not see Lucien in the press of people. Had he left, appalled by her confession? Well, it was for the best, she reminded herself again. He had appeared so enamored, he was obviously confusing her with some ideal of his own, and she believed he would certainly be disappointed with the reality. Irish from her father, English from her aristocratic mother, Rosaleen really was not sure where she belonged. Even as a wealthy colonial heiress, she was not at ease among these powdered and bejeweled English people. Nor was she fitting in at home in Virginia with her candor. Though determined to assist the Irish Catholics here, Rosaleen felt very alone right now, for there was no one with whom she could share her true feelings and thoughts. Lucien would never know his attentions tonight made her painfully aware of her lack of conformity. It left her lonelier than she'd ever felt in her life.

As she glanced about the room, Rosaleen suddenly spotted a girl her own age, sitting silently with the older ladies. The straight-haired girl reminded Rosaleen of how her mother might have appeared at that age, and something touched her.

The duke came over to her minutes later and asked for the next dance.

"Your Grace, I would be more grateful if you would ask that young lady on the other side of the room, the one sitting in the midst of those elderly dowagers. I have noticed since my arrival she has not danced once this evening."

Irritated Rosaleen was again putting him off, Lucien frowned in the direction she indicated. "You mean the mousey one who looks ready to bolt for the door at any second?"

Rosaleen gave him a level stare. "You are a titled, handsome man, so you have never known what it is like to feel out of place, especially where looks are concerned." She thought of her mother's gentle ways. "If you dance with her, Your Grace, the other gentlemen here will take your lead. It is such a trifling to you, but I know it will mean a lot to the young lady. Please," she added.

Lost to the pleading in her sweet voice, Lucien asked, "How can I refuse you anything?"

"Thank you, Your Grace. I can think of nothing that would make me happier."

"But there is a price for my compliance."

Wariness with English aristocrats was a difficult habit to break. "Your price may be higher than I can pay."

He looked bemused by her remark. "A dance before you leave is all I ask."

Rosaleen smiled her relief. "Yes, I promise you a dance."

For a tall man, his movements were graceful, she thought, as he walked over to the girl. Rosaleen could not hide her pleasure as she watched the young lady stand up, before Lucien escorted her over to the two lines of men and women. Taking her place on the side with the other ladies, the girl blushed and moved awkwardly at first. Then Lucien spoke to her, encouragingly, Rosaleen was certain, for she saw the transformation when the girl became more secure about her abilities.

At the conclusion of the minuet, Lucien saw the lady back to her chair, bowed deeply over her hand, then left the smiling, radiant girl. He returned to Rosaleen.

"Her name is Emily Cramer. A pleasant young woman," he added, clearly surprised. "I did enjoy dancing with her more than I first thought."

"If only men would look beyond the surface, they

would not miss such rewarding experiences. Oh," Rosaleen whispered with delight, "there goes James Winthrop over to ask Emily for a dance. You have done it, Lucien. How marvelous."

Lucien was moved by the clear enjoyment she took in another girl's happiness. Few women of his association would have bothered about a plain country mouse. The more he learned about this colonial girl, the better he liked her. "The dance?" he reminded. "If we join the minuet, you can spy more easily on your lamb."

"Oh, yes," she agreed, not taking offense at his humor. "I will be happy to dance with you now."

"There you are, Miss O'Rahilly." Henry Lorens came over to take her arm before Lucien had a chance to offer his. "This is our dance, I believe."

Rosaleen bit her lip. It was true; she had promised Henry the next dance. Apologetically, she looked at Lucien, then allowed Henry to lead her onto the parquet floor. She would dance with the duke later.

The room seemed too warm, and as Lucien watched Rosaleen and Henry perform the intricate steps of the minuet—their hands touched, they stepped back, then smiled at each other—he felt the need for fresh air. It appeared Miss O'Rahilly was still reluctant to dance with him. Had she made that promise merely to get him to dance with Emily?

Half an hour later, Lucien opened the French doors leading back to the ballroom. He'd spent the time walking in the Lorenses' gardens alone, trying to sort out his thoughts. It was clear he had not handled things well this evening. Of course, Miss O'Rahilly probably thought him the "ass" she had rightly called him for his odd behavior. Still positive of his feelings, he realized he never should have declared himself so quickly and with such fervor. Even though he'd never experienced such an instantaneous attraction before, a lady like Rosaleen was probably terrified of such declarations upon their first meeting as adults. He smiled when he remembered her long confession. What an adorable little angel she was, he mused, then headed back to the earl and James Winthrop.

"Where have you been, Montrose?" Henry complained. "Pru's been after me to find you. Says you promised her another dance."

"Sorry. Just getting some air." His eyes searched and found Rosaleen. Women on one side, men on the other. Rosaleen's new partner this time was a scarlet-coated officer. He recognized Colonel Percy Bembridge.

"I'll say this, Montrose, Miss O'Rahilly has captured all the hearts of Kinsale's eligible bachelors' this night. I couldn't even get another dance with her. We're all smitten with her."

With a deep sigh, Lucien had to agree with Henry. It was clear the dark-haired beauty had made a number of conquests tonight. But, he thought, feeling suddenly confident after a walk about the gardens, a logical plan of action seemed called for. Miss Rosaleen O'Rahilly was not like other English ladies of his acquaintance; he was certain of it now. He would have to approach her differently. She would not be impressed with an adoring swain bumbling about her ankles like a lap dog. When the colonel escorted his partner back toward them, Lucien kept his features politely impassive.

Accepting a glass of ratafia from Henry, Rosaleen saw the fastidiously dressed colonel's features change to astonishment when he saw the duke. "Montwose, didn't know you were back in Kinsale. Sink me, does her gwace know you are here?"

His question jarred the younger man, and his back took on a more military posture. Lucien reminded himself Percy had been a source of solace to his bereaved mother after Calvert's death. She always spoke warmly of the colonel. Well, he thought, his young, widowed mother deserved happiness, and if she chose it with Colonel Bembridge, Lucien was not her judge. "I left London in a hurry, sir. The idea of a Grand Tour did not appeal to me, so I decided to see my estate here in Kinsale."

"Pwease give your mother my regard when you write her tonight to inform her where you are."

Lucien did not miss the colonel's meaning. Percy could not know Lucien had written Garnet before his ship sailed for Cork. "Yes, I shall do that, Percy."

"Oh, Colonel Bembridge, the very man I wish to see." Prudence Lorens pulled her escort over to the group of people standing near the duke.

In his late forties, Percy Bembridge had risen rapidly through the military ranks. Attention to detail was his motto. He bowed to Lady Prudence and listened while the Englishwoman expounded her version of the encounter with Black Ned.

Rosaleen stood listening to the colorful story, for tale it was. Prudence did have a vivid imagination, but it was to Black Ned's advantage. Pru now began describing Black Ned as over six feet tall, with shoulders the size of tree trunks.

Percy took advantage of the lady's need to stop for air and added, "Ah, yes, the chief magistwate has informed me of the details, your ladyship. Pwease have no fear. We will capture that Irish vermin and his scurvy partners. Hanging will be too good for them."

Rosaleen felt her slender chin come up, but she vowed to remain silent.

"Bunch of thieving hooligans," Henry added as the crowd about them nodded in agreement. "Like all Irish in this land, ignorant rabble. Why, one Englishman is worth ten Irishmen with their superstitious religion and criminal ways. If it weren't for the Irish, Ireland would be a pleasant place to live."

Rosaleen's gloved fingers tightened at her sides. "Though without them, you would probably last all of three minutes with no Irish servants to fetch and carry for you, or tenants to work your lands." Because she was a rich heiress from Virginia, dressed in an expensive gown, did all these English people forget what blood ran in her veins? She could not even look at Lucien. Did he feel the same way as they did?

"Surely you are not defending a criminal like Black Ned?" Colonel Percy Bembridge demanded.

Rosaleen felt their rapt attention. Never should she have come here, even at Aunt Edna's insistence. She did not belong here. Her cousins were the earl of Holingbrook's children, raised as proper English Anglicans like their father. How easily they fit into this English world, hardly ever mentioning their mother being Irish Catholic. Even her aunt appeared more comfortable as Edna Fitzroy, Countess of Holingbrook. That she was the former Irish groom's, Taggart O'Rahilly's, younger sister—no Englishman ever mentioned it. Rosaleen did not set herself above anyone else, but she could never stifle that part of her legacy. "You seem to forget I am an Irish Catholic."

Henry brushed her words aside. "Oh, Ross, we all think of you more as Lady Millicent's daughter and the earl's niece. No one blames you for your father being Irish."

"How magnanimous," Rosaleen snapped. "However, I happen to be proud of my Irish heritage, too."

Lucien took in the shocked expressions about him at Rosaleen's declaration. He could have throttled Henry for his condescending remark. Feeling an overwhelming protectiveness for her, Lucien sought to deflect their reaction to himself, but he suspected this independent beauty was not going to appreciate his interference.

"As well you should be proud, Miss O'Rahilly. Ireland has a rich, if troubled, history, with gallant warriors and courageous ladies. Despite what you may believe, Ross, I do see more than one side to this Irish-English dilemma. Those highwaymen appeared decidedly underfed to me, even through their masks and black rags. Much to my shame, my estate and tenants have gone to ruin through my absentee landlordship. Through my negligence, I now realize I added to the hardships of the Irish here, something I intend to rectify. In the morning, the workmen arrive to assist my tenants in repairing their cottages. Then I plan to purchase more sheep and cows, organize the planting of more crops. I need to hire a great many Irish workers, especially since I mean to restore Montrose Hall to its former beauty. It will be a long process, but I hope to prove to my tenants how much I regret letting them down in the past."

Rosaleen could not help showing how much his words pleased her. "Oh, Your Grace, I am sure you will succeed."

"However," the duke went on, holding up his right hand when he saw Henry and the colonel open their mouths to protest. "I will never countenance breaking the law as an answer to their Irish problems. Lady Prudence's brooch belonged to her grandmother. Henry's and my stickpins, along with our coins, belonged to us. There is a decided difference in the alms I choose to give freely to the poor here and in London, as opposed to being forced by the business end of a pistol to hand over what is legally mine."

"Here, here," said a few gentlemen listening about them.

"Pru," Lucien addressed his hostess, who stood next to James Winthrop. "I heard your vivid description of Black Ned. You think most highwaymen are like the stories you've read, similar to ones about the notorious Dick Turpin, do you not? Romantic hero, ladies?" The duke shook his blond head. "Dick Turpin was a butcher by trade, his face marked by smallpox. It was documented Turpin was not averse to holding the ladies of the house over an open fire until they confessed where the family wealth was hidden. From Newgate prison, his life ended in 1739 at Tyburn gallows."

His Grace's eyes focused on the dark-haired lady. "Black Ned and his fellow criminals—yes, Ross, I said criminals, for they are breaking the law. They take property they do not own, frighten English passengers only intent on returning safely to their homes. Irish patriots? No. They are Irish hooligans who steal what is not theirs."

"Just as England stole Ireland from the Irish, Your Grace?"

Even Lucien was taken aback by Rosaleen's boldness. It was treasonous to speak such words, even in this relaxed atmosphere of a party, and she had shouted the words in front of one of His Majesty's chief military officers. God, he thought, didn't she realize the danger? All his logical attempts to show her and his English friends the complexities of the situation in Ireland now seemed for naught. Uneasily, Lucien saw Percy stare at Miss O'Rahilly, as if seeing her for the first time. The gasps of horror and unfriendly looks from some of the gentlemen and ladies shouted one thing to him: Logic be damned; he'd better diffuse things quickly.

Lucien forced a languor in his cultured speech he did not feel. "Gad, Miss O'Rahilly, next you'll be wanting me to apologize for a thousand years of history. No matter what anyone says, my sensitive nature convinces me I was solely responsible for Attila the Hun." He stifled a yawn behind his right hand. "All this talk of politics is dashed fatiguing. Reminds me of the time I chased you about the food tables at your uncle's party years ago."

Giving the impression of unruffled congeniality, the duke was relieved to see the people about him relax — all except Rosaleen O'Rahilly. He was certain only he could discern the meaning of that pinched look about her nostrils; but he ignored it, for it was partly her own fault she was in this predicament. "Remember, Bembridge, how my mother almost had you arrest the little hoyden? Course you do. Bless me, I ruined my best silk coat trying to protect myself from this amazon warrior."

Shorter than all the gentlemen present, Rosaleen saw many of them grin at the duke's absurd reference.

"I do recall it, Your Grace." The colonel gave a hearty laugh. "A little brawler even then."

"Oh, you can laugh," His Grace went on, sounding petulant. "Only I had the devil's own time until I pushed her into a bed of flowers. The jarring contact with her dignity seemed to get the brat's attention. Got a flower bed I can use, Pru? If this naughty guest keeps spouting such political twaddle, I may have need of it again."

Rosaleen heard the open laughter about her. Ladies tittered behind their fans; gentlemen grinned. James Winthrop gave Lucien a knowing wink. Deliberately, Lucien was making a fool of her in front of these English snobs, making certain anything serious she could counter with now would only be met with ridicule.

"Careful, Your Grace," Henry warned his friend with a chuckle. "Else Rosaleen will give you another lump on the jaw to remember her by."

Lucien appeared befuddled. "What? Just because I say Black Ned is nothing more than an underfed runt with bad tailoring? Bless me, a good Paris suit with clean lace at the cuffs would reform the fellow." With a blank stare, he looked about the jovial crowd when their laughter became more raucous.

The source of their amusement spoke privately to her hostess. "Pru, would you please tell Elizabeth I have gone back to Fitzroy Hall. No need for her to leave this soon. I shall not require the Fitzroy coach."

Taken aback, Lady Prudence said, "Of course, Rosaleen, but you must allow me to arrange your transportation home."

Rosaleen made no attempt to hide the coolness in her features as she glared up at the faces about her. "No thank you. You have all done quite enough for me for one evening. Good night, ladies, gentlemen."

As the crowd dispersed to line up for the next dance, Lucien kept his eyes on Rosaleen. Before he could follow her, he felt Percy's hand on his arm.

"As a . . . a fwiend of your dear mama's, I feel I must warn you. I am certain Her Gwace would not approve your chasing after that Irish girl. A duke should aim higher than a mere colonial with money, a Catholic at that. She will only bring you trouble and disgrace. Your youthful dalliances are better spent with English girls."

"Thank you for your concern, Colonel." All pretense at congeniality departed his blond features. "Now, kindly take your bloody hand off my coat."

Such was the cold fury in the duke's voice, Percy found himself releasing the young man's arm. Grimly, he watched Lucien leave by the side door in the opposite direction from Miss O'Rahilly. He smoothed one of the side curls of his bagwig. Nothing to worry about, the officer decided, for Lucien was clearly taking his advice and staying away from the girl. Young buck just wanted to have the last word, that was why he had sounded so autocratic just now. All the same, the colonel knew where his duty rested. Percy decided to send an urgent message to Garnet this very night. He would use his diplomatic contacts to get the note to her immediately.

Never looking back, Rosaleen walked quickly from the ballroom. She slipped the servant girl two coins to retrieve the purple cape. Miss O'Rahilly was determined to walk the few miles back to Fitzroy Hall rather than be beholden to any of these English for a carriage. Down the long drive toward the dark road leading home, Rosaleen pumped her legs as fast as her attire allowed. How she wished she had on her comfortable breeches now. It was easier to walk in boots than these heeled dress slippers. Sean Kelly was right. All these English were cruel, heartless, self-indulged . . . "Snobs," she muttered.

"I beg your pardon?" said a familiar voice in front of her.

She looked up to spot Lucien standing next to his carriage. He had his leather gloves and tricorn hat on, clearly ready to leave. She recognized the Montrose crest on the door. A driver in gray livery sat atop the coach. When Brian Fogarty exited the vehicle, she could not help greeting the short Irishman in his fifties. With his close-cropped white hair and sparkle emanating from his green eyes, he'd always reminded her of a mischievous-looking leprechaun. "Brian, it is good to see you again."

"Good evening, Miss O'Rahilly. 'Tis a grand night for a party."

"Yes, quite. However, I have decided to leave early. Good night," she finished, nodding to both men.

"Please wait, Miss O'Rahilly." Alarmed, Lucien went after her. "Rosaleen." He stepped out in front of her when it appeared she was not going to halt on her own.

"Well." She was still apparently upset over his treatment in front of all those guests.

"I should like to offer my carriage to see you home," he stated, wishing her expression did not force him to such formality. "I cannot allow you to walk home alone unescorted, especially with Black—" best not bring up her hero again. "It would not be proper or safe to wander about Kinsale's roads alone in the dark. My coachman is armed, and I carry a pistol in the carriage now. Please accept my small protection."

Rosaleen's features did not change. "The

highwaymen you all seem so afraid of and disgusted by would never harm me, for as you and your friends made clear tonight, I am part Irish. Frankly, Your Grace, I am particular about the company I keep, and right now I feel Black Ned and his band are the only true gentlemen within twenty miles of here." With a regal sweep of her purple cloak, she walked around him to resume her course down the road.

Now what? Lucien ground the backs of his teeth in frustration at her stubbornness. "Get in the carriage," he told Brian, in a tone he rarely used with his servant. Then he bounded up the two steps and plopped down on the seat across from his valet. "Drive slowly," he ordered out the open window to his coachman.

"Damnation," Lucien cursed when he spotted another carriage of late arrivals heading up the drive. He would not make a scene, for there would be enough talk about Rosaleen O'Rahilly after her outburst tonight. And the lady made it clear she wanted no part of him, but he could not allow her to walk home unescorted at such a late hour.

"Oh, stop the coach," a lady called to her driver from the next carriage. A plump woman of about fifty, pink plumes in her elaborate peruke, leaned precariously out her window. "For shame, Lucien, leaving the party so soon?" said Lady Carstairs. "My four daughters will be so disappointed."

Manners made him stop his coach in order to accept the woman's greeting. All the while Rosaleen was getting away from him. "Devil's own headache, my lady," he said, thinking of a certain Irish lass.

107

"But I am sure there will be many more chances at future balls to meet your charming daughters." He heard the titters from inside the carriage, signaling the girls heard his remark.

"We shall hold you to that, Your Grace. Drive on," she told her coachman.

Arms folded across his chest, Lucien sat scowling out the small carriage window as they made their journey down the drive.

His Irish servant and confidant since childhood spoke first. "Sure and Miss Rosaleen has always been different from the other girls here, Your Grace. I can still see her chargin' across your lands each summer when ya let me come home for a visit. She'd give a wistful glance about, then dash off on one of her uncle's uncontrollable beasts. Last year she got that big black devil on four legs. A jaunty wave, then she'd leave me shakin' in me boots for fear she'd break her neck, but the lass only laughed when I spoke me fears ta her. Went on ta pat my hand like I was a child, not old enough ta be her grandfather. 'There, there, Brian, says herself, I ride this way all the time in Virginia.' " He sighed, then shook his head. "A sweet girl but always so alone. Used ta go out with her aunt and female cousins on their rounds ta the Fitzroy tenants. Stopped about three months ago. Now appears ta prefer solitude. They say in the village she's had English and Irish suitors a plenty come ta court her, but she turns them all away. Strange girl. Beggin' yer pardon, Yer Grace, but she may not wish yer attentions either."

"Devil take it, Brian, I just want to give the young woman a ride home, not father my first child." Tonight's blunders made Lucien realize he would have to be more careful in the future. Approach this scientifically, he told himself. She seemed a skittish filly for all her courage in the face of that crowd back there. "Good Lord, what can you do with a woman who won't let you protect her?" he asked aloud, realizing this was not going to be easy, especially since the source of his interest seemed to hold him in contempt right now. It did nip a bit of the romantic edge off his intentions to woo her in the courtly manner.

"Stop the coach," he shouted when he spotted her a few feet ahead. Jumping out of the conveyance, Lucien swooped down on her. "Miss O'Rahilly, for the last time, cease this folderol and get in my coach."

His irritation mirrored her own. "I would rather meet Black Ned in a peat bog at midnight. Now, kindly . . . sod off."

He blinked, at first thinking he'd heard incorrectly. Never had any lady spoken to him like this. "Bloody hell" came out in clear, masculine anger. In an instant his left arm encircled her waist; the other slipped under her legs as he hoisted her against his hard chest. "My first impression of you at the age of ten was correct. You are still a rag-mannered gypsy."

"And you're still the most arrogant—put me down this instant. Lucien, do you hear me?" Struggling against his muscular chest was like pushing against one of the elm trees along the side of the road. "This is your last chance, brigand, put me down!"

Chapter Six

The duke ignored Rosaleen's protests, stalked over to the open door, then dropped her on the plush cushions of his coach. "Now, sit there and behave yourself for once."

Her immediate attention was taken up with straightening her voluminous skirt, petticoats, and hoop that billowed about her. Horrified, the colonial girl felt Brian must be shocked to get a glimpse of her lavender stockings.

In a lithe movement, the duke reentered his coach and wedged himself next to her, instead of sitting across from her as she expected a polite gentleman to do.

He saw Brian get up. "There is no need for you to leave," the younger man told his servant. Then he stretched his long legs out in front of him, thus barring Rosaleen from any hasty exit out the carriage door.

The Irishman continued his retreat. "I will ride with the coachman atop, Your Grace." He looked at the furious girl sitting next to Lucien. "I shall be ready to come to your aid if you need me."

Rosaleen gave an appreciative nod to Lucien's Irish servant. "Thank you, Brian. I shall take comfort from your kind offer."

"Oh, no, Miss Rosaleen, I was speaking of rescuing His Grace."

The twinkle in Brian's eyes and the leprechaun smile splitting his craggy face was her undoing. Rosaleen could not keep the dimple at the right corner of her mouth from popping out. She giggled despite herself. "I should keep a sharp ear, Brian. His Grace has felt my fists before."

When they were alone and the carriage was making an unhurried ride toward Fitzroy Hall, Lucien spoke first. "Rosaleen, I realize you are a trifle ruffled because of my remarks in the ballroom, but I—"

"A trifle ruffled? You are too modest, Your Grace." Her bosom heaved with the return of strong emotion. "How dare you make a fool of me in front of that herd of sheep!" Two spots of color blossomed on her cheeks. "I am quite certain they now believe I am nothing more than an amusing, outspoken child."

"That is precisely what I wanted them to think."

"Yes, I am sure you did. Another form of control over the unworthy Irish rabble." Inching her way to the farthest side of the coach, Rosaleen turned her back on the duke.

Her tight-lipped silence irritated him. "Damn it, Rosaleen, you are no longer in the school room. Your statement in front of witnesses tonight could have gotten you in a far worse predicament than being made to look like a sulky brat. If you had listened to what I said before your unguarded tongue put you in that difficult situation, you would realize I am not a man of singular thought. I was trying to get you out of the danger you were too angry to see, even if it meant you might never speak to me again, so do not push me too far," he warned with lost patience.

Despite his command, Rosaleen did not miss the frustration in his tone. Yes, she had heard his words earlier. At first, when he'd come to her defense of the Irish, she had been moved by his declaration and humility, along with his plans for Montrose tenants. That's why it had hurt so much when he had followed his wonderful words with making sport of her in front of everyone. She turned to look at him. He was watching her, waiting, an uncertainty in his eyes. She grappled with her temper.

"I am used to taking care of myself without assistance. It becomes a habit with time. Your Grace, why did you involve yourself?"

Her voice had returned to that light sweetness. Taking this as a good omen, Lucien moved slowly toward her on the leather upholstery. With gentle fingers he lifted her chin up so that he could study those midnight eyes once more. "Because I care what happens to you, dear angel. Since that afternoon by the pond, you have not been far from my thoughts. I've gone about Kinsale trying to find you. A few times I thought I was going mad, having just dreamed you up. You will never know how overjoyed I felt to see you here tonight, for I feared you were lost to me."

112

Rosaleen knew she should turn her head away, protest "angel" was certainly no apt description of her, but she was too aware of his warm fingers on her skin to make a quick decision right now.

When she did not pull away, he bent his head to touch his lips to hers. He was surprised and delighted to feel her response as he began to learn her soft little mouth. The sweet taste of her lips, the faint scent of lilacs clinging to her smooth skin—everything about this young woman enchanted him. Increasing the pressure from his lips, he caressed the small line of her jaw with his right hand, then moved to the velvet softness of her earlobe. Finally, it was Lucien who pulled away as her unexpected fervor to their first brief kiss made him aware of the danger to continue. He felt his healthy body respond in a way he'd never experienced with any other woman before—all from a mere kiss.

Rosaleen had meant to pull away immediately, but her first kiss had changed everything. Lucien's mouth had been gentle and coaxing, causing a fierce longing for more of his firm mouth on hers. Her skin felt on fire even beneath her gown and petticoat, where his hard body had pressed against the soft curves outlined under her thin cloak. What must he think of her, for he'd been the one to pull away first? The answer that crashed against her mind made her want to cry, an indulgence she rarely allowed herself. It was totally her fault, she reasoned. Apparently, Lucien now wished to pursue her on merely a physical level. Gone were the flowery phrases. This man meant to get right down to business.

Trying to get his heated thoughts under control, Lucien reminded himself he had to proceed slowly. However, his brief experiment proved enlightening. Rosaleen's intense nature was not confined solely to politics, and the discovery pleased him. When he looked at her again, he was perplexed by the dejection on her face. Umbrage at his forwardness he might expect, but sadness? He saw her move away from him once more as she hovered next to the other side of the coach.

"Rosaleen?"

Silence.

"Rosaleen, if I misread . . . if I offended you just now, I am truly sorry, for I only intended to—"

"No, Your Grace," Rosaleen interrupted in a soft monotone. She kept her gaze straight ahead. "You have nothing to apologize for. You see, I realize I am to blame for that kiss. Coming upon a girl swimming naked in your pond, my confessions tonight about my true failings, shared with you to cure you of your misguided infatuation—oh, no, Your Grace, any man would come to the same conclusion you did."

"And pray what conclusion might that be?"

Her answer was matter-of-fact. "That I am a woman of easy virtue, accessible to an English duke for a brief tumble in the hay. As an Irish Catholic, like the tenants here, I am of little consequence to any aristocrat in need of a quick release from his unbridled lust."

Unprepared, a squeak escaped Rosaleen's lips when she felt herself firmly grasped about the waist, moved up, then down to sit across a pair of hard thighs encased in tight black breeches. She swallowed when she chanced a look at the man glowering across at her. For the first time, Lucien appeared positively dangerous. She shivered despite her cloak and the balmy evening air.

His words came out in a clipped fury. "Never are you to even think, let alone say, such a vile thing about yourself. I also find your low opinion of me insulting."

She tried once to wriggle off his lap, but he shook his blond head and pressed her firmly back down where he wanted her. He possessed a strength she had not realized. His usual English reserve and fastidious attire had given her the impression of docility—until now. One hand held her slender waist; the other encircled the back of her shoulders. Always sure of her own strength and ability to stand up for herself, it astonished Rosaleen to realize, while he was not hurting her, she could not alter her position.

"I have not lived the life of a monk, but never have I forced my attentions on any woman. Had I even the remotest inclination for a brief tumble, as you call it, I could have shoved your naked form beneath me that afternoon and taken you on that bank with no one to stop me." The icy blue of his eyes penetrated her. "But it is not my way. The thought of force at such a time fills me with nothing but repugnance. And as for my unbridled lust . . . well, young lady, self-control is not solely a woman's prerogative. For instance, you are sitting on my lap while I attempt to talk with you in a calm manner, proving I have mastered my first inclination to toss you across my knee and paddle your impertinent backside."

Rosaleen could not hide her shock at his words. Never had anyone spoken to her in this manner. It left her feeling quite unsettled.

A roguish grin came to his lips when he felt her uncertainty from his last remark. "At least I finally have your undivided attention." He relaxed his hold on her.

"I am no green boy, Rosaleen. Never have I spoken such phrases to any woman. I meant every compliment I gave you tonight, for I have never met anyone who captivated me as you have. You think you are the only one with faults? I've tons myself, and if we had five hours this night, I would attempt to catalog them for you. Though my friends deride me about my interest in peering at things under a microscope or mixing liquids together in glass tubes, for all my time spent with books, I cannot explain what has happened to me. There is no logic to it. All I am certain of is I want to know you better.

My intentions are honorable," he continued, "but I've learned enough about your ways to realize you would never believe me if I told you now my hopes for your future. However, I promise to let you set the pace of our relationship, for I know you will not be pressured into doing anything you do not choose. You ran off after your declaration of your dark sins," he added, a hint of amusement in his voice, "before I could tell you I would have you as you are." His features became more serious. "I want only truth between us."

He stopped, afraid he'd gone too far in opening to her. Her silence buffeted his vulnerable feelings. "Have I been so wrong, sweet elf? I thought you felt something of this magic between us, too."

The touch of his hands on her waist and shoulders was almost a caress now. She felt his warm breath next to her ear, delighting in the scent of the sandalwood soap that clung to his clean-shaven face. Tentatively, she raised her fingers to brush back a strand of blond hair that had escaped from his neatly tied queue at the back of his neck. The sincerity she read in his blue eyes as he waited for her answer touched something inside her. Only truth between them, he'd said. What of her other life, the dark side of her, the secrets she had to keep because others depended on her? Would this honorable Englishman feel the same way about her if he found out she was also Black Ned? She closed her eyes, trying to find an answer.

Part of Rosaleen wanted to spend time with Lucien so that they could become better acquainted. As she continued sitting on his lap, she felt secure with his arms about her. He did not seem to look down on her because she was half Irish. His gentleness at the pond still filled her with the warmest feelings. To ease her embarrassment, he'd quickly bundled her into his coat and closed his eyes as she dressed. He was correct, she realized. He could have easily taken advantage of the situation. She felt a beginning trust melt her enforced coolness. Never having felt so drawn to a man before, she found these new sensations both thrilling and frightening.

Of course, he could never learn of Black Ned,

but surely she was intelligent enough to keep that part of her life hidden from him. And from the beginning, Sean Kelly had said her joining his group was only temporary, for they always knew she would return to Williamsburg with her parents. As Lucien sat holding her, waiting so patiently for her answer, Rosaleen came to a decision. She relaxed and nestled her head on his shoulder. "Oh, Lucien, you are so comfortable."

He chuckled when she snuggled closer. "Ah, yes, my lot in life, to be mistaken for an overstuffed chair. Does this mean you are not filled with revulsion to learn I will call on you tomorrow at two in the afternoon?"

The intensity of her look almost took his breath away.

"Lucien, the thought of seeing you again only fills me with happiness. I should warn you, though, many of the English here, including my cousins, feel I am too direct for a female. I keep trying to curb my nature, to fit in, but it is difficult for me." The uncertainty returned to her voice. "After a few days in my company, if you regret your declarations, I beg you to tell me, for I will not hold you to any permanent commitment because of this evening. Agreed?" She held out a gloved hand to him in the manner of sealing a bargain.

"I have met many ladies who have tried to impress me with their virtues. You, sweet elf, are the first one determined to show yourself in the worst light." Despite her outward bravado, he suddenly realized how fragile her self-confidence must be. He suspected others had pointed out her nonconformity since childhood. Though he wanted to seal their bargain in a more intimate manner, he accepted the significance of her gesture. "Agreed, Miss O'Rahilly." He took her slender fingers in his hand and gave her a gentlemen's handshake.

The duke felt the carriage slow, signaling their arrival at Fitzroy Hall too soon. Or perhaps it was just in time, he told himself, for he was very conscious of her soft curves against the muscles of his thighs right now.

"You are home, my dear." He helped her move off his lap to sit on the cushions next to him. He could not help smiling at her awkward attempts to refasten her cloak, while pushing back a stray black curl he'd caressed earlier. "Here, let me help." He found her flustered expression adorable but forced himself to concentrate on redoing the cloth-covered buttons of her cape. Lilac colors suited her, he mused.

"Please," she said, concern in her eyes. "Will you have the driver stop near the back of the house?" She did not want anyone to see the Montrose crest on the carriage.

Though puzzled by her odd request to enter the house like a tradesman at the back door, he complied, giving an order to the driver and Brian atop the coach.

Lucien stepped out of the carriage first, then assisted Rosaleen.

Murmuring good night to Brian and the Montrose coachman, she felt dazed as she accepted Lucien's arm.

Rosaleen led him through the damp grass around

to the back of the Fitzroy mansion. When they came to the elm tree, she said, "This is fine, Your Grace. My room is just up the back stairs."

"Which one is yours, adorable elf?" His romantic side wanted to know.

Automatically, she pointed to the window alongside the large tree limb. "It was my mother's old room when she was young." She cleared her throat and stopped walking. "Thank you for seeing me home. Good night."

He smiled but shook his head. "I will see you properly to the door. Come." Tucking her gloved hand in the crook of his arm, he resumed walking.

Rosaleen realized she had no choice but to follow.

"Even if our relationship until now has been rather unconventional, I intend to do things properly," Lucien said as he escorted her up the stone steps. "Shall I speak with your uncle in the morning or would you prefer I write directly to your father in Williamsburg requesting his permission and stating my intentions?"

His proper suggestion alarmed her. The last thing she wanted now was the attention any formal declaration would generate. Part of her success at slipping out her bedroom window at night was that no one took much notice of her. And what was he talking about, his intentions? All they were going to do was spend time getting acquainted.

She forced a casualness into her voice. "Oh, pray do not be so formal right away, Lucien. After all, you did say you would allow me to set the pace of our relationship. Besides," she teased, "you have agreed to tell me by the end of the week if you regret your hasty words. I own, you will thank me for sparing your embarrassment when you find your only goal at the end of the week is for sanctuary with Father Collins. I suspect a little of my company goes a long way."

Though he accepted her self-deprecating humor, it was clear she still doubted his sincerity. It seemed prudent to keep his own plans to himself for now.

Hearing voices outside, Colleen Mulcahy opened the door. Rosaleen swept in, then turned around to look up at Lucien, who stood on the other side of the threshold. "I hope you will forgive me if I do not invite you in." The less her relatives saw of the duke, the fewer questions she would have to answer. "I am fatigued after an enlightening day."

"Of course." The polite formality returned to his voice. Doffing his tricorn hat, he executed a perfect bow. He came back up in time to see her beguiling smile — just before she shut the wooden door in his face. Even the elderly cook behind her could not hide her shock at the girl's action.

Patience, Lucien reminded himself, as he turned to walk down the back steps to his waiting carriage. He needed to approach this like a scientific experiment.

True to his word, a few moments before two the following afternoon, Lucien Huntington, Duke of Montrose, called at Fitzroy Hall. If he was surprised to find Rosaleen waiting for him with her horse saddled and ready to go, he was far too happy she had not changed her mind to question the lady's almost eccentric punctuality and eagerness to be off.

He could hardly keep his eyes off her as he lifted her up on her sidesaddle. In yellow riding skirt and coat, a matching tricorn perched saucily on her black curls, Rosaleen was a vision of loveliness. He took his hands away from her small waist far sooner than he wished.

Rosaleen read the admiration in his eyes, and it pleased her. "You look quite dashing in your riding clothes, too, Your Grace." She saw his blond features color for a second, almost as if he were not used to receiving such compliments. As he swung his booted foot up in the stirrup to mount his reddish-brown stallion, she realized for a tall man, his strong body possessed a natural grace. "Henry Lorens says he can tell a great deal about a lady from her horsemanship. Shall we see how I fare on my first test? I have only a week to ensnare you, Your Grace."

If only she knew she'd already captured his heart, he thought.

"Oh, and my friends call me Ross," she added, with a coquettish smile "See if you can keep up with me, Lucifer," she tossed over her shoulder. In an instant she went racing down the path that led across Fitzroy lands.

He recognized her childhood name for him. "We shall see who's the better man, Ross." With an unbridled laugh, he charged after her.

As he gave Jasper his head, the duke was not surprised to find Miss O'Rahilly an excellent rider, but that barely controlled beast she rode was hardly the one he would have chosen for her. They kept up the racing pace for a long time, reaching the edge of Fitzroy lands where the trees thickened into a dense forest. Laughing and out of breath, they stopped to rest the horses.

Not waiting for him to assist her, Rosaleen jumped off Bradai's back and ran to the base of an old oak. Dismounting, he walked slowly toward her.

Rosaleen's black hair tousled about her face from their race, and there was a smudge of dirt on her cheek, kicked up from her horse's hard contact with the road. Lucien thought her gamine face enchanting. "I scarcely kept up with you."

"Oh, Lucien, I did enjoy that. Isn't it wonderful the way the wind and sun on your face make you feel so free?" She saw his blue eyes take on a darker hue as he smiled down at her.

He liked her best this way, laughing, open, no cool reserve or talk of politics between them. He did not miss the longing in her voice. "I should think a wealthy colonial heiress, beautiful niece of an earl—is freedom so rare for you, sweet elf?"

Leaning back against the tree, Rosaleen became thoughtful. "Did you ever swim in a pond on a summer afternoon, ah . . . in the natural state?"

"Of course. Many times."

"And when you go out for a ride, like today, must you take a valet or a stableboy with you, or report to an older person exactly where you are going and when you will return?"

Her questions puzzled him. "Of course not. I come and go as I please."

"Precisely," she stated. "I suppose that day you

123

found me in your pond, I was enjoying a private rebellion of sorts. Those small privileges you take for granted have been denied me since childhood because I am a girl." Her eyes clouded with remembrance. "I even pulled out the blasted embroidery one afternoon when company was present, and they were giving poor Mama a hard time because she did not insist I master it. Whatever would those stiff-necked dowagers have said if they knew my parents allow me to ride astride in my brother's breeches, as long as I stay on O'Rahilly lands at home?"

This bit of news did take Lucien by surprise, for no female of his acquaintance ever wore breeches, let alone rode astride. But he continued to listen without interruption.

"How would you feel if you had to report to someone every time you just wanted to get on a horse and ride out on a beautiful day until you couldn't go any faster? Or if you had to take a maid or female relative with you if you left the house? Or could only swim with the ladies in Bath trussed up with brown flannel from head to toe and a lacy mobcap pushed over your hair, surrounded by a lot of other women who spoke only of their ailments or the latest gossip?"

"Well, I have to admit," Lucien answered, "I had not thought of it that way. In truth, Ross, I'd have to say I would resent such restrictions."

She sensed no censure in his reply. Indeed, he seemed to be considering his next words carefully.

"However, as we have agreed to speak our minds with each other, can we not balance your freedom with my concern for your safety and reputation?"

"Oh, my, this is beginning to sound like the prelude to a lecture. Perhaps I should sit down."

He did not mind her teasing. In fact, he took it as an encouraging sign. "If ever you wish to swim in my pond again, I must insist you let me know ahead of time."

"What, friends for a short time and already you are giving orders?" Mischief sparkled from her dark eyes. "Well, Your Grace, if you want to spy on me, you shall have to come up with a more original excuse."

"Rosaleen, you are an intelligent woman. If some other fellow had come upon you instead of me that afternoon, you might have come away with more than an injured foot. While I sympathize with your need for a little adventure, I intend to see to your safety at those times. You have my word I shall keep my back to you." He tried pushing home his advantage. "At the very least someone known to your family could have spotted you. One of the tenants might have happened by. In a small town like Kinsale, gossip spreads quickly."

"Please, Your Grace, do not concern yourself with such matters. I take full responsibility for my actions. You do not have to—"

"I tried to explain yesterday, both your safety and good name have become important to me."

"Lucien, I do appreciate your regard, but it is such a lovely day. Can we not discuss this another time—perhaps on a rainy day when we have nothing better to do than cogitate on my reprehensible habits?" Laughter hovered close to her lips. "I dare say, if you continue in this vein, even the squirrels will be snoring in a few moments."

Tempted by the lilt in her pleasant voice, he almost gave in again to her Irish ways, but something held him back this time. He gave her a reproving look. "If you wish to see me again, you shall have to comply with that request."

She saw the gentle breeze ruffle a strand of his tawny hair against his cheek. Hands clasped behind his back, he looked so handsome to her. Boots gleaming, buckskin breeches hugging his muscular legs, outer coat buttoned even on such a warm day—did he perspire or appear rumpled only when fencing? she wondered, then stifled a giggle at such an inappropriate observation. However, when she looked back at his face, she thought she read uncertainty, almost fear for a moment.

Rosaleen walked a few steps to her right, pondering his words. His request did make sense. It made her realize how lucky she'd been to go undetected those afternoons for this long. Turning, she faced the tall Englishman. "All right, Lucien, I agree, though at the moment I am not so certain I will feel like venturing near your pond in the future. Part of my Irish nature Papa says—to put up my fists, then talk later." She became more serious. "Risks are best kept for more important things," she added, thinking of her hidden life as Black Ned.

His whole body relaxed. "Thank you, Ross."

"Why did you appear so wary before I gave you my answer?"

"Game playing is not my nature. I am a man of

my word, and I was afraid you might just tell me to sod off again."

She smiled, then moved closer to him. Reaching out, she touched his hand. "Oh, Lucien, you have more power over me than you suspect, for I find the thought of never being in your company again a most dismal prospect. I would miss seeing your attractive face, hearing the low laughter that bursts from you when something amuses you, or the sky in your eyes when you look down at me, like you are doing now. The artists are wrong to show the devil as a creature of shadows, for I think Lucifer was blond and blue-eyed, a seductive smile on his lips, with honeyed words that could melt a woman's heart. You are a conjurer of spells, my Lucifer, for being with you has become so important to me that the thought of never seeing you again could bring me close to tears."

Moved by her declaration, Lucien could not speak for a moment. Unlike last night when he did not ask, he wanted this to be different. "Rosaleen, may I kiss you?"

Tilting her face up to his, she answered, "I should die if you do not." She felt his arms go about her waist and shoulders as he supported her body. Similar to their first kiss in his carriage, she experienced Lucien's gentle coaxing as he captured her receptive mouth. However, this time the familiar warmth turned to a blazing fire as the kiss went on and on. . . . She had to reach for his broad shoulders to steady herself.

With a soft moan of surrender, Rosaleen pressed herself against him. Not knowing what she wanted, the young woman was aware this contact between them caused her to desire more of him. She felt the corded hardness of his body as he held her tightly against him. When his hand moved lower to rub the tip of her linen-covered breasts, her skin tingled with the return of that weakness in her legs. The sky and tall trees seemed to spin about her. Certainly, she would have fallen if his arms weren't about her. She must pull away. At least this once, she should show him she was not a wanton. However, the touch of his lips, the feel of his firm hands on her soft curves, made her open her small mouth to learn more of him.

Lucien felt the heavy tightening in his lower body. Getting a grip on the situation, he pushed himself away from his sweet Rosaleen. His breath came in shallow gasps as he was forced to turn his back on her to readjust the front of his riding coat over his breeches. He ran a shaky hand through his tawny mane, amazed to feel the silk black ribbon still held his hair in place, for he felt uncharacteristically disheveled, confused, and on the verge of losing control.

After a few ragged moments, he turned back to her. The trust he saw in those large dark eyes unnerved him. God, he thought, she did need a keeper. What the devil was wrong with her father in Williamsburg or uncle here in Ireland to allow her to go about the countryside free as the summer breeze? Just because he was a duke, he was still made of flesh and blood. Hell, were she his daughter or niece, a maid and two bodyguards would chaperon her at all times. "I . . . I think the horses have rested enough. We'd best be on our way back."

Rosaleen tried to hide her disappointment that their pleasant few hours were over. Why did he sound so cross all of a sudden? Perhaps she should have pulled away first. Was he scandalized because she was not more reserved? They still did not know each other well. And here she was practically throwing herself at him. The open show of her feelings probably shocked him. She resolved to be more circumspect in the future. Prudence Lorens said men could not resist a lady who showed a polite but cool reserve. Perhaps Pru was right.

During their sedate ride back to Fitzroy Hall, Lucien did some serious thinking. If her relatives chose to act irresponsibly, he must take charge of Rosaleen's well-being. "If you do not mind, I think I shall ask Henry and Prudence to accompany us on our ride tomorrow. Might I suggest you ask your cousin, Elizabeth, also to come with you."

Oh, dear, she must have displeased him by showing her honest pleasure at his attentions. "Yes, of course, Your Grace."

He looked across at her. "Stop a moment."

She gave a brief tug on Bradai's reins and waited. His expression softened, giving her hope she hadn't frightened him off. Was he going to kiss her again. Never had she been kissed on a horse. How romantic.

Reaching into the pocket of his riding jacket, Lucien took out a lacy handkerchief. "Lean forward." When she complied, he wiped her left cheek. "There, now you look more presentable. Can't return you home looking like a grubby urchin." His eyes gave her a critical once over to be sure everything was in place; then he indicated they could proceed.

Grubby urchin? Rosaleen tried to stifle her devastation. It was obvious he did not think of her as a tempestuous siren at all. Bradai must have felt her feelings, for he increased their speed, signaling he too wanted to run away.

Yes, the duke mused as he watched her gallop ahead of him, he would have to be even more careful in the future. Only a bounder, he told himself, would spout about protecting a lady's reputation, then get her into a dense forest, kiss her, and God knows what else he might have done if his father's teachings hadn't nudged him. Well, he knew one thing about Rosaleen's relatives. They certainly possessed some peculiar notions about allowing Miss O'Rahilly to dash about Kinsale on her own.

The fierce whinny from Bradai as his front hooves pawed the air shoved Lucien's attention back to the matter at hand. His breath caught in his throat when he saw Rosaleen pitch backward on her saddle while she attempted to stay on her mount. Pressure from his legs on Jasper's sides brought the blond-haired man next to her instantly.

"Easy, Bradai. We have to go slow today." The thrashing stallion brought his front legs down hard on the dirt road. Snorting, the horse shook his head, signaling his displeasure with her actions. Calmly, Rosaleen patted Bradai's sleek neck. She knew he was not used to this lumbering gate, or her tight-fisted hold on the leather straps in her hands. In truth, she would rather pick up the speed, too.

However, it appeared His Grace was more comfortable at this grandmother pace. The thought caused her to chuckle.

Once he was certain she was all right, Lucien's censuring words came out before he could curb them. "You should be on a docile little mare, not that cursed fire dragon, for he is too dangerous for you."

Her chin came up. "First the ultimatum about my use of your pond, now this. For a man only a few years older than myself, you are beginning to sound like a pompous old poop."

Astride his horse, Lucien's military posture returned, signaling her barb struck a nerve, but he was not given a chance to make a verbal response.

"My father gave me this horse when we visited Ireland last summer. He knows I am an excellent horsewoman, as does my uncle Dunstan, who is in a position to judge, for he raises those chestnuts, similar to the rather barrel-chested nag you are riding. Papa is a very open-minded gentleman. A self-made man of intelligence and hard-working pragmatism, he is unincumbered by aristocratic stuffiness where women are concerned."

Lucien recognized the quicksand under his feet. The last thing he wanted was a quarrel now. "Your pardon, Rosaleen. My fear for your well-being made me a bit testy."

Her usual good humor returned. "It was kind of you to be concerned, but really, Lucien, it was not necessary."

As they resumed riding side by side, she spoke again. "You could not know my father allowed me the same tutors along with my brothers. Papa has always encouraged independence in all his children. He is a kind, intelligent man. I can understand why Mama adores him. There are so few men like him." Lucien did seem to regret his comment. "You see, Papa loves me, but he also respects my need to make my own decisions. He is a rare parent indeed, and I know you will find him as wonderful as I do when you meet him."

Remembering Taggart O'Rahilly only from that party at Dunstan Fitzroy's rose garden years ago, Lucien did want to meet her father again, so that he could ask him why he was not supervising his handful of a daughter. The duke's thoughts became more disconcerted. He'd done his share of rowdiness in his younger days and enjoyed giving and receiving pleasure from the ladies. Yet, no woman had ever called him that name before. Good Lord, he thought, where Rosaleen O'Rahilly was concerned, was he actually beginning to act like a "pompous old poop"?

In a gesture of conciliation, Rosaleen made sure she stayed with Lucien's sedate pace as they returned to Fitzroy Hall. From lowered lashes, she stole a brief glance at the gentleman riding across from her. Adorable man, he did appear troubled. "Lucien, I am not angry with you," she said, thinking he tormented himself over his verbal misstep about her horse.

"How relieved I am to hear it. Now I will not have to kill myself."

Whatever brought that sarcasm on? she asked herself, but went back to concentrating on the area between Bradai's ears. Lucien was complex. One moment he was kissing her quite thoroughly; then they were quarreling. Now he seemed almost annoyed. Well, she thought, her manner brightening, a few weeks in her company, and he would come around to her way of thinking. Poor Lucien was not used to independent females, that was it. Like so many men, he just required reeducation. A good thing she had no aim of ever marrying. Imagine having to deal with a man's prickly feelings every day? However, something told her to hold off informing the duke of her firm intention never to be encumbered with a husband. Later, once he saw how much fun they could have together, she was certain he would be pleased to learn her intentions. After all, what man would not welcome his freedom?

Chapter Seven

"My word, Rosaleen, I do not know what is the matter with you." Concern showed on Elizabeth's thin face as she peered down at her cousin. "Perhaps we should have Dr. Wexford look at you. Even Mama commented the other night you appeared ready to fall asleep over the rice pudding."

Sitting on the edge of the taller girl's bed, Rosaleen watched Elizabeth's maid fasten the buttons at the back of her cousin's afternoon gown. She stifled another yawn. In the past, no one had commented on her habit of staying abed until noon a few days a week. Now it was not possible after a late night on the highways, for during the last two weeks, Lucien had insisted on seeing her almost every afternoon. Even Sean Kelly took a dim view of her time spent with his employer's son, reminding her again English aristocrats could not be trusted. Then there were three evening parties. She and His Grace danced until the wee hours. Though she never remembered enjoying a time more, this new social life took a toll on her opportunities to rest.

Dressed in similar gowns of flowered muslin, wide-brimmed straw hats over the ruffled pinners on their heads, both ladies went downstairs to the Fitzroy carriage.

This afternoon she and Elizabeth were to call on Henry, the earl of Dunsmore, and his sister. Lucien would be there.

Hidden under her clothes, on a gold chain about her neck, Rosaleen wore the gift Lucien had presented to her the day before. She felt the pendant nestle between her breasts. At first she'd refused to accept the beautiful diamond and amethyst cluster of lilacs, with costly emeralds for leaves. However, the duke had brushed all her protests away with his charming ways, insisting she accept a small token to commemorate the end of the week and his steadfast intentions. Confused by his mention of intentions again, Rosaleen had accepted the lovely present only after he'd declined to speak any more on the subject. If he felt disappointed at her restraint in keeping the pendant hidden next to her skin, rather than showing the expensive present off, he said nothing.

A footman assisted auburn-haired Elizabeth into the coach first. "Papa likes the duke; I can tell, Ross. They had a long talk before you came downstairs yesterday. I do not know exactly what was said, but both men came out of Father's office smiling." Her gray eyes sparkled when she studied her noncommittal cousin. "It is quite clear he is smitten with you. Of course, I overheard Mama say your father might not approve of the duke. Uncle Taggart is frightfully sensitive about English aristocrats. I shall never understand why, for he married one."

"Mama just goes by Mrs. O'Rahilly at home in

Virginia." Rosaleen felt uneasy that her relatives seemed to read more into the situation than she wanted. And it shocked her to learn Lucien had spoken privately with the earl without telling her. Warning messages flashed inside her head. Though Liz could not know, Rosaleen felt her father had good reason to dislike titled Englishmen. She remembered the time as a child racing into her parents' room with the happy news of a new foal's birth. Her father, dressed in breeches but no shirt, had his back to her, and for the first time she saw those deep scars across his shoulders where Geoffrey Fitzroy, her mother's late father, had beaten him brutally and often. The vision still brought tears to Ross's eyes. It was good Lucien fired Tom Bennet, after the way he'd beaten poor Sean Kelly. How could the English be so cruel? Uncle Dunstan was the only Englishman above the rest. No, she would never put herself in the position of having any Englishman her lord and master.

Shaking herself, Rosaleen forced a lighthearted tone into her voice. "Oh, Liz, Lucien and I are just friends. Pray, enjoy the afternoon without becoming so serious. I've no intention of encumbering myself with an English duke. If Uncle Dunstan has his heart set on an additional aristocrat for the family, he has a brood of better-looking children who can easily accomplish the task."

Elizabeth giggled. "Oh, Ross, you do have Uncle Taggart's outrageous way of speaking."

"Sure and I do me best," Rosaleen countered, with the return of her humor. " 'Tis true, I've always felt more Irish than the other part. Besides, my brothers will certainly wed in the future; thus, the O'Rahilly line of scoundrels will continue. The family history will lose nothing if I die an old maid with a colorful past."

As her cousin went into peals of laughter, Rosaleen feigned an interest in the scenery on her side of the landau. It was evident Liz did not realize Ross was serious about her determination never to marry. Why should she marry? the nineteen-year-old asked herself. With all the money she'd ever need in a few years when she was older, the family would no doubt accept her desire for even more freedoms. No, she could see no logical reason to take on the restraints marriage would surely impose. Her mother was happily married, but she was not like Millicent. Rosaleen knew her fists came up too quickly, and she did not suffer fools lightly. Though the duke of Montrose was the most interesting man she had met, she would never allow herself to become trapped into marriage. Only, it was not going to be a simple task. Hadn't she awakened this morning with the warm memory of his passionate kiss tingling her moist lips? A pity His Grace had not repeated the pleasurable experience since that afternoon when they went riding. During the last week especially, Lucien had seemed distant. It caused her to wonder if she'd been too forward those two times they had kissed. Was he afraid of her or still shocked because she had not been the one to pull away first?

James Winthrop was also a guest at the Lorenses' this afternoon. Dressed similar to Lucien and Henry, the barrister wore a linen coat and breeches, unpowdered hair tied neatly at the back of his neck with a black ribbon. "They tell me in town you've had wagon loads arriving daily at Montrose hall with tools, paint, and supplies. Didn't I ride by yesterday to see a tall, blond-haired duke mixing mortar along with his Irish tenants?"

Lucien accepted the other man's teasing good-naturedly. "Faith, I am probably more in the way than anything else."

Henry put his china cup and saucer back down on the mahogany tea table in front of him. "What, Lucien Huntington working like a common laborer?" A hoot of laughter filled the room. "I don't believe it. This can't be the same lad I went to school with."

The three ladies appeared perplexed. Rosaleen spoke first. "Why should His Grace doing physical work amuse you so, my lord?"

Henry's mirth increased, while James Winthrop merely smiled.

"Oh, do tell us," Prudence encouraged. "Was Lucien a wicked fellow at Cambridge?"

"Well," said Henry, wiping his eyes, "as you ladies probably know, peers away at school usually hire one of the younger lads to fetch and carry for them."

"Yes," Prudence answered, "but why should Lucien having a toady cause so much merriment?"

"Because His Grace is the only man at Cambridge I ever knew to hire six lads to report to him four times a week for three hours at a time. Why, James, you were one of them as I recall."

"Yes, quite." James nodded his brown head but appeared uncomfortable.

"Don't look so guilty, James." The earl grinned back at the ladies. "My friends and I tried every bribe imaginable to get those six lads to tell us what went on during those sessions. Wouldn't give us a clue. All very hush-hush."

Rosaleen caught Lucien's silent warning to James when Mr. Winthrop appeared ready to say something.

"I like my creature comforts," Lucien drawled. "Upon my honor, I needed six to take care of me. High standards, don't you know."

"Gad, man, you had Brian Fogarty with you. What ever could the others have done for you?"

Lucien appeared bored by the discussion. "A duke needs more waiting on than an earl."

Henry looked cross for a moment at the reference to his lower rank. "Well, as a successful lawyer now, James, I bet you wish you could get a case against His Grace?"

Rosaleen sensed many things were left unsaid on this topic. A definite aura of tension sprang up among the men.

James seemed disquieted by Henry's remarks. "I have no complaints."

While the dark-haired girl knew about the tradition of toadyism among the English, she felt disappointed to learn Lucien was not above exploiting the poor or younger students during his university years.

"Used to refer to them as the Montrose Club," Henry went on. "All the same, if James is correct about you mucking about with stones and bricks on your estate now, you have certainly changed since the old days."

Unruffled, the duke smiled at Henry. "It gives me something to do in the mornings while my Rosaleen is snoozing."

His words flustered her. "I had no idea you called in the morning, Your Grace."

"I asked your uncle not to disturb you last week

when I rode over. His lordship told me you usually do not rise until after one in the afternoon. So, to pass the time until I see you, I get in the way of my tenants. After all," he added, a roguish twinkle in his blue eyes, "the sooner I get their homes in order, the sooner the men will be available for hire to do the repairs on Montrose Hall. I plan to hold a large party when the place is refurbished." His tone became more intimate as his gaze rested on Rosaleen. "Then we can welcome our English and Irish guests alike, hmmm?"

His use of the word "we" unsettled her. The outlandish scene of her telling him the reason she might not be able to comply washed over her: "Sorry, old cock, can't play congenial hostess at your party, for I have ta pound the highways as Black Ned this evening." A nervous giggle escaped before she could catch herself.

"Oh, well," she managed in a more reserved tone. "It is a long way off. A lot can happen in a few months."

Lady Prudence gave Lucien a beguiling smile. "Rosaleen sounds just a bit reluctant, Your Grace. If you need a hostess for the housewarming, I would be most pleased to assist you."

Lucien gave the blond beauty a gracious smile. "Thank you, Pru. I just might take you up on the offer." Turning away from Rosaleen, he made small talk with Henry and Pru while Elizabeth and James spoke with each other.

Though he attempted to ignore her remark, Lucien remembered this was not the first time Rosaleen had made him feel they were playing chess. During these last two weeks, he'd gone out of his way to be certain

140

they were never alone, trying not to rush her into a formal commitment. He knew to be alone with her would probably lead to his taking her in his arms again. While he'd enjoyed their days of riding in the afternoons with their friends, taking tea at Lorens or Fitzroy Hall, all of it only added to his longing for her. More and more he found it difficult to be around her, yet not able to touch her, kiss that warm mouth, or bury his face in those midnight curls. Embarrassed at how run-down things were at his own mansion, but feeling his tenants' homes needed attention first, Lucien believed he could not ask his friends to visit his home yet. All of them seemed to understand. Yet, he had to admit he did miss being alone with Rosaleen—the way she'd been in his carriage and that afternoon when they rode across Fitzroy lands. Somehow, she seemed more aloof in the company of these people. It puzzled him.

Rosaleen saw Lucien go over and whisper something to James; then James smiled and went over to Henry. Before she could protest, James and Henry were escorting the other two women out the sitting room door for a stroll in the garden. However, instead of feeling gratitude, she experienced that warning inside again. Standing up to follow the others out, she was waved back from the door by a grinning James Winthrop. Only Prudence looked irritated by this deliberate maneuver of Lucien's to insure he had a few moments alone with Rosaleen. Yet, Prudence had no opportunity to protest when James started pulling her along after him.

It hardly seemed reasonable to make a scene about it. With a shrug of her shoulders, Rosaleen went back to her seat on the brocade-covered sofa. She kept her hands in her lap as Lucien shut the door of the sitting room, then stood watching her, an enigmatic expression on his face.

She attempted the offensive with a disarming smile. "If you would like to walk in the garden with the others, Your Grace, I assure you I will understand. Solitude is not a hardship for me."

"Does my company displease you, then?"

His pointed question surprised her into a direct answer. "No, Your Grace. I cannot remember ever having enjoyed a time more than the last two weeks."

He stayed where he was, leaning against the closed door. "Then, why do you address me so formally? And when I attempt to get close to you, all in a proper manner, why do you check me? Politely, yes, but you have kept me at arm's length all week. I thought we agreed to become better acquainted. Rather difficult if you build walls between us. It would seem your reserve would be better spent on Henry, for his lordship is quite besotted with you."

Her dark eyes widened. "Henry? Oh, you are mistaken, for Henry certainly does not—"

"I know the signs, Ross." With a self-deprecating look, he ended the physical distance between them. "Why should I not, for I see the same expression in my own mirror each morning. I know you are not mean-spirited, Rosaleen; you just have not noticed Henry."

Could she have been so blind with the earl? "Poor Henry, I shall speak with him at the earliest opportunity."

"Right now, my dear, I am more concerned that you and I come to an understanding."

Keeping her gaze lowered to the pair of dark brown

boots standing in front of her, Rosaleen experienced that trapped feeling again. "If you recall, Your Grace, it is by your instigation we always meet in the company of others."

The strain of the last two weeks was taking a toll on him. He sank down on the cushions next to her, then took her hand when she made a move to rise. "Please, Rosaleen, do not shut me out like this. I have tried to give you time, for I smugly thought two weeks ago I could easily wait."

"And I appreciate your patience, Your Grace." ·

His hands went to her shoulders to give her a gentle shake. "Can you not call me by my name?"

The anguish on his face made her feel ashamed. "I never meant to cause you pain, Lucien. I, too, have been trying to act correctly," she added, then confessed part of her reasons for her recent behavior. "I thought my . . . my eagerness from your two kisses shocked you; therefore, I resolved to try to behave in a more . . . English manner. Your approval does matter to me."

His whole demeanor changed. A boyish grin lit his features. Impulsively, he reached out to draw her hand to his lips. "Oh, my precious darling, what a dunderhead I've been. It never occurred to me you did not realize how delighted I was at your warm response." The brilliant blue of his eyes captured her wide-eyed gaze. "My love, you must believe me when I tell you I would have you as you are. And the reason I insisted we not be alone after that ride together was because I find your proximity makes it difficult for me to refrain from taking you in my—" He did not want to talk right now. She was in his arms before he finished the sentence. Holding her close, he ran his hand along her back to touch one of the black curls at her neck. His lips found the soft pulse at the base of her throat. "I have missed holding you, sweet elf."

Would she always feel that melting in her legs when he touched her? Rosaleen wondered. She gave herself up to the enjoyment of his embrace. When he did not kiss her mouth but moved back abruptly from her, she found it impossible to mask her disappointment.

His expression became self-effacing. "I now recall why I promised myself not to be alone with you." He had not missed the look of regret on her face when he'd pulled away. It pleased him to know she was not as immune to him as he'd thought. God, he could not wait until they were married.

"Oh, Lucien, I wish. . . ."

His blue eyes darkened with desire while his arms came about her slender shoulders once more, only this time he made certain he just held her. "What do you wish, sweet elf?"

Her voice was barely a whisper. She snuggled closer. "I wish you would kiss me again. Please," she added.

He stifled a groan at the pleading tone, then felt her small hand on his knee. "That would not be a good idea," he stated, then removed his arms from her and inched over to the right of the sofa. "What we need to do is discuss some important matters."

Not to be put off by his unexpected coolness, Rosaleen took more initiative. She shimmied over to him. Glad for cloth panniers today instead of hoops, she went to her knees on the overstuffed sofa. "That's right, Lucifer, sit there like a stern schoolmaster," she challenged. She bent her head and brushed her soft, pink lips on the corner of his mouth. "I do adore the sandalwood scent that clings to your skin." She heard a stifled moan come from his throat, but he did not move. Closing her eyes, she indulged in placing feathery kisses along the lean, strong jaw, over his left cheek, ending near his earlobe. "Yes, Lucifer, do not move." When she blew soft puffs of air close to his ear, she saw beads of sweat break out on his forehead. He clutched his right hand on his knee.

This initial feeling of power delighted her. What should she do next? She smiled when she remembered something he'd done to her. Steadying herself, she reached for the back of his white neckcloth and unfastened it. As she ruffled the material away from his skin, Rosaleen could not mistake his indrawn breath at her actions. "This is quite enjoyable, Lucifer. Now, stay as you are," she reminded again in wicked delight. Leaning closer, she kissed his neck, then moved down to find the rapid pulse at the base of his throat. She touched the faint blond wisps of hair at the top of his muscular chest, just above his lawn shirt. It surprised her to feel her own body begin to heat as she continued. What she'd begun as a game was turning into something she had not counted on. He was not touching her, but she felt her young body throb at this new experience. Her breasts seemed sensitive to the material of her chemise and gown. The lacings of her corset were now too tight. Her face felt hot against the faint roughness of his cheek. Using her tongue, she traced the shape of his earlobe.

With a growl of overheated arousal, Lucien's arms darted up and captured her by the shoulders. Before

145

she could blink, he had her on her back across his legs. Her gown rode up as it billowed about them.

"Oh, my," she said when she read the smoldering desire in the depths of his eyes.

He felt the corners of his mouth quirk upward at her guilty expression. "Yes, that's right, my dark-eyed gypsy, be afraid." His left hand turned her head up toward his; then his mouth swooped down on hers. This time he did not hold back. His lips and tongue against her mouth showed her exactly how far her game playing had pushed him.

Rosaleen felt dizzy as the fire of his passionate kiss consumed her. And she admitted it; she wanted to burn, to feel him. Her tongue met his intimate embrace. She felt him caress one of her nipples through her thin gown. His fingers made circles, outlining it until it became a hard pebble against his hand. She moaned, her own intense nature rushing to the surface. He made her experience such a fierce wanting. Her hands came out to run along his arms as she pushed herself closer to him, needing more of him, yet not understanding exactly how she could get it. When she felt his hand reach under her skirts to caress the insides of her stocking-clad thighs, a raw shiver of desire coursed through her body.

"Oh, Rosaleen, I ache for you." He took the soft skin of her ear between his teeth and gave it an erotic bite. "You make me want to nibble every delectable inch of you."

"Yes, oh, yes, Lucien, I want this, too. But—" She glanced over his shoulder. "Should you not lock the door first?"

Her words made him remember where they were. Despite his urgent desire, the duke took an unsteady

breath and mentally yanked himself from the dangerous precipice. He gave her inner thigh a soft pat before he released her. It took a few minutes for his
breathing to return to normal.

"Your earlier naughty maneuvers made me . . . almost forget what a child you are in some ways."
Moving away from her, he was certain her disheveled,
flushed appearance must match his own. He busied
his hands with awkwardly redoing his neckcloth. "I
am delighted to learn what a passionate woman you
are, Rosaleen O'Rahilly." More in control, he looked
back at her. "But you also learned something just
now, did you not?"

Heat permeated the fine-boned features of her
face. She nodded in agreement, not able to speak.
Again, he was the one who'd pulled away first. Was
she not to his liking, then, when it came down to it?
Right now he looked displeased with her. She
smoothed down the wrinkles of her gown and tried
to readjust the black hair that escaped her ruffled
pinner. "If you knew I would feel this way, why did
you let me continue?" She could not hide the reproach in her voice.

The duke's frown deepened at her words. "Because
you would learn a better lesson if you experienced it.
You are not always amenable to words, hoyden.
Complaining like a spoiled child denied a treat does
not become you."

"But it was cruel to make me want you, then . . .
toss me aside like an old bone you'd tired of playing
with."

He shook his blond head. "Ah, the overdramatics
again." He would never forget the feel of her ripe,
full breasts, and the curve of her bottom. "Your

analogy is the most absurd rot imaginable. That deliberate teasing you played at just now was unfair to me because you knew I could do nothing proper about it in our present circumstance. Rest assured, I did not come through this unscathed," he added, thinking of the receding ache between his legs.

She looked unconvinced. His usual air of the self-disciplined Englishman seemed in place. "What do you mean, unscathed? I am the one you rejected, humiliated, find not to your . . . aristocratic tastes."

His faced heated. "Never mind; just accept that your needed lesson also cost me a measure of discomfort."

Not understanding much of this, Rosaleen only knew she was sad to have the duke cross with her again. "Oh, Lucifer," she sighed after a few silent moments. "Sometimes things seem so complicated."

Her forlorn expression caused some of his irritation to depart. "It will not be this way much longer, I promise. You did say your parents will be here in another week. I must admit, Ross, it is pleasant to know you are not repulsed by my . . . my attentions."

"Oh, no, Lucien, I never felt this way before, and I like it." Her face took on a crimson hue at such a blatant admission.

"Come along, let us join the others in the garden before I forget all my honorable intentions." He smiled as she preceded him out the door. "You can tell me all about your costume for your uncle Dunstan's masked ball. Will you be my partner as a dark-haired little angel? It would suit you, you know."

The dimple popped out at the corner of her saucy mouth. "No, it is a secret. I want to surprise you."

"Shouldn't our costumes match?"

"Oh, Lucifer"—she giggled—"we are not bookends. We can wear different costumes, even though I intend to dance with no one but you all evening."

Her words pleased him. "I do adore you, sweet elf." With a longing glance back at the blue sofa, Lucien realized how close he'd come to finishing what she had merely started in mischief. Soon, he promised himself. In a week, he would ask her father for her hand. Whatever would she say if she knew he already had a special license to wed her without the usual delays? He'd tackle that later. By now his mother should have received his letter, telling her of his marriage plans. Yes, things were progressing wonderfully. Scientific strategy and patience—that was the way to handle his Rosaleen.

Lucien arrived back at Montrose Hall whistling an Irish tune Calvert had taught him as a child. He felt so happy all his plans were working out. He was positive Rosaleen would enjoy being his wife, for this afternoon dispersed any doubts he possessed about her feelings for him. Indeed, he mused with a chuckle, it had better be a short engagement, judging from his provocative darling's behavior this afternoon. After a footman took his hat and cane, Lucien walked toward his sitting room. He did not expect to see Brian Fogarty standing outside the closed door with a black scowl on his face.

Brian came over to his employer in a hurry. "Sure and we've trouble ta spare. I didn't know if I should have one of the grooms race over ta the Lorenses' or not. After thinkin' about it, I decided bad news could wait."

Still in good humor, Lucien smoothed back his hair and prepared to greet his company. Perhaps it was Father Michael Collins returning his call, for he'd made a point at Liam's suggestion to call upon the physician's brother upon his arrival. He reached out for the brass doorknob as Brian stepped out of the way.

" 'Tis her, more's the pity," Brian muttered.

"Her?"

"Her Grace, lad. She arrived here this morning with three carriages of luggage. Looks like she's plannin' ta encamp here."

"Capital," Lucien said, happy to be able to tell his mother the good news in person. Ignoring his servant's sour expression, he opened the door.

"Mother, how marvelous to have you with us," he said in warm greeting. Automatically, he went over to the rose-marble fireplace, where she stood with her hands clenched in front of her.

At the sight of her tall, handsome son, Garnet Huntington's expression softened.

Lucien embraced her. Still the pouty mouth, pale, blond frailty in the translucent skin, but at forty-seven, the Englishwoman's figure had ripened. The once tiny waist was now plump; the breasts, always voluptuous, had taken on a pendulous appearance, proved by the generous view from the low cut of her white Paris gown. It was a gown for a much younger woman, but Lucien made it a point never to criticize his mother's taste.

As he kissed Garnet's powdered cheek, the duke was engulfed in the scent of white roses. When she patted his arm, he was positive she would welcome his news. He offered her the best chair in the house, the one without frayed material. He took the wing chair opposite her. "Would you like me to ring for tea?"

"No, I believe we have business to discuss." Folding her hands in the lap of her sheer cotton gown, she fingered the diamond necklace at her throat. "I was under the impression you were going to France, Switzerland, then Italy this summer."

Lucien looked apologetic. "I know, Mother, but I really was not keen on a Grand Tour. I am of more use here than traipsing about art galleries and ruins. There are enough ruins here on Montrose lands in dire need of repair."

Hair powdered white and worn high as the current fashion, the duchess tapped her closed fan on the arm of her chair. "Sean Kelly tells me you fired Tom Bennet."

"Yes. Mother, I realize your trusting nature caused you to believe that scoundrel when he wrote you how well things were going here, but he lied. I am even more remiss for not taking over my responsibilities here myself. Kelly told me Bennet wouldn't even let him keep the stables clean. Sean warned me Tom would try to put the blame on him, and he was correct."

Garnet was not surprised to learn Sean Kelly had come out unscathed by her son's conscientiousness. As a spy over the years, Kelly, she knew, could take care of himself. Bennet meant nothing to her, but she did not like the enthusiasm in her son's voice as he described his plans for his property in Ireland.

"The tenants are in rags, their cottages mere hovels; raw sewage floats in what could hardly be called drains. With Liam Collins gone, only seventy-year-old Dr. Murphy is left. It's too big a task for him. Wexford is only interested in coming down from London once a year to see his titled English patients."

"Lucien, you are hardly to blame because these tenants have no physician."

His dark blue eyes pleaded for her understanding. "But I am responsible for the tenants on Montrose lands. Father loved this land, this house, the people here. Mother, I want to try and rebuild things here. We're nearly finished refurbishing the tenant cottages. I've drawn up charts and schedules for the next planting, purchased more sheep and pigs. I intend to replant the gardens in the back where father used to putter with his roses. Oh, it will be a grand place again." He smiled self-consciously. "I have managed a few spare hours to resurrect my old laboratory downstairs. In any event, Dr. Murphy has already asked me for more of my simple herb and plant extracts."

"Becoming quite the apothecary, are you not?" his mother commented. The knuckles of her hands turned white with the pressure she exerted to keep them folded on her lap. "Pray, when did you intend to tell me you had returned to this bucolic haven?"

"I assure you, Mother, I never meant to worry you, and I did write you before I left Cork and again last week to tell you I—"

"If Colonel Bembridge had not been so considerate as to send his urgent letter in a military dispatch, I would never have known you were here. Oh," she added, reaching into the cloth bag inside the narrow slit at the hip of her gown. She retrieved a lacy embroidered handkerchief to dab at the corner of her right eye. "You are all I have. What if I became ill and needed you? Imagine my despair if I'd sent a message to your London mansion, only to find you were missing." Giving the impression that a deluge of tears would soon burst forth, she stood up and walked over to the marble fireplace. "But you must do as you see fit; for you are the duke of Montrose now, and this property in Ireland is yours. You know it is not my nature to interfere with your life. I am only the woman who brought you into the world, even though it almost killed me, a widow alone, with no other relative in the world."

To mention Nigel and Edwin Somerset, her two brothers, Lucien knew would be a mistake. Shaking his head over Garnet's melodramatics, he got up and went over to comfort her. "Dear, Mama, I will always be here for you. Haven't I signed over the chateau in Paris to you and always provided a sizeable income?"

Garnet allowed her son to comfort her. "You are always generous with me. Only, I . . . I never liked this house."

He patted his mother's back. "I would never insist you reside here, Mother. You should always live where you are happiest."

She felt her self-confidence return. He was always kindhearted, even as a boy. Yes, nothing had changed. She could still mold him to her purpose. "You are such a devoted son," she said, holding on to his arm.

"I did write you, but you clearly missed my letter by leaving Paris. However, I am most pleased you have come. Now I shall be able to share my good news with you in person."

The boyish smile returned to his features. "I have met the most delightful young lady in the world. You met her years ago, too. Oh, Mother, she is everything I could ever want for my wife—full of life, humor, intelligence—and she does not hesitate to stand up for those less able to defend themselves." He laughed openly. "Though she may surprise you at times with her directness, for I know what a proper Englishwoman you are, dear Mama. Yet, I'm convinced with time her youthful rambunctiousness will mellow. I cannot wait for you to meet my sweet angel."

Garnet forced a smile. "How wonderful. Lady Prudence Lorens is a delightful girl. The last time I was here, oh, how many years has it been? Well, I can still see little Prudence's blond head as her mother introduced her and Henry to us. Sweet child could not take her eyes off you."

Lucien appeared chagrined. "Well, no, you see— Pru's a fine girl, but she is not the young lady I was talking about."

"No?" Taking the closed fan that hung on her right wrist, the duchess tapped her son across the hand. "La, sir, you have been a naughty boy. Pray, what other eligible females have you been courting behind your mama's back?"

Garnet's kittenish ways right now began to grate against her son. He flushed, then blurted, "Though I have not formally proposed to her, it is my intention to ask the lady's parents next week when they arrive from Virginia. You see, Mother, the girl I intend to marry is Rosaleen O'Rahilly."

It was worse than Garnet feared. Percy's note merely pointed out that Lucien was back in Kinsale, and he'd met Miss O'Rahilly briefly at a gathering at Lorens Hall. Only the colonel's missive could have instigated her return to this godforsaken part of the world.

Incensed her son should even be within twenty feet of that O'Rahilly's vermin, Garnet now realized it would take all her skill to get them safely out of this debacle. Aware Lucien watched her, she stifled her rage and only allowed him to see her horror at his declaration. "Merciful heaven," she cried, taking a step toward her son.

"Mother?" Her white face alarmed him. "What is it? Mother?"

"Oh, oh, I cannot bear it," she whimpered; then her small body swayed.

"My God." Automatically, the duke caught her before she reached the frayed Oriental carpet at his feet.

Chapter Eight

While Louise, Garnet's French maid, hovered about her mistress, Brian Fogarty brought in brandy without being asked. He set the silver tray, crystal decanter, and two glasses down on the dusty end table next to the sofa. "Will His Grace require anything else?" he asked in his most formal tone.

Distracted by his worry over the unconscious woman prostrate on the sofa, Lucien did not answer at first. "Yes — no — wait a moment."

The trim, brown-haired woman in her late thirties held a bottle of smelling salts near the duchess's nostrils. The Frenchwoman shook her head.

"Louise, I do not think it is working. Mother still has not stirred."

"Dangle a diamond necklace in front of her snout and she'll come around," muttered Brian.

"What? Did you say something?"

The picture of angelic concern, Brian offered, "I was askin' if I should have Sean Kelly fetch Dr. Murphy?"

"Yes, good idea," stated his employer.

Instead of leaving right away, the white-haired servant poured two generous snifters of brandy. Placing them back on the tray, he took the two glasses over to Lucien. "Me mother always said a spot of spirits down the gullet gets the heart started. And His Grace appears ta need one, too."

Lucien looked aghast. "Good God, Mother never takes anything stronger than sherry, and that much brandy would kill her." He took one of the glasses off the tray. "However, I believe I do need this."

The servant bowed, then shuffled back to the table, the unneeded glass still in his hand. He eyed the decanter, the full glass, then shot a quick glance at the two people whose full attentions were glued to the fragile flower. Should he pour the brandy back in the decanter? he wondered. He shook his head, tightened his mitt about the bulbous crystal and gulped down the contents. " 'Tis more sanitary," he said under his breath. A hiccup escaped, followed by a hasty hand to his lips and a furtive peek over his shoulder. Safe. "Well, Yer Grace," he said, a new thickness in his lilt, "I shall now see ta . . . ta fetchin' the good Dr. Murphy."

Before Brian could get a steady hand on the brass doorknob, a moan came from the sofa.

"Calvert, are you there?"

Turning about, Brian saw his master go quickly to Garnet. Louise stepped back, and the duke sat down on the edge of the sofa.

The duke took his mother's delicate hand, cradling it in his strong fingers. "Mother, it is Lucien. You are safe."

"I . . . I was dreaming of your father." She added a pathetic mewl to her voice. "Oh, how I miss that dear old man." Her teary gaze focused on the worried young man hovering over her. "I do not need a doctor, least of all any Irish one." The effort of speech appeared too much for her. Garnet sank back against the needlepoint pillow under her head. "Dr. Liam Collins was enough." She snatched her hand from her son. "Oh, Lucien, tell the others to leave," she added, her voice drifting off like the faint cries of a dying lark. "I can take no more."

Lucien saw the pain in his mother's blue eyes. "Thank you for your help," he told Louise and Brian. "I believe I can see to Her Grace now."

When they were alone, Lucien got up and moved a chair next to the sofa. He sat down, distressed when his mother began weeping again. "Mama, don't cry. You will make yourself ill."

"It does not signify. I do not want to live. Oh, my darling, please do not hate me."

Her sobs tore at him. He stood up, feeling more parent than child right now. He sat down on the couch once more and took her in his arms to console her. "Please, Mother, tell me what is tormenting you, for I do not understand why this news has devastated you."

Garnet leaned her head on her son's firm shoulder. "I fear you will never forgive me for what I have done to you. Have you never wondered why I was so adamant against your returning here?" She pulled back to look into his eyes.

"Mother, I know you dislike Ireland. I suppose it is too rural for your exuberant nature. The bustling life of London and Paris have always suited you."

"Would that were all." Anguish brushed Garnet's face. "Constantly I prayed this terrible day would never come. I thought it could be avoided if I kept you away from here, made sure I knew everyone who would be at the parties we attended. All would be well, I told myself. You would marry soon, a proper English girl of your own class; then the problem would be solved forever. The secret would die with me." Forced to stop speaking, she dabbed at her eyes again. "Then no one else would ever know my shame."

Though tempted to comfort his mother as before, something in her expression caused him to return to his wing chair across from her. He waited.

Clearly gathering her reserves, the duchess swung her small white slippers to the floor. "You must not interrupt, my dear, or I shall never be able to confess the truth to you." Her eyes were a picture of sympathy and horror as she stared at him.

"You remember your father and I speaking about Sir Arthur Lyncrost in London?"

"The wealthy investor?"

"Yes." Nervously, Garnet twisted her lacy handkerchief in her fingers. "Though Calvert was not feeling well, he insisted I go to Sir Arthur's that evening. We had only been married a short time. The large party was in honor of George II's birthday. Unknown to me, Taggart O'Rahilly, former groom at Fitzroy Hall, was now the wealthy owner of Williamsburg Shipping. I rebuffed his crude advances. Men of his sort are not easily dissuaded. His insulting manner and the press of people caused me to step out onto the terrace for a breath of air. Louise had just left to fetch my shawl, when out from the shadows a hand clamped across my mouth. I fought him as best I could, but his overbearing strength crushed the breath from me before I could scream for help."

Garnet saw her son's hands tighten on the arms of his chair, but he continued to listen without interruption. "O'Rahilly lifted me in those laborer's arms of his and carried me back into Sir Arthur's garden. Then . . . Taggart . . . raped me right there on the damp grass, surrounded by those boxwood hedges. I can still feel his rough hands on my tender flesh as he forced my legs apart. He was a raging beast. Oh," she sobbed, burying her face in her hands. "He was so disgusting, vile—I wanted to die."

Removing her hands from her face, Garnet looked at her son. His practiced English reserve in the face of adversity made it difficult to tell what he was thinking. She went on. "After he . . . he had his way with me, I ran back to the terrace, thankful no one had witnessed my degradation. Louise found me in a huddled mass on the stone walk. She helped me wash my face and straighten my gown. All I could think of was hiding my shame. The scandal. You do not know how cruel people can be—they could not understand that the wide gap between our ages only made me cherish my husband more. And you know Calvert would have called Taggart out. For Calvert's sake I said nothing and went back to the party. But my humiliation was not to end," Garnet wailed, scraping at her eyes once more with the rumpled piece of lace in her hands.

"Then Taggart married Lady Millicent Fitzroy and became our neighbor. Calvert doted on the young O'Rahilly couple. He and Taggart even went hunting together. A short time later, when I found I was carrying Taggart's bastard—" Garnet saw Lucien blanch. "I am sorry, my precious, it was O'Rahilly's crude word, not mine. I met the unfeeling man for

160

the last time in secret. The blackguard laughed in my face when I told him I was pregnant. Because of his advanced years and delicate health, there was no way Calvert could have been your father," she said for emphasis. "Oh, I cannot tell you all Taggart said to me, for it humiliates me even now just to think of it. The sordid language—O'Rahilly called me a . . . a whore. I made certain I never saw him alone after that terrible day."

Bile rose in Lucien's throat, threatening to choke him. His mind and body reeled at this mortal blow. Unsteadily, he got to his feet and walked over to the fireplace. Forced to take in this horrible news, he pressed his hands against the cold marble to steady himself. A glimmer of hope made him turn about to speak to Garnet. "Mother, you cannot be sure. I mean, these things are difficult to tell. Father was still your husband, and I assume. . . ."

Sadly, the duchess shook her head, causing her son's words to drift off. "Do you not think I wanted it to be otherwise? Alas, no one better than I knew of your father's fragile condition. My darling boy, there is no way on earth Calvert could have been your father. The night I learned I was carrying Taggart's child, I made sure your father had more wine than was his custom. Though it may shock you to hear this, I went to Calvert's bed that night. In the morning, I teased him for his ardent attentions during the night. Clearly, he could not remember, but he delighted in the knowledge he'd made passionate love to his young wife. You see, he always believed you were his rightful son and heir. It was the one gift that meant the most to him, and I take consolation I gave it to him." A Madonna's smile crossed her features.

161

"And father never suspected, never knew?"

"Until today, no one but Taggart O'Rahilly and I knew the truth. Taggart threatened to denounce me publicly as a whore if I ever breathed a word of the truth. Now, as a wealthy businessman, he would never allow anything to jeopardize his friendship with the present king, especially scandal. No, not even poor Calvert ever knew of Taggart's treachery, for I could not hurt that dear, old man. How could I tell Calvert his best friend betrayed, humiliated both of us?"

My God, Lucien thought, feeling as though his world had collapsed about him. It was like the shock of the death of someone close. His mother's loud crying nudged him, and he went back to comfort her. All he could do was hold her, for speech eluded him.

"Please do not hate me, Lucien. I could not bear it if you hated me."

"Shhh, Mother, do not distress yourself. You will become ill with such weeping." His heart was moved by her inconsolable grief. "I do not hate you," he told her truthfully. "None of this is your fault. You were only an innocent victim." As he and Rosaleen were now, he thought. A strangled groan of raw pain escaped his lips.

Garnet pulled away from his comforting arms, ready to press her advantage. "Now you can understand my reaction when you told me you are in love with your half sister."

Her last word made Lucien wince as the knife went deeper into the core of him. "Was in love," he forced himself to correct.

Winning always made Garnet the epitome of congeniality. "You know it has to be this way, my poor boy."

"Yes." Physical torment buffeted him.

"And we must never talk of this again, either to each other or anyone else. Even to speak of it now almost killed me. There is dear Calvert's memory to guard from scandal. You do see the necessity for secrecy, do you not?"

"Yes, of course." It amazed him when he could still speak. He brushed a hand across his eyes to clear his vision. "I will leave you to rest, Mother." Bowing, he excused himself and walked slowly out of the room.

A long sigh of relief escaped Garnet's lips when her son finally left. She sauntered over to peer at her reflection in the large gilt-edged mirror hanging on the right wall. Making a disapproving sound with her tongue against her teeth, she attempted to wipe away the moisture from around her eyes. Cucumber slices on them would relieve the puffiness, but salty tears were bad for the complexion. These scenes always took so much out of her, like with Calvert years ago. Wetting her dry lips, the duchess was sorry her son's manservant had taken the decanter away. She could do with a stiff brandy right now. After readjusting a flower that had come out from her elaborate coiffure, she went in search of a footman to summon Sean Kelly to her son's study. With Lucien sequestered in his suite of rooms upstairs, Garnet knew she would not be disturbed.

Sean Kelly had rarely been inside the house since Lucien's return. He took the wooden chair opposite the massive desk. Running a hand through his short red hair, peppered with gray, he could not hide his smirk at the woman sitting across from him on the duke's leather chair. " 'Tis good ta see ya back in charge, Yer Grace."

The duchess returned the pug-faced man's smile. Uncouth lout, Sean might be, but this Irishman had proved a useful spy years ago. Had prison muted his ferret ability? She had no illusions; the money she paid him was the only thing that kept him loyal. Never, she vowed, would she allow Lucien to marry an O'Rahilly—not after Taggart had killed the only man she had ever loved. Though reasonably sure her performance this afternoon strangled any plans Lucien might have about the scheming chit who'd bewitched him, Garnet had learned the importance of contingency planning. She leaned back in the leather chair and came to the point.

"Kelly, I need something I can use against the earl's family. Taggart and Millicent O'Rahilly will be arriving Tuesday. I want you to use your cunning ways to pump one of their servants. It must be something I can hold in reserve in case situations change."

Sean rubbed the stubble on his chin with a dirty finger. "Won't be easy. Them Fitzroy servants are a tight-lipped group. They have some daft notions about loyalty."

"Pray, do not look so appalled, Sean. There are a few incorruptible people in the world. Yet, I have never met one who did not have a price. Try that Fergus sot." She reached into the desk drawer and pulled out a few coins. "I remember his fondness for whiskey. A few bottles on a summer night should loosen his tongue. He's known Millicent since her childhood. If there are any skeletons, he'd know them. One evening away from your highway revels should not matter."

For the first time, Sean looked uncomfortable. "Why, I'm sure I don't know what ya mean."

Amused, Garnet dismissed him with a wave of her hand. "Sean, I do not give a tuppence whose carriage you and that band of Irish clods waylay. As Black Ned, you can steal all the wealth from Kinsale as far as I am concerned, as long as you touch nothing that is mine or my son's." A hard look came into her eyes. "And, Kelly," she added, before the man could open the door, "I want no sloppy job this time. After you question Fergus, there must be no trail that could implicate me, understand?"

Though a warm night, Kelly shivered, reminded of the cold, putrid cell he and his late brother had shared. "I understand, Your Grace." After he made sure no servants were about, he slipped away.

For the second night, Lucien was jarred awake by the same dream. His hard body was covered with sweat. Still in the throes of his nightmare, he reached out to the space next to him. "Rosaleen?" he called. In his mind, he saw her running from someone—a man covered in black with a leather mask over his face. Lucien tried to save her and reached for his sword at his hip, but someone always got in his way. A man with dark wavy hair, a dimple in the center of his chin, blocked his way. It was Taggart O'Rahilly in the mist who shook his head in warning, holding himself between Lucien and Rosaleen.

Lucien's dark gold hair tangled about his shoulders. He swore at the Irishman's name when realization swiped at him once more. His rage against the man who was the cause of his suffering grew. Leaving the rumpled, damp sheets of his bed, the duke walked over to stare out the window of his bedroom. The darkness was in tune with his thoughts. He felt the heavy tautness between his legs. Aware he could inform his mind logically Rosaleen was now out of his reach forever, his body was a different matter. He could not go back to bed; for the dream would come back, and the torment would start all over again. For hours he sat on a worn, overstuffed chair, peering out into the night. What would he tell Rosaleen? He was certain she adored her father and had no idea he was such a vile bastard. Part of him wanted to shout the truth for all to learn how despicable Taggart O'Rahilly was. Yet, he knew the truth would devastate Rosaleen. However, she would have to be told something. As the night dragged on, the duke could think of nothing. His own pain was still too intense.

"Bessie wants ta know if Yer Grace would have a little kipper this morning?" Brian Fogarty asked. Until the duke hired more house servants, Brian tried to help out when he could. The Irishman added a lightness to his manner. "Sure and she's startin' ta wonder if you've suddenly taken a dislike ta her cookin'. You've not eaten a proper meal in four days."

"Just tea," Lucien stated. "Mother still abed I take it?"

"Yes, Yer Grace. Louise tells me Her Grace never sees the world until late in the afternoon. The party the colonel's aunt gave last night must have been a social triumph, as the gentry say. One of the maids says she saw Her Grace and Bembridge drive up after three and—"

The duke slammed his fist on the cloth-covered table, causing the blue and white china to rattle up then down. "Damn it, Fogarty," he shouted, "I will not tolerate servant gossip in my house! Now, fetch the blasted tea and go about your business."

Mutely, the older man went back to the kitchen. He shook his head. Dark circles under the young man's eyes, the haunted look on his face again—what had happened behind those closed doors four days ago when that woman arrived? Brian wondered.

Returning with a steaming cup of tea, cream and sugar, Brian set them down in front of the duke. He studied the younger man pouring out his tea. "Suppose Miss Rosaleen already told ya the news from Fitzroy Hall," Brian attempted again.

Lucien frowned. "I have not seen Miss O'Rahilly this week. What news are you blathering about?"

Fogarty shrugged his shoulders. "Two fishermen found Fergus Mulcahy's body washed up along the harbor. Poor old fellow had too much whiskey again. Slipped and hit his head on the rocks. Probably drowned before he knew where he was. Only a matter a time before somethin' like that happened. Drank somethin' chronic. Too old ta be wanderin' about after dark." Brian realized the duke hardly knew the Fitzroy retainer, but he was hoping to lead into finding out what was troubling him. "Shall I have Kelly saddle Jasper for yer ride ta Fitzroy Hall? Miss Rosaleen will probably tell ya all about Fergus."

Lucien shook his head. "No, I will not be going

out today." After only two sips of tea, he got up and headed for his library.

"Is there no other way out of it?" Lucien asked his mother. The last thing he wanted was to attend a costumed ball at Fitzroy Hall.

Garnet looked patiently at her son. "Your father always attended the Fitzroy mask when he was in residence each summer. Now that you have chosen to live here, propriety means you must attend the party in two weeks."

"But I cannot face her, Mother. It has been four days, and I have not been able to get any words down on paper to send her. She has not contacted me, either. I thought perhaps she might be concerned when I did not come over to see her."

"Well, she is probably caught up in all the activity with the arrival of her parents. Then, of course, everyone at Fitzroy Hall was sad to learn of their old servant's accident. I did not know him myself, but they tell me he'd been with the family since Millicent and Dunstan were children. A pity."

Garnet's expression became firmer. "Lucien, you must make an appearance. You will not be able to tell Miss O'Rahilly the truth, of course, but you cannot run from her forever. While I know it is not easy for you, I am quite certain you know why I cannot attend. Seeing that man again would kill me."

"Of course, Mother. I never meant you should go." Sighing, he realized his mother was correct. He could not avoid them forever. "All right, I will attend."

Sympathy tinged her reply. "You go along now. A ride will do you good. Leave everything to me. I shall arrange a suitable costume and have Lady Prudence attend with you. Such a charming girl, why don't you ride over to the Lorenses' this afternoon?"

"I don't think—"

"Go on. Henry and Pru will take your mind off all that serious thinking you do. It will be fine, Lucien. Together we can face any hardship. We must focus on the bright side of things."

Relieved his mother had recovered her usual equanimity, he did not share her enthusiasm for the future. However, he realized he needed the exercise if nothing else, and a ride on Jasper might help distract his troubled thoughts.

When her son was out of the house, Garnet again summoned Sean Kelly to the study. The speed of his arrival told her he'd been lurking about the grounds.

"You returned the letter?" Garnet demanded.

Kelly nodded. "Made sure no one else was about. Miss Rosaleen met me outside," he explained, making sure to leave out the part of their usual meeting at night when she rode as Black Ned. No need for the duchess to know she was wrong to assume Kelly was Black Ned. After all, hadn't he learned from the duchess how useful insurance for the future could be?

Garnet could not hide her pleasure. "And she said nothing?"

"Just looked sad to have her second letter returned unopened. I told her His Grace confides nothing to me, just that I was to return them unopened, as with any future missives from her."

"And she does not know I am here."

"Not yet."

"Splendid. That can come out at the party. Now,

Kelly," Garnet went on, "I take it you have something else to divulge. Louise told me of Fergus Mulcahy's accident. How ingenious of you to make certain the old coot will never identify his assailant."

Kelly gave the lady a self-satisfied smirk. "It took a few bottles ta loosen his tongue. He kept saying he couldn't tell, that Lady Millicent and the earl were like his own children. A little encouragement from me, and I managed ta choke it out of him."

Garnet's eyes narrowed. "Do not attempt to play the coy maiden with me, Kelly. Get to the point. What did Fergus tell you."

Leaning across the duke's carved desk, Sean whispered what Lady Millicent had shouted to her husband in the Fitzroy barn nine years ago.

A serene smile transformed Garnet's face as she rested back against the leather chair. "So, Lady Millicent is kinswoman to Father Michael Collins and his brother, Liam." Millicent was right to be concerned for her brother, Garnet thought. The information that she and Dunstan were part Irish Catholic could easily ruin the honorable earl. All knew the law. No Catholic could inherit land, title, or vote in Ireland.

"Well?" demanded an eager Kelly. "When are ya gonna spring the trap."

Blond brows shot upward. "This information is too valuable to waste when it is not needed. I shall hold it in reserve, in case there are any . . . complications with keeping that bitch away from my son. You have done well. Now, leave me."

Sean's freckled face reddened. He got up but stated, "I was thinkin', since it's so valuable ta ya and all, ya might see yer way ta a hundred pounds for me trouble and —"

Any congeniality galloped away. Garnet glowered at the Irishman. "You do precious little for the money I pay you, and I know how you love stealing my son's sheep, hens, and any other four-legged creature you can get your grimy paws on. Then there is the bounty you pilfer on those occasional evening jaunts."

Kelly did not like the way the duchess was looking at him. How did she know so much about his activities? he wondered. Did she have a spy looking after him? Hastily, he left as ordered.

Millicent O'Rahilly could never remember seeing her daughter so subdued. "My dear, is there something you would like to talk about?"

Rosaleen's father had gone out with his brother-in-law and her cousins to the stables. Uncle Dunstan was eager to show off his new horses. She and her mother were alone in Rosaleen's room. "I am fine, Mama."

The bespectacled woman looked about the room that had once been hers as a child. "My, this place brings back memories." She read her daughter's wish to be alone. "Then, I shall leave you to rest. If you do find you want to talk, anytime, Ross, please come to me, all right?"

With a smile of appreciation for the auburn-haired woman, Rosaleen answered. "All right, Mama."

After her mother left, Rosaleen sat in the wing chair next to a small writing desk. The hectic arrival of her parents distracted her thoughts for a time. But after a few days, she became more uneasy when Lucien did not call for her. At first she put it down to his dedication to renovate his estate. Then she wrote a note to him, inquiring after his health. However, last evening when she slipped out to meet Sean Kelly, her friend had returned her second letter unopened. When she pressed him, all Sean could say was that His Grace was not ill.

Try as she might, Rosaleen could not come up with a reason for the change in Lucien. There was only one thing to do, she told herself. She must swallow her pride, ride over to Montrose Hall this very morning, and simply ask him what was amiss.

Chapter Nine

Arriving early at Montrose Hall, Rosaleen was told by Brian Fogarty that his master was at one of the tenant's cottages. "Will ya be wantin' ta wait?" he asked, a hopeful expression on his face.

"Well, I . . . no," she answered, determined to see this through while her courage lasted. "Thank you, Brian. I know where Sally and her family live. I will ride out to see His Grace."

"Very good, miss." Brian could have hugged the girl for her pluckiness. She was probably just what Lucien needed to pull him out of these low spirits of the past week.

Rosaleen could hardly believe the change in Sally O'Brien. Gone was the pale, hopelessness on her face. She had gained a few needed pounds, and her skin glowed with a new healthiness. The woman was bending over to talk with her five-year-old son. Rosaleen jumped down from Bradai's back. "Sally, I would hardly recognize you," she admitted with a warm smile.

The woman in her mid-thirties looked up. "Why, Miss Rosaleen, sure and 'tis His Grace deserves more than the thanks me and me husband can give him." She turned back to her youngest son. "Now, you mind the duke and don't get in the men's way."

With a mischievous grin at Rosaleen, the boy went charging up the embankment behind him.

Weeks before he'd been sickly, and the change brought a misty feeling to Rosaleen's eyes. How proud she felt of Lucien, for he had kept his promise to help these people. Looking about her at the women cooking in the open and laughing, the children playing—it was clear they were better fed. Though their clothes were simple and not new, Ross could see no one in tattered rags as before. She shook her head. "I cannot believe how wonderful you all look."

Sally pushed back a wayward strand of her brown hair that escaped her mobcap. " 'Tis all because of His Grace. And we ain't the only family the duke's helped with food, clothes, and fixing up our place. Imagine His Grace even ridin' about with Dr. Murphy this week, dispensin' salves and medicines the doctor says the duke put together himself. Though the duke's not a Catholic, Father Collins said it would be all right when me boy asked loud as ya please if we could all say a prayer for the duke at Mass."

Sally lowered her voice and stepped closer to Rosaleen. "I know ya won't be tellin' on us, for even though yer from the colonies, everyone here thinks of ya as one of us. Some of these English would have Father Mike before the magistrate, though 'tis gettin' better than it was. The soldiers don't seem quite so

174

quick ta enforce the letter of the law as before."

"It pleases me to see the duke of Montrose doing such fine work," Rosaleen commented.

Mrs. O'Brien shook her head in wonderment. "His Grace has been out here every morning ta nightfall all week. Never thought I'd see one of them English aristocrats workin' like a farm hand. Even made a plan on paper for the size of the barns. Never saw anything like it. All drawn out with numbers and lettered what goes where."

Hope sprang in Rosaleen at Sally's words. This might be the reason Lucien had not been over to see her. Yet, why had he returned her letters unopened? "Sally, is Luci—I mean His Grace nearby?"

Her older companion's smile widened. "Sure and he's just up near the ridge. Mind where ya walk, for they've got lumber, bricks, and tools strewn everywhere."

Rosaleen made her way up the grass- and stone-covered hill. She returned the greetings and waves from some of the tenants she knew. Stopping when she reached the spot of most activity, she saw Lucien first.

Never had she viewed him like this. Dressed only in serviceable dark breeches, scuffed boots, a brown leather apron over a blue-gray workman's shirt, the duke was pounding nails into the main support beams of the new barn. Shirt sleeves rolled up, his blond hair tied back with a thin leather thong, he was dressed similar to the Irishmen laboring about him. The skin on his face and arms had tanned from his work outside in the summer sun. Something warmed her heart to see him working with his tenants this way. She smiled, then called his name.

However, when he looked down to see her, Rosaleen was taken aback to see the expression of raw pain on his face. He put the hammer down, said something to one of the men up on the boards with him, then slowly climbed down the wooden ladder.

Shocked by his haggard appearance, she was certain it had little to do with the work or clothes he wore. The dark-haired woman reached out automatically to touch his arm. "I have been worried about you. Lucien, you have been ill?"

Instantly, he pulled his arm back, then looked almost apologetic. "No, I have not been ill. Thank you for your concern."

It was as though her touch repulsed him. His formal air alarmed her. There was no hostility, yet no warmth. Rosaleen tried to keep her voice level. "You have made some lasting friends among your tenants. The people now have hope you will care for them and your lands here in the future."

Her words caused his features to soften. He studied her for a moment. She was dressed in a simple riding skirt and jacket in her favorite lilac color, without hat on such a sultry day, and had tied her black curls back with a matching silk ribbon. The duke shut his eyes for a moment.

"I am trying to face my responsibilities" was all he said to her words of praise.

What was wrong? He was treating her like a stranger, not the woman he said he adored.

Only after a deep breath could he look back at her. "It took me a few days to compose what I would say to you. I meant to ride over to see you this afternoon."

"You once agreed to tell me if you changed your

mind about your feelings for me. I am not a child, Lucien. I can see you have something to tell me. Best be direct about it."

He did not miss the way her small body stiffened, as if she prepared herself to take a blow. His rage mounted against Taggart O'Rahilly, the man responsible for debasing his mother, along with ruining his and Rosaleen's life. Though a part of him wanted to tell her what a cruel, heartless bastard her father really was, something held him back from shouting the truth at her. It was clear she idolized that unworthy cur, and Lucien found he could not confess the truth that would certainly wound her even more. Yet, the time he'd been dreading all week had arrived, and he prayed this would soon be over for both their sakes.

The duke led Rosaleen over to a spot away from the others, where they could speak in private. When she leaned against one of the tall elms, he could not help looking down into her eyes. They were gypsy eyes with their obsidian color, and he knew it would be the last time she ever looked up at him with such gentle encouragement. He straightened to his full height. "I believe it would be better if we do not see each other in the future. Things have changed, you see."

"You mean in the way you feel about me?" she asked, confused. "You no longer lov—care for me?"

"Just so" was his clipped reply.

Rosaleen clenched her gloved fingers to her sides. "I see." Now she understood why he'd returned her letters without reading them. Had he felt this way from the start? forced its way into her thoughts. "I was just an amusement for a few weeks. A chance for you to sample a bit of local Irish color."

He started to say something, then clamped his lips together. Better for her to believe him a bounder than hurt her more with the truth about her father. God, how he hated Taggart O'Rahilly at this moment.

Was that loathing she saw flicker in his eyes? Hurt gave way to a more heated emotion as she realized what a fool she'd been to ever believe — he was a golden devil, with honeyed words and kisses that had made her forget everything but how much she wanted to be near him. While all along, he'd felt nothing. Hadn't he been the one to pull away first when they shared those two kisses?

"Was I another of your scientific experiments, Lucifer?" she demanded. "A challenge because I did not swoon in your arms upon first meeting you, like the rest of London's simpering misses so eager to snare you?" Only the narrowing of his blue eyes told her she had penetrated his reserve.

His words were matter-of-fact. "I will tell Henry and the others you have informed me gently that you could not consider me as a suitor, but we have mutually agreed to remain friends. That should satisfy any gossip's speculation."

"How efficient, Lucifer. Have it all neatly taken care of, everything in order, the perfect scientific solution for disposing unwanted baggage."

"Damn it, Ross, don't goad me," he warned from his own private hell.

Her dark brows rose in mock reproach. "My intent is to be just as efficient in tidying up loose ends." Turning her back on him, Rosaleen quickly unfastened the first two buttons of her riding jacket. She reached for the slender gold chain about her neck. After readjusting her jacket, the young woman turned, took his right hand and placed the lilac necklace in his palm.

He frowned. "It really is not necessary to return the pendant. I designed it for you and meant for you to have it."

She shook her head. "I want nothing from you. You do not need to pay me off to get rid of me. Oh, and I take it you will not be escorting me to Uncle Dunstan's ball this Saturday?"

"Under the circumstances," he said, looking embarrassed, "I believe it would be better if I do not. As the representative from Montrose Hall, my late fath—as Calvert used to do, I must make an appearance. It will cause more talk if I am absent when everyone knows I have returned to Ireland. So you will not hear it from anyone else, my mother is visiting Montrose Hall and has arranged for Lady Prudence Lorens to accompany me."

"How nice of you to tell me not to expect you as my escort. I am free, then, to accept dear Henry's invitation to be my partner for the masquerade. Why, hasn't it all worked out splendidly?"

Lucien felt something ignite inside at her flippant tone; then he quickly told himself he had no right to feel jealousy where Rosaleen was concerned. Yet, he was learning his heart did not always accept what his mind told it. He still awakened night after night, reaching out for Rosaleen, then cursing the darkness when the horrible truth slammed against him once more. She was lost to him. "If you will excuse me," he finished, with clear unease. "I must get back to help Sally's husband and their neighbors with the barn."

Though he'd hinted she would be part of his future, never had he come out and formally asked her. Why should she be upset? After all, she'd already promised herself never to wed. Only, why did she suddenly feel like crying? Her chin jutted up at that familiar angle. "Yes, of course, Your Grace. Forgive me for taking up your time." She turned, back straight, dark head held high, and walked down the hill to where Bradai was tied.

As she rode away from Montrose lands, Rosaleen swiped at the tears on her face. She could live without him. Pride pushed her painful thoughts into another direction. How could she have been so gullible to believe him when he complimented her, kissed her, held her, gave her the impression of a man in love? Sean Kelly was right; she should never have trusted any Englishman. Never would she make this mistake again.

Dressed in her Turkish costume, Rosaleen moved the ivory-handled mask away from her face to get a better look at the partygoers. Uncle Dunstan was dressed as a simple groom, while Aunt Edna appeared as a shepherdess. Both the earl and his wife stood at the entrance of the ballroom greeting their guests. Chairs and benches lined the periphery of the large room. The polished hardwood floor was filled with costumed neighbors attired as everything from clerics to animals, milkmaids, and pirates. Edwin Somerset, dressed as a red devil, hovered over Rinaldo. In the guise of a gondolier, the prince was laughing uproariously at a comment Edwin seemed to make after spotting Rosaleen. Had Lucien bragged to them of how he'd made such a fool of her?

Rosaleen's father opted for his usual elegant black evening clothes with a black half-mask over his tanned features. The dimple at his chin became more pronounced when he smiled at her. "What, not dancing this set?"

Rosaleen forced a smile while cooling her face with her lavender, plumed fan. "I have danced every minuet since we came downstairs, Papa. You know, I believe there are more people here this year than last."

"And I saw at least two swans and a black crow," said a familiar voice behind them. Lady Millicent, clothed in a dark brown dress with matching feathers sewn on the material, came up next to her husband and daughter. "I think I should have opted for the nearsighted duck outfit." Then she laughed.

When Taggart bent his dark head, the lines about his eyes deepened as he grinned across at his wife. "You look adorable to me, sparrow."

She held her feathered half-mask away from her face. The gray eyes behind her round wire spectacles filled with mischief. "You are only being kind because I am your wife and you feel sorry for me."

"Hellion," said the Irishman. "You will pay for that remark later."

"I am counting on it," said his wife, with another saucy look. "Why did you not come as a black Irish stallion?" she asked innocently.

"Growing bolder still, I see," challenged Taggart, adding a roguish leer at his tall, slender wife.

Rosaleen realized, even after so many years of marriage, her mother and father still loved each other deeply. Touches of gray hair, deepening lines about their faces—none of it mattered to them. But theirs was a unique case, she told herself. Many couples at this party probably had the typical English marriage. Cold politeness, if they talked at all with each other.

"Though you are the handsomest man here, Papa," Rosaleen said, "why do you never wear a costume at Uncle Dunstan's yearly masked party?"

Merriment sparkled from his dark eyes. "Sure and I've always felt dressing in the trappings of a gentleman's evening togs was masquerade enough for me. There are many English aristocrats, I am sure, who would agree with me."

"Oh, look," said her mother, "isn't that the duke of Montrose? Edna told me he's finally returned to Kinsale. My, he has turned into a handsome man."

Reluctantly, Rosaleen followed her mother's gaze. The duke of Montrose was dressed in a Roman officer's tunic with gleaming armor. Without mask, he wore a golden helmet and carried a flat, Roman sword at his left hip. Golden leather sandals that laced up his muscular calves completed his magnificent costume. Caught up in her attention to Lucien, she did not see his companion right away. Lady Prudence Lorens was a vision as Venus, the Roman goddess of love. Clothed in an ivory-colored tunic bordered with gold embroidery, the gown draped straight down to her slender ankles which were encased in matching gold sandals like her partner's. Clearly, Prudence had sacrificed the use of hoops and panniers for historical authenticity. Her blond hair was pinned up at the sides, but the back billowed about her slender shoulders in a halo of blond curls. Rosaleen heard the admiring murmurs pass through the crowd at the handsome, golden couple. Even Aunt Edna blushed when the duke bowed over her hand as he and Prudence made their proper greetings to their hosts.

When Rosaleen felt her mother's shrewd eyes studying her, the dark-haired girl blushed, then accepted the next minuet with Henry Lorens, her escort for the evening.

Gentlemen on one side, costumed ladies on the other. Rosaleen held her lilac mask up to glance down the row of costumed gentlemen. Lucien was fourth from Henry. When he looked her way, she quickly turned to curtsy to her partner.

Dressed in the round turban of an Arab potentate, Henry had a simple white half-mask tied about his elaborate turban. "Good thing I've my breeches on under these robes. If I slip on these flat sandals, at least I'll keep my modesty. Have I told you how enchanting that harem costume is?"

"At least three times, my lord." Rosaleen completed the intricate steps in her lavender slippers.

"I adore women of daring, lovely Rosaleen. You are the only woman here so scantily covered."

She stepped back with the other ladies, turning to the left and right as the dance required. When she took the earl's arm after the dance ended, she said, "For shame, my lord. I am fully clothed from the lilac plumes on my head to my pointed slippers."

"Yes," said Henry with an indulgent smile, "but those sheer pantaloons and that frothy material elsewhere do tempt a man's thoughts." Peering over the top of her dark head, he spotted someone, then frowned. "Good Lord, James Winthrop looks positively foxed. Not like James, the staid barrister, but he's got reason tonight, poor devil."

Rosaleen took a quick glance over her shoulder toward the far side of the room. The brown-haired Mr. Winthrop staggered next to an older lady who clearly did not wish his attention. "What ever caused him to be so imprudent?" she wondered aloud.

"That spoiled sister of mine. Sorry, Ross. Shouldn't be airing the family linen in public." Clearly, he saw the concern on her face as she watched James continue making a bad impression on Kinsale's finest. "He could certainly harm the law practice he's trying to start here if word gets about he can't hold his liquor in public. Nobody gives a fig how much he drinks in private, but insulting the earl's guests here won't get him more clients."

The truth of Henry's comments distressed her. "My lord, let us go over and get him out in the air for a bit."

Rosaleen and Henry arrived just as James was brandishing a pistol at Vicar Nigel Somerset, dressed as Punchinello. His wife Abigail, her plump form pushed into a dainty Columbine costume, was attempting to inch herself away from the inebriated man dressed all in black.

"And she wasn't even impressed to see me as Black Ned," complained James below his black half-mask. "I've a mind to go out and rob a coach. What has Black Ned got that I can't top?" Mr. Winthrop demanded of no one in particular. "Dare say, I could be divine, too, if I worked at it."

Rosaleen saw that Abigail and poor Nigel were upset at being singled out for James's attention.

"Ought to give Pru a plate of those mushrooms, eh, Vicar?"

When Nigel Somerset took off his mask, his face was ashen. "I . . . I have nothing to do with mushrooms anymore, young man. S-So painful to remember. . . ." His voice drifted off as he stared into space.

"Oh, Nigel, I feel quite faint," Abigail cried. Her pudgy hands reached up and untied her white mask as her husband had done. It was clear both Somersets felt the need for more air in this press of people.

The vicar took his wife's arm. "Bless my s-soul, Abbie, please do not faint. S-somebody, please. My wife's ill."

"Henry," said Rosaleen, taking charge. "Take the vicar and his wife to the next room where the food tables are set up. It will be less crowded in there now. I shall get James outside for some air."

Nodding, Henry led both Abigail and the fifty-five-year-old vicar out of the ballroom.

Rosaleen got a no-nonsense hold on James Winthrop's black-coated arm. "Come along, Black Ned," she ordered.

James gave her a toothy grin below his black half-mask. "Miss O'Rahilly, you look positively exotic in that Turkish costume. She turned me down, you know," he added. A sob, then a hiccup followed his forlorn declaration. "Laughed in my face. Said I might be a lawyer with a successful future but pointed out I'm not an ar—aris—don't have a bloody title." Hiccup. "Was that me? Beg your pardon."

She patted his arm in sympathy. It was now clear to Rosaleen that smitten James had asked Lady Prudence to marry him, and the lady had let him down cruelly. At least Lucien did not jeer at her, but it still hurt to think of him. "Come along, Black Ned, you can tell me all about it on the terrace."

"You like my costume?"

Humor lit her eyes when she took in his black tricorn, shirt, coat, breeches, and shiny boots. "Why, James, I believe Black Ned himself would applaud your dapper costume."

With another lopsided grin, James allowed the petite harem girl to lead him toward the French doors. "I might even tell you a little se-secret," he slurred, holding up the pistol in his right hand.

Having danced three minuets with Lady Prudence, Lucien was relieved when a Harlequin gentleman came over to claim the next set with Venus. He attempted to keep his reserve in place when he spotted Rosaleen heading out the French doors with James Winthrop. But what the devil was the matter with her father to allow Ross to wear such a revealing costume? The thin pantaloons left no question about the shape of her lovely legs.

God, when would he be free of such thoughts of her? the duke wondered with despair. Night after night, coming awake in a sweat, the result of those erotic dreams where he is holding the black-haired gypsy in his arms. He was forced to close his eyes against the pain once more. When would he start forgetting her?

"Montrose, I said I need to speak to you."

"What?" The duke opened his eyes to see the concerned features of Henry Lorens. "Sorry, Henry, what is it?"

"Abigail Somerset just told me James was bragging about his costume as Black Ned."

"So?"

"You could tell he's completely foxed, and Ross is

out there with him. Will you come out to the terrace with me? I may need your help."

Totally reluctant to see Rosaleen that close again, Lucien tried to beg off. "Really, Henry, I think you can get someone else—"

"No, Lucien," the earl cut off. "You're the only one I can trust to be discreet. Please." Worry etched his features as he came closer to whisper about James's emotional state concerning his rejected marriage proposal.

"And," continued Henry, "the vicar's wife just told me James confessed to her that the pistol he's carrying is loaded."

Instantly, Lucien was on his way toward the French doors, with Henry following close behind. All the while, fear for Rosaleen's safety gripped him.

Lucien's eyes took a moment to adjust to the darkness of the Fitzroy terrace. He listened for a sound, then saw the outline of a figure. With relief, he recognized the pair of legs when the candlelight from inside the ballroom silhouetted her form. He became puzzled when she dropped something into a potted shrubbery on the terrace. Then she slipped quickly back to Winthrop. When Henry came up behind him, Lucien and he walked slowly over to the couple.

"Good God," Henry cried, "Ross has got the pistol."

"Quiet. Don't startle her," warned Lucien. "Having no experience with firearms, the girl could accidentally blow all our heads off."

When she heard someone approach, Rosaleen immediately turned the pistol about and held it awkwardly by the muzzle end. It would not do to have anyone suspect she knew anything about firearms, let alone how to disarm them. "Oh, James, I never feel comfortable around these things," she squeaked. "What ever shall I do with it now?"

"She made me face it—I'm not divine," said James, lost in his foggy thoughts of Prudence.

"James, please take this . . . awful thing back."

Seeming to dismiss the pistol, James blubbered into the sleeve of his black coat. "Pru thinks I am unworthy of her. And it's true. My family was poor. I never could have remained at Cambridge after Papa died if it weren't for—"

"Winthrop, stop this carrying on at once!" ordered a masculine voice from the shadows.

Such was the tone of command, James looked up, blinked, sniffled, then stumbled back to lean against the stone railing behind him.

"That's right," said the voice again, this time in a soothing manner. "Stand there and take deep breaths."

Out of the corner of his mouth, His Grace added, "Henry, go over and keep James right where he is."

Henry went over to the other side of the terrace to place a friendly but firm hand on James's arm.

Lucien kept his eyes on Rosaleen. "Now, stay calm, Ross. The vicar's wife alerted us about James's pistol."

She looked to the right to see the Roman officer heading her way. Lucien had taken off his helmet and carried it under one arm. The concern she read in his expression almost undid her, but she remembered her part in protecting the real Black Ned's identity. "Oh," she cried, "I think I am going to faint." She swayed, still holding the long muzzle of the pistol between her fingers.

"No, you are not going to faint," reassured Lucien, with more conviction than he felt when he saw her face. Blasted thing could go off with her descent to the ground. "Rosaleen, I am going to take the pistol from your fingers. Just stand perfectly still; there's my good girl."

"James says it is loaded," she whimpered, purposely adding a note of hysteria to her soft voice. "I am so frightened."

"Yes, I know, but I won't let anything hurt you, little one."

His endearing words almost brought tears to her eyes. Why couldn't she put him out of her heart? His concern felt cruel right now after his declaration that it was over between them. Over before it really had a chance to. . . . When she felt his warm arm come about her waist in support while his other hand took the pistol from her, Rosaleen nearly sobbed at the contact. Close to his chest for a moment, she heard the hard beating of his heart. She felt a little ashamed for pretending to be in danger. Had Lucien really been concerned for her safety? she wondered. However, when he stepped back and turned-the-pistol around to hold it in the proper manner by the butt handle, she saw the reserve return to his handsome features.

With care, Lucien checked the weapon. He looked surprised at the findings. "It is not loaded." He shook his head at Henry. "It appears our concerns were unfounded."

"I'll be a—" Henry caught himself. "I've never known James to lie, but in his state, Montrose, I'm sure he believes he is Black Ned."

Lucien returned the earl's expression of relief.

"Henry, would you be kind enough to take James out to my carriage? Tell my coachman I wish him to return after he sees Winthrop home. Here," he added, giving Henry the empty pistol. "Return it to him in the morning with our compliments. You might remind him he owes Vicar Somerset and his wife an apology for frightening them."

Henry nodded. "Certainly, Lucien." Smiling, now that the danger was over, he put a comrade's arm about James Winthrop. "Come along, old boy, time for Black Ned to be in bed. Hope you don't have a case tomorrow. Something tells me you're going to have the devil's own hangover in the morning."

"Thanks, Henry," babbled James. "You, Lucien . . . and little Rosaleen are such good friends." He gave Henry a glassy-eyed stare. "Prudence said I was a nobody. It's true. Your sister even speaks French. Yo-you know what that means?"

"That she can converse as vapidly in French as she does in English," answered the lady's exasperated brother.

"Did I tell you she refused me?"

The earl rolled his eyes toward heaven. "God's nightshirt, here we go again. All right, Winthrop, you can tell me again in His Grace's carriage. When I return, I'm going to need a drink."

Despite his initial fear for her safety, followed by the discovery there never was any danger, when Lucien got a closer look at her costume, he felt his emotions careen in another direction. "By God, your father is an irresponsible fool to allow you to appear in that . . . that indecent getup."

Taken aback by his words, Rosaleen's reaction rushed to the surface. "That is not the first time you

190

have criticized my father, and I want an end to it," she ordered. "Kindly remember, I am not James Winthrop, one of your old toadies from Cambridge that you can boss about to do your bidding." Hardly pausing for breath, her earlier hurt gave way to unleashed temper. "This costume covers every inch of me, which is more than I can say for your blond Venus and her bare left shoulder."

"At least Lady Prudence's lovely costume hides her legs."

"Perhaps she's bowlegged and needs to conceal them. Anyway, Henry said I looked enchanting."

"He's besotted with you; what would he know? Henry hasn't a clue what decent ladies should wear." Lucien's irritation increased a hundredfold when her chin came up at him. Though he did not wish to probe why too deeply, something irritated him in the way Henry and the other young bucks had gushed over Rosaleen tonight. "Prancing about in that obscene Turkish costume, your legs and breasts practically bare—" His baritone rose an octave. "Any English gentleman would be mortified to be seen in your company. You look like a Haymarket tart displaying her wares."

"Oh, how dare you . . . that you could . . . you insufferable . . . !" Automatically, her right fist came up in an arc, and she punched him on his left jaw.

His head snapped back with the impact. At first he could not believe she'd dared strike him. Then the pain in his jaw confirmed she had most effectively socked him. In an instant, he let go of the helmet in his right hand, allowing it to clatter to the stone floor. He grabbed her by the shoulders.

Rosaleen stifled an outcry when her feet came off

191

the cold stones. She was appalled to see the angry red swelling where her doubled fist had clouted him below his left cheek. What had she done? Her cursed temper had gotten the better of her again, and she bitterly regretted it — not only because of the fury she read in Lucien's eyes.

"That is the second time you have punched my face. Be warned, virago. You are not ten years old now, and I feel no compunction to hold on to any code of honor at such treatment, least of all from anyone by the name of O'Rahilly. Never punch my face again unless you are prepared to take the consequences." None too gently, he placed her back down on the gray stones of the terrace.

Shaken by her own lack of control and the measure of Lucien's outrage, Rosaleen raced toward the French doors to return to the safety of the crowded ballroom. He really must hate her now, she told herself. Well, even if he found her not to his liking, did he think no other Englishman would look at her? Tears swam before her eyes, but she managed to get them under control before she opened the French doors and stepped inside.

MORE PASSION AND ADVENTURE AWAIT... YOUR TRIP TO A BIG ADVENTUROUS WORLD BEGINS WHEN YOU ACCEPT YOUR FIRST
4 NOVELS ABSOLUTELY *FREE*
(AN $18.00 VALUE)

Accept your Free gift and start to experience more of the passion and adventure you like in a historical romance novel. Each Zebra novel is filled with proud men, spirited women and tempestuous love that you'll remember long after you turn the last page.

Zebra Historical Romances are the finest novels of their kind. They are written by authors who really know how to weave tales of romance and adventure in the historical settings you love. You'll feel like you've actually gone back in time with the thrilling stories that each Zebra novel offers.

GET YOUR FREE GIFT WITH THE START OF YOUR HOME SUBSCRIPTION

Our readers tell us that these books sell out very fast in book stores and often they miss the newest titles. So Zebra has made arrangements for you to receive the four newest novels published each month.

You'll be guaranteed that you'll never miss a title, and home delivery is so convenient. And to show you just how easy it is to get Zebra Historical Romances, we'll send you your first 4 books absolutely FREE! Our gift to you just for trying our home subscription service.

BIG SAVINGS AND FREE HOME DELIVERY

Each month, you'll receive the four newest titles as soon as they are published. You'll probably receive them even before the bookstores do. What's more, you may preview these exciting novels free for 10 days. If you like them as much as we think you will, just pay the low preferred subscriber's price of just $3.75 each. *You'll save $3.00 each month off the publisher's price.* AND, your savings are even greater because there are never any shipping, handling or other hidden charges—FREE Home Delivery. Of course you can return any shipment within 10 days for full credit, no questions asked. There is no minimum number of books you must buy.

4 FREE BOOKS

TO GET YOUR 4 FREE BOOKS WORTH $18.00 — MAIL IN THE FREE BOOK CERTIFICATE T O D A Y

Fill in the Free Book Certificate below, and we'll send your FREE BOOKS to you as soon as we receive it.

If the certificate is missing below, write to: Zebra Home Subscription Service, Inc., P.O. Box 5214, 120 Brighton Road, Clifton, New Jersey 07015-5214.

FREE BOOK CERTIFICATE

4 FREE BOOKS

ZEBRA HOME SUBSCRIPTION SERVICE, INC.

YES! Please start my subscription to Zebra Historical Romances and send me my first 4 books absolutely FREE. I understand that each month I may preview four new Zebra Historical Romances free for 10 days. If I'm not satisfied with them, I may return the four books within 10 days and owe nothing. Otherwise, I will pay the low preferred subscriber's price of just $3.75 each; a total of $15.00, *a savings off the publisher's price of $3.00*. I may return any shipment and may cancel this subscription at any time. There is no obligation to buy any shipment and there are no shipping, handling or other hidden charges. Regardless of what I decide, the four free books are mine to keep.

NAME

ADDRESS   APT

CITY   STATE   ZIP

(   )
TELEPHONE

SIGNATURE   (if under 18, parent or guardian must sign)

Terms, offer and prices subject to change without notice. Subscription subject to acceptance by Zebra Books. Zebra Books reserves the right to reject any order or cancel any subscription.

Lucien grabbed her roughly by the shoulders. Not

Chapter Ten

Lucien gripped the cold granite railing and forced himself to take slow gulps of evening air. Only when he felt the return of his self-control did he bend down to retrieve his Roman helmet. Placing it on his head, he tied the leather strap under his chin, then felt the area where his throbbing jaw puffed. At least the strap would hide his bruised jaw. For such a tiny woman, Miss O'Rahilly had a dockside bully's right cross.

Spotting the potted shrub on his way back to the ballroom, he went over to it. In the dim light of the terrace, he felt about, under the green yew. His fingers hit something. He pulled it out and brushed the soil particles away from the round object.

The duke walked over to an area where the light was better, then peered down at his open palm, which held black powder and the round ball from a pistol. The discovery added to the duke's puzzlement about the elusive Miss O'Rahilly.

An hour later, Lucien attempted to play the attentive partner to Lady Prudence. Having recently discovered her treatment of his friend James, the duke experienced a bitter taste as he stood by Henry's sister. She sipped punch with other English guests. However, he realized, as the lady's escort for the evening, certain proprieties must be adhered to no matter his personal feelings right now.

"Look, there is Sir George Lindenwood dancing with Ross. See, he is the one dressed like a buccaneer, next to the boxwood hedge costume."

Pru eagerly went on to tell the group what she knew about Sir George. "They say he killed a man in a duel over an earl's wife in London. Had to come here until the scandal dies down. King George will never receive him back at court. It is all too divine for words."

As the evening progressed, so did Lucien's unusual consumption of brandy. To his already frayed emotions, the added burden of having to watch all these Englishmen pay court to Rosaleen was almost more than he could stand. He reached for another glass of the amber liquid after a white-gloved footman passed by.

When Lucien saw Taggart O'Rahilly move toward the French doors, clearly intent on getting a breath of fresh air, he plunked the empty glass down on the cloth-covered table, then followed.

Lucien's fevered mind tormented him with the realization three lives were ruined because of Taggart O'Rahilly, the man Rosaleen believed the most wonderful man in the world. Whether from the brandy or flower-scented air, the duke felt a brief dizziness. Or was it Ross's clout to his jaw that suddenly unleashed his desire for revenge against this Irishman?

"O'Rahilly!" he yelled to the man with his back to him.

From a few feet away, Taggart turned, his streetwise instincts sensing danger. He removed the black half-mask and slipped it into the pocket of his coat. Recognizing the Roman officer as Lucien Huntington, the Irishman saw the duke's unsteady gate. Was the lad merely foxed?

"That is my name, though I am your senior enough to be addressed more respectfully as Mr. O'Rahilly. Now, what can I do for you?"

This Irishman's censure did nothing to assuage Lucien's emotions. For a minute he studied the man. Yes, they were the same height, similar muscular build. As he made these physical comparisons, he felt rage consume him. With wrenching anger and pain, he blurted, "Damn you, I wanted to marry Rosaleen!"

"By Saint Patrick, you've gall, Montrose." Remembering Garnet's treachery, he felt appalled then outraged at Lucien's declaration. "Never," Taggart bit out between his teeth, "would I allow my daughter ta marry the likes of you. She'll wed a real man, not some pansy-dressed milksop, an English aristo ta boot."

The last week of torment and the brandy almost unhinged his mind. "As well you know I can never marry her, you Irish bastard!" From his left hip, the duke unsheathed the broadsword and raised it with both hands like an avenging angel above Taggart's head.

"You are mad," Taggart spat, but felt sweat break out on his forehead.

195

"Stop!" Rosaleen cried, rushing in front of her father. With Lucien's behavior of late, something alarmed her when she spotted him heading out after her father earlier. It frightened her to see the wild look in his blue eyes. "Please, Lucien," she cried, terrified at what he was about to do. This was nothing like the Lucien she had come to know and—no, she could feel nothing for this man. He had practically told her he despised her. "Please," she repeated, tears forming in her dark eyes.

From what seemed a long distance, the duke of Montrose heard the soft, lilting voice of his beloved. He blinked, trying to clear his mind from the black nightmare that ensnared him. With sickening reality, he looked up to see the sword in his hands. Then it registered in his fevered mind what he'd almost done. And he might have killed Rosaleen! His troubled eyes darted to her. She looked so grave. God in heaven, he must be going mad, he thought, then tossed the heavy sword to the ground. With a strangled cry of pain, the blond-haired man rushed out into the darkness of the garden.

Automatically, Rosaleen prepared to race after him, but her father's hands on her arms stopped her. Her initial fear, confusion, then despair over the last few days were all too much for her. Without warning, she burst into tears.

Taggart held Rosaleen close as she sobbed against his chest. Never had he seen her cry this way before, almost as if her heart were breaking. As he continued to comfort her, he did not like what he suddenly discovered: His beloved daughter was in love with Lucien Huntington, that young Englishman who had appeared quite ready to decapitate him just now.

By the next morning, Rosaleen's practical side had returned, and she decided to ride over to Montrose Hall to hear from Lucien himself why he had attempted to kill her father last night—a man she was positive His Grace hardly knew. Enough of his bizarre actions; she wanted answers.

However, when she arrived at Montrose Hall, Miss O'Rahilly was surprised to have Garnet Huntington answer the door. Remembering her manners, Ross executed a proper curtsy and smiled in greeting. "Until the duke mentioned it a few weeks ago, I did not know you had returned to Kinsale, Your Grace."

"It was my unexpected present to dear Lucien." The duchess smiled.

"I . . . I should very much appreciate seeing His Grace this morning."

With a mewl of regret, Garnet added, "I am so sorry, my dear, the duke is out riding this morning with Lady Prudence Lorens." When she saw the girl's crestfallen expression, Lucien's mother knew she had been wise to get her son out of the house early. This O'Rahilly chit was more persistent than she'd anticipated. So like her father, the duchess mused, taking in the nineteen-year-old's dark hair, eyes, the determination in the chin. "Pray, come in. I would like to see you for a moment, if you can spare the time. Young people are so driven these days."

"Of course, you are most kind, Your Grace." Following the lady dressed in a ruffled pink morning gown, Rosaleen was taken aback to find the duchess already had her hair powdered and a heart-shaped patch at the corner of her lightly rouged mouth. Only half past eight, yet the duchess appeared as if she'd been up for hours.

Garnet had put on more weight than Rosaleen remembered her having nine years ago, but she was still a strikingly attractive woman. Large diamonds dangled from her delicate ears. Looking at her, Ross began feeling better already. Who but a devoted mother would know her son's heart? And Lucien was so distant now, he would never confide in her again, she was certain.

When they were seated and Rosaleen politely declined tea, she tried to come to the point. The duchess sitting across from her in a wing chair helped with her sympathetic expression.

"Take your time, my dear. I can tell this is not easy for you. That it concerns my son, I have already guessed." Garnet understood why her son was attracted to this young woman. Not a beauty in the classic sense like herself, but Rosaleen did have a certain sultry allure. Unlike her superior Paris tastes, mused Garnet, this girl seemed to prefer an understated elegance. The hunter-green riding habit was simple but expensive, she concluded, sizing up her adversary. Mentally, Garnet completed the final touches on her plan to ensure Lucien and this unsuitable baggage would never come within arm's length of each other again. The girl was clearly inexperienced where men were concerned, but she had courage. This one wasn't apt to have an attack of the vapors. But then, Garnet thought, this was the sort of skirmish she enjoyed.

"At first he seemed so friendly and happy in my company," Rosaleen went on. "Then suddenly. . . ." She blushed. "He cannot even bear to have me touch his arm, even for assistance into a coach. Indeed, Your Grace, my very presence now appears to . . . to be repugnant to him." She swallowed. Best not tell his innocent mother about his attempted assault on her father. She would wait and speak to Lucien alone on that matter. This genteel lady would probably faint if she knew. "I have gone over it in my mind; I can find nothing I have done to cause his . . . thorough contempt."

When Garnet saw Rosaleen successfully master the threat of tears, the older woman discovered she had arrived from Paris just in time. This little nobody was clearly in love with Lucien, even if she did not realize it. Yet, the girl was no fool. It would take strategy to put her off for good. Garnet reached into the cloth bag inside her gown and took out her pocket handkerchief like one setting up props for a performance. She patted her eyes with the square of lace.

At the sight of the woman's tears, Rosaleen went over to sit next to the duchess on the overstuffed sofa. "Oh, Your Grace, the last thing I wish to do is cause you distress. I want to assure you His Grace has always been the perfect gentleman with me." She blushed but knew she had to reassure his poor mother she was not in that sort of difficulty. Automatically, the dark-haired girl placed a comforting hand on Garnet's arm. "Please, Your Grace, I never meant to upset you." Her smile was rueful. "Indeed, neither you nor your son can be blamed because His Grace finds me not to his liking. I only sought your insight into why he has suddenly changed toward me. In truth, madam, I believe he loathes the very sight of me now."

Garnet stared across at the colonial girl. She shook her head, clearly attempting to gain more control of her emotions. "How young you are, my dear. How innocent. Bless you for that."

Rosaleen felt more confused.

"You see, child, Lucien is not like other men. He can only be—oh, this is so difficult to put into words." She touched the cloth to her blue eyes once more. "Lucien can only be fulfilled with another man."

"Your Grace, I do not understand what you are saying."

"I'm sure he told you I wanted him to take his Grand Tour. I never wanted him to return to Ireland, especially when I knew my brother and his lover would be in Kinsale for a summer visit while Edwin checked on his estate here. You must remember Prince Rinaldo, the Italian gentleman in his thirties? You met him at the Lorenses', then the party last evening?"

Ross did not probe how the duchess was so well-informed. "Yes, I have seen your brother, Edwin, and the prince during my summers here. Forgive me, Your Grace, but I fail to see what they have to do with—?"

"They visited us in Paris last summer. I thought it

was only a young man's infatuation, but Lucien is so constant in his feelings. Picnics, late suppers—then there was that week Edwin was not able to join them when he caught a cold. Well, I am sure from your sad tale, Lucien tried to fight his true feelings by attempting unsuccessfully to court you. Such a paragon of English virtue, he probably believed he could overcome his true nature. I've lived in fear these past months, praying to God Lucien would find peace in a woman's arms. But I see now I was only fooling myself, as Lucien was to think he could ignore the inherited curse of the Somerset men. It is in the blood," Garnet finished, capturing Rosaleen's wide-eyed stare. "You see, my dear, Lucien has been hopelessly in love with Prince Rinaldo for over a year now."

Stunned by this disclosure, Rosaleen could not speak for a moment. Lucien in love with Prince Rinaldo? She looked back at Garnet. "But . . . Your Grace, those two times when we kissed—" She stopped. "That is, the duke seemed happy in my company during the beginning."

Garnet gambled on her son's code of honor. "Ah, my dear, I venture to guess it was my son who pulled away first from you, is that not so?" Rosaleen's downward gaze shouted her victory.

"Has Lucien ever . . . ever told the Prince how he feels?"

Garnet's expression of horror was real. "Oh, no, he would be far too shy to make such a disclosure. Besides, he knows any outward flaunting of his true nature would be suicide as far as his title and position in society is concerned. Never must you dis-

201

close to him or anyone else you know of his . . . his unrequited love. I have already spoken to him about a match with Lady Prudence. He is agreeable to it, for he knows it is the only decent thing to do. Prudence is a sensible girl and will accept my son without his physical attentions. Poor man, only I know of his inner suffering. Every time he looks at Prince Rinaldo, a sadness comes into his deep blue eyes. Neither Edwin nor the prince are aware of Lucien's inclination either. Since his school days, I have known of my son's preferences, but a mother always hopes with the right woman . . . alas, it will never be. Prudence already accepts this. The Montrose line will end here."

Instantly, Rosaleen remembered the Montrose Club. Heat stained her cheeks at the thought of what those six boys had been made to do by Lucien for payment a few days each week. Things began falling into place with tragic rapidity. Answers to many questions forced their way into her mind. The two times Lucien kissed her, he had always been the one to pull away first, ending their kiss far sooner than she desired. He had always been chivalrous, even when, Rosaleen now admitted, she would have welcomed more physical responses from him. Apparently, he had made a gallant effort to conform, then found he could not go through with the lie that she attracted him.

"Then, you understand?"

The duchess's question shoved Rosaleen back to the present. "Yes, of course, Your Grace. You may count on my discretion."

* * *

That evening, Black Ned and his men saw a man charging across Montrose lands past midnight when they were on their way to work. Staying in the shadows until the stranger passed, Rosaleen was aghast at the reckless rider. Dashing over boulders, fallen trees, the lunatic seemed to have little regard for himself or his hard-driven horse. She gasped when moonlight splashed across the hatless man's face. It was Lucien pounding across the dark landscape as if a demon were after him.

"There he goes again, tearin' out at night. For a week now he's taken ta ridin' out like seven banshees were after him." Sean Kelly shook his head. "Jasper or His Grace—don't know which one is gonna break his neck first. Never knew the stuffy duke ta be so foolhardy. English are all daft; 'tis in the blood."

Despite her resolve to stay uninvolved, to accept it was over between them, Rosaleen felt moved by the wild, forsaken look on the duke's drawn features just now. Too ashamed and shy to speak of his love, he was killing himself in lonely torment and self-loathing. Perhaps his agitated state, along with his uncharacteristic consumption of liquor, had caused him to lash out at Taggart. Did her father remind Lucien of the darkly handsome Rinaldo? Pity for his unfortunate plight made her suddenly determined to try to assist him in secret. There must be a way to help him.

"Lucien, what a delightful surprise." Father Michael Collins shouted his greeting from the bed of

203

turnips and potatoes he was pulling from the ground. Dressed in frayed black robe, sash about his slender waist, the priest's once carrot-colored hair had muted toward white. However, the Irishman in his late fifties got up from the earth with the ease of a younger man. He motioned the rider over. Brian Fogarty had asked him earlier to have a word with the troubled young man if the opportunity presented itself.

The priest did not miss the reluctance in Lucien's face but saw him dismount and walk over.

"Good morning, Father Collins." Politely, Lucien doffed his tricorn.

Michael took in the dishevelment—dust-covered boots and clothes, redness about the blue eyes, hint of stubble on the usually well-groomed face. Heavy sweat foamed across Jasper's sleek body, proving both rider and beast had covered a lot of ground the last few hours. "Up early I see."

Lucien shook his head. "In truth, Father, I have not been to bed yet."

"Will you join me for some chocolate or tea? Please," he added for the Irishman realized now Brian Fogarty's concern was well-founded. Something was gnawing at this man, and it robbed him of sleep and the prudent interest to care for himself. From the way the clothes hung on his tall frame, His Grace had also lost weight, Collins noted.

Too bone-weary to refuse, Lucien accepted the hospitality. Lowering his head, he entered the priest's small cottage. Rough wooden planks hardly covered the dirt floor. Something was boiling in an earthenware pot over a peat fire.

Lucien watched Michael go about setting up the tea. He glanced about the sparsely furnished room. With Taggart O'Rahilly as his father, Lucien realized he was now part Irish. Not that religion had played a large part in his life up to now, but he felt more Anglican from his upbringing. "Father Collins, do Catholics believe they are the only ones with the true religion?"

Smiling, Father Collins gestured for Lucien to sit down. He then poured out the tea in two chipped cups. "I try to teach my flock we are all God's children with the potential for His salvation."

"But what of our birth? A duke or an Irish groom—you have to admit, it makes a difference to the world we live in."

"I cannot deny in Kinsale the English dominate in terms of money, laws, power, and lands. But we are all ashes in the end. I doubt God sorts the dust from a duke or an Irish groom's son.

Lucien took a slow sip of the hot tea. It seemed to soothe his agitation. If only he could sleep without that recurring dream, he thought. His mother was right; he never should have come back to Ireland. Then he would not have met Rosaleen again, the one woman forbidden to him. "But if a man finds out he has been living a lie, that he is not the person he thought he was—I mean, if through no fault of his own, say his birth—" He stopped when he saw the priest watching him intently. His mother had warned they could tell no one. Her honor was more important than his own confused feelings on the matter. Abruptly, he rose from the wooden chair. "Thank you for the tea, Father Collins. Faith,

I must be fatigued. Please forgive my nonsensical rambling."

As the priest stood in the doorway of his cottage, he watched the duke of Montrose get on his chestnut horse and ride toward Montrose Hall. Liam had asked him to keep an eye on the lad if ever he returned to Kinsale. Through Lucien's disjointed phrases, Michael Collins had recognized the journey of a tormented soul seeking answers. All the business about a lie and birth led the shrewd priest to a decision. He would write a hasty note to Liam in Italy telling him his suspicions. His brother had stayed close to Lucien through their correspondence. Perhaps Liam could shed some light on the duke's odd behavior.

"What did she say when you told her the earl of Dunsmore asked for her hand?" Taggart asked.

Lady Millicent moved her spectacles up to a more comfortable position on the bridge of her nose. "She smiled and said she would be happy to do whatever you and I decided was best for her. Now, what do you think of that?"

Taggart's expression mirrored her concern. "Docility was never one of Ross's strong points. And did you see the way she picked at her food yesterday?"

Millicent came over to her husband and snuggled against his chest when he opened his arms to her. "I am worried, darling. Since we returned to Kinsale, I have been struck by the difference in Ross. She is quiet, listless, never seems to voice opinions any-

206

more. Though there are nights she retires early to bed, the child looks exhausted, even after rising at one in the afternoon. And there is something else." Lady Millicent stepped back to look directly into her husband's dark eyes. "I saw the way she looked at Lucien Huntington when he first arrived at my brother's masked ball the other evening. Ross has many admirers here and in Williamsburg, but never has she taken them seriously. I believe that has changed with Garnet and Calvert's son."

For days Taggart had been trying to coax his only daughter to confide in him. Clearly, Millicent had met with equal failure. Not wishing to alarm his gentle wife, the Irishman never told her about the incident on the terrace when the source of Rosaleen's unhappiness had tried to separate Taggart's head from his body.

He kissed his wife briefly on the lips and patted her shoulder. "It is probably nothing serious. The first childhood crush is always difficult. I doubt Ross will consider Henry, and I must admit I'd rather she married an Irishman. Don't worry, sparrow," he finished with a quick hug. "Things have a way of working out."

After leaving his wife to rest in their room, Taggart headed for the Fitzroy stables. His black servant, Caleb, was waiting for him. "Well, is she finally gone?"

Caleb nodded. "Yes, sir," said the Jamaican in his cultured voice. "I found out the duchess just left Montrose Hall for a short visit to London. One more thing, sir," Caleb added, as his employer headed for the saddled horse.

After swinging up on one of his brother-in-law's horses, Taggart looked down at Caleb. He did not miss the loyal servant's reluctance to continue. "Out with it."

"The groom at Montrose Hall. I recognized him from years ago."

"So?"

"It was Sean Kelly."

Blood drained from Taggart's face at the mention of that Irishman. He and Sean had once been childhood playmates, but they had taken different paths. So, he had not died in prison along with his older brother, Patrick. And Garnet had Sean back at his old post of spying, he wagered.

"Thank you, Caleb. You know I value your discretion. If my family asks, please tell them I have gone for a ride into town." Putting his knees to the horse's flanks, Taggart rode out in the direction of Montrose Hall. At least he'd made sure that woman would not be present when he confronted the duke of Montrose.

Chapter Eleven

Positive his unhappy daughter was keeping something from him, Taggart was determined to see the duke, and with Garnet out of the way, they would not be disturbed. When a young groom saw to his horse, O'Rahilly was relieved to be spared seeing that weasel, Sean Kelly.

Walking past a footman who informed Taggart the duke was out, the Irishman marched through the familiar Montrose entry corridor and opened the door to Calvert's old study. As he expected, he found Lucien working on a stack of papers behind his desk.

Lucien bounded to his feet. Outrage replaced shock. "You barge into my home, unannounced, certainly unwelcome. By God, sir, your audacity has no limit."

Taggart closed the door behind him, then walked unhurriedly into the room. "The polish I tried to learn at William and Mary years ago has a way of sloughing off when I sense danger to my family. You might call it an ethnic advantage for survival. I also recognize when a man wants to kill me."

209

His hands came down on either side of the wooden desk. "What I want to know is why?"

"I can hardly believe you dare ask me that after all you have done."

"Is that all you have to say?" Taggart lost some of his belligerency when he read the pain behind the lad's words. It was clear Lucien was suffering some inner torment, but how in hell did he expect Taggart to guess what was the matter? He only knew Rosaleen's unusual behavior had something to do with this man.

The Irishman leaned back from Lucien's desk as the duke walked around to confront him. Perhaps if he tried another tactic, the younger man might open up. "Well, maybe it does not signify, especially since Henry Lorens has asked for Ross's hand in marriage." He saw a spark of life in Lucien's face and pressed harder for a response. "Do you hate my daughter, then, is that it?"

"Hate her?" Lucien echoed. "I lov—no, I do not hate Rosaleen, Mr. O'Rahilly." His blue eyes turned glacial. "It is her father I have reason to wish dead." Angrily, he told the Irishman what his long-suffering mother had confessed.

After a few astonished moments, Taggart found his voice. "I am definitely not your father," he stated in a grim tone. Inwardly, he was amazed Garnet's perfidy would extend to her own son.

Yes, the duke mused, he would expect such a coward to deny it. "And I say you are a liar and raper of defenseless women."

Taggart felt the blood race through his veins.

"Be careful, Montrose. Sure and I've overlooked much from you for my daughter's sake. You'd best remember I've killed men for less." As often occurred, his brogue returned with his strong emotion. "Many faults I have, but tellin' lies isn't one of them. You want the truth, do you? Well, here's more than I've told anyone. When I first came back to Ireland after making my fortune in Virginia before I married my Millie, I stopped in London with a cargo of tobacco and cotton. Sir Arthur Lyncrost was hosting a party in honor of King George II's birthday. Your mother did not know I was the former O'Rahilly groom. She wanted no names that night. Nearly swooning when she came upon me in Sir Arthur's garden where I walked alone, Garnet arranged to have me meet her at an inn outside London. However, when I asked her if she wished to know who I was before we came together in her suite of rooms at the inn, she insulted me for keeping her waiting and ordered me to get down to business. I lost my temper and yelled at her, after which your delicate little mama drew a jeweled stiletto from under her pillow and got my complete attention by brandishing the point over the area between my legs. Though I was tempted, Montrose, I never spilled my seed into her. Is that blunt enough for you?"

Lucien could only remember his mother's horror and anguish as she confessed this Irishman was his father. "The brutality of your attack still haunts her. My lady mother would never lie about such an intimate thing."

"Your mother would fabricate Christ's parentage if it suited her purpose."

"Irish scum," Lucien snarled, than came at Taggart with his fists.

The two men scuffled, seconds away from exchanging blows. Using some of his old dockside maneuvers, the man nearing fifty got a rough hold on Lucien's arms and twisted them behind his back while shoving a knee into his spine. "Damn it ta hell," he bellowed, "any officer in His Majesty's Horse Guards could be your father, Montrose. If you don't believe me, go to the Inn of Three Cranes outside of London and ask for Mistress Louise's rooms." Then he let the Englishman go.

Lucien was forced to massage his painful right shoulder where the ox of an Irishman had almost pulled his arm out of the socket.

Taggart saw a hint of uncertainty in Lucien's eyes. "You think she is visiting Sir Arthur Lyncrost and his family in London? Go and prove me wrong if you're not afraid of the truth," he challenged. As he watched the younger man fight an inner battle, part of Taggart almost regretted having to hurt the lad this way, but it was time Lucien knew the truth. If his uneasy fears that Rosaleen was in love with this man proved correct, Taggart knew Lucien would have to face Garnet's treachery. Not pleased to learn her son might become his son-in-law, nonetheless, the Irishman now realized Garnet loathed the idea even more. Why else would she tell Lucien such an abominable lie?

Taggart reached out to put a hand on Lucien's shoulder, but the Englishman pulled away with a look of hatred. "Lucien, Calvert was a good friend. I give you my word I never did anything to dishonor his friendship."

"So you say."

Remembering Calvert, Taggart forced back his temper. "Then, sir, it will be for you to tell my daughter the truth. I shall not lift a finger to help you." Coolly, he left the duke's home.

For the rest of the day Taggart O'Rahilly's words gnawed at Lucien. Finally, he decided the only way to prove him wrong was to set sail for London himself. Then he would come back and challenge that lying Irishman to a duel to the death.

Upon arriving in London, the duke was taken aback to learn his mother was not staying at the Lyncrost's town house. Covering Sir Arthur's bewilderment, Lucien told the Montroses' longtime friend that Garnet had probably gone directly home to Paris. Though it was getting dark, Lucien declined Sir Arthur's hospitality and started the long ride to the secluded Inn of Three Cranes outside the city.

Lucien was glad he'd brought his pistol and sword. The large brick structure was covered in ivy, set back in a thick grove of tall elms. The young innkeeper, son of the original owner, smiled and directed him up the stairs to Lady Louise's rooms on the third floor.

The second floor had a long hallway with a series of doors. From the male and female sounds coming from behind the closed doors, the duke realized quickly this inn was also a brothel. He reached the third floor, walked about the corner to a dimly lighted hallway, then stopped at the only entry door. Ahead to his left he saw a narrower set of stairs, probably used by servants to discreetly enter this floor.

The duke of Montrose stood alone outside the closed door. All that he'd ever believed about his mother could be reinforced or wiped away with a single knock. Just before he could raise his fist to the door, he heard a pair of booted feet coming up the servants' stairs. The Englishman darted back around the corridor to stand in the shadows.

Lucien watched as Colonel Percy Bembridge arrived. Dressed in his scarlet and gold uniform, the colonel raised a gloved hand to knock softly at the carved wooden door. It opened, and the duke got a view of opulent white and gold furnishings in the French style. Bouquets of white roses on either side of a white and gilt-edged sideboard gave off a heady scent. It was Lucien's mother who answered the door, but he had never seen her dressed like this. She had on tight black breeches, and her powdered blond hair was tied back in a ribboned queue, like a gentleman. He saw her smile up at the colonel. When Percy reached about to lift the short woman up to his height, Lucien watched as his mother placed a dainty arm around the colonel's neck and kissed him full on the mouth.

"I thought you would never get here," she complained, giggling when he placed her booted feet back on the white and gold Oriental carpet. Then she closed the door behind them.

Lucien told himself Garnet was a widow and entitled to have the colonel as her lover if she wished. Though her manner of dressing as a man surprised him at first, no doubt she did it to please Percy, and they rightly felt the necessity to keep their liaisons secret. It still proved nothing. However, when Lucien was about to go back down the main stairs, the arrival of three young officers coming up the servants' stairs stopped him. An uneasy feeling bit at his insides.

The three officers were obviously the worse for wine, but they managed to straighten up before pounding on his mother's door. Garnet answered, smiling flirtatiously at the tall young men. With a pretty pout she told them they'd chosen the wrong evening and should come back to visit her tomorrow. The lurid comments by the three lieutenants and Garnet's returned suggestive banter left a sour taste in Lucien's mouth.

Lucien had to shut his eyes as shock and pain coursed through him. He leaned his blond head against the hard wooden wall and waited for the three rowdy young men to leave. After hearing his mother's childlike laughter and Bembridge's lisping words of submission, the duke walked slowly past the door to return down the main stairs. When he reached the first floor of the Inn of Three Cranes, the well-fed proprietor spoke to him.

"Want to make an appointment for later? 'E don't usually stay the whole night."

Without answering, Lucien raced for the door. He felt the bile rise in his throat and just reached outside before he was ill on the grass and dirt.

After he wiped his face with his pocket handkerchief, the duke went back over to his horse, which stood tied to a clump of shrubs. Weary in body and sick at heart, Lucien began the long ride back to London, not caring that it was dark and he was alone on these roads. With the discovery of his mother's promiscuity came the doubt of her story that Taggart O'Rahilly was his father. But who the devil was his father, and why would his mother lie to him about Taggart? His emotions felt too raw to sort out the meaning of things tonight. All he wanted to do was take the fastest packet back to Kinsale.

When the duke finally returned to Kinsale late one evening, he was in no mood to face the visitor waiting in the sitting room. Why would his uncle Edwin's lover be here at this hour?

"And this is the third time in two weeks he's come over ta see ya," Brian Fogarty explained. "Edwin and he probably had a tiff, and he wants ya ta talk ta yer uncle, I'm thinkin'."

Lucien entered the room, with Brian right behind. He tried to appear welcoming but felt exhausted from his hasty trip. "Prince Rinaldo. My uncle is well, I trust?"

Not as tall as Lucien, Rinaldo was dressed in evening clothes, a silver ribbon holding his thick black hair against the back of his neck. The man in his thirties flashed a smile. "Edwin is always in perfect health, though he does not know the nature of my visit." Pointedly, the Italian stood peering down at Brian. "What I have to say is in the nature of a private matter."

Lucien turned to his Irish servant. "Thank you, Brian, you may go to bed now."

"Your Grace." Brian bowed and left the room.

Lucien was aware of the contrast between the impeccably groomed prince and his own disheveled appearance. When his visitor did not come directly to the point, Lucien suggested, "If you are not adverse to informality, I should like nothing better than listening to your news upstairs while I wash some of this dust off."

Rinaldo seemed to relax. "Certainly." He followed Lucien up the marble staircase leading to the duke's suite of rooms.

After indicating an overstuffed chair next to a small wooden table, Lucien stripped to the waist. He went about washing and attending to his toilet.

"Mio Dio, you shave yourself?"

Through a myriad of soapsuds, Lucien could not hide a smile as he brought the sharp razor across the stubble on his right cheek. "When possible, I have always preferred to wait on myself."

"Ah, I see. The touch of the common man," the prince stated, followed by a flash of white teeth that contrasted with his swarthy skin.

Though the comment was innocuous, Lucien could not help frowning at his reflection in the shaving mirror. His mother said Taggart was his father; the Irishman denied it. After rinsing his face, the duke peered deeply into the mirror. Just whose son was he? Did he have more in common with men like his groom, Sean Kelly? If there was Irish blood in his veins, would that explain why he often felt more at home here in Ireland, away from the people with which his mother wished him to associate? Rubbing the moisture from his face and chest with a clean linen towel, Lucien turned about to face the now standing Rinaldo. "If you do not mind, Your Highness, I am tired from the long trip. You told Brian you have urgent news for me?"

Rinaldo studied the Englishman. There was an appreciative gleam in his dark eyes as he took in the blond hair about broad shoulders, clean skin, narrow waist above tight buckskin breeches. Appearing unable to stop himself, Rinaldo reached out a graceful hand and touched Lucien's hard chest. "Sweetheart, *baciami*."

"God's teeth," Lucien swore, stepping back so abruptly he nearly toppled the wooden table behind him. "What in bloody hell do you mean, kiss you?"

Not the least offended, Prince Rinaldo's smile widened. "You do notta have to be shy, my blond Apollo. The signorina, she told me everything."

Reaching for the clean lawn shirt Brian had placed on the large four-poster bed, Lucien pulled the shirt quickly over his head. His hands were unsteady as he buttoned the top buttons. Years of

218

practiced reserve came to his rescue. He tied his cravat, then put on a plain waistcoat and blue outer coat. All the while, he attempted to control his outrage and confusion. "Pray, sir, who is this lady, and what has she told you about me?"

"The sweet little dark-haired girl, she came to my town house last week late at night, and—"

"Rosaleen O'Rahilly went to your rooms, alone, at night?" Blond brows shot to his hairline.

"*Si*, she made sure Edwin was at Somerset Hall. She is very discreet. Made certain no one saw her come or leave."

Lucien went over to the table and grabbed for the decanter. "Sit down, Rinaldo. I believe this is going to take a little time. I need a brandy. How about you?"

Sitting back down on the overstuffed chair, Rinaldo accepted the glass from the younger man.

His Grace pulled up a straight-backed chair from next to his bed and sat down across from his guest. "Please tell me everything the lady said."

Rinaldo's dark eyes softened in remembrance. "Ah, such a shy little beauty. If nature had changed things, how I would pursue such a one. Expressive dark eyes, voice like an angel—she admits to being nervous about coming to see me, but her affection for a friend overcomes her fears. First, she makes me give her my solemn promise no one but you will ever know of this meeting. The one thing I refuse to promise is not to tell you who has arranged this gift. I thought you might wish to tell her secretly your gratitude, no?"

"I wish to tell her something all right," Lucien bit out between his teeth. "Pray continue."

"The little Madonna informs me Lucien Huntington, Duke of Montrose, has a grand *passione* for me, but he is too shy and ashamed of his feelings to ever speak openly about it to me. He is losing weight, does not sleep. She says she is alarmed at your failing health. Never will she divulge how she knows this secret love, only assures me it is true. She hands me a bag full of coins and asks me, if I am not adverse to it, if I will give you a night of romantic bliss — her words exactly."

"The devil you say?" Lucien's fingers tightened around the crystal glass in his hand. He shoved it down on the table, then stood up abruptly, turning his back to the prince in order to hide what he felt.

Confused, Rinaldo put down his brandy, then walked over to the blond-haired duke. "Do you not understand, Lucien? I, Rinaldo, am your gift for the night."

Lucien whirled on Rinaldo. "By hell, she dares to —" With effort he swallowed his livid rage, aware Rinaldo was not to blame for this misunderstanding. "Do you have the money she gave you?"

"Yes, it is right here." Rinaldo reached into his dark coat pocket and held out the small cloth bag. "I did not want to take it; she insisted."

The scent of lilacs still clung to the material. Lucien went over to a drawer near his bed. He returned quickly with a large bag of coins. "I would be grateful if you'd take this instead and give me your word to say nothing of this to anyone. As we both know, the lady's reputation would not fare well if this became known. Rinaldo, I am no one's judge, and your relationship with my uncle Edwin is your own affair. I am getting the distinct impression you have read more into my politeness at our meetings than I intended. The lady's incorrect information has added to the confusion."

Comprehension etched across the Italian's face. He shrugged, then gave Lucien the smaller purse. "The lady was wrong, then?"

"Yes, she was definitely incorrect."

Rinaldo shook his head when Lucien forced the heavier bag of coins into his hands. "No, it is not necessary. I do not do it for the money anyway. You give me a king's ransom. Too much."

"Take it, sir, I insist. If nothing else, you deserve payment for being placed in such an awkward situation. I understand my uncle is the jealous type. I have no wish to have him challenge me to a duel over you." A speck of humor returned to the duke's voice.

Even Rinaldo smiled as he accepted the generous bag of money. "It would not do me any good to have this get out. I have always been faithful to Edwin, but as you say, he is more volatile than we Italians in his jealousy. Yet, I do not think Miss O'Rahilly was—how you say it? It was not a prank to her. I could tell she felt affection for you. I know of no other woman who would have the courage to arrange such a gift to help someone."

Help him? Lucien almost choked but forced himself to show the prince politely to the door. "Yes, only Rosaleen O'Rahilly would dare such a thing," he agreed under his breath.

"Do you wish me to have my servant return the coins in the morning?"

"No," Lucien answered, giving the Italian a level stare. "I shall return them to the lady myself, with my compliments." Only the coldness in his blue eyes shouted the true extent of his rage at her latest audacity.

After seeing the prince to his carriage past midnight, Lucien charged to his stables and saddled Jasper himself. The memory of Rosaleen smirking past him on the arm of Henry Lorens did little to stifle his fury.

Arriving at Fitzroy Hall, Lucien was aware no servant would let him in at this ungodly hour. Recalling their first meeting when he saw her home in his carriage, Lucien went around to the back of the estate, tied Jasper to a nearby tree, then looked up at the large elm tree outside her room. He hoped he still remembered how to climb trees.

His strong emotions egged him on, and he began climbing up the tree. She had pointed to a thick limb and stated her room was just inside. Hoping he was correct and not bounding into the earl's bedroom, Lucien lifted the window and swung his booted feet into the dimly lighted room. No fire was going on such a warm night, but a candle still burned on a nearby night table, clearly forgotten before sleep. As he walked quietly into the room, he felt reassured by that faint lilac scent he always found arousing.

Rosaleen's eyes were open. Having just washed and gotten into bed after a night as Black Ned, she attempted to inch her way to the bottom of her bed to her wooden chest, where she kept her sword and pistol. But she only made it halfway down the bed before she felt a masculine hand brace about her mouth. She struggled, but the man's strength easily overcame her. A sack of coins landed in front of her on the bed.

"I am returning your coins, madam, since I had no use for your gift." He kept his hand about her mouth. "So," he growled into her ear, "you think I am as useless as a gelded sheep, do you?"

Chapter Twelve

Rosaleen felt the duke free her mouth. Even in the dimness she recognized him. "Lucien," she whispered, turning on her knees to peer up at him. Of course she knew the feel of his strong, graceful fingers on her skin. His sandalwood soap mixed with the scent of leather and a fast ride through a forest on a warm summer night. She wanted to fling herself into his arms, just to have him hold her briefly for one last time, but she knew it was impossible. As his long-suffering mother confessed, Lucien could only be fulfilled with another man. His tone told her the extent of his feelings. However, what did he have to be vexed about? It had taken a long time for her to get up enough courage to arrange this discreet gift for him. He sounded anything but grateful. As he continued glowering down at her with menace, Rosaleen's chin came up. "Did something go wrong?"

"Let us say, something went awry with my night of romantic bliss." Anger got the better of him, and he came down on the bed next to her. The small bed creaked in protest at the unaccustomed weight.

Lucien grabbed her roughly by the shoulders. Not groggy or warm from sleep, her skin felt cool through the thin material of her nightgown. However, he was too far gone to contemplate the meaning of anything except his fury. "Have you any idea how dangerous it was to go to that part of town at night, alone? How did you manage to get out of the house without a servant or your parents, or even that uncle of yours spotting you?"

Without fear, her dark eyes met his. "That is my business. You need not thank me for arranging your gift." Her soft voice was rich with sarcasm.

He gave her a quick shake. "Thank you? By God, I thought of nothing but throttling you with my bare hands all during the ride over here. How in blazes did you come up with that harebrained notion I'm one of those finger twirlers?"

She blushed at his coarse remark. It was not true? But how could his mother be so mistaken? Then came the thought perhaps Garnet had other reasons for telling her Lucien desired Prince Rinaldo. Rather than cause enmity between Garnet and her son until she was sure of things, she did not answer his question. "Then, you are not a . . . ?" Suddenly, her world became less bleak. "You see, I thought you would be grateful that I was helping you when you were too reticent to arrange things for yourself."

"Yes," he countered in a tight voice. "A man appreciates knowing the woman he loves assumes he's a sodomite."

"You do not have to be crude about it."

He gave her an arched look. "I believe we have

passed the stage of party manners, Ross."

"Well, I suppose . . ." Then the more important word he'd spoken penetrated her confusion. "You love me?"

For the first time in many days, amusement sparked in his clear blue eyes. "God help me for telling you so soon because you will no doubt toss it in my face when next you lose that hot temper of yours, but, yes, hoyden, I do love you. I think I've felt this way since that first time I caught sight of you in my pond."

The implications of his words hit her. "Oh, you are a horrid beast," she berated, pulling back from his arms. "You say you loved me all that time, yet you were so cruel to me that morning I came to you near Sally's cottage. How could you toss me aside like some Irish trull you'd tired of?"

He read the hurt behind her angry words. Then he told her what his mother had confessed to him and recounted his conversation with Rosaleen's father. He did not leave out his trip to the Inn of Three Cranes. "While I take the greatest joy in now realizing your father spoke the truth, you can understand my regret finding out my mother is a — she is not all she seems. I will not rest until I find out who my true father is."

"Oh, Lucien, you should have told me this before." She touched his cheek with her fingers. "We could have gone to my father, and he would have told us the truth immediately. I thought you hated me, or at the least looked upon me as merely a summer's diversion."

"Never would I feel that way." Lucien's arms

came about her, tenderly this time. "Oh, Rosaleen, I have missed you so much." He kissed her smooth cheek, then found he needed more of her soft, warm body.

"God, Ross, I was never more angry than when Rinaldo blithely told me about your arrangement of my gift. You could have been attacked, robbed. You rush about without using the brains God gave you. You're far too rash for your own good. Never are you to go near that part of Kinsale again, do you hear me?"

She'd already promised herself never to go near there, but his autocratic tone right now did not sit well. Memory of her hurt at his cold rejection weeks before caused her to pull back from him. "You have no right to order me to do anything, Your Grace. That privilege is reserved for Henry Lorens, the man I intended to marry after you severed our relationship."

Instantly, she recognized her flippancy was a mistake. Lucien's hands came about her waist, and he lifted her easily across the mattress to trap her upper body. One arm came about her shoulders, while the other forced her chin up to meet his penetrating stare.

"You cannot mean to marry the earl, not after what I declared tonight. Look me in the eye and tell me you love him."

Rosaleen sought the offensive. "Unhand me at once and leave my bed. Go paw one of your English whores for the night!"

All his pent-up longing now mingled with his wrath. He brought his mouth down hard on her soft lips. At first he wanted to punish her; then something changed as he continued kissing her. His lips gentled on her flesh. He stroked the back of her shoulders in an effort to coax her into yielding.

Initially, Rosaleen pounded his back with her fists to get free, but as his kiss turned to the familiar tenderness, she found it impossible to fight against her own feelings. "Lucifer," she moaned his name.

He could not seem to get enough of her. His arm supported her upper body as he cradled her close to his heart. His fingers laced in her thick black curls. He caressed her slender throat, lingering where the rapid pulse fluttered under his lips. "Oh, sweet elf, don't you know how empty my life has been without you?" He placed soft kisses along her cheeks, her impudent little nose, her closed eyes, delighting in the way her hand began stroking the back of his neck. Returning to her lips, his tongue came out to taste her sweetness. He reached down where her nightgown bunched about her thighs. Running his warm hand along her hips, it nestled in the down of black curls that covered her most secret treasures. As he continued their heated kiss, he cupped the little mound with his palm. "I can feel your warm honey welcoming me, my love," he whispered next to her ear.

"Oh, Lucifer, please. I want —" Rosaleen had never felt this way before, completely cherished yet vanquished at the same time.

He stopped and moved his fingers away. "Yes, love, what do you want?" He felt the heat and dampness against his fingers and knew from the tight heaviness between his legs his own arousal was becoming difficult to restrain. But he wanted them both to have no doubts about their feelings for each other. "Tell me, Ross, what do you want?" teased the blond-haired devil, before planting another kiss on the sensitive flesh of her earlobe.

She could not help writhing in his arms. "I want . . . I don't want you to stop. Please."

The darkness hid his thoroughly masculine look of triumph. Back and forth across the soft core of her, he kept up the steady caress with his fingers.

Rosaleen encouraged him with her heated actions as she moved her hips to match his erotic rhythm. Her legs clenched and unclenched as she sought something she could not name. As Lucien continued the sensual onslaught with his fingers, the tension mounted within her. Suddenly, she felt her body convulse when something pulsed deep within her, and she collapsed across his arms in her first feminine release. She felt completely drained, and for a moment she could only bury her face against the folds of his coat. He soothed her, murmuring soft words of love, while he brushed back a strand of damp hair from her face.

"Oh," she murmured when she could speak normally once more. "I never realized it could be so — you do that very well."

He stifled his laughter at her open admission. So like his Rosaleen — without coyness, to the point. "Thank you."

When he stood up to place her gently back against the pillows, Rosaleen's hand accidentally brushed the area between his legs. "Oh, my," popped out. "I . . . am so sorry . . . I mean, I never meant to cause you—I should not have made you continue."

His smile was rueful. "I will recover, sweet elf. Thank you for your concern, but I knew what I risked. I wanted to give you pleasure." She appeared so contrite, he could not help placing a chaste kiss on the tip of her nose. "You look ready to cry," he said, amazed at her reaction. He sat down on the edge of her bed once more.

"It's because. . . . You see, Lucien, while I don't say I know everything, Papa insisted my mother tell me early about . . . what takes place between a husband and wife. Mama said Father did not want me to go to my marriage bed as terrified as Mama was, having lost her mother when she was only a child. Mama says a lady should never . . . well, purposely get a gentleman in such a condition, for it is very painful, unless she is his wife and can . . . ah, remedy the discomfort." Warmth suffused her face, but her concern caused her to speak her heart. "I . . . I now realize what I did that afternoon on the sofa when we were alone at the Lorenses'. You were right to be displeased with me."

She could not tell Lucien she loved him, for she was still uncertain of her feelings. Old habits of distrust were hard to break. She only knew she cared for him, more than any other man she had ever met. But her work as Black Ned was still not finished, and this man, for all his talk of love, was still an English aristocrat. She looked up to find him watching her with an unreadable expression on his face.

Lucien was moved by her honest declaration and

concern for him. An intriguing, lovely woman, he told himself. Would he ever solve the mystery of Miss O'Rahilly? And their problems were still not over. "We have more important things to discuss, darling. It must be clear to you by now that my mother and your parents have little liking for each other."

Rosaleen looked down at her hands. "Yes, my father has already warned me to stay away from you. And the lie your mother told you about your parentage was probably a ruse to keep you away from me." She was also thinking about her work as Black Ned. "Oh, Lucien, we will never be together. It is such a muddle."

He brought his fingers under her chin, so she was forced to look into his eyes. "I will speak to your father in the morning. I know he loves you, and it is time this hatred between our families ended. The Montroses and O'Rahillys must let the past die. I will not let either of them ruin both our lives over things that happened before either of us were born. I know now Taggart is not my father. We will be married very soon. Enough of this interference from our families."

Rosaleen was unnerved by his resoluteness. Married? She had not meant a wedding; she was talking of a more open arrangement so they could be together. Her work as Black Ned was too important to give up just yet. Besides, she'd already decided never to marry anyone. Yet, something in Lucien's expression told her that right now, as she sat next to him on her bed, was not the time to divulge her own plans for their future relationship. "Your

Grace, I think we should wait, perhaps another month. There is really no hurry and—"

"Rosaleen, is there a reason you do not wish to marry me?" he demanded. "This is not the first time you have sought to put me off from posting the marriage bans."

"Well, I just do not wish to rush into marriage."

"So you say." His manner was skeptical; then another darker thought occurred to him. "Is it because I do not know the identity of my father that now makes marriage to me less palatable?"

"Oh, that you can even think me so shallow to— that was a typical stiff-rumped English remark."

"Yet you do not deny it. You would not be the first potential bride to change her mind at the thought of marrying a bastard."

Fire in her eyes, she glared across at him. "That word suits you because of your inane remark, sir, not your issue."

"Damn it, answer my question."

"No, for I will not be bullied by anyone, least of all an English duke who snaps orders at me in such a tone of superiority. Now, kindly leave my room the way you came before I toss you out the window myself."

His eyes narrowed. "One day," he said in a dangerously quiet tone, "you will push me too far with that cursed temper of yours. You tell me we must wait but will not explain why. Very well, miss, I will give you three days to make up your mind whether you will wed me now or not. It is either yes or no. I will not be held on a string by anyone again. My life is my own now, no matter who my father was.

There will be no more of these intrigues. I suspect some dark secret is partly why you keep putting me off from a formal commitment between us." He saw her blanch at his veiled threat. "Yes, that is right, Irish gypsy, be uneasy. Though I loved Calvert Huntington as the only father I knew, now I'm aware I could be any blackguard's off-spring. Thus, I feel freer of constraints to always act the gentleman. The gloves are off, Rosaleen O'Rahilly, and I give you fair warning. I will use any methods I need to protect you from your own folly. Therefore, I will leave you alone until your decision is made."

Before she could reply, Lucien went over and re-opened her window. He swung his long legs over to the tree limb.

His last words haunted her, and she did not fall asleep for a very long time.

Lady Millicent turned over in bed. "Taggart?" she said, nudging the man next to her. "I thought I heard someone outside." At first her husband did nothing but reach for her to pull her back under the sheet. She turned over and swung her long legs over the side of the bed and walked barefoot to the window. Peering out into the darkness, she saw nothing but her brother's lovely gardens. Strange, she thought she heard a rider close to the house. Smiling, she recalled the time she had snuck out her old room by climbing down the elm tree in order to come to her brother's aid. So long ago.

"Are you all right, sparrow?" The dark-haired

Irishman rubbed the sleep from his eyes.

"I must have been dreaming, darling. Sorry I woke you." She walked back to bed and snuggled against the arms that reached out to her. "You know, Taggart, I've been trying to find the right moment to talk to you about Ross."

"Umm, waiting until I'm befuddled, are you?" His mind on other matters, he pushed the straight reddish-brown hair away from his wife's slender neck to place little kisses against her skin.

Millicent knew this might be her best opportunity. "Darling, it is not Lucien's fault for the problems we had with Garnet and John Nolan years ago." She felt Taggart move away from her.

Had Lucien gone to the Inn of Three Cranes? Taggart wondered. "Millie, beneath his cool reserve, I sense the young duke might very well be a fine man, but I certainly don't intend to have Garnet as an in-law."

"But Ross is in love with him?"

Taggart's eyes darted to her face. "She told you this?"

"Not in words, and I do not think she realizes it herself. But surely you must see the change in her since we arrived. Why, she has not even gone with Edna on her rounds in weeks as she always did in past summers here. And did you not see the way Lucien's eyes watched her at Dunstan's masquerade? It is clear to me he is in love with her, and I should not be surprised if that young man approaches you soon to ask for Rosaleen's hand."

"But she is an Irish Catholic, and he's an Anglican duke. No vicar would marry them."

"Now you sound like Garnet." His wife moved closer and sighed with contentment when her Irishman's arms encircled her once more. "Your sister married my brother. Vicar Nigel Somerset could perform the Anglican ceremony; then Father Michael could marry them. Ross could practice her Catholic faith in private, as Edna does. Besides, things are changing in Ireland. Father Collins says Mass now in his thatch-roof cottage, and the soldiers look the other way." When she felt his lips nuzzle her ear once more, she knew Taggart was close to bending. "We cannot always choose where are hearts lead us. Certainly, you remember that, my love."

"Oh, sparrow, you have a way of leading me like a docile lamb to market. Sure and I'm even ready to hand you the cleaver."

Giggling, she tipped her face up to his. "It's part of my Irish ways."

"Shhh, not here," he said in warning. "God, you know we agreed never to speak of it openly, for Dunstan's sake."

Contrite, Millicent added, "Yes, my brother could lose everything if the truth of our Irish heritage came out. I'm sorry. But, Taggart, will you reconsider your position on the duke and Rosaleen?"

A crooked grin made the dimple at his chin widen. "I might be persuaded." Boldly, he ran a hand along his wife's curved hip.

"You mean I shall have to wrestle the snake of Ireland one more time?" she asked, with mock reluctance.

"Hellion," he whispered next to her ear, then nipped at the lobe. "For a woman in her late forties, you are still a handful. Poor Lucien does not know what he is getting himself into with the women of this family."

Smiling, Millicent began toying with the gray hair that touched his temples. "I dare say, Rosaleen will soon put him in his place." A stifled cry of surprise escaped her lips when her husband tossed her on her back and came down on her with a quick maneuver of his own.

Mr. O'Rahilly chuckled as he stared down into his wife's shocked eyes. "From what I observe in Lucien Huntington, Rosaleen may just have met her match in that outwardly reserved duke. He is nobody's fool. I wager he'll never be anyone's doormat either. And that includes our adorable but strong-willed daughter."

Two nights later, Lucien awoke again after midnight, unable to sleep. The question of why Rosaleen was putting him off about marrying him kept gnawing at him. Finally, he decided a ride in the cool night air might clear his head. Keeping his word, he had not gone near her, but tomorrow was the last of the three days he'd given her to answer whether she would wed him or not. And he was now beginning to worry her silence meant no. Had he been unwise to give her the ultimatum?

As the duke began his ride, from habit he nudged Jasper in the direction of Fitzroy Hall.

The leisurely ride helped to ease his troubled

thoughts. Part of him felt justified in taking charge to get her to make up her mind. Since the beginning, he'd been positive he wanted to marry her. Had he been mistaken in her feelings for him? In truth, never had she actually told him she loved him. Was he a romantic fool to desire to hear the words from her lips, too? Why did he have this persistent feeling she was in danger and was keeping something from him?

Forcing Jasper into a run, he decided he must stop these troubled musings for tonight. His mother would be back next week; then he would confront her with her lie that Taggart was his father. It was not a meeting he looked forward to. "Faster, Jasper," he said, pressing his knees against the horse's flanks. He raced to forget, to tire his body so sleep could refresh him once more.

Keeping his horse back in the shadows of the grove of trees, Lucien halted near Fitzroy Hall. He looked up at the darkened window that was Rosaleen's room. He could not help smiling when he thought of her up there in her maidenly nightdress, her black hair in a riot of curls about her lacy pillows. Her small hand was probably pressed under her cheek as she slept, the dark-haired angel of his dreams. His romantic reverie halted when he saw her window open, and a dark figure moved on the ledge to reach for the limb of that elm tree outside her window. Automatically, the duke reached for the sword on his left hip. A bold thief attempting to rob Fitzroy Hall? And what of his sweet Rosaleen? Had the churlish bandit harmed his love? Preparing to confront the scoundrel, Lucien brought Jasper up with a start when he heard the robber's voice — God, it was Rosaleen!

She was dressed in a pair of men's black breeches and dark shirt. Her hair was hidden under a round felt laborer's hat. His eyes grew large as he stayed back in the shadows. A man about her same height came out from the thick hedges with another horse's reins in his hands. Lucien saw Ross climb on the back of the horse without assistance; then the two people rode off.

Without hesitation, Lucien followed but kept far enough away to avoid discovery. What was she up to? A clandestine tryst with another man? What could she possibly be doing dressed like that at this hour? Nothing came to mind.

Still keeping hidden, Lucien halted when they made a brief stop at the old O'Rahilly cottage. Rosaleen entered alone. He dismounted, ready to come to her aid. What's this? he thought. He could not believe his eyes when the petite figure of his Rosaleen reappeared dressed all in black, a full mask covering her face. A sword hung from her left hip, while she armed the pistol in her hand with the skill of one accustomed to its use. He suddenly recalled the night at her uncle's party when he'd found the ball and powder in that potted plant. Obviously, Rosaleen had disarmed James Winthrop herself.

The man with the same height called her "Ned," as she mounted her horse. Lucien's mind filled with horror as the truth crashed against him. He raced for the figure all in black. "Wait!" he called, running out to stop her. His hand brushed the front of her coat. "Rosa—"

The butt end of a pistol against the back of his skull cut him off. Lights ignited within his brain. He felt his legs crumple under him as his body moved closer to the hard ground.

Chapter Thirteen

Hours later Lucien came groggily awake to find Jasper looking down at him, munching the grass near the duke's head. Groaning, the Englishman reached behind to feel a painful lump on the back of his skull, obviously the source of his severe headache. Someone had thrown a horse blanket over him. He tossed the warm, rough material off and tried to get his thoughts in order. He remembered reaching out to the black figure and feeling . . . a firm breast. Good God, he wasn't hallucinating. Black Ned was his Rosaleen!

What was he going to do? He couldn't turn Ross over to the chief magistrate, for she would certainly be hung for treason. But he had to stop her folly. That was the damn secret she'd been keeping from him. Standing too quickly, he was forced to grasp Jasper's reins to steady himself.

He knew he needed help. Her father might not like him, but Lucien was positive Taggart loved his only daughter. Bracing himself against the throbbing in his head, he swung up on Jasper's back and started for Fitzroy Hall.

Just before dawn, he arrived at Dunstan Fitsroy's estate.

Still in their bed gowns and outer robes, Lady Millicent and Taggart came downstairs after a servant informed them the duke requested to see them immediately.

Millicent made the duke sit down while she tended the back of his head. "Your Grace, how ever did you come by such a blow?" she could not help asking.

Unwilling to speak the truth in front of Rosaleen's gentle mother, Lucien stated, "I fell off Jasper."

A bark of laughter burst from Mr. O'Rahilly; then a pointed look from those gray eyes behind his wife's wire spectacles made him suppress his mirth at the young man's plight. "Never mind, we understand. A lad in love is apt to be a bit clumsy."

The duke appeared nervous. "Mr. O'Rahilly, I would first like to apologize for the words I said at our last meeting."

Taggart understood his meaning. Apparently, Lucien had visited the Inn of Three Cranes. "I should not have lost my temper." Taggart now felt sorry for the man, forced to ride about at late hours because he was lovesick over his Rosaleen. "I know why you are here at such an unusual hour," the Irishman began. "You have finally got up the courage to ask for my daughter's hand in marriage, is it not so?" He could see from his wife's smile, Millicent was pleased at his congenial manner.

This was not going to be easy, Lucien conceded. "Ah, yes, I do wish to wed Rosaleen, but . . ." He looked back at Lady Millicent. "Please, Taggart, I have something of a personal nature to speak with you about."

Nodding, Millicent curtsied to the gentlemen, then left.

When the door closed, Lucien went over to stand in front of the older man. "I need your help, sir."

"Now," Taggart encouraged. "Do you wish to discuss Rosaleen's dowry?" he asked. "No need to be reticent with me. Rosaleen owns lands in Virginia, has investments in my shipping business that go with her when she marries, her stocks in—"

As Taggart went on about the wealth Rosaleen would bring to the man she marries, Lucien's fear for her safety caused him to bluster, "Hang the bloody dowry. I'm trying to tell you Rosaleen is Black Ned!"

Taggart's booming laughter echoed across the earl's study, nearly rattling the windows. "The blow to your pate must have jarred your wits," he pointed out when he could speak.

"Damnation, I am attempting to warn you that your daughter is in danger, and all you can do is laugh your bloody head off."

"Now, you just remember who yer talkin' with, Montrose. You charge in here before daybreak with some flimflam about Black Ned. . . . While I can appreciate the absurdity of my little Ross even knowing how to hold a pistol, much less fire one, you'll meet me at dawn if you go spreadin' that sh—that fabrication about."

"By God, you are as pig-headed as your daughter," Lucien shouted, losing what remained of his composure. "Since the beginning of time, fathers have spoiled their daughters, indulging them until

242

they become bad-tempered hoydens. Then it is their unfortunate husbands who must deal with the pampered brats when they marry."

"Don't you preach to me about parenthood, Montrose. I saw enough of how you English aristocrats raise your children — cold, restricted. I made sure my little girl would run free, learn the same as my sons, think and act on her own."

"O'Rahilly, I have no quarrel with her excellent education. It is her rash, headstrong ways I censure. You call it freedom; I say part of her upbringing included neglect. She plunges into danger without thinking through the consequences."

Taggart smirked with pride. "I was a hell-raiser myself at her age."

"And your daughter is just like you. You've given her everything but the self-discipline to restrain her anger."

"After venting yer spleen, I'm left to wonder why you intend to marry her, then."

"Because I love her, despite her fault of a very bad temper, something I intend to help her curb."

The dark-haired man showed his disbelief. "You? Making up that hogwash about my sweet angel being Black Ned proves you are not the man for Rosaleen."

"If you do not believe me, ask your daughter to come down right now and confront her with the truth."

Taggart's gaze locked with Lucien's unyielding blue eyes. "All right, curse you, I'll prove my baby is no highwayman. You're a lunatic to even suggest it." Without hesitation, he stalked across the room in his slippers, pulled open the study door and

243

shouted for a servant. He asked the befuddled footman to request that Miss Rosaleen come downstairs at once.

"I don't know who in blazes yer father was, but tonight you've proved insanity runs in yer family," muttered O'Rahilly. Sitting in a nearby chair, he watched the duke pace up and down the room, his hands thrust behind him. It was clear from his disciplined posture, His Grace was controlling his emotions with effort.

When told who waited downstairs, Rosaleen knew she had to act quickly. Prepared, she tapped lightly on her uncle's study door and entered.

The picture of innocence, her black hair brushed loosely about her shoulders, Rosaleen was attired in a white ruffled nightgown, over which her maidenly robe buttoned from neck to ankles. Pink brocade slippers on her tiny feet, Miss O'Rahilly floated into the room and smiled up at her father. "Papa, you wished to see me?"

He walked over to her. "Yes, little one. Lucien here says he—"

"Oh, Papa," she interjected, looking aghast. She hid behind Taggart. "I was not told you had anyone with you," she fibbed. "I am not attired to greet anyone but family."

Taggart sought to put her at ease. "Well, this is one time we can overlook the proprieties. Lucien thinks he saw you tonight, and what is more, Rosaleen, he believes you are Black Ned."

Too many people depended on her. She could not risk Lucien ruining everything by his unfortunate discovery. She chanced her first look at the duke. "Oh, Your Grace, you cannot be serious?" She giggled, then saw her father grin at the absurdity of it all.

"That's what I told him, Ross."

Lucien's frown was glacial. Rosaleen swallowed but knew she had no choice but to call his bluff. Did he have any idea the harm he might cause by his interference? Changing her tactic, she accused, "You are serious." Her face crumpled. "How could you say you loved me, wish to marry me, then accuse me of being a highwayman—oh, it is too horrid to contemplate." She blubbered into the top of her father's velvet robe. "Upon my honor, Lucien, you have hurt my feelings beyond repair."

"There, there, *Gleoite*," Taggart soothed, clearly trying to comfort his daughter. He shot the blond-haired man an unfriendly look. "Sure and Lucien's probably sorry he wrongly accused you. A man in love does daft things."

Sniffling on cue, Rosaleen moved her face to the right of her father's arm.

Lucien ground the backs of his teeth to keep from marching over to show this termagant exactly what he thought of her performance. Her expression right now reminded the Englishman of the time when she was ten and her father comforted her. He could almost see her mouthing the word "bastard" at him.

However, Lucien reminded himself he was no longer a boy. He would protect her, even if the exasperating woman wanted none of him. He forced his tense features to relax. "I apologize to you both for my . . . obvious mistake." Challenge in his blue eyes, he captured Rosaleen's surprised glance. "I have splendid news for you, my dear. Your father has given us his consent to marry. Not believing in long engagements either, I should like to announce our formal betrothal at a party here next week."

"One week? I don't—" Taggart stopped his protest when he recalled his wife's request. "Yes, I suppose that will be for the best." He turned indulgently to his daughter. "You see, Ross, Lucien still loves you. Now, dry your eyes, there's a good girl. All is well. He just had a nitwit attack. Happens to English aristos all the time. Don't fret about it. He's normal now."

Rosaleen stepped back from her father. Expecting him to refuse to allow her to marry Lucien, she felt trapped when she could not come up with an immediate way out of this new quagmire. Both her parents knew she was fond of Lucien, but she did not believe it was love. Right now her displeasure at his interference was at the forefront of her thoughts—especially when she had told him two days ago they must wait to marry.

Keeping his countenance of affability in place, Lucien temporarily ignored the source of his irritation. "Mr. O'Rahilly, may I please have a few moments alone with Rosaleen?" His smile was self-effacing. "I am sure you can understand my need to make a more private apology to my intended for those idiotic remarks. As you observed earlier, a man in love is apt to be clumsy. It appears my trepidations about asking you for her hand caused me to inadvertently wound your daughter's sensitive feelings."

Taggart could not hide his pleasure at the duke's

humble words. It was clear the man adored Rosaleen. Despite his earlier misgivings, the Irishman admitted he was beginning to like this Englishman. "Of course, Lucien." As he moved past his mute daughter, Taggart whispered, "Your mama was right. She said Lucien was the right man for you; I'm glad to see you so happy."

Happy? Rosaleen thought, as her father shut the door behind him. She was ready to strangle the duke of Montrose with her bare hands. She whirled about to confront him. "Never will I forgive you for enacting this farce for my father's benefit."

Lucien walked the three paces over to stand directly in front of her. With barely controlled fury, he demanded, "Just how long have you been masquerading as Black Ned?"

With a toss of her black curls, she answered, "Since April."

Horror chilled his heated blood when he thought of the danger she'd been in these last three months.

His expression made her defensive. "My work is important to the tenants. The money and jewels we acquire goes toward buying these Irish Catholics a better life."

Hands on either side of his waist, Lucien looked heavenward, pleading for self-control. "If you were not sleeping your mornings away after those evenings of highway philanthropy, you would still be going with your aunt Edna on her morning rounds. Then you would see many here are no better off than they were in the spring, especially on the Lorens estate. I suggest you take it up with the man who does your accounts on the booty taken."

What was he talking about? True, she could not

spend time with the tenants as she used to, but Sean assured her they were being helped in secret. No, she would not give an inch to this arrogant devil. "I hardly think an English duke is in any position to judge the well-being of Irish Catholics. I feel honor-bound to help them, since it appears most Englishmen here are too selfish to help anyone but themselves."

"And I hardly think a naive little hellion who spends her evenings carousing the dark roads of Kinsale for adventure because she is bored with her lot in life is in any position to lecture me about moral obligations."

Her dark eyes narrowed with the upward jut of her chin. "You have no right to make my patriotic work into something frivolous."

"Patriotic—? You are breaking the law. Highway robbery is a criminal offense, punishable by hanging in case English jurisprudence was one course you skipped with your tutors."

"If these Catholics waited for any lard-assed Englishman to help them through legal means, they'd all be dead before anything was accomplished. English law is just for the benefit of Anglicans, or haven't you noticed, Your Grace?"

Hands back at his sides, Lucien fought for the return of his reserve, but it seemed a losing battle. "So enthralled with your theatrics as Black Ned, you clearly have not kept up with what is going on around you. Things are changing, Ross. The Penal Laws have been relaxed because England is preoccupied with the rebellion in the colonies right now. They fear the Irish might take the same course of action. Father Michael can now say Mass openly.

The soldiers look the other way at Catholic activities that would have meant arrest even a year ago."

His last words muted her displeasure. With other things on her mind these last few months, she admitted this came as news to her. Had she proof Sean aided the tenants? She must speak with him tonight.

Lucien felt his muscles uncoil as he studied her expression. It was clear her logical mind was considering his truthful words. "We seem to be making progress."

His comment had the opposite effect on her strained nerves. "That still does not excuse your underhanded methods in maneuvering me into this formal announcement." Though it was hardly the atmosphere she planned, he had forced her hand. "I do not wish to wed anyone."

At first he was amused by her words. "You are just piqued with me for taking charge this time."

"No, Your Grace, you misunderstand." Serious dark eyes held his. "From the very beginning, I never intended marriage. As I began to feel an attraction for you, I hoped you would accept my plan for a mutually beneficial arrangement."

Something sparked in his blue eyes, but his voice was dangerously calm. "Pray, madam, what exactly did you intend offering me?"

She wet her lips. "While I will not deny I have always been drawn to you, I do not believe this is love. Perhaps I shall never love any man, for I value my freedom too much to see it destroyed through marriage, especially an English one. My parents' marriage is an exception; most I have seen, particularly with English aristocrats, seem only cold, dull prisons for women. With no desire for a duke's money or title, I . . . I hoped you would see the logical solution that I should become your . . . your mistress."

Color stained his blond features. "I told you I loved you. I tried to show you my honorable feelings through a proper courtship, and all this time you have only been dallying with me?" Her guilty expression shouted her answer. "And you had the audacity to accuse me of using *you* for a summer's diversion." He turned his back on her and walked over to the closed French doors on the other side of the room. He shoved his clenched fists behind his back, for the first time not sure he could trust his restraint.

Rosaleen felt confused. "I believe most men would jump at the chance to have what they desire, without any legal encumbrance."

Lucien confronted her from across the room. "If all I wanted was a woman's body, I could have saved myself weeks of aggravation trying to court you, thinking I'd lost you forever when you might have been my half sister, then scared out of my wits to learn you are Black Ned. Damn it to hell, Ross, I want a wife, not a whore."

"Lucien!" She was aghast by his phraseology. "I would never take money from you."

"And you think the exchange of coins is the only thing separating the two?" His laugh was harsh. "You can fence and shoot a pistol with the skill of a seasoned campaigner, but you are a child in this area of relationships."

"That is not true. I know what goes on in the bedroom."

"From all your experience in the field, no doubt."

"Well, how would you know my . . . my past?"

He arched a blond brow. "I know from the way you kiss and respond to my touch you are still a virgin. You may know about the physical details, but you clearly know little of matrimony. Did no one ever talk to you about friendship in a marriage, laughter, enjoyment of a family, sharing good and difficult times, helping each other, taking pride in what we could build together?" He shook his head when she remained silent. "For all your worldly adventures, Miss O'Rahilly, you never learned what is truly important between a man and woman. It is strange," he mused aloud. "I was raised by a gentle older father and a beautiful young mother who seldom showed outward affection toward the man she married, yet I still believe happy marriages exist. You, on the other hand, were raised by a man and woman I can see adore each other, but you seem to view marriage as a trap to be avoided at all cost."

She lowered her gaze rather than let him see his words stung her. All her life it seemed she had been busy with taking forceful stands against injustice, rebelling in her own way against being told by society what she could or could not do. Never had she considered a potential lover could be a friend, too. "It appears there is no more to be said, Your Grace. I shall make an excuse to my parents that we changed our minds."

"But I have not changed my mind. I still intend to make you my wife."

Her head darted up. "But I have already stated I will never mar—"

"Miss O'Rahilly, you will marry me, and it will be tonight on my terms."

Rosaleen could read little emotion in his stance. The light from the fireplace cast shadows across the room, making him appear more formidable.

Yes, he thought, he was beginning to learn how to handle her. A good thing he'd already spoken to Father Collins. "Tonight you will slip out of the house as always, only this time, I will be the man in the shadows waiting for you."

"I cannot. My men will be expecting me."

"You will send a message to one of them, informing him that Black Ned will not be able to attend their soiree this evening." He gave her no opportunity to think or protest this time. "Father Michael will marry us this evening with Brian Fogarty as witness. I will arrange everything. You will spend the evening with me."

"But . . . Lucien, if I promise not to go out as Black Ned, surely you can trust me—"

"Not for an instant." He was unmoved by her pleading expression. "You see, virago, I am learning your gypsy ways, and if you are not down near that grove of trees by midnight, I'll climb up that elm and fetch you myself."

"I'll tell my father, and he'll stop you."

"I am prepared to fight a duel for you. If you wish your father's death as a wedding present, I can arrange it."

"You are mad if you expect me to marry you now. This haste is indecent. You're too old to act like an overheated youth escaping to Gretna Green."

"Nevertheless, I think you will be down there, especially since I promise to have the chief magistrate arrest you as Black Ned if you are not. The scandal would ruin your family and your uncle in one swoop." He did not flinch at the stark fear on her face, for he realized he had to be harsh if she was to believe he'd really see this through. She'd left him little choice in her confused loyalty to her family and those Irish hooligans she called patriots. "And I shall expect you to present yourself as a willing bride to Father Collins. I know this Catholic ceremony will bind you to me far more securely than an Anglican one." There would be time enough to have the formal wedding with Vicar Nigel Somerset performing the ceremony later.

Frantically, she sought a logical solution to this new danger. Nothing came. "I never expected you to be so devious, so cruel. How can you force me to marry you when I have told you of my feelings?"

He saw her try to fight the moisture at the corners of her dark eyes, but he pushed a menace into his tone. "Perhaps there is more of my mother in me than I realized. Let us say, I have learned new fighting methods." He moved away from her, congratulating himself on winning. However, he knew he had a long day ahead to finalize his plans before nightfall.

When she realized he left her no choice, her hurt feelings careened in another direction. "By God, Montrose, I vow to make your life a living hell for this underhanded treatment."

His hand on the door, he scowled back at her. "It already is, hoyden."

Lucien had ridden less than a mile away from Fitzroy Hall when a cloaked figure stepped out into the road. Cursing, he brought Jasper up quickly. "Damnation, woman, I might have—" When the woman brushed back the hood of her red cloak, Lucien's expression turned to amazement. "Lady Millicent?"

Millicent could not hide the urgency from her voice. "Please, Your Grace, a word in private?"

He could have closed his eyes and seen Rosaleen speaking. Their voices were identical. "Certainly," Lucien answered, then jumped down from Jasper's back. He took the reins of the lady's horse and followed her into a more secluded area on Fitzroy lands. When they came near a cottage, she turned to face him. He recognized it as the old O'Rahilly place Black Ned had used earlier that night.

"Taggart told me your accusation. I did not share his amusement." Her bespectacled gray eyes bore into him. "You see, Lucien, unlike my husband, I believe you. While I, too, love Rosaleen, I am not as blind as Taggart to her unbridled outrage for the less fortunate or her desire for adventures. The question now is how do we protect her?"

Lucien felt he could trust this tall, practical woman, and he took her into his confidence.

When he finished, she shook her head. "While it is not the wedding night I would have chosen for my little girl, I understand her impetuous nature has brought her to this state. I own she has a lion's courage. If only her father had not been so adamant about her upbringing," she admitted, a rueful expression on her face.

"I give you my word to care for your daughter."

"I would not be here if I believed otherwise. Now, to the details. You will need a proper place for . . .

for this evening. My nieces and nephews used to play in this O'Rahilly cottage behind me. I can promise no one will disturb you, and it is quite hidden among these trees."

He showed his relief, for this was one part of his plan he'd not been able to work out. "Thank you, my lady." Impulsively, he reached out and took the lady's gloved fingers in his hand, then raised them to his lips. "I will not forget this kindness to me, and your trust."

Her gray eyes mirrored his gravity. "Not only my daughter's but my future is in your hands, Lucien Huntington, for if my husband ever learns of my role in this night's activity, my marriage would be at an end, I have no doubt."

Bringing the red velvet hood up over her straight auburn hair, Lady Millicent allowed the younger man to assist her back on her mare.

The duke waited until he was certain Millicent was safely away, then remounted Jasper. Rosaleen, he mused, was not the only O'Rahilly woman with courage.

Chapter Fourteen

Positive Lucien would follow through on his threats, Rosaleen made sure she was down by the grove of trees at the appointed time. To her consternation, the duke had only Jasper with him. Without hat or gloves on this cooler evening, she wondered why he wore only a light cape over his clothes. But she was still too incensed for polite inquiries. "I take it this is part of your new treatment of me. I am to walk behind your horse all the way to Father Collins's cottage?"

Unruffled by her sarcasm, he grinned, as if considering her words. "Now, that is a thought. The walk might improve your prickly attitude." Without ceremony, he bent down and scooped her up to sit in front of him. "No, stay there," he ordered, when she began inching herself away to hold on to the pommel of Jasper's saddle. With ease, he brought her slender form back across his thighs and snaked an arm about her waist in case she thought of protesting. Dressed in her breeches and dark shirt, he frowned at her attire. Every time he saw this blasted outfit, it reminded him of her danger in parading about Kinsale as Black Ned. "Could you not even wear a simple gown for the ceremony?"

Ignoring his testy manner, she craned her neck about to glare back at him. "I almost didn't take a bath today, just to show you what I think of your despicable behavior."

His voice was scathing. "You took a bath just for me? How kind. A bridegroom appreciates these little courtesies."

"Bastard," she snapped.

"How true, at least technically."

Pushing further, as he started them off in a slow trot, she added, "Your father was probably some gin-soaked sailor who made a practice of debauching women, just like his son."

"Oh, I do not think so. Never touch gin; I've always preferred brandy."

Was he laughing at her? In the dark she could not tell. "I bet he was hung for piracy or poaching on property that didn't belong to him. That is something English scum parading as a duke could relate to." She was rewarded by the sound of him clamping down on the back of his teeth, signaling her arrows were not missing all their targets.

"You can continue riding comfortably as you are in silence, or I can toss you facedown across Jasper's back and let you contemplate the road for the rest of the trip. The choice is yours."

The polite menace was back in his clipped speech. Rosaleen bit down on her lower lip to keep from telling him her true feelings.

Lucien increased their speed.

When they arrived at Father Michael's cottage, Rosaleen was further irritated to find everything ready for them. Brian Fogarty was attired in his best clothes; Father Collins had on his Sunday vestments. He was clearly overjoyed to be performing the romantic couple's wedding. Taking charge of everything, Lucien gave her a warning look when he saw her reaction after he took off his cape. Dressed in gold silk coat and breeches, with a waistcoat of silver and green embroidery, he was dressed as a bridegroom.

Lucien could tell Father Michael was shocked at the bride's attire. "She had to slip out of her room by the elm tree, so we thought this more practical."

The priest looked sad for a moment. "I cannot help regretting you did not confide in your mother, Rosaleen. When she came to me last week to discuss you and Lucien, I felt she was most receptive to the match."

"Mother came to you about this?"

"Oh, bless my soul, no. She never hinted you might run off like this. She merely said she assumed you would be marrying the duke in the future."

Astonished by this bit of news, Rosaleen allowed Lucien to lead her closer to the kneeling bench. When she caught his intent, she pulled back, but he already had her hand firmly in his. "Rosaleen," he said, both as a reminder and a warning.

She thought of all the tenants, Sean Kelly and his men who depended on her, then her family and poor Uncle Dunstan who would be ruined by the scandal. She knelt down. Turning her head to the right, she saw Brian. Only he seemed to share her distress over this fiasco. The Irishman looked worried.

The ceremony was shorter than Rosaleen hoped. Hiding her expression from everyone but Lucien, she glowered up at him when he placed a chaste kiss on her forehead. All attempts to keep them from leaving the priest's home met with defeat.

With the impression of a smitten bridegroom anxious to be alone with his wife, Lucien hustled them out the door. Jasper was tied behind the cottage, and Brian acted as coachman atop the hired carriage. Rosaleen was too proud to ask where they were going.

Next to her, Lucien folded his arms across his chest in silence.

Was he taking her to Montrose Hall? she thought with distaste. When the carriage stopped at the former O'Rahilly cottage on Fitzroy lands, Rosaleen could not hide her bewilderment. "Your Grace, you intend for us to spend the evening here?"

"It is the one safe place to insure secrecy. At Montrose Hall, I cannot vouch for the discretion of all my servants, something I have yet to remedy by hiring my own staff," he added, almost in way of an apology. He got out of the carriage and held up his hand to her.

She saw him color when she ignored his offer and jumped down from the conveyance on her own.

"Then, I assume you would not take kindly to being carried over the threshold according to custom?" Her glare answered him. He let her walk past him to the door.

Despite her anger, she was amazed at the appearance of the cottage. The place had been cleaned, a welcoming fire kept out the chill of the night, and the table had been set with dishes she suspected came from Montrose Hall. There was ham, fresh bread, cheese, a bottle of wine. The duke was helping Brian lift two trunks from the back of the carriage. She watched Lucien swing the larger of the two on his shoulder and carry it through the doorway. Something touched her that he would go to all this trouble to make the place comfortable for—then she spotted the new piece of furniture at the left side of the room. It was clearly the largest bed one could fit in such a tiny cottage. She wet her suddenly dry lips.

When Brian went back outside for a moment, she walked over to Lucien. She tried to keep the nervousness out of her voice. "Your Grace, you have your way. According to my religion, I am your wife. Can you not leave it at that?"

"You mean a marriage in name only?"

She brightened when he caught on so quickly. "Yes. Under the circumstances, as an English gentleman, you can hardly expect me to—"

"Just as you had intentions concerning me, I also made plans upon first meeting you, and I can assure you, madam, a marriage of convenience never entered my diagram."

Stifling her disappointment, she gave him a wintry look. "I might have known, for only a true son

260

of Calvert Huntington would be honorable enough not to force a lady to his bed."

He winced at her words but said nothing.

Instantly, she regretted her speech, for until now she'd always found him to be a man of integrity. "Lucien," she pleaded, "why do you insist on going through with this? I concede, you have defeated me. I told you I never meant to hurt you. You made it clear you do not want me as your mistress, but you must understand I do not wish to be a wife to you or anyone."

"I've done with words, Ross. You make it abundantly clear you do not feel the same as I do. So be it. But I intend to make certain you never ride out as Black Ned again. Now, I could do that by just keeping you here each evening, but I know you, Ross. You would not stop until you'd found some way to get your own way. I'll admit it; I am being selfish in making you my true wife. And it won't be force, gypsy eyes, for I know your passionate nature."

His last words unnerved her, especially when she remembered how her body had betrayed her before from this man's touch. He had a disquieting knowledge of both her body and her mind. It would be almost impossible to stay unmoved by his lovemaking. And he would show her how much she desired him, she was positive. She saw the resolve in his blue eyes. "I shall never forgive you for what you are doing tonight."

"We shall see," he stated. "Now, I must tend to the horses before our night of wedded bliss," he tossed over his shoulder.

Fuming, Rosaleen plunked down on one of the wooden chairs in front of the table of food. Having eaten nothing all day, she still felt no appetite. Brian came back in and began unpacking the two trunks. Lucien's robe, slippers, a clean set of clothes for the morning. When the servant went to the large trunk, she gasped when he took a sheer lilac nightgown from the leather case. It was followed by a matching silk robe, with satin slippers. He hung a pretty yellow morning gown in the wooden wardrobe next to Lucien's garments. When Brian began pulling white stockings and various lacy undergarments from the luggage, she could not stop from going over to him. "Please. Brian, I shall finish unpacking that trunk." She could not keep the embarrassment from her face.

Nodding, Brian stepped out of the way. "Very good, Your Grace."

It was the first time she had been addressed this way. She was now the duchess of Montrose, but the title only reminded her of the difficult situation. However, she could not hold back a murmur of pleasure when she took out the ivory brush and comb set. And there was a mirror and pins. "Your master certainly sees to details."

Brian busied himself unpacking the rest of the food. He took out two crystal glasses wrapped in a white napkin. The table silver with the Montrose crest was set out. "His Grace usually shows splendid judgment."

Pleased, Rosaleen realized Brian was on her side

in feeling this marriage was a mistake. She sat back down on the chair and watched him finish his task of setting out their wedding supper. "I can see that you are concerned, Brian."

"Yes, Miss Rosaleen, 'tis fearful worried I am."

Her features softened at her old friend. With more assurance than she felt, she tried to allay this Irishman's distress over her welfare. "Part of this unusual predicament, I admit, is of my own making, for I have yet to learn when to hold my tongue. You are very dear to be so upset on my behalf, but I truly believe His Grace is not a cruel man."

The white-haired man set down the last piece of silverware, then turned to look down at the woman sitting on the other side of the table. "But, Miss Rosaleen, I know ya'll come to no real harm from the duke. 'Tis your husband I am worried about."

Well, she thought, a little miffed. "Afraid I'll overpower him with my superior muscle, are you? I have neither sword nor pistol, so have no fear I'll take advantage of his delicate constitution in the middle of the night."

Patiently, Brian waited for the young woman to finish. "That's right, blow the storm clear. Then we can talk." Ignoring her, he went back over to close the empty trunks and place them neatly next to the wardrobe.

Rosaleen remained silent as she waited for Fogarty to come back to the table.

He smiled that leprechaun way when he read the compliance in her expression. "Now, keep you gob closed until I have me say." Without asking, he

263

pulled out the chair across from her and sat down. "If ya're not too puffed up with yer own feelings of being wronged, ya might take me advice to watch that O'Rahilly temper. The duke has the patience of a saint, but even he has limits."

"I am listening," she said, trying to encourage the man to continue, for she welcomed anything that could help her out of this current dilemma.

"What I was talkin' about is this here and plain: I don't want ta see Lucien hurt, for that gentle young man has never given his heart so openly to any woman." At her skeptical look, Brian grinned. "Oh, he's had his share of women before, but none of them ever captured his heart. And those ladies instigated the liaisons on their own without the duke havin' ta chase them."

"Brian, I do care for Lucien, but I abhor his manner in forcing me into this marriage."

"Did ya give him any choice, then?" The older man did not wait for her reply. "Paradin' about as Black Ned, then blithely tellin' him, rather than be his wife, ya'd prefer becomin' his mistress. What did ya expect him ta do?"

She colored at his words. "I had no idea His Grace was on such intimate terms with his valet."

"Don't get on yer high horse with me, Ross. I care for Lucien as if he were my own son."

Her eyes widened. "Any chance you really are his fath—?"

"Not a one. Can ya see Garnet, that she-cat, co-zyin' up ta the likes of me? I couldn't even tell Lucien how bad things were on Montrose estate when

264

I visited, else the duchess said she'd give me the sack. Lucien needed me; I couldn't risk it. I don't believe that woman ever loved anyone in her life, save the squire, John Nolan."

"Does Lucien know of the late squire?"

"This morning when he was so troubled, he told me all this, and I mentioned Nolan. Of course, how to prove it? The duche—I mean the dowager duchess now," he added with obvious glee, "won't be back until next week. Only she can give the lad the truth. Hard to say, for faithfulness ta one man was never her strong point."

Shocked by Brian's disclosure, Rosaleen admitted, "I know so little about His Grace. What I hear seems at cross-purposes." She thought of James Winthrop. "What of his years at Cambridge when he had those six toadies waiting on him. Just what was the Montrose Club?"

Uncorking the bottle of brandy on the table, Brian poured himself a generous amount into an earthenware cup he'd obviously packed at the bottom of the wicker basket. "Though Lucien will have me head for tellin' ya, here's the truth of it. He chose those six younger boys from the poorest families and paid them three times the going rate ta meet with him each week. He tutored them in science and mathematics and swore them to secrecy. It is his quiet way not ta shame a man in need of assistance. The boys were only too happy ta have everyone believe the Montrose Club was a den of dark arts and forbidden pleasures. Think of the razin' they'd of taken if it got out His Grace made

265

them spend more than six hours a week working on their lessons? All the lads passed their examinations and went on ta make a fine livin'. Why, Winthrop would have dropped out of school that summer his father died if Lucien hadn't arranged an anonymous scholarship for him."

All this time Rosaleen had been taking in this new information about her husband. As the Irishman went on about Lucien's childhood—being packed off to school, forbidden by his mother ever to visit Ireland—she felt something melt inside her heart. Then there was that difficult business about his parentage. She felt ashamed by her taunting remarks earlier. Until now she did not realize how different his lonely childhood had been from her happy one.

The cottage door opened, and Lucien entered.

Rosaleen took a closer look at his features and saw how drawn he appeared. There was a sadness in his eyes, but when he caught her looking at him, that mask of detachment returned to his face.

When Brian finished his drink and rose to leave, she leaned over and murmured, "Thank you for sharing this with me."

The Irishman searched her eyes; then a smile softened his craggy features. "Ya don't hate His Grace, then?"

She shook her head. "In truth, Brian," she whispered for his ears alone, "I never did. It will not be easy, but I can only promise to try and work things out with him."

" 'Tis a start, then." Appearing happier than he

had all day, Brian got up, bowed to His Grace, then left for Montrose Hall.

Feeling the strain of the day's trying events, Lucien did not speak but knelt on one knee to stoke the fire once more. Now that the time had arrived, he realized he felt nervous. Did she despise him? It was clear she intended to fight him at every step. This was not the way he'd wanted it. Was he too romantic to wish their first time would be in the master bedroom at Montrose Hall, after a banquet with their friends and family? He continued brooding into the flames. Yet, the thought of her safety overcame his regret in manipulating her into this marriage. Her role of Black Ned was no game; she could have been killed. His blood still ran cold when he thought of that night she'd waylaid the Lorenses' coach. He might have seriously wounded her in that duel. It was more than clear no one had taken charge of her. If she hated him for it, so be it. At least she would be alive.

Rosaleen began slicing some of the fresh bread. She tried to think of a way to coax the duke away from the fire. Of course, her earlier behavior, she knew, gave him little reason to wish her company. "Will you have some supper, Your Grace?"

He stood up and began walking toward the table. When he saw the faint smile that made the dimple at the right corner of her mouth more visible, Lucien decided not to inspect his good fortune too closely. He'd eaten little all day. Taking a deep breath, he said, "Thank you, Ross, I should like some cheese and ham." As he sank down on the chair across from her, he could not hide his surprise at the change in Rosaleen's demeanor. She set about placing things on his plate. He was puzzled, yet he felt things were still so fragile between them, he did not wish to break the truce with serious conversation. "Would you like some claret?"

"A small glass would be lovely." She watched as he reached for the bottle on the table and uncorked the vintage wine. He poured two glasses. Tempted to toast their future, he stifled his romantic side, unsure of how Rosaleen would take it. They still had so much to learn about each other, he reminded himself.

As they finished eating, Rosaleen frowned when she looked down at her breeches, for the first time wishing she'd worn one of her lovely gowns tonight. From lowered lashes, she studied Lucien. He'd removed his outer coat and placed it over the back of his wooden chair. The ruffles at his neck and wrists only accentuated his graceful strength. The golden threads of his waistcoat caught the light from the candles and fireplace. His tawny hair was tied neatly at the back of his neck with a black silk ribbon. She closed her eyes and inhaled the faint scent of sandalwood. A woman could do worse than this handsome man for a husband, she told herself, then blushed at her blatant perusal.

"What are you thinking, sweet elf?"

At the sound of his sensuous voice, her eyes flashed open. The heat on her cheeks made her look away.

He enjoyed this peaceful time between them.

"You looked like an adorable angel at her prayers, or are you plotting more mischief?"

This time she smiled at his teasing. "Alas, sir, I feel you may regret having me for a wife. I have tried to warn you of my failings, and—"

"Enough," he cut off with a chuckle. "You will never get me to see you in that dark light you insist on shoving yourself into." Wiping his lips on the large napkin on his lap, he pushed himself away from the table. He raised his glass to her. "To my beautiful wife. Will you at least drink to a small truce?"

She caught her breath at the warmth in his blue eyes. Raising her own goblet, she saluted him. "To my . . . patient husband and . . . a truce." His boyish smile made her heart lurch. She did not look away when he touched his glass to hers; then they both took a sip of their wine.

When they finished, she spoke first. "I will clear these things away. Why don't you pull your chair near the fire and relax."

"Thank you."

While she busied herself with cleaning the plates and putting the leftovers back in the wicker hamper the cook and Brian had prepared, Lucien stretched out his long legs before the fire. The diamonds on the square buckles of his dress pumps sent sparks of light across the room. He felt more content than he had in a long time. How he wished tomorrow would never appear. He had to return her to Fitzroy Hall before dawn, so she could slip in her room unnoticed. Their wedding before the vicar and all of

Kinsale would not come soon enough for him. He knew he was playing a very dangerous game right now. He only hoped he could follow through with his honorable intentions tonight.

When Lucien felt two soft cool hands begin massaging the tight knots at the back of his neck and shoulders, a husky moan of pleasure escaped his lips. "You will never know how sinfully wonderful that feels."

"You are as tense as a coiled spring," she commented, clearly amazed.

He reached around his head to grasp both her hands. Gently, he brought her about to stand beside him. "You assumed you would be the only nervous one tonight, hmm?"

"Well, until a little while ago, I thought you were nothing but an overbearing Englishman, but I see I was mistaken. Wrong about so many things," she added, pleading with her eyes for his forgiveness and understanding.

He'd never seen her this way. Her cool hands, the slight tremor in her voice, told him she was a little afraid about tonight, yet she was giving the full impression of willingness to keep the vows she made before Father Collins. Tenderly, he coaxed her down across his lap and was rewarded when she gave a contented sigh before resting her dark head against his shoulder. He breathed in the welcoming scent of lilacs that always clung to her clean skin. For a few minutes he said nothing, just pleased to be holding her close, having her trust him. He felt her even breathing, which signaled she was beginning to relax. He lowered his head to place a soft kiss near her temple. "Are you tired, sweetheart?"

"Mmm . . . no . . . I mean yes, if you want me to be," she finished, lifting her head to look into his eyes.

This docile Rosaleen was new to him. Had he cowed her with his earlier anger? "Are you afraid of me, Ross?"

She looked away. "I am not afraid you will hurt me physically, if that is what you are asking. I mean, I know the first time is often a bit painful for a maid, but I've no doubt you will be a gentleman."

"You do have an interesting way of putting things. Yet?" he encouraged. He ran his hand along the smooth material at the back of her wide-sleeved shirt.

"I . . . I am afraid what I feel for you may not be enough to sustain a lasting relationship between us. Besides, you have not considered I may not be to your tastes once you have the object you believe you desire."

"That's the old cynical Ross again. Tell me, are all the Irish so morbid about love?" Not offended by her words, he smiled down at her bent head. "You know, wife, it appears I am the romantic of this family, and you the confirmed cynic. It is a puzzlement to me that you can casually dismiss what you have never tried. I am attempting to show you I do not want a servant, or a rabbit, for a mate." His warm hand under her chin forced her to look up at him. "I told you before I would have you

271

as you are. Admittedly, I would appreciate a less volatile temper. However, kindly allow me the privilege to make my own observations where you are concerned, hmm?"

His words did please her. "All right, Lucien. I will try, though old habits are hard to break."

He ran his fingers along the smooth skin of her jaw. "In my frustration over your safety, I know I behaved badly at Fitzroy Hall this morning. In truth, Rosaleen, I am prepared to sleep on the sofa tonight while you have the bed. However, make no mistake, duchess, I intend to see you in this cottage every night until we are formally wed by my uncle, for your days as Black Ned are over." He began stroking her thick dark hair. "There will be time enough in the future for the equally delightful physical part of marriage."

"But. . . ." She bit her lip, not sure how to phrase it.

"Come," he said, easing her off his lap. "I will turn my back, and you can get on your night things, then slip into bed." Not waiting for a reply, he walked over to the bed and turned back the covers for her. Then he reached for a coverlet on the bottom of the bed and proceeded to the overstuffed couch on the other side of the room.

She stood near the chair where he'd left her, trying to find a delicate way to inch him toward what she desired. "But, Lucien," she finally blurted. "I want you to make love to me tonight."

Chapter Fifteen

Rosaleen clamped a hand over her mouth. Would she ever learn a less direct approach? Lady Prudence would never say such a bold thing. Turning away, she cursed herself for acting like an idiotic rube.

Lucien came up so quietly, she gave a start when his hands turned her around to face him.

When he saw the tears in her eyes, he was lost. "Ross, are you sure you want this? You'll not call foul in the morning, or toss it in my face when next you become vexed with me?"

"No, Lucien. I really want this. If you do not make me your true wife tonight, I know I shall die. Only, I am so sorry I'm dressed so shabbily." She glanced down at her boots. "I resemble a stable hand, not a bride."

"You look beautiful to me." He bent his head and placed a tender kiss on her moist lips. When he tasted the salty moisture from her eyes, he pressed his mouth firmer on hers to blot out all her doubts about how much he desired her. His hands roamed freely over her back, then lower to fondle her luscious hips encased in the tight breeches.

She could not get enough of him as he continued the arousing onslaught with his mouth and hands. When she felt the hard muscles of his leg nudge between the softness of her thighs, she nearly swooned at the erotic sensations he was making her feel. As he moved his hard body across hers, Rosaleen was forced to pull her mouth away for fear she would actually faint. The room seemed to spin, causing her to grip his arms. When his warm hands went to the buttons of her black shirt, she lifted her arms to allow him to slip the soft material over her head.

"Shame," he admonished, upon seeing the binding about her chest. "It is a sacrilege to tie those gorgeous breasts so tightly." He undid the cloth strips as if he were unwrapping a long-awaited present.

A deep sigh of relief escaped her lips when she was free to take a deep breath in comfort. No wonder she'd felt near to swooning just now. "It did help in my disguise. Yet, it's no more uncomfortable than the laces we are expected to use to cinch our waists and push up the bosom."

"But we are through with disguises, are we not?" He kissed the top of her shoulder, encouraged to feel a shiver course though her healthy body. "I want you, sweet Rosaleen. You have haunted my dreams since I first met you." Caressing one of her firm, full breasts in his hand, he lowered his lips to the pink nipple. When he heard the moan deep within her throat, he stepped back to place an arm about her waist, then lifted her high against his chest. Walking over to the bed, he placed her on the edge, then knelt to remove her boots and stockings. As he unbuttoned her black breeches, he could not help smiling. "This new fashion you've started makes it easier to get a lady out of her garments than dealing with corsets, hoops, and petticoats."

"Please, Lucien, do not tease me about my clothes. Just think how I feel to know your memories of our first time together will not be of a bride in her lovely wedding gown. Your memories will be of me in these ugly boys' clothes."

He looked up into her sad face. "Oh, no, Rosaleen, I assure you, I will only have the most erotic memories of my lovely, dark-haired wife." When he had her undressed, he made an unhurried study of her full, ripe breasts, narrow waist, and black triangle between her pale thighs. "Beautiful," he whispered. Standing up, he removed his neckcloth, waistcoat, and shoes, then he came back to her. Bending over her lithe form, he started kissing every inch of her, from the smooth skin of her face, down her slender neck, to that sensitive area along her collarbone. When he began using his tongue on her breasts, he was amused to hear her gasp, then clamp her lips together, almost as if she thought it more appropriate to appear unmoved. "Tell me what you feel, darling. Open yourself to me, not just your delectable little body. I want all of you, enchantress. Say the words for me. I want to hear them."

"Oh, Lucien, I am on fire. Yes. Please. Do that with your mouth again." When he did, she arched her hips automatically. She could not hold still at his skillful seduction. Something was building inside her, and she could not help wanting more of him. However, when she felt his kisses move lower, she wriggled back toward the headboard away from him. "Surely, it is not proper to—"

He lifted his head, his blue eyes glazed with desire and amusement. "Yes, dear wife, it is quite proper." It was clear she did not know everything about making love. "Come, will you trust me to have a care for you? I only seek to give you the sweetest of pleasures."

"But I want to give, too, Lucien. Your enjoyment is equally important to me. I . . . am quite aware you must remove more of your garments in order to . . . complete . . ." Heat scorched her face, and she could not finish the sentence.

His love showed in his smile. "Rest assured, Rosaleen, we shall both have pleasure tonight." He got up and divested himself of his remaining clothes.

She watched him from the bed, aware that even now he remained orderly. He placed his garments neatly over the back of a chair. His golden hair touched his shoulders, matching the faint wisps of blond across his chest. His legs were well-muscled, especially his thighs. When she peeked at the area between his legs, she could not ignore the fully aroused maleness of him. "I . . . I never expected you to be so—there is a great deal of you."

Lucien successfully stifled his laughter. He returned to their bed. So like his direct Rosaleen. Even in this new experience, she spoke her thoughts. "I am very much like any other man,

276

little one." He reached for her once more. "Let me see, where was I?" he teased, gently placing her on her back once more. He pressed lingering kisses along each breast. "No, I believe I was lower." With maddening slowness, he kissed his way down her stomach, then sauntered to the dark nest of curls between her legs. Purposely, he saved the core of her womanhood for last, only after he felt the honeyed dampness with his fingers. "So welcoming, my love. It's almost as if you were made for me, for I adore every delicious inch of you, inside and out."

"Lucien. Please. I don't think you should do that." Every part of her felt ablaze with this wanting hunger. Her dark hair billowed about her as she moved her head from side to side in an effort to stay in control.

"Do you want me to stop?" He looked up at her, waiting.

"Oh, no, please," she whimpered. "Touch me there again." Boldly, she ran her fingers though his thick golden hair, and when his head came up to her, she used the soft pads of her fingertips to caress the chiseled lines of his straight nose and lean jaw. "Please, oh, please make me yours tonight, Lucien. I want to yield everything to you."

Her words pushed him over his own precipice, and he increased the speed and pressure of his tongue on the soft petals of her skin. Back and forth, he was incited by her passionate arousal.

"Yes, oh, yes, darling!" she cried out as the tight coil within her pulsed and carried her in a burst of throbbing ecstasy. Unlike that first time when he'd only used his fingers, Rosaleen found this release more powerful. When Lucien moved up to take her back into his embrace, she began kissing his neck. She ran her pink lips down across the hard, golden mat of his chest. Her riotous black curls teased his body, making her aware his skin was as hot as her own.

Never had he expected such a fiery response this first time between them. She learned so quickly. He closed his eyes in an attempt to hold back. "Easy, love, this is not a race." A sound of frustration escaped his lips when he felt her small hand on his hard shaft. "Temptress, I am trying to be a gentleman on your first journey," he grated, only half in jest. "Faith, if you continue touching me there with those inquisitive hands, I shall find it almost impossible to be gentle."

Rosaleen's head nestled in the area of his flat stomach. "But, Your Grace, I wish to learn your body, too. Do you like this?" she asked, then slid her hand up and down his pulsing manhood.

"So much that you are going to kill me if you do not stop."

Distracted by two beads of moisture that nestled on the tip of his jutting manhood, she held him still for a moment. Bending her head, his wife ruffled her tongue over the white droplets. She leaned back to concentrate on this new discovery. "It tastes faintly salty. Shall I kiss you there again?"

"God, no" came out in a strangled reply. He saw her brief disappointment. Reaching down, he easily lifted her up beside him. "Another time I shall adore your sweet offer, but tonight I. . . ." He felt his own face color as she stared up at him with those fathomless eyes. "I will spend too soon, my love, if you continue your very pleasurable exploration, for I am near to bursting from holding back."

She began to understand. A faint smile fluttered across her lips. "Forgive me for interrupting you. Pray continue."

He saw the amusement in her passion-filled eyes. "You are a rascal, gypsy eyes." He kissed her lips again, long and hard, his tongue stealing out to capture hers. He placed her on her back and positioned himself between her parted thighs. The thought that he might hurt her muted his own pleasure, and he sought once more with his mouth and hands to raise her desire to a fever pitch. When he pressed slowly into her, he felt the impediment and saw her eyes open in surprise as she braced herself but did not cry out. Her gesture caused him to pull back.

"No, please, Lucien, I want this." The tender look in his blue eyes melted her initial apprehension, and she strained her upper body forward to kiss him full on the mouth. When he began moving against her once more, she felt a fullness between her thighs. He was now holding her firmly against him; then he made a quick, deep thrust inside her. His mouth on hers muffled her outcry of pleasure and pain.

Lucien held himself still within her tight sheath. "Done, thank God," he breathed against her hair, both for his sake and hers.

When she opened her eyes, the distress she read on Lucien's features took her breath away. "I am fine, Lucien." She brushed a damp strand of thick blond hair away from his face. Never had she imagined a man could be so tender. Her heart lurched as the depth of her feelings for this man forced their way into her mind. But she became too lost in the wicked images Lucien was causing her to experience for any coherent declaration right now. Slowly, she moved against him. She heard his groan of unfulfilled desire. In a purely feminine instinct, Rosaleen wrapped her legs about his waist, urging him to move back and forth within her. He was murmuring words of love and desire, kissing her, holding her in an embrace that both cherished and conquered her. She closed her eyes. "Yes, Lucien. I want you so much," she cried, admitting her aching need.

Lucien reached for the pocket handkerchief he'd placed under the pillow earlier in the day. Both their bodies were covered with perspiration from arousal and their pleasurable exertions. Gritting his teeth, he forced himself to run through a memorized list of plant extracts and their use. God, he hoped he could follow through now that the time was on him, but he knew he wanted to hold on until Rosaleen—he heard her cry out his name as she climaxed once more. His body tensed with his forced self-mastery. Only seconds from his own release, he pulled abruptly out of her and thrust his pulsing manhood into the handkerchief he held in his left hand. An animal outcry of anguish pushed from his lips at the frustration and loss he felt in not completing their lovemaking within her. It was almost physical pain that assailed him. Forced to close his eyes, he leaned back on his heels, trying to steady his erratic breathing.

It took Rosaleen a few moments to realize what had occurred. She opened her eyes. Though it was her first time with a man, she knew full well this was not the way it was supposed to be between husband and wife. Her initial shock gave way to another emotion as she continued watching him. Without a word, he rose from the bed, tossed the cloth into the fire, then went over and put on his velvet robe. To her sensitive feelings, he seemed quite indifferent — his blasted English reserve in place. No word of explanation beforehand, he dared act as if nothing unusual had happened. Her hands shook when she grabbed for the flowered robe at the bottom of the bed. He was rejecting her, she told herself, as she clumsily fastened the cloth-covered buttons. Was it because she was not an English aristocrat? They were husband and wife before her Catholic faith. Yet, he probably thought she was not good enough to make her his true wife. He could spout words all he wanted, but when the time of truth came — yes, she understood all right. This was just a new form of putting her in her Irish place.

Her hurt gave way to rage. Bounding off the bed, Rosaleen charged over to him. "Oh, how dare you insult me in this base manner!" she screamed.

"What are you talking about?" His own emotions felt near to breaking, and he was in no mood to deal with one of her outbursts.

"You know perfectly well what I am speaking of? Why did you wish to wed me? Is it my money, or just to humiliate me for having the brains to refuse marriage of my own free will?"

He swiped an unsteady hand through his tousled blond hair. Logic. He had to stay calm, he told himself. Along with her virginity, he'd assumed she would be none the wiser for his quick maneuver. And he'd made sure she had her release first. It never occurred to him to discuss his intention with her beforehand, for he knew she was still a maid. "Rosaleen, I only wanted to spare your sensibilities at such a time. It appears I misjudged your knowledge of these intimate matters."

"You certainly did, Montrose. And you said you loved me," she scoffed. "Yes, those honeyed words trip off your tongue, more fool I for believing you. My father made sure I knew a loving husband does not treat his wife like some . . . some pox-ridden whore he vaults from to avoid contamination."

"Young lady, you will cease such vile language at once." He felt a vein in his right temple twitch. "Bloody hell, I might have guessed Taggart O'Rahilly would be sure you knew all about such things. Now, if you will just allow me to explain, I can—"

"Bastard," she screeched, forcing herself to see the truth. He did not love her, for he could not even stand to stay within her at such a personal moment. "Do you think I'll listen to any more of your meaningless flattery?" Rosaleen knew she had to get out of this cottage before she burst into tears and mortified herself further. Oblivious to her attire, she started for the door.

Lucien bounded ahead to bar her exit. This time his hands were rough when they encircled her shoulders. "Damn it, Ross, you can't just fire your weapons, then retreat when you bloody well please. You're going to listen to me, and—"

"Let me go! I hate you. I wish to hell you'd never . . . never started making love to me, to end it in that insulting, vile—"

"Believe me, madam, I vow I'll not touch you in that way again until Nigel Somerset performs that damnable Anglican ceremony. Now, be quiet and let me explain."

"I don't want to hear more of your lies and coaxing words. Get out of my way, you English son of a bitch."

"By God, you go too far." Lucien stood his ground.

Incensed, Rosaleen tore from his grasp, raised her doubled right fist and punched him square on the jaw. She saw his head thud back against the wooden door with the force of the impact.

As always happened with this man, instantly she felt appalled at her lack of control. With no one else did she ever react so violently. Yet, he'd insulted and wounded her in the most intimate way a man could hurt the woman he says he loves. She saw the crimson mark on the skin above his left jawbone. However, when her eyes glanced higher, she read the livid rage in the depths of his icy blue eyes.

"By hell, madam, I warned you about coming at me again with your fists." White-hot anger sent sparks before his eyes, but he gave in to the feeling this time. Clamping an arm about her waist, he hoisted her easily against his right hip. Her struggles and kicking of bare toes against his robe-covered legs were no match for his resolve. Two strides brought him next to the table, where he pushed the wooden chair out with his bare foot. Sitting down, he wasted little time tossing the outraged woman across his knees.

"Lucien, you let me up at once. Brute. Don't you dare lay a hand on me." She kicked her legs in an effort to get free, but when she reached back to swipe his chest with her right fist, he grabbed it and pushed it firmly against her back. "What of your code?" she yelled.

"Devil take the ruddy code. It is time you learned I am your husband, not your punching bag." He raised his right hand and brought it down hard against the center of her silk-covered bottom. "You canceled the code—" he swatted her again—"when you punched me in the jaw for the third time."

She could not believe his strength. Wiggling and kicking her legs—she was still unable to get free from his ironclad hold on her waist. "I'm warning you, English bully. My father will kill you for this. Lucifer, let me up at once."

With slow deliberation, Lucien reached for the hem of her robe and pushed it up past her waist. "The mention of Taggart O'Rahilly right now, hoyden, only makes be more determined to do this thoroughly."

"No, wait. You can't—ow!" she yelped when his punishing hand landed on her bare right cheek. The silk material offered little protection before, but he now seemed to be calculating the intensity and rhythm of his swats. Her angry shouts turned to pleading by the sixth well-placed slap on her vulnerable bottom. "Please stop, Lucien, I—ouch!" His hand came down again on her stinging flesh. "I'm sorry I punched you. I won't do it again."

"You're bloody well right, you won't do it again." He punctuated his words with a volley of smarting slaps on her reddening backside. Then, as he reached the number he had planned beforehand, he stopped but kept her facedown across his lap while he spoke to her. "I am counting on the memory of that smarting sensation in your behind to send a prudent message to your brain when next you are tempted to pummel me with your fists."

Calmly, he lifted her up to stand to his right. Ignoring her tear-stained face, he rose from the chair and went over to place another log on the dying embers.

Unable to put it off any longer, Rosaleen reached around to massage the painful throbbing across her silk-covered backside. Her skin felt puffy and on fire. "I knew you would beat me one day, Englishman," she accused.

From his hunched position near the fireplace, he gave her an arched look. "That was not a beating and you know it. I gave you a well-deserved, controlled spanking which consisted of ten swats on your plump little bottom."

His words sparked her resentment. "I have never been treated this way."

He came to his full height and faced her. "That is more than evident, for if your father had taken you in hand when you were a child, you might not possess such an ugly temper. There is nothing endearing about a grown woman throwing a tantrum or her fists."

Her chin jutted upward. "Since the age of ten, I've never punched anyone but you in my life."

"Forgive me if I fail to appreciate the honor. I assure you, virago, I shall feel this throbbing in my jaw longer than you'll find it uncomfortable to sit."

Though she tried not to, the dark-haired girl found her face coloring at his words. In truth, the stinging sensation was receding in her southern region, but she refused to agree with him. After he walked over to stand in front of her, she glanced up to see the purplish swelling on the left side of his face. It did appear a painful bruise. Feeling defensive, she added, "Well . . . I felt hurt that you were rejecting me."

He sighed with a combination of understanding and exasperation. "Would you care to listen to my explanation now?"

She nodded. "Please."

His arm about her shoulders, he led her over to the bed. "If you, ah, recline on your side, I believe you will be more comfortable."

"It really does not hurt much now," she blurted, despite her earlier resolve.

"Good."

She looked up at him but read no amusement in his expression. Indeed, he went over and grabbed the chair he'd used earlier. He brought it back and sat down next to the bed. It was almost as if he were attempting to keep her embarrassment to a minimum.

Shrugging her shoulders, his wife went over to

the bed and relaxed on her side, so she could study him while he talked.

"Would you like a cup of tea or more food?" he offered in a courteous manner.

"No, thank you."

He rested his chin on the hand he braced on his knee. "I never counted on my virgin wife knowing all the details about making love. Leaving you at such a time was one of the most difficult things I ever had to do in my life," he admitted.

When she said nothing, he went on. "While we are married according to the Catholic religion, by English law you are still not my wife until we are wed in an Anglican ceremony. Therefore, I must protect your honor and reputation."

"But we know we are man and wife; that is all that matters."

"My darling," he said patiently, "what if you became pregnant with our child before Uncle Nigel weds us?"

Comprehension washed over her. "I never thought of that. According to English law, it would mean our child was a bastard and I was a—"

"Something I will not allow my wife or our child to face. Yet, there is a more serious matter to resolve before we decide on children, Rosaleen Huntington."

"Yes, Lucien?"

"The dark side of your fierce temper troubles me greatly. I could not even reach you earlier. You made no effort to hold back, to listen to me, to pause for one moment in your physical response. Children misbehave sometimes. Even if you did not mean to and deeply regretted it later, what if you grabbed one of our children with more force than necessary?"

Blood drained from Rosaleen's face. She sat up quickly, her body feeling chilled by his question. "Dear Lord, Lucien, I would never. . . ." Her words drifted off. Terror consumed her, for she could not say with certainty she would never lose control of her anger again. The thought devastated her more than if she'd been stabbed with a knife.

He was affected by her reaction. "Darling, it is in your favor that I am the only one you have ever clouted, but you do understand my concern?"

"Yes. It is well-founded. Lucien, what if I ever hurt a child? Until now it never occurred to me my cursed temper could endanger someone in my care. I want to change, but I do not know if I have enough character to do it." Disturbing visions buffeted her, and she could not continue for a moment. Then she looked across at him. "Your Grace, you should not have let the spur of the moment entice you into marrying me. You have made a poor bargain."

Never had he seen her so dejected. "I will be with you to help," he said, affection showing from his eyes. "That you desire to change makes all the difference in the world. We can face this together, darling."

She did not share his confidence.

"Spur of the moment?" he echoed when she remained mute, for he knew this continued self-consternation was not good for her either. "I always intended to marry you from the moment I saw you at the Lorenses' party. However, it appeared the source of my honorable intentions wanted nothing to do with me or my marriage proposal. When I found out you were Black Ned, I used that information to force you to wed me. Though it may sound arrogant, I thought I could show you marriage to me would not be the abhorrent trap you envisioned. You see," he added, a scoundrel's smile on his face, "I am not a total gentleman beyond redemption."

"And you are not a milksop either, as I first supposed."

He laughed openly at her audacious remark. "And here I thought to charm you by acting the adoring swain at our first dance. Or was it the spanking that convinced you I am not a man to be ignored?"

A gurgle of laughter escaped her parted lips, despite her efforts to quell it. "It is impossible to be a haughty matron, Lucifer, while you're draped naked across your husband's knees contemplating the knotholes in the floor."

"Brat." Yet, he delighted in the return of her trust enough to be impudent with him. The tops of her full, creamy breasts peaked out from the area where the buttons of her robe had come undone. He felt his body tighten with desire. He smiled at his reaction. Somehow, he had a feeling Rosaleen would always affect him this way.

Her thoughts became more serious as she watched him. "Lucien, it was your kindness in tending my foot the day at your pond that first touched me. You showed a care for my feelings as well as my injured body. Few men, Irish or English, would have acted so nobly." He appeared embarrassed by her praise, so she let the matter rest.

Then Rosaleen glanced behind him to see the beginning light through the small window. Dawn. It was time for them to leave. She felt sad at the thought of departing their enchanted place. This Irish cottage would always be special to her now.

Sensing her mood, Lucien caressed her with his gaze, letting her see all the love he felt. "I am glad you are my wife, sweet elf. Tomorrow we will continue our . . . discussion," he added, humor and longing in his manner. "Jasper and I will be waiting in the same spot at midnight."

His words reminded her of his resolution that she would not be allowed to ride out as Black Ned again. Half of her felt relieved to have that part of her life over, yet there was that independent streak—the part where she felt those poor tenants needed the money the English seemed too tight-fisted to dispense legally. No, she still did not like Lucien making this decision for her. However, tonight she had experienced a side of the duke she never suspected; it made her pause before protesting his directive openly. Rather, she asked, "Will you keep your word about not—that is, not to make love to me until your uncle performs the Anglican ceremony?"

Her question made him wince inside. Of course, tonight showed him how difficult it was for him to end their coming together earlier than normal, but something cut at him to learn how she seemed intent on holding him to his ill-chosen vow. His nod of compliance was somber. "I am a man of my word. Unless you ask me, I will not touch you in that way until Uncle Nigel weds us in the presence of our family and friends."

He could read nothing in Rosaleen's expression as she got off the bed and began dressing for the ride back to Fitzroy Hall.

Chapter Sixteen

Lucien cast another glance about the area. "All right, I shall wait here until you are safely in your room. Have a warm bath in the morning," he whispered. "It will help soothe some of those parts unaccustomed to a husband's attentions."

Attired again in her breeches to allow an easier climb up the elm tree, Rosaleen was glad the darkness hid her embarrassed reaction to his well-meant advice. It was a bit disconcerting to realize Lucien knew so much about her body.

Tenderly, he lifted her by the waist and set her down on the grass next to Jasper. "Go along now, and be careful climbing that cursed tree."

The dimple at the edge of her mouth popped out at him. "I was climbing trees before you learned to fence, Your Grace."

Leaning on the pommel of Jasper's saddle, the duke of Montrose returned her impudent grin. "I can well imagine. If we are blessed with little girls, I assure you, hellion, they will not grow up as headstrong as their mother."

She gave an impertinent curtsy to the gentleman barely past his mid-twenties. "Spoken with the pomposity of a confirmed old poop. We shall see just how they turn out, Your Grace" was all she would concede.

As she began edging up the elm tree, Rosaleen realized a great deal had happened since she climbed down hours ago. She was now a married woman with a handsome husband, and the lovemaking part had been more pleasurable than she ever dreamed possible. Yes, perhaps being married to the duke would not be such a terrible fate after all. Distracted by her happy thoughts, she briefly lost her footing and stifled an outcry of alarm before her short legs swung up to reach the limb outside the window ledge. Holding on to the branch above her, she peered down at the ground. Lucien was off Jasper and standing by the tree. Quickly, she sought to reassure him by giving him a cavalier wave.

God's nightshirt, thought the distraught duke when he was able to breathe once more. When she smiled and gave another airy wave, he muttered a few colorful expletives. Assured she was back safely in her room, Lucien climbed atop Jasper and started back to Montrose Hall. Though he admitted loving Rosaleen with all his heart, the duke realized he was going to have to set some ground rules—else, his young wife's shenanigans were going to make him a candidate for Bedlam.

Rather than give in to the sleep her body desired, Rosaleen washed and changed into a pale amber morning gown. She was ready a short time later to accompany Aunt Edna and her female cousins on their rounds to the Fitzroy tenants.

Carrying a basket of food and some outgrown clothes of her cousins', Rosaleen knocked on the splintered gray door. She heard Annie's gravelly voice and entered the small cottage.

No fire in the fireplace on this summer day, the widow Kelly sat in her old wooden rocking chair, smoking a long clay pipe. Teeth missing, bent posture, short gray hair tucked under a once white mobcap, Annie Kelly appeared far older than her early fifties. Her face wrinkled into a smile at seeing her visitor. "Why, Miss Rosaleen, 'tis a grand surprise. Must be three months since ya came by."

Looking about the sparsely furnished room, Rosaleen tried to see any indication Annie was better off than a few months earlier. Setting her parcels down next to the older woman's chair, she accepted a seat on the round stool in front of the hearth. "How are things with you, Annie?"

Still puffing on the pipe at the corner of her mouth, Annie shrugged her bony shoulders. " 'Tis the same, except me body don't move as fast as before. Old injuries. I don't hold with cursin' the dead, but them broken ribs Pat gave me on one of his drunken nights still pains me when it gets damp. If it hadn't been for your mother's courage, sure and I'd of been under the sod meself years ago. Course it was a bad way for Pat ta go, in that fearful prison."

Arms resting on her knees, Rosaleen looked at the older woman intently. She'd heard tales about

Sean's deceased brother, Patrick. Her family, along with many here in Kinsale, still retold the story of how Lady Millicent charged into Fogarty's pub and pointed what later turned out to be an unloaded pistol at the barrel-chested Irishman's private parts and convinced him to take an oath that he'd never beat Annie Kelly again.

"All the babes are grown now." Mrs. Kelly glanced about her. "Seems odd ta have it so quiet, but Caren brings her brood over when she can spare the time from Edna—I mean her ladyship." Annie chuckled. "Seems strange ta have Edna O'Rahilly married to an earl."

After a few silent moments, Rosaleen cleared her throat and asked, "Annie, has Sean helped you in any way during the last few months? I mean, did he give you any money?"

Annie rolled her eyes. "Lord love ya, Ross, Sean Kelly never parted with a guinea in his life. Sure and I haven't seen that weasel up close in more than a year. What ever caused ya ta ask such a daft question?"

Frowning, Rosaleen was forced to see Lucien had been correct. The ride through town this morning had convinced her the tenants in the neighboring states were no better off materially than they'd been before Black Ned took to the roads. "I . . . I just thought he might have helped you a little. Many of the Montrose tenants looked better. I wondered if Sean had anything to do with it."

Removing the pipe from her mouth, the old woman's face brightened. "Why, Miss Rosaleen, 'tis the duke of Montrose that's responsible for helpin' those people, just as your uncle and his lady helps us." Leaning closer, she lowered her voice. " 'Tis the Lorenses' tenants that are in a bad way, now that Henry's taken over from his late father. All the earl of Dunsmore is concerned with is makin' his mansion a showplace ta match the richest toff in England. Him and that snippy sister of his. All know she's got her hooks out ta bag the duke of Montrose."

The vision of Prudence in her Venus costume on the arm of a blond Roman officer flashed across the dark-haired girl's mind. Rosaleen experienced a stab of something which both hurt and angered her. However, she forced herself to concentrate on the grim truth that Sean never had kept his word to give all the booty collected to Kinsale's needy Catholics.

Taking her leave of Annie Kelly, Rosaleen wasted little time riding over to Montrose Hall stables. She found Sean Kelly stretched out in a soft bed of hay, sound asleep. "Kelly," she snapped at the snoring man.

With a grunt of protest, Sean opened one eye. He ran a hand through his rumpled short hair, then yawned loudly. "Why, Ross, never expected ta see you up and about so early." He smiled a greeting and stood up. "And a vision in yellow ya are."

"Save your blarney for your three companions. It is lost on me." She frowned across at the man she'd unwisely trusted. "I know you haven't given a farthing to the tenants. You lied to me, Kelly. Just what did you do with the money and jewels we've taken these last three months?"

The expression in Sean's puffy eyes became more belligerent. "No need to get in a lather. Me and the boys are kinda holdin' it in trust, ya might say. Things is gettin' riskier with Colonel Bembridge back in Kinsale. He's made the chief magistrate increase the patrols. Me and the lads are takin' all the risks. 'Tis our necks facin' the hangman. Why shouldn't we keep the money we earned?" he demanded, pushing out his chest.

"We stole that money, and I helped you only because you promised to give it to the tenants." Rosaleen's dark eyes narrowed. "Right from the beginning you intended to keep it for yourselves, didn't you? Why was I so privileged to be part of your club in the first place?"

Sean never expected her to find out the truth so soon, but he could not hide his pleasure that revenge against the lady's parents was within his reach. "Ya did help us get more loot than we'd of managed plannin' them raids alone. Yer access to the society parties was a needed boost ta me and the lads."

"Kelly, I am not letting you get away with this. You distribute that money to the tenants discreetly, especially the Lorenses' tenants, within the week, else I'll hand you and your three accomplices over to Sir Jeremy Cartgrove."

Sean took a menacing step toward the angry woman. "Don't threaten me, Ross, for I've friends in high places, too. When the duke's mother denounces you as Black Ned, how do you think the O'Rahilly and Fitzroy families will fare under the scandal? And won't yer father be proud ta have his only daughter hung by the neck for treason?"

Despite her efforts, her face turned ashen. Trapped in a web of her own making, she searched mentally for a rope. "It might prove awkward for Garnet to denounce me, especially since my father is hosting a party Friday to announce my engagement to Lucien Huntington, Duke of Montrose."

"The devil ya say?" Sean could not hide his shock at this news. Convinced her son would never come near Rosaleen again, Garnet had gone to London. Though the duchess was expected back in Kinsale tomorrow, even Kelly doubted her ability to handle this new situation before Friday. "From all I hear about the proper, staid duke of Montrose, the knowledge that his little bride-ta-be is the notorious highwayman, Black Ned, might make him a bit queasy ta follow through with the marriage, if ya follow me."

It was Rosaleen's turn to appear smug. "Lucien already knows I am Black Ned. He is more liberal-minded than you suppose." Now that she realized Kelly was nothing but a lying traitor, the colonial woman had no intention of telling him of her marriage before Father Michael.

"Well," Kelly sputtered, more conciliatory, "Sure and I'm a reasonable man, especially for old time's sake. Me and the lads have a mind ta go ta France, for things is gettin' too hot here ta continue our excursions in Kinsale. You just come with us as Black Ned one last time, and I promise ya half the take ta give ta whomever ya like. One more ride as Black Ned, then me and the boys will have enough ta stay in France for the rest of our lives. And none of us

298

will say a thing about Black Ned. He disappears from the earth after Friday."

"I wouldn't go along with you again for the crown jewels."

"Ya got no choice. If you turn me in, 'tis yer own neck that stretches, too. And that family of yers ends any hope of a respectable future. Got brothers who might want ta make a good match someday, I hear." Sean touched the wrinkled area of his neck, above his worn linen shirt. "I've a mind ta have a small country place outside of Paris. Me neck was never meant ta dance at the end of a gibbet. Suppose yers would be even more sensitive to the knotted rope."

His words sent shivers down her spine. She was not an English aristocrat, and she knew her Irish Catholic father had many enemies just waiting for him to fall from grace with King George. She could not ruin her family as a result of her misguided actions. And her honorable uncle would be devastated by the scandal. His children could not suffer because of her folly. There appeared no other way out. Lord help her, how ever would she get away from Lucien? "Have you a night for this final ride in mind?" she demanded.

Scratching the stubble on his cheek, Sean grinned as a marvelous plan began forming in his brain. "That I have. Friday night just past midnight."

"You cannot be serious. That is the night of my engagement party."

Now that he'd won, Sean could afford to be magnanimous. " 'Tis the perfect time. There will be good pickings from the guests as they drive home."

299

"But except that night with the Lorens coach, we've never robbed people I actually knew. Englishmen or not, I cannot ask these people to my party, then pay them back by robbing them."

Sean's pug nose wrinkled in disgust. "Ain't like ya ta be a hypocrite. Stealin' is stealin' no matter who it is."

Lucien's words about breaking the law came back to haunt her. He'd been right all along. She should have found another way to help the Irish Catholics. Her rash nature got her into this predicament, and Rosaleen blamed no one but herself right now. She knew she had little choice but to ride out as Black Ned this last time. At least if she was there, she could make certain none of the guests came to any real harm. And, she conceded, there would be less chance of her discovery in the future if Sean and his three partners were out of the country for good.

"All right, Sean, I will meet you Friday night. But I am going to see you and your companions on that boat for France myself. This is the last time Black Ned rides, understand?"

"Yes. Upon me mother's soul, I swear this is the last raid for Black Ned."

"Lucien!" Garnet called in her little-girl voice. She directed her three footmen and maid to take the trunks upstairs immediately. She spotted Brian before he could make a hasty retreat back to the kitchen. "Fogarty!"

Trapped. Brian turned about and attempted an air of politeness. "Welcome back, Your Grace. We were not expectin' ya until tonight."

Never wasting charm on servants, Garnet pursed her lips. "Pray forgive me. I had no idea I needed your consent to return to my own home." Her blue eyes narrowed when she took a closer look at his attire. "Your livery coat has a spot on it. I will not tolerate sloppiness among you Irish. Change it at once. Where is my son? He should be here to greet his mother."

"His Grace is in the sitting room."

When Brian did not move after she headed toward the door, she snapped over a lace-draped shoulder, "Well, clod pate, open the door." She brushed past the servant. "Darling boy," she gushed into the room, raising her arms for her son to come to her.

Having dreaded this meeting, Lucien rose slowly from the sofa and put down the plant book he'd been reading. He could not feign exuberance. He walked over to place a brief kiss on her powdered cheek. The scent of white roses engulfed him. He stepped back. She looked radiant, he had to admit. Dressed in her usual white shade, her gown was the latest Paris creation, with a row of aqua-colored bows from bodice to the open skirt where a petticoat of embroidered white roses nestled on a panel of pink silk. Pear-shaped diamonds dangled from each delicate ear. He saw her pout at his cool reception.

"What is wrong, to greet your mama with such formality? Have I done something naughty again?"

Her childish manner grated on his nerves right now. "Please sit down, Mother. I should like to speak to you."

Sizing things up, Garnet moved sideways, careful to keep her hoops and skirt clear of the table legs. She sat down on the unfrayed wing chair. After Lucien went to the worn chair across from her, she said, "Faith, do not be too long, my boy, for I am fair to collapsing from the trip. Do you know, Daisy Lyncrost kept me out every day in the shops. La, the woman knows every milliner in town." Garnet opened her ivory fan and wafted it across her face. "I shall be glad to return to Paris for a rest."

Lucien frowned as his mother rattled on with the lies about her full days as guest to the Lyncrosts. He looked across at her when she finally ran out of steam. "Mother, I know you were not staying with Sir Arthur's family. There is no need for subterfuge. I am aware of your . . . your quarters at the Inn of Three Cranes."

Garnet blanched, hardly stifling a lurid curse. Who had blabbed to him? "The bitch, Rosaleen; she told you, didn't she? Probably got her father to confide in her using who knows what sordid methods."

"Miss O'Rahilly knew nothing about this until I told her." For the first time in his life, the duke looked at his mother with a scientist's eyes. "She does not deserve your rancor. I also know Taggart O'Rahilly is not my father. It would please me to hear the truth of my parentage, Mother."

Garnet took a defensive posture. "Then, whose malicious gossip have you been listening to?"

Growing impatient with her games, the blond-haired man closed his eyes to retain his self-control. "I spoke to Taggart. At first we exchanged a few

302

heated words. Suffice it to say, he led me toward the Inn of Three Cranes. I believe Percy Bembridge was a caller. I left after you postponed those three young officers until the next evening."

Mentally, Garnet cursed Taggart O'Rahilly for still being a thorn in her side. Never had she dreamed Lucien would learn of her rooms in London. "You had no right to spy on me."

"I'm not setting myself up as anyone's judge, Mother. I just wish to know who my father is. You say it is not Calvert. I believe you. However, we both know why you lied to me about Taggart."

Her face was a mask of disinterest. "I believe Miss O'Rahilly will not trouble us further. Let us just say, I have straightened her out on the facts of life."

"It was you!" he accused, dangerously close to losing his control at the discovery. "Rosaleen would not tell me how she came to such a false conclusion. I wager you never counted on my sympathetic Rosaleen going to Prince Rinaldo to arrange a 'gift' for me. Imagine my . . . surprise . . . when Rinaldo landed on my doorstep like a suitor with flowers? By God, madam, you take my breath away with your audacity."

Garnet clenched her hands about her fan. Things were going completely awry. It was not like her to step into a trap this way. That dark-eyed witch was even bolder than herself.

"Mother, I am waiting. Who is my father?" When the woman refused to answer him, Lucien bounded from his chair. He peered down at her. Until now, he'd thought of her as a fragile, bereaved widow, someone to be protected. He leaned down and gripped the arms of her chair. "Damn it, Mother, do you know the hell you put me through, making me think Rosaleen was my half sister? God, I almost went mad during those tormented days and nights. What a perverted sense of revenge must beat in that tainted heart of yours to use my feelings so cruelly."

She looked up at him, her blue eyes cold against his heated anger. "I have nothing further to say on the matter." She got up when he stepped back from her chair. Inwardly, she was livid at the turn of events. And she'd just discovered something more horrible than she could have imagined: Lucien was still in love with this Rosaleen creature.

When she heard her son storm from the house, she wasted little time summoning Sean Kelly to the study. Before she could berate him for his dereliction of duty, Brian Fogarty knocked at the door with a white envelope on a silver salver.

"I was told by the Fitzroy servant 'tis most important, Your Grace. Beggin' yer pardon fer the gravy stain still on me coat."

With a wary look at Brian's impassive features, Garnet snatched the envelope and dismissed Lucien's servant.

With Sean on a chair at the other side of the desk, Garnet sat down. She tore open the envelope when she saw the crest, wondering why anyone from Fitzroy Hall would be writing her. As she scanned the printed card, her cheeks took on a crimson hue. "It is an invitation to attend a bloody engagement party Friday evening for Dunstan

Fitzroy's niece." She tossed the offending card on top of the wooden desk. "The earl is giving that baggage and Lucien a party to announce their upcoming marriage, and I first learn of it from a flimsy invitation." Instantly, she realized Lucien deliberately planned this insult, letting her find out his intentions in the most calculated manner. Getting up from her chair, she forgot Sean's presence as she paced back and forth in front of the marble fireplace.

Even Sean was amazed at her lurid words as she cursed all the O'Rahillys, her dead husband, Calvert, and every Irish Catholic in Ireland. Never could Kelly remember the duchess in such a state. He decided to remain silent until the gale blew over.

Garnet whirled about to focus her spleen on Sean. "And you, you inept jackass, why in blue hell do I pay you so much for such bumbling? A rodent dead three weeks would prove more useful in getting information to me." All her work and scheming for nothing, she shouted at herself. "Leave me," she ordered, giving the quaking Irishman a disdainful glance. "You are fired. I want you packed and off this estate by morning."

"But . . . ya can't. I got no place ta go. Sure and I'm too sick ta work in the fields."

"Quit whining. You're no foundling, and I'm not charity-prone. Do not let me see your repugnant face again. Get the hell out of here."

"Now, just a second, Your Grace." Sean got to his feet. "I've given ya years of service, as did me late brother. Ya got no call ta be dismissin' me like I was dirt under yer dainty shoes."

305

At his tone, Garnet turned and reached into the slit at the side of her ruffled gown. This time it was not a handkerchief she retrieved. She held the item behind her back while staring at her former employee. "Dirt is too kind a word for you. My son is about to marry that O'Rahilly's spawn, and he'll never be as malleable as before. If there is one species I know, it is men, and I saw the way he looked at me tonight. If you had been doing your job, I would have been forewarned of his confrontation. Then I could have planned a course of action beforehand to insure he'd stay at my side, instead of having to sit there like a bucolic clot, similar to most of the bovine idiots who populate this stink hole."

Sean tried his most persuasive voice. "There now, and I understand yer feelin's exactly. Only I have a way to insure the duke never marries Rosaleen O'Rahilly. And ya won't have ta dirty yer beautiful hands with blackmailin' her mother about them Collinses. 'Tis himself offerin' ya a miracle."

Garnet kept her right hand behind her back as she glowered at the pug-faced Irishman. "And what is this miracle going to cost me?"

"Ah, I like a woman who comes to the point. Well, I'm fixin' ta take a trip. Ya might say, for me health. France is more receptive to Catholics, and I've got a nice little spot all mapped out. For two thousand pounds I'll deliver ya yer heart's delight."

"Two thousand—? Every Irish vermin from one end of Kinsale to the other isn't worth a tenth of that amount, you thieving swine." With practiced ease, Garnet brought her right hand up and pointed

306

the jeweled stiletto at Sean Kelly's throat. "Your penchant for banditry has fogged what few wits you ever possessed if you think you can outswindle me. I've dealt with your scum before, and I never lose; nor do I pay more than I bargained for."

Sweat seeped out above Sean's upper lip as he tried to step back, only to have the Englishwoman follow. She moved the point of her blade from Sean's jugular to an area farther south.

"Of course, cutting your balls off will be redundant, since you've never possessed any courage to speak of," she stated, brandishing the knife just over the area between his legs.

"Don't . . . don't ya want ta know me secret before ya kill me?"

"That you're a stinking lout is no secret."

Kelly did not flinch this time. "No, I mean about handin' ya yer heart's desire on a platter."

"I'll hand you your cock on a platter in a minute."

For the second time, Kelly did not back away.

Garnet thought Sean looked less a sniveling coward than usual. She lowered her knife. Did he know something of value? Pulling the diamond clips from her small ears, she tossed one to him. "One earring now. The other, only if I like what you tell me. If I do not, I will slit your throat right here."

Shoving the greasy strands of spiky hair away from his forehead, Sean peered down at the expensive jewel in his palm. Then he told Garnet the true identity of Black Ned.

Garnet turned and walked back to the leather chair behind her son's desk. She returned the dagger to the soft leather case she always carried on her person or kept under her pillow at night. A smile, almost of one in a state of grace, transformed her features. She looked back at Kelly. "I will pay your price."

Chapter Seventeen

"You look beautiful," Lucien whispered close to Rosaleen's ear, when he could snatch a moment alone with her. It pleased him to see her wearing his gifts—the returned lilac cluster pendant, and the matching earrings he'd presented to her this afternoon.

Rosaleen's black curls were arranged in a becoming upsweep. She had chosen the gold silk gown with care, for she wanted Lucien to be proud of her.

Standing next to her in his blue coat and breeches, Lucien could not hide his happiness. "Our Anglican wedding will not come soon enough for me."

She noticed his eyes had taken on a darker hue. Did he realize she regretted his vow not to make love to her until Nigel married them or she asked? Just talking and resting until dawn in the O'Rahilly cottage was straining her nerves, too. "Lucifer, I . . . Come, Your Grace, we must attend to our guests."

Sighing, Lucien offered his arm to her.

Rosaleen's thoughts kept returning to the night ahead. It would take all her persuasive skills to slip out for a final run as Black Ned.

Making a spectacular entrance in ivory silk and lace, Garnet Huntington was the last guest to arrive. In his dress uniform, Colonel Percy Bembridge stood next to her. They walked regally over to the guests of honor.

"Never did I expect Mother to attend," Lucien whispered to Rosaleen. He reached for her hand and tucked it in the crook of his arm.

Executing a deep curtsy to her future mother-in-law, Rosaleen attempted politeness. "Your Grace, you honor us by your presence." She allowed Percy to bring her gloved fingers to his lips.

Aware all eyes were on her, Garnet smiled a greeting to Taggart and his wife, then turned back to the happy couple. "It has taken me a long time to realize it, but I have learned the folly of parents interfering with their children's lives." She reached out her gloved fingers to take their hands in her own. "Though I have to admit I was astonished at the haste in making this announcement, I recall how dear Calvert pressed me until I consented to wed him." A tearful expression entered her eyes. "All the happiness you deserve, my dears."

Many of the guests began clapping and adding their words of congratulations to the young couple.

Lucien felt relieved his mother was not going to make a scene. When she freed his hand, he bent his blond head close to her ear. "Thank you, Mama. I appreciate the effort this cost you."

For someone who created the illusion of fragility, the duchess had strong fingers, Rosaleen discovered. She tried not to wince at the pressure Garnet exerted when she gave Rosaleen's fingers another congratulatory squeeze. Then Garnet and the colonel went to line up for the next minuet.

After Lucien excused himself to speak with Henry and James, Lady Prudence Lorens came over to Ross. "Well," she huffed, holding her aqua fan in her gloved fingers. "It appears a great deal has happened since the masked ball at Fitzroy Hall."

"Yes, I heard you turned James down," Rosaleen said, deliberately misinterpreting the tall girl's meaning.

"I am not speaking about Winthrop, you idiot. I am talking about your underhanded methods in getting Lucien to propose. His mother promised me he would ask for my hand by the end of the week."

"Then, Garnet was mistaken. No one speaks for His Grace. Even I have learned that."

Prudence compressed her pink mouth. "I can guess why the duke is marrying you."

With effort, Rosaleen tried to put a chain around her temper. "My lady, if you will excuse me, I must see to my other guests."

"You've shackled poor Lucien by getting a brat in you," she accused. "Counting on His Grace never learning the child probably isn't his?"

Her fingers tightened into fists, but Rosaleen closed her eyes, trying to remember her resolve to rein in her temper. Without another word, she turned from Prudence and began walking toward the French doors. The Irishwoman only knew she

311

had to get outside before she lost control and punched Lady Prudence in the nose.

The duke was laughing at something James told him when he glanced up to see the distraught features of his beloved as she raced past their guests. With a polite word to the men about him, he turned and made a path for the Fitzroy gardens outside.

"Rosaleen?"

She heard the duke call her name in the dark, but she would not answer because she did not want him to see her this way. Clutching her arms across her chest, she bit down on her lips to quell the physical pain that assailed her from trying to hold in her anger.

Lucien found her leaning against the elm tree outside her room at the back of the house. "Darling, what is it?"

So lost in her private battle, she could not speak at first. "Please. Leave me." Blood pounded against the veins in her head.

Her anguish tore at him. "I cannot abandon you in such a state." He thought for a second. "I saw you speaking with Pru. Did she insult you?"

She could only nod, caught up in trying to press her arms tighter about her chest.

"Mmm, I can just imagine what that snip said to you." Sizing up the situation, he grabbed her arm. "Come on."

"What? Lucien, let go." He appeared so grim, she misunderstood his actions. "I swear, I did not lose my temper. I never touched Prudence."

"I know. Now move your legs." Without preliminaries, the duke dragged her behind him as he charged toward the tall hedges beyond her uncle's flower garden.

Out of breath from the effort to keep up with his long-legged stride, she still did not understand what he was about. "You're walking too fast. Slow down."

"Then, pump your lovely limbs faster, for we are going to get that rage out of you before you really harm yourself. You cannot tie a piece of string over an overextended bellows filled with gunpowder."

Then she understood his intent. He was showing her a method to expel her anger in a way that would not hurt anyone. Making every effort to keep up with her athletic husband now, Rosaleen increased her stride.

For twenty minutes they raced up and down the intricate maze. Finally, out of breath, Rosaleen signaled she had to stop by frantically waving her right arm. "Please." Her laughter made it difficult to speak. She looked up to find her husband grinning at her. "My anger has dissipated, sir, along with my ability to think one coherent thought. I shall collapse onto this gravel path if we continue." The physical pressure of attempting to contain all her rage inside had gone, replaced by a healthy tiredness. "I do hope you know the way back, darling, for I can scarcely remember where the path is."

Lucien did not miss what she had called him. He went behind her to begin massaging the back of her neck. "I am very proud of you, dear wife. You've done it. You controlled your temper."

"Ooo, that feels marvelous," she said, as his

313

hands performed their magic on her previously tense muscles. "I could not have done it without your help, Lucien. Thank you for being with me. I intend to use this method often. Our servants will think I've gone dotty, but it works. What an intelligent man I married," she exclaimed, then impetuously turned about and stood on tiptoes to take his face in her hands. She kissed his warm mouth, then delighted in the feel of his hands on her waist as he assisted with her embrace. "Come," she teased, "we must return to our guests before they construe we've left for a scandalous tryst in the garden."

"I wish. . . ." He removed his arms from her. That cursed vow. "Do you have anything to ask me?" he said, a hopeful longing in his blue eyes.

Rosaleen knew he wanted her to ask him to make love to her in the O'Rahilly cottage tonight. How she wanted to, but it was impossible now. "Only a request. May we go back in now. The night air has turned cooler."

He attempted to hide his disappointment. "Yes, of course."

The rest of the evening's festivities progressed smoothly. However, as it got closer to midnight, Rosaleen became more anxious. All her efforts to get the duchess to leave failed. Lucien's mother appeared in no hurry.

What now? Time was running out. She had to get Lucien and Garnet out of here. Stifling a yawn behind her hand-painted fan, she said, "Oh, pray excuse me."

314

Smiling down at her, Lucien whispered, "Can this sleepy kitten be the same little rogue who used to stay up late riding the highways?"

She imitated a pretty pout and kept her voice lowered. "Faith, sir, you must admit you do interrupt my sleep by insisting I go with you after midnight to the O'Rahilly cottage, just to sleep," she added pointedly, reminding him of his kept vow. "Besides, with all the preparations for this evening and the wedding, I am no longer able to sleep until noon." She yawned behind her fan once more. "Pardon, Your Grace. I fear I am becoming quite a boring hostess." She fluttered her eyelashes, giving full evidence she battled an overwhelming urge to curl up right here on the parquet floor.

The duke looked down at her with a combination of sympathy and wariness. He admitted it was becoming painful to sleep in the same bed with her, yet not make passionate love to her the way he desired. Perhaps one night would not hurt. "You give me your word you will stay put in your bed upstairs?"

She hated lying to him. It was difficult to hold his piercing gaze. "I promise if you give me leave, I shall politely say good night to your mother and our few remaining guests, then go right upstairs to my bedroom."

Tempted by the tender look in his eyes, she almost blurted everything to him, but loyalty to her family made her stifle the inclination. Never could she let Sean ruin the Fitzroys or O'Rahillys. And she was positive Kelly would follow through on his threat if she did not comply. Soon, she told herself, it would all be over forever, and Sean and his three mates would be on their way to France.

Lost to the pleading in the depths of her midnight eyes, Lucien nodded his approval. "All right, sweet elf, tonight you stay upstairs. In truth, I have been toying with the idea of trusting you for the duration of our engagement." His smile was chagrined. "I find it decidedly uncomfortable to keep my hands off of you while your warm curves cuddle into me."

"Lucien!" she admonished, shocked by this open declaration with people about them. "Please, someone might hear you."

"I made sure they would not." He did notice the shadows under her eyes. "Run along now, for you do look in need of sleep."

Worry over tonight had made sleep impossible for the last few days, but she forced herself to go about saying her adieus to their guests. Then she dashed upstairs.

A half hour later, all the guests had departed, and her parents had gone up to bed. She looked at the silver clock on her writing desk. Dressed in her black breeches and shirt, she went over to the window. It was time to leave.

Sitting across from his mother and Colonel Bembridge, Lucien leaned back against the leather cushions as the two people chatted on about Paris. He felt positive about the future. Rosaleen was going to become his wife, this time freely before the vicar. He had found happiness here in Ireland, as

Calvert had years ago. Perhaps his mother's change of heart meant she would now tell him who his father was. After all, he wanted no specter at the wedding ceremony to come forward. Lord, he hoped it wasn't Bembridge.

The duke watched the preening officer with his lisp and fussy mannerisms. He smiled at the thought of his wife's reaction if it proved true her new father-in-law was none other than the English colonel. The slow, comfortable ride caused his own eyelids to feel heavy. Folding his arms across his chest, Lucien decided to catch a nap before they arrived back at Montrose Hall.

When he heard pistol fire, the duke bolted upright, knocking his head on the roof of the carriage. Bembridge's frame made it impossible to peer out the window.

"Halt!" shouted a man's voice. "Stand and deliver!"

Lucien experienced a sickening lurch in the pit of his stomach. He leaned across to get out of the carriage, but Percy barred his way.

The colonel reached under the seat and retrieved a pistol. Shoving his wig-covered head out the window, he yelled, "Form your lines!"

Lucien heard the sound of horses. He tried once more to move past Percy.

The colonel pointed his gun at the young man. "Pway, remain seated, Your Gwace."

He darted a look at his mother. She showed no fear or shock. Indeed, there was an expression of triumph on her face.

"Oh, let him step out for a second, Percy. But remember, dear boy, you are to stay back here with me for your own safety."

Lucien followed Percy out of the carriage. The colonel assisted Garnet. He made out at least thirty English soldiers on horseback surrounding a group of scruffy riders. With a growing dread, he forced himself to study the five riders in dark clothes and face masks. The one holding back near the trees got his attention. Small boned, slender shoulders. He knew it was Rosaleen immediately. Fool, he berated himself, he should never have underestimated Garnet's capacity for evil. And his ire rose at Rosaleen for having broken her promise, putting her life in danger once more.

"Lieutenant Gage," Percy shouted, "keep your pistol on that man away from the others. I want him alive."

Lucien saw the officer nod and move his horse closer to Rosaleen. He aimed his loaded pistol at her and ordered her to drop her weapon. She tossed it to the ground.

"Arrest them all," Bembridge ordered.

"What?'" one of the men shouted. He charged his horse toward the three people standing near the Montrose coach. "Bitch! You told me I'd go free. Ya promised me."

Garnet looked bored by Sean Kelly's outburst. It confirmed her earlier decision, for he was proving far too dangerous to keep on as a spy.

The masked Kelly raised his loaded pistol and pointed it toward the duchess; however, Bembridge fired first.

The colonel's bullet hit Kelly in the stomach.

Slumping over his saddle, Kelly kicked his horse in the opposite direction. Horse and rider went racing off past the coach.

The other three men began to panic and raised their pistols.

"No," ordered Percy to his men, as they got ready to charge after Sean. "Get those four other robbers. Let that one go. He's a dead man, for I know my aim was straight."

Lucien watched the mortally wounded Kelly ride back toward the thick grove of trees not far from the O'Rahilly cottage. Taking advantage of the commotion, he darted toward Rosaleen's horse in an effort to get her out of the way.

"All right," Garnet ordered, "do it now. Don't let him reach that man."

Garnet's strapping footmen bounded from atop the carriage.

Instantly, Lucien felt the three men grab him from behind before he'd made it even two strides from the carriage. Struggling with all his might, a bellow of rage burst from him before they roughly tied his hands behind him, followed by a gag across his mouth. They shoved him back into the shadows of the coach and wasted little time securing his hands to the brass door handle of the Montrose carriage. They hobbled his legs with a sturdy rope against one of the wooden carriage wheels. It was all over quickly and efficiently. Lucien recognized his mother's touch in this.

In horror, the duke of Montrose could only watch as Bembridge raised his arm and commanded his men to fire. Noise and smoke from their rifles filled the night. After the mist cleared, Lucien saw blood spew from their multiple gunshot wounds. The three masked riders crashed to the ground before they could fire a shot. He did not miss Rosaleen's shudder of terror as she sat atop her horse in the distance.

The ropes bit into the duke's wrists as he tried desperately to get free. The rough cords burned his skin when he twisted and pulled without success. A hatred he'd never felt before rose against his mother.

"Cease firing," Bembridge ordered. "Check those three men on the ground."

A soldier dismounted, walked over and kicked the bodies with the toe of his boot. "All dead, sir. Just this one left," he added, pointing to the outlaw atop the horse, "and the fellow who got away."

"Never mind him. He'll be dead by morning. Excellent work, men." The colonel walked over to the unarmed bandit. He reached up and pulled the short fellow roughly off his horse. "Irish bastard." Bembridge backhanded Ned across the face, sending the masked highwayman to his knees.

A furious growl came from deep within Lucien, muffled by the tight gag over his mouth. He felt blood run down his hands as he tried again to free himself. All he could do was watch with sickening reality as the colonel grabbed for his fallen prey once more.

"You've led me a disagreeable chase for months," Percy complained while he tied a rope tightly around Ned's wrists. "Yours is one hanging I do not intend to miss." When Ned began struggling, Percy went for the robber once more. However, his eyes widened when his hand pressed against the front of Ned's chest.

Rosaleen realized Percy now knew Black Ned was a woman. She clamped her lips together beneath her mask, determined not to cry out to Lucien. She would not ruin his life before society or the law by implicating him in her crimes. Frightened, she forced herself to stand erect. She was prepared to take the consequences for her actions. Though she could not see Lucien, she knew he was either in the carriage or near it. He had not called or come to her. A man of honor, he probably now believed she deserved her fate. She was hot in the leather mask and heavy coat. The part of her face where Bembridge hit her throbbed and felt swollen. When she wet her dry lips, she tasted blood from a cut at the corner of her mouth. All Ned's group were dead now. The bitter irony swept over her, for she realized not one Catholic had benefited from all her efforts as Black Ned.

From the slit of her mask, Rosaleen's nose twitched when the scent of roses assailed her. Garnet.

Turning her back on the black-draped highwayman, Garnet smiled and whispered to Percy. "I thought you should be the only one to enjoy this present before you turn her over to Sir Jeremy Cartgrove in the morning. Use Sean's old shack on Montrose lands. No one will disturb you." She ran a gloved hand along the colonel's upper arm. "I know how much you adore girls in tight breeches, and I assure you, this peasant wench is of no consequence. Why not keep the mask on her face to add

321

mystery to your unrestrained pleasure? Time enough to let the whole of Kinsale see her in the morning when you parade her through the streets on a leash behind your horse."

Percy could not hide his arousal at the duchess's suggestions. He raised her gloved fingers to his lips. "As always, Your Gwace, you are so understanding and generous with me. Leave it to you to find out the truth."

Garnet beamed. "I have always known how to get what I want." She turned to walk back to her carriage. "Oh, and colonel, Lady Prudence Lorens and her brother will be my son's guests tomorrow evening for a private supper. You will join us, will you not?"

"Delighted, my dear."

Bembridge roughly tied Rosaleen's booted feet to the stirrups of her saddle while her already secured hands were lashed to the pommel in front of her. Percy allowed no one else to come near her.

There was nothing more to say. Lucien was lost to her, she concluded. If she did not love him, why did this truth fill her with such sadness and regret? She was glad no one had removed her mask, for it hid the moisture in her eyes.

Purposely giving Bembridge time to get away, Garnet had kept her three servants waiting near the coach. During the last hour, Lucien had made no attempt to break free of his bonds. She felt it was safe to step two feet in front of him. Warily, she said, "I do hope you are not going to be tiresome

322

about this. If I order Richard to untie you, will he have to use his pistol?"

Lucien moved his head from left to right.

"Good. I counted on your scientific bent to keep you reasonable." She made a motion, and the footman cut Lucien free.

After the tight gag was removed from his mouth, the duke stepped awkwardly away from the carriage. While he rubbed the rope burns and cuts below the lace at his wrists, he reminded himself Rosaleen's life depended on his ability to keep his head. Many things became clear while he'd been shackled to that coach, forced to watch his beloved being manhandled by Percy while his mother stood by gloating.

Garnet moistened her lightly rouged lips. "When Sean told me that hussy said you knew she was Black Ned, I could not bear it. It hurt me more than you will ever know."

Lucien could not believe she was again resorting to that pathetic little-girl act. Though it filled him with revulsion, he forced himself to place an arm about her shoulders. "Please do not cry, Mother. Until this evening, I never believed she could be Black Ned. We quarreled over something silly, and she lost that horrid temper of hers. Jeering at me, the minx told me she was Black Ned. I thought it was a childish prank. However, when I saw the outline of her form on that blasted horse tonight, I knew she was telling the truth. I was such a blind fool to think I cared for her. She was just toying with me. I was a challenge against her hatred of all Englishmen. Heaven only knows what she did alone with those four brigands she rode with."

Garnet craned her neck to study her son's face. She saw the hurt in his eyes. So, this Rosaleen had made a fool of him. The Irish girl was more clever than Garnet suspected. "You do understand now, do you not? I had to have my footmen tie you, for I thought the girl had bewitched you. When you started to go to her rescue, I ordered—"

"Rescue?" He appeared incredulous. "I was so furious at her deception, I wanted to strangle her with my bare hands. She made such a fool of me, Mother, letting me believe she was a lady, an untouched flower. Never could I marry anyone who had such contempt for England and her laws. My father might not have been Calvert, but I still bear his proud name. I will not allow anyone to soil the Montrose name again," he added with feeling.

The duchess was surprised at the intensity in her son's voice. "Well, then it is settled." She laughed nervously. "You shall have your revenge, dear boy, for only you, Percy, and I know of Ned's true sex. Percy thinks she is a peasant girl, and I have given her to him as a gift for one night. Imagine Percy's amazement when he unwraps my gift tonight. He has an old score to settle with Taggart O'Rahilly himself, for that brutish Irishman once socked Percy on the jaw. Yes, the colonel will delight in turning Miss O'Rahilly over to Sir Jeremy in the morning. She will be subdued by then, I assure you. Take joy in that, poor darling." She patted her son's arm with affection. "We can go on as before, the two of us. Prudence will make you a good wife, and she is such a sensible English lady." Garnet rubbed her gloved fingers along his coat-covered shoulder. "No one will ever come between us again."

Lucien kept his expression unreadable. "You know me so well, Mother." He returned her smile.

It was going to be all right, Garnet told herself as she looked up at her handsome son. "When you smile like that you do remind me of your father. Your darker blond hair comes from him. He had dark brown hair, and the way you have of clenching your jaw is just like he used to do when he became vexed with me, which was very rare. I still miss him so much. If Taggart O'Rahilly had not murdered him in that duel, we would have run away to Paris together."

Lucien held his breath, certain she was getting ready to tell him the identity of his father.

When Garnet took her son's hand in hers, she was horrified to see the blood on his wrist. Her whole demeanor changed. "Oh, my poor darling, you are hurt. It was too bad of Richard to tie your bonds so tightly. Come," she added, pulling him by the hand. "I will get you right home to tend to your wounds."

Lucien allowed Garnet to fuss over him in the coach as they drove back to Montrose Hall. He tried to quell his impatience to leave. Yes, he concluded, fighting the urge to pull his hand away, Garnet believed every word he'd said tonight. And why not? Hadn't he learned well from this mistress of deception?

When they arrived home, he thanked his mother but said Brian could tend to his wrists.

"As you say, dear boy. Well, then, I am for bed. It has been a most active day. I do need my beauty sleep. You may kiss me good night."

Bending his tall frame, Lucien placed a brief kiss on his mother's powdered cheek. He yawned behind his hand, then stepped back. "I shall be lucky to stay awake for Brian to tend me." He watched his mother go up the stairs, then waited until he saw Louise enter her rooms.

Instantly, he raced toward his laboratory in the cellar. There wasn't a moment to lose. God, he hoped this would work, for it was his last hope.

Chapter Eighteen

Rosaleen stood on the far side of the rough shack, her wrists tied to a wooden peg above her head. Percy had taken only two soldiers, along with a peasant and his wife to see to his needs. The soldiers were standing guard outside the door.

"Come on," he said to the gray-haired woman bending over the open hearth. "Get that stew cooking. I do not intend to wait all night for my meal." He brushed past the Irishwoman's husband, who was laying out the colonel's tableware and linen as ordered. Percy looked down at Black Ned. "Or to wait for my night of pleasure." He ran a possessive hand across the swell of Black Ned's hips. "Get out," he told the two Irish servants, clearly needing to be alone with his prize.

They got up to leave.

However, the cottage door crashed open before they reached it.

"God in heaven," the Irishman said as he peered up at the deathly apparition.

The hooded figure dwarfed everyone in the small

cottage. A cape billowed about him like a predator's black wings.

" 'Tis the devil himself," cried the peasant's wife, crossing herself.

Percy drew his sword from the scabbard on his hip. "Who in blazes are you?"

"I have come for Ned," growled the intruder, taking a menacing step toward the English colonel.

"Pway think again. You are a madman or drunk," Percy jeered, raising his sword, "if you believe you can just saunter in here and steal Black Ned from Percy Bembridge."

Beneath the hood covering his head, his even white teeth gleamed where an opening in the full mask was cut. "That is precisely what I intend."

"Oh, give him up, Colonel. 'Tis Beelzebub comin' after his own." The Irishman put a hand about his wife's quaking shoulders.

"Gage!" Percy shouted to his lieutenant stationed outside the door.

"I am afraid your two soldiers will not be able to help you for at last a few hours." The intruder floated to the right.

The colonel and his two servants peered toward the open door. Both guards were facedown on the damp ground outside.

"God, he's killed them," shrieked the plump Irishwoman. "He's gonna murder us all and take our souls. We're gonna die."

"Stop your wife's caterwauling," Percy ordered the Irishman. "If anyone dies, it will be this black-draped nuisance." Advancing on the mysterious visitor, Percy raised his sword. "I was a dragoon," he boasted.

"Now you're a nincompoop." With lightning speed,

the stranger doubled a fist and knocked the rapier from the Englishman's hand. It clattered to the dirt floor.

Incensed, Bembridge raced over to his coat to get his pistol.

The cloaked figure reached into his cape, then tossed something into the fire. Smoke and the strong smell of sulfur permeated the cabin.

"Blessed Mary, save us, it is the devil," shrieked the hysterical Irishwoman.

Smoke blinded him, but the colonel fired across the room as he raged at the audacity of this stranger. Racing to the right, Percy cursed when he collided with the Irishman. "Out of my way, you lumbering oaf. After him." Charging out the cabin door, Percy heard the sound of horse's hooves, but he could see nothing in the darkness.

The Irishwoman clung to her shaking husband. " 'Twas the devil himself rose up from hell ta take Black Ned back with him."

Percy stalked back and peered about the room as the smoke began to clear. Cut ropes were on the dirt floor below the wooden peg, but Black Ned and that demon from hell were gone.

Grateful for the rescue by this mysterious knight, nevertheless, Rosaleen was irritated when she felt herself enveloped in his thick cape and dumped facedown across the saddle in front of him.

He continued their suicidal pace through the thick forest, jumping over obstacles, racing across a pond so quickly she felt cold water penetrate the cape and slits in her mask.

Once she tried to right herself, but the demon snapped his displeasure and pushed her roughly back down.

Finally, the unknown rescuer pulled his horse up with an abrupt tug on the reins. She felt the stranger dismount. When he lifted his cape from her and set her on her booted feet, Rosaleen had to grasp the horse's neck to steady herself. "There was no need to throw me across the horse like a sack of potatoes. I know how to ride." She bit her lower lip, reminding herself this odd-behaving man just saved her, and she owed him gratitude, not sharp words. Glancing up, she saw he'd put the cape back on. The hood and mask covered his face once more. She looked at his black horse but recognized nothing that might assist in the man's identity. When she peered behind him to see the O'Rahilly cottage, she could not hide her relief. She was back on Fitzroy land.

As the cloaked figure tied his horse to a nearby tree, she tried to compose a proper speech of thanks. Perhaps poor Sean had sent him, with his dying breath requesting one of the Irish tenants to rescue her. She knew Lucien had washed his hands of her. Hadn't he just sat in the coach and let Bembridge overtake her?

She cleared her throat. "You have been most kind in helping me. I gather you wish anonymity, and I shall respect your desire, sir. Now, I pray you, please get safely away, for I should not forgive myself if you are caught."

Expecting a gallant bow before he took his leave atop his horse, Rosaleen squeaked in protest when the devil incarnate thrust an arm about her waist and under her knees, then lifted her. Instantly, she began

330

wiggling to be put down. "Sir, you forget yourself. Unhand me at once."

The demon tightened his hold about her and began walking toward the cottage.

Rosaleen tried another approach. "You must let me go, even though I am grateful for the rescue."

Menace in his guttural voice, the demon growled, "You will not think this is a rescue, I promise you."

Truly uneasy now, Rosaleen began to struggle harder. However, the horrid beast kicked open the cottage door with his booted foot and strode in with her still in his arms.

When he set her on her feet, he easily made it to the door before she could make her escape. Holding her wrists above her head with one hand, he reached into the folds of his cape and pulled out his sword from the scabbard at his hip. Then he freed her hands while blocking her way to the door.

Rosaleen swallowed, wondering if this was some irate Englishman she had once robbed who somehow found out Black Ned was in Percy Bembridge's clutches. In a last effort, she reached up and removed her hat and mask. Her black curls tumbled about her shoulders. "I am Rosaleen O'Rahilly. My . . . my father will pay you a great deal if you return me unharmed right now to Fitzroy Hall."

Her captor continued to point the sharp end of the rapier at her throat. His mask muffled his low voice. "They told me you were married to the duke of Montrose. Wouldn't your husband pay more to get his wife back?"

"How did you find out about that private ceremony?" she demanded.

No answer.

"Another of Garnet's spies," she grumbled, chiding herself for not remembering how the duke's mother paid others to insure she kept informed. His taunting words only caused her pain, for she knew Lucien's heart now. "His Grace would not pay a farthing to get me back. The Catholic ceremony will not be recognized by English law, and he will be free to marry Lady Prudence Lorens."

The phantom lowered his sword for a moment. Close to her, he whispered, "Are you so certain he does not love you, Ross?"

Instantly, Rosaleen became more alert — the coaxing tone of his voice. She inhaled deeply. The clean scent of sandalwood played against her nostrils. It was Lucien!

Stunned by her discovery, she forced her gaze to the floor while she tried to think. Why was Lucien keeping his identity from her? Was it to punish her for breaking her word in resurrecting Black Ned this one last time? Well, she fumed, if the duke thought he could frighten her, he had a surprise coming. Much of her usual spirit returned. She stamped her booted foot. "Kill me then and have done. I'll tell you nothing more. Finish what you came for."

"That I will." The gruff voice was more intimidating. He stepped back but continued threatening her with the foil. "Strip," he ordered.

"What?"

"You heard me. Get out of those clothes."

She did not move. "Who are you?" she demanded, hoping to get Lucien to end this pretense.

The figure all in black took a step closer. "Someone not to be trifled with. Now, take off all your clothes or I shall do it for you. And I promise, you will not like my coarse methods."

Rosaleen read the warning in Lucien's tone and knew from his stance he meant every word. Looking about the room only made her aware of how different things were since the last time she was here with him. On shaky legs she went over to sit on the wooden chair near the table, then glanced at her boots. It seemed the safest place to start. Two lighted candles on the table sent diabolical shadows across the cottage walls. She moved slowly, pulling off one boot then the other.

"Hurry up."

"You might at least turn your back."

Nothing.

"Do you intend to stare at me while I disrobe?"

"That is part of my entertainment for the evening. Get on with it," he commanded, swiping the air in front of him with the sword.

She went to the three buttons of her black shirt. Her nervous fingers took longer than normal. She lifted the shirt over her head and deposited it at her feet.

"The bindings, too," said the demon.

The old O'Rahilly fire entered her eyes. "You truly are an ascendant from Hades," she snapped at her husband. "Certainly no gentleman."

"Tonight I am not a gentleman," agreed the devil, flashing a grin through the slit in his mask. "But then, you are not dressed as a proper lady either. Now, the breeches."

Lucien was obviously trying to humiliate her, Rosaleen decided, as she unbuttoned her breeches at the waist and knees, then pulled them off. Naked, she turned her back on the black demon, determined to keep the intimate front of her away from his eyes.

She heard the clank of the sword as it landed on the wooden floor boards. When she turned her neck about to peer over her shoulder, it was just in time to catch her tormentor reaching out to lift her in his arms once more. "I detest being carried," she protested. The hold on her naked waist and shoulders showed her blackguard of a husband had removed his leather gloves and cloak. His hands were warm against her cool skin. He said nothing but walked over to the overstuffed couch and placed her against the cushions with unexpected care.

Before she could sit up, he was tying her hands with a silk cloth. It was looser than the painful rope Percy had used, but Rosaleen angrily realized she could not free her hands. "Why are you doing this?"

Her husband continued his work of securing another silk scarf about her ankles.

His touch did not hurt her, but he was firm and quick in his efforts to hobble her. "You unspeakable English ruffian. How dare you treat me this way. I'll run a sword through your liver. I shall have Henry Lorens call you out."

"View the earl of Dunsmore as your champion, do you?"

"Well," she grated, trying but failing to keep her right ankle out of his reach. "Henry is a more polite man than that uncivilized lout I married."

"Earlier I thought you sounded regretful Montrose was out of your life."

Mutiny tinged her reply. "I am beginning to get used to the idea. Right now the duke's absence would fill me with nothing but delight."

In seconds he'd effectively stripped her of her clothes and her means of escape. She was truly outraged when the apparition hovered over her form, as if admiring his handiwork. With hands and ankles tied, Rosaleen could not move. A spasm of fury ripped though her naked body. "I would rather you kill me than use me for your . . . your perversions."

The disguised duke misread her reaction. "Do not be afraid, little one. I'll only do things you will enjoy."

"In a pig's eye, you black-draped bastard." Rosaleen looked up at his masked face. "Untie me at once, do you hear me?" When she felt a hand on her arm, she tried to move away, but the bindings prevented it.

He caressed her shoulders, then moved up to her jaw. "That is right, Rosaleen, there is nowhere to run. I have you, and I intend to do exactly what I wish. You will want more than my hands on you in a moment."

"Never, you loathsome cur."

The hands grew bolder as he made a leisurely exploration of her chest, along the sensitive skin below each breast, then mischievously darted across the curve of her hips.

When Rosaleen felt him fondle the soft skin inside her thighs, she could not smother a gasp. No, she would not yield to him. "Stop. Your attentions are sickening."

She closed her eyes tightly to keep her mind focused on what she was telling this unspeakable knave she married. Her words must have worked, for she felt Lucien stand up. But then he came back at her, and she knew he was not defeated yet. Still, she refused to look at him, because she feared her eyes might give her away. It was wrong, she told herself, to feel anything but abhorrence for this treatment.

Lucien ran his skillful hands up across more intimate parts of her skin. She held her breath when she felt his lips and tongue on her flesh. It was clear now he'd removed his cape and mask. "I hate this," she said, in a desperate move to get him to stop before she humiliated herself. "Your touch is disgusting."

"Your body says otherwise," the devil countered.

Unable to stop himself, the blond-haired man took his captive's face in his hands and kissed her with all the fierce desire he'd held at bay until they could live openly as man and wife.

"You—" she accused, but her lips were seduced once more before she could call him another name.

"Yes," said her captor, in his own familiar voice. "It is Lucifer," he added, using the nickname she often berated him with.

Though grateful for her husband's earlier rescue, when the Irishwoman raised her arms to receive more of her husband's skillful lovemaking, she was nudged back to reality by the silken cloth at her wrists and ankles. Anger surged through her. "Devil you are." Sparks shot from her eyes. "You frightened me, bullied me, treated me monstrously."

Matching her anger, the duke hovered over her like an avenging angel. "I could have thrashed you within an inch of your life when I saw you on the road tonight as Black Ned. Just because I love you to distraction does not mean I take kindly to being lied to. Damn it, Rosaleen, you were inches away from being killed or raped by Bembridge." He reached down and gave her a forceful shake. "Why did you do it?"

She told him about Sean's threat to turn her over to

the authorities and ruin her family unless she went this one last time. "I honestly believed he and his three companions meant to go to France. Of all they did, it was a bad end, for I know Sean never counted on your mother handing him over to Percy."

"No, I am sure my mother probably told him he would be allowed to escape. Poor fool was not the first man to believe her, then live just long enough to regret it." Lucien gave Rosaleen a pointed stare. "However, I still want to know why you didn't come to me when Sean threatened blackmail. I am your husband; I would have helped you."

"No, Lucien, it was my problem. Sean could have ruined my family and the earl with the scandal. I had to see it through myself."

"Maddening woman," he snapped. "You'd sacrifice yourself without even considering how empty my life would be without you."

Tears swam before her eyes. "I—"

"Now that you are here in one piece, madam," he cut off, "have you thought about what Bembridge will tell the chief magistrate?"

She looked defensive for a moment. "Well, he only knows I am a woman. Sean and his men are dead. Only you and your mother know Black Ned's identity. Come, untie me. I will have to speak to your mother so that she will not give me away."

"Oh, no you won't. From now on you are out of this whole Ned business. You have made a fine mess of things up to now, and I will not allow you any more rope. It tightened enough about that luscious neck of yours this night as far as I ever want to see happen again."

His phraseology sparked something within her.

337

"You won't allow?" she grated, struggling to sit up. "It could ruin you if word of your rescue got out. I will not have you sacrificed for my errors. If you imagine you can begin setting down rules for—" Her words were cut off when her rogue of a husband began tying another silk square—this time about her mouth.

"I must remember this method in years down the road when you start to get out of hand." He dared an amused smirk down at the woman glaring up at him. "You know, Ross, dressed in three silk scarves and nothing else does become you."

No words made it through her gag, but sounds of pure rage sputtered out.

"Yes, I know you love me," he teased outrageously. Getting off the couch, he went over to the chair and picked up his cloak. "In case it gets cooler when the fire goes out." He draped the long cape over her naked form, taking care to tuck it about her feet and legs. "I shall be back for you before daybreak." At the alarm in her eyes, he lifted one edge of the silk against her mouth. "Are the bindings too tight?" he asked, showing his usual concern for her comfort.

"No." So distracted, she told the truth. "Where are you going?"

"To bury Black Ned," he answered, then replaced the cloth about her lips. "And this is the only way I know to insure you stay out of trouble until I return." Without another word, the duke went over and picked up her discarded clothes. When he left the cottage, he locked the door behind him.

Frustration, rage at his tactics, then fear for his safety raced through Rosaleen's mind as she was forced to lie there in the darkened cottage. What was he going to do? She only knew he was risking himself to save her life and her family's honor.

Suddenly, she heard the sound of a pistol firing nearby. Her body tensed. She felt chilled despite the cloak about her. Tears stung her eyes as she suddenly felt devastated at the thought of losing him. He could be bleeding to death in some peat bog. He might die never knowing the truth—she loved him. If she had not been so stubborn and prejudiced against all English aristocrats, she would have realized it sooner—before it was too late to tell him.

She sobbed against the darkness. Her gallant husband was no match against their enemy. And Lucien probably did not even realize his mother was their most dangerous adversary.

Chapter Nineteen

Lucien wasted little time riding back to the secluded area where he'd hidden Sean Kelly's body.
As directed, Brian Fogarty was waiting for him.

He dismounted, then grabbed the two bundles
across his saddle. In one hand, he carried Rosaleen's clothes. The other knapsack contained the
fox he'd just shot.

He arranged Rosaleen's shirt over the shrubbery
to his right, then walked back to kneel over Sean's
body.

"Please hold the lantern steady, Brian."

The older man turned his head away but tried to
use both hands to keep the light focused where his
employer wished. " 'Tis downright macabre what
you're doin'."

Lucien continued his clinical study of the wound
in Sean's stomach. "Entered at an angle, then
there's another hole up closer to the sternum." He
rose and walked over to Jasper to retrieve two
loaded pistols. Standing far enough from the shirt
draped over the hedge, he raised first one pistol
then the other and fired in a calculated manner to

duplicate the holes in Sean's shirt.

Lucien went back to Sean's body and methodically divested the corpse of his clothes. "These I'll burn at Montrose Hall." He rolled them in the knapsack that formerly held the dead fox.

"Ghoulish business," muttered Brian. His employer said nothing but continued dressing the dead man in Black Ned's clothes.

"Hand me the hat."

Still holding the lantern, Brian reached over to get Rosaleen's black felt hat. "And what makes ya think ya can pull this off?"

"It has to work. This is the only way Ross will be free of Black Ned forever. By now those two servants have spread that superstitious nonsense about the devil stealing Ned. Bembridge will not rest until he has Black Ned arrested and hung. One thing I have learned about Percy, he will do anything to avoid appearing foolish." He grabbed the dead fox, took out a knife from his coat and slit its throat. "Blood is still warm," he commented with a scientist's observation. He held the animal over the newly dressed corpse.

"Oh God, sure and I think I'm gonna be sick." Brian turned his head away once more as the younger man spattered Sean's shirt with the fox's blood.

"It has to look like his own blood, Brian. Remember, all the soldiers were concentrating on the four accomplices. They expect four corpses only, for one rode away, probably, they thought, to end up in some ditch or washed away in the harbor. No one cares much about that rider who was shot. Bembridge only cares about getting Black Ned.

There," Lucien finished. "Ross and Sean are the same height. What was baggy on Ross just fits Sean." He read Brian's reaction to his grisly actions. "God help us, it has to work."

"And I tell you, Sir Jeremy, the bold fellow threw something into the fire that made the place fill with smoke; then he road off with Ned."

A linen dressing gown hastily buttoned over his white nightshirt, the chief magistrate scowled once more at Percy Bembridge. "Well, it is a fine day when you have to come here at this hour to tell me Black Ned has escaped again. The English here are not going to take this well. They've been sending letters to His Majesty since April, begging him to supply more troops to rid them of that cursed highwayman. When I got your note that you'd captured Black Ned, I—Come in," he shouted in response to the knock at his office door.

A young soldier came in, followed by Lucien Huntington.

"Montrose." The older man rose. "Percy told me it was your carriage waylaid by that despicable wretch, Black Ned. What brings you here at this awful hour? The duchess was not harmed, I hope? Percy said the villains were armed, but—"

"Mother and I were not injured," Lucien reassured, trying to keep his manner relaxed. "Of course the shock did not do her any good. Mother went straight to her bed. Then I went back to the spot where Bembridge shot Black Ned. He did not get very far, as the colonel wisely suspected. I have his body over my horse. I assumed you would want it for identification. It turns out Black Ned was none other than our groom, Sean Kelly."

"Shot Black Ned, you say?" Sir Jeremy lifted his brocade cap to scratch his bald head. "Bembridge, I thought you said the fellow escaped from you and your two soldiers?"

It was clear Percy Bembridge felt confused, for he thought he'd mortally wounded one of Ned's men. Was the fellow he shot Black Ned? The girl—was she just a joke Garnet was having with him? "I . . . that is I. . . ."

Lucien spoke up with an air of English comradery. "The colonel is too modest to tell you himself. However, I saw it as did my mother and the colonel's men. Percy shot the scurvy knave in the stomach. I shall bring the body in." Immediately, Lucien went outside. He returned with the corpse slung over his left shoulder. Where should I . . . ?"

"Upon my soul," gasped Sir Jeremy. "The other three bodies are out back. Well, put him on the bench over there against the wall."

Lucien did as instructed.

Sir Jeremy moved his spindly legs over to peer down at the corpse. "Black felt hat, just as Lady Lorens and the others described. Short stature, black coat and breeches, as you said. God's nightshirt, Bembridge, that's Black Ned all right. What in thunderation were you babbling about Ned escaping from you, rescued by some dark apparition?"

The colonel looked first at the frowning chief magistrate, then at the unruffled duke. Finally, he

343

seemed to find his voice. "Pwease understand, Sir Jeremy, this is not —"

"What the colonel is trying to say is, this is not the way he intended to have Black Ned brought to you," Lucien cut in. "He was going to have his soldiers bring Ned to you tomorrow with a procession through Kinsale. However, with the strife between England and her colonies, offending the Irish Catholics with this corpse through the streets would serve no logical purposes. A quiet announcement could be made in the morning, with mention of the colonel's dedication."

Sir Jeremy thought for a moment, then looked back at the bewildered officer. "This will probably mean a promotion for you, Bembridge."

At the mention of advancement, Percy's expression changed. "You are too kind, Sir Jeremy. I . . . I only did my duty."

"Of course, and most effectively," Lucien added, clapping the officer on the back. "And Ned was such a strong, cunning fellow, it took all your courage and strength to subdue him. I understand he didn't die right away but managed to find your small encampment on my lands. Hit your two guards on the head with the end of his pistol, I heard."

"Here now, what about that Irish couple blathering about the demon from hell?" the elderly magistrate asked.

Lucien laughed outright. "Sir Jeremy, you know how superstitious these Irish can be. Surely, you and Percy are not going to believe all that foolish gibberish about devils from Hades. Can you see the

344

English here and King George's reaction in London if you seriously considered such poppycock? Leprechauns and black-cloaked demons? Mind you, Sir Jeremy, I realize it is your decision if you wish to dismiss the physical evidence of Black Ned quite dead over there on that bench." Lucien stifled a grin as he watched Percy. Clearly, the Englishman was fighting a losing battle with his conscience. The duke was certain Percy would never pass up the chance for another promotion. And the last thing Bembridge would do was make himself a laughing-stock by telling everyone Black Ned was really a slip of a girl.

Finally, Sir Jeremy seemed to come to a decision. "Colonel, I misjudged you when you went on about losing Ned. My advice is to forget that silly business about black-caped ghosts. Probably been working too hard. Know I'm partly to blame. Pressed you too hard about catching the bandit. You've done well. Got all four of the blighters, so take a week or two off in London. I'll take care of the necessary paperwork here. I can almost promise you that promotion," he repeated.

Lucien congratulated Percy, then prepared to take his leave. "Both Mother and I feel dreadful that a trusted employee in our household could be such a traitor to our beloved England."

As he accompanied Lucien to the door, Sir Jeremy gave him a look of sympathy. "Now, Your Grace, you must not blame yourself. Everyone knows you and your lovely mother are loyal English subjects. That has made me even more determined to keep this whole business as quiet as possible.

We'll bury the four blackguards quietly. You leave it to me, eh, Bembridge?"

Percy stood at attention when he looked at Sir Jeremy.

"We've got four corpses," the magistrate stated, "proving to my satisfaction, only four existed— Black Ned and his three accomplices. It ends here, understand, Bembridge?"

"Yes, sir," answered the colonel.

"I knew I could count on you and the colonel for assistance," Lucien said, his face a mask of serious appreciation.

After leaving the magistrate's office, Lucien raced back to the cabin to get his wife. As he hustled Rosaleen into a dress he'd brought with him, he told her what had occurred.

Fully intending to light into the duke for leaving her behind, Ross felt too relieved he was safe to berate him. She marveled at his cool audacity. "And they truly believe Sean Kelly was Black Ned?"

"Indeed they do. Be thankful Percy's ambitions and pride outweigh his need to tell the truth."

As Rosaleen mounted the horse Lucien brought back for her, she could not help looking across as he swung up on Jasper's back. "Lucien, I am truly grateful for all you have done for me. You humble me with your courage and regard. Had you been harmed tonight, I would never forgive myself."

The blond-haired man moved his horse closer to her smaller mare. "You know, wife, if I did not have to get you back up to that cursed room at Fitzroy Hall before daylight, I would take full advantage of this situation, vow or not, and make love to you until you did swoon." Leaning to the right, he was pleased when she met him halfway. Their kiss was full of promise and love.

When he pulled away, Rosaleen looked back at him, for the first time letting him see the depth of her feelings. "I was so wrong to think all Englishmen were untrustworthy. You should have a better behaved wife, someone who will not lose her temper, or get into such horrible scrapes. Lucien, I do not deserve you."

Amusement etched across his face. "How true, but then I cannot imagine my future with anyone else. You are a hellion, Rosaleen Huntington, but I happen to like hellions."

"I . . . I love you, Lucien. No matter what happens now, I wanted you to know that."

"I suspected you might love me, sweet elf."

"But how could you?" she asked. "At practically every opportunity I told you I would never marry; I never knew myself until—"

"I suppose it's the calculating scientist in me," he teased, "but I looked at your actions, not your words. And the way you responded to me when I held you, or your kindness to the tenants, and your efforts to protect me even at your own expense. I hoped in time you would come to realize it, too. Only I never counted on that Black Ned business."

"You know, Your Grace, there is a bit of the scoundrel in you for all your gentlemanly ways."

"At times, Irish elf. At times." Then he nudged Jasper's sides.

Rosaleen followed. However, her smile faded when something occurred to her. "Your mother, darling. I will still have to face her."

The look he shot over his shoulder made her shiver. "No, I will deal with my mother."

"But Her Grace is still asleep," Louise hissed. "No, you cannot go in. She left specific orders not to be disturbed."

"Louise, you will kindly go to your own room, for I intend to speak to my mother alone right now."

At his authoritative tone, the small maid left.

Lucien entered his mother's sanctuary. He went about pulling back the drapes to let in the morning sun.

"What the devil—? Louise, I told you I—" Garnet sat up against the fluffy pillows when she saw the imposing figure near her bed. "Why, Lucien, how unexpected."

Hands at his waist, he looked down at her. Without the pounds of makeup, powdered wig, tightly laced corset, and diamonds, she appeared this morning more like an aging courtesan who was turning to fat. He wasted little time telling her what had occurred with Black Ned. Not giving her a chance for more interference, he kept his marital status with Rosaleen a secret.

Garnet clenched the white silk bed covers in her hands. When Lucien finished speaking, she gave him an unfriendly look. "So, your words in the carriage were just an act."

"Quite so, Mother, for you have taught me well how to give an effective performance. Be thankful

348

Ross wasn't harmed, or I would not be standing here talking with you in such a calm manner."

"I only sought to protect you. You have no idea how dangerous that O'Rahilly family can be."

"I only know first hand how scheming you are, Mother." His features remained impassive when she snatched a handkerchief to dab her eyes. "You will be well provided for, but I want you out of Ireland right after my wedding. That will keep the gossips satisfied that nothing amiss has occurred between us. You have the house in Paris, and I will see that you never want anything materially. But never, never do I want to see you again."

The picture of Calvert telling her he was divorcing her flashed across Garnet's mind. She could not believe the venom in Lucien's voice. All she had done was solely for her son, she told herself. "Lucien, please," she cried out as he turned to leave. "You cannot mean to shut me out this way? Lucien, you are all I have in the world! Lucien!"

Never looking back, the duke closed the door behind him.

Garnet punched the pillows with her fists, then let out a string of colorful phrases. Reaching for a cobalt-blue and gold cupid on her night table, she hurled it across the room. The porcelain crashed into tiny pieces against the white door of her room.

For the first time since her true love was killed, authentic tears of rage and despair formed in Garnet's eyes. It was all because of those damned O'Rahillys, she told herself. Everything she had suffered was because of them. It had been so long since she'd given in to these feelings, she wasn't sure she could control them. Her face was wet with genuine tears. She reached under her pillow and took out the knife she always slept with. Turning the ruby and emerald dagger over in her hands, she felt close to using it. How would it feel to press the point into her creamy-white breast?

Then she caught herself. The thought of experiencing physical damage always frightened her; then there would be the mess. With the weapon in her hand, the duchess felt calmer. She caressed the hilt of the stiletto in her fingers, as though it were a talisman.

The movements quieted her frayed emotions. She must think. Calm, that was what she needed. Never did Garnet Somerset give up, she reminded herself. She was not some dotty crone to be pushed aside. Lucien was making the same mistake that old fool, Calvert, had done if he thought she'd go meekly to Paris forever. She didn't give a rat's ass what happened in Ireland. But she would not be tossed aside or allow her only son to wed an O'Rahilly.

An image washed across her mind. It cleansed away her brief consideration of self-destruction. She smiled. Swinging her legs over the side of the bed, she reached for her lacy dressing gown and embroidered slippers. She tied the white sash about her waist, then went over to her writing table and sat down.

Taking the quill pen in her hand, she prepared a letter to Lady Millicent Fitzroy. "My final card," she said aloud, then laughed, enjoying the sound as it reverberated about the room.

With Taggart and Lucien gone to Cork to meet Liam Collins's ship, Rosaleen and her mother worked in the attic room upstairs, which now served as a sewing room for the wedding preparations. Edna and the children were three flights down working on the food and entertainment plans.

Rosaleen helped thread another needle while her mother finished a white on white shamrock on the hem of Rosaleen's wedding gown.

"It will be good to see Liam again," Lady Millicent mused. "I think when our men come home tonight, Liam will shed more light on the duke's parentage. Father Michael was wise to write his brother."

"I do hope so, Mama, for Lucien is adamant about knowing the truth before we are married."

Continuing to concentrate on her stitches, Millicent remarked, "And with Black Ned deceased, Kinsale can now rest easier without that notorious highwayman cavorting our roads. I can well believe Sean Kelly was Black Ned."

Ross could rarely recall her mother speaking ill of anyone deceased. "But, Mama, I thought you hardly knew Sean."

The older woman looked up from her embroidery. "Sean Kelly and his brother, Patrick, were employed by my father to look after his stables after Taggart went to the colonies. When your father and I married, the Kellys delivered Nolan's forged notes to Fitzroy Hall. Unknown to us, John Nolan was paying them to spy on the happenings here. It al-

351

most ended our marriage that first year. After Taggart fired them, they went to work for the Nolans."

A sadness came over the auburn-haired woman. "And I am still convinced it was Sean and Patrick Kelly who waylaid me that night I was coming home from visiting the tenants. They tied me to a tree and would have . . . raped me had your father not come to my rescue. Your brother, Redmond, was not our first child. Only a few months' pregnant, I lost our first babe from that horrible night. Your father would have killed the Kelly brothers had not Sir Jeremy been prudent enough to have them quickly imprisoned away from Kinsale."

"Mother, I . . . I never knew." Rosaleen reached out to touch her mother's cold fingers.

Millicent's expression relaxed. She patted her daughter's shoulder. "There was no point in telling you, to cause you pain. Bad things are best left in the past."

"But, Mama, why does Garnet still hate us?"

She gave her daughter a bemused look. "You have matured during these months in Kinsale. You are correct about Garnet's feelings for us. I shall tell you what I suspect. Garnet cared deeply for only one man that I know. But John Nolan was Irish and married to a wealthy Englishwoman. John loved money and power more than anything. He readily became Anglican, trying to blot out any connection to his Irish heritage. Nolan was probably flattered to have young Garnet's adoration. My father was deeply in debt to Nolan, and the squire hoped to control Fitzroy lands through my marriage to Garnet's brother, Edwin Somerset; but Taggart dashed that notion when he carried me off on my wedding day. Feeling cheated, Nolan tried every way in secret to ruin us, then later challenged your father to a duel. He lost, and Garnet has never forgiven Taggart for killing Nolan.

"Enter," Millicent called when there was a knock at the door.

Out of breath from the climb up three flights of stairs, a red-faced footman handed Millicent a note, then left.

"Oh, I hope this is from Virginia. Your brothers should be home from school by now." However, Millicent's expression lost all of its congeniality as she scanned the missive.

Alarmed by her mother's reaction, Rosaleen took the note from her white fingers.

"Oh," Millicent breathed, placing a hand to her heart. "Poor Fergus. We all thought it an accident. How could she have that old man murdered?"

"God, Mama, she writes Sean Kelly killed him." Ross finished reading the startling news of her mother's connection to Father Michael Collins and his brother. "Does father know you are part Irish?"

"Yes, I told him of my Irish heritage on our wedding night. But it was not until Liam was arrested unjustly for Calvert's death that I was forced to reveal the Collinses are my kinsmen. No one else knows, and it must remain so." She stood up and headed to the door.

Rosaleen placed the letter in the pocket of her apron and went to her mother. "Mama, where are you going?"

"I have to meet her as she orders. Garnet could

ruin Dunstan and all of us with this declaration. I know my brother. He would not shrink from the truth. All his lands and titles would be lost. I must speak to her, beg her not to do this wicked thing."

"Please, Mother, you cannot go." Rosaleen's dark eyes pleaded with her mother, for she was certain Millicent had no idea how treacherous Garnet could be.

The taller woman shook her head. "I must go, Ross. Perhaps I can persuade Garnet to spare us. She is only angry now because Lucien intends to marry you." Mrs. O'Rahilly did not mention she already knew Father Collins had wed the duke and her daughter.

Rosaleen forced a smile. "Perhaps you are right, Mama. You always see the good in everyone. At least help me put my dress back before you go."

"Yes, but then I must be off before the men return." She laughed nervously. "Men are so overly protective when we women need to see things through."

Rosaleen inched her mother toward the open closet where it was dry and warm, the best place to store the wooden form holding her wedding gown. With the vaulting motion of a skilled fencer, Rosaleen stepped back and shut Millicent in with the gown. She shoved the bolt across the door.

"Rosaleen!" Millicent shouted and began pounding on the door. "No, Rosaleen. Garnet will do as she threatened if her instructions are not carried out. I must meet with her. Ross, let me out!"

Rosaleen knew none of the servants would venture up here for at least a few hours, when Aunt

354

Edna noticed they did not come down for tea. It would give her the time she needed.

Garnet arrived at her chosen meeting place, pleased to find Lady Millicent already waiting for her. Lighted candles had been placed on either end of the rough wooden bar. The taller woman stood behind the bar, her face and slender form covered by the familiar red cape.

"Are you not suffocating in that hooded cloak, Millie?"

"I . . . I find it difficult to look you in the eye, Your Grace. This is a painful meeting for me."

The duchess sounded mildly sympathetic. "Vanquished after you took such care to keep your secret must be a blow." It was clear she intended to enjoy the moment to its fullest. "Fogarty's son is so accommodating. He did not even want to know why my maid wished the use of his closed pub on a Sunday evening. Probably thought she had a rendezvous with a groom, you having set the precedent by marrying your former head of stables. Of course, I suppose the coins I had Louise give him were more than enough to keep his curiosity to a minimum. Now, his father, old Fogarty, would never have been so amenable. Then, you and I have seen a lot of changes since the old days, have we not, Millie?"

"I beg of you, Your Grace, please tell me why you have sent for me."

"Still the same sweet manners," Garnet remarked, with a touch of amusement. "La, Millicent, you really should discard that ratty old cloak. Military capes are more in style with the ladies now, not that homespun red thing. Then, Millie dear, you were never one to follow fashion. I have always wondered why a fastidiously tailored man like Taggart ever looked twice at such a plain, bespectacled giant." The duchess smiled when she saw her old adversary's gloved fingers press harder on the rough wood of the bar.

"Your Grace, please get to the point."

Dressed in an aqua-blue riding skirt under a jacket of ivory linen, Garnet walked farther into the small pub. She turned her powdered head to the right. "I cannot understand why the rustics enjoy sitting in such a dingy room." She sniffed. "Filthy sty probably hasn't been cleaned since old Fogarty died."

"Your Grace, please," the cloaked figure interjected, as she leaned against the curved wood of the bar. The anguish was clear in her gentle speech. "My brother and his family will be ruined by this disclosure. It will also cause difficulties for your son, from the resultant scandal to his future bride."

"Ah, yes, you have hit the crux of the matter," Garnet pointed out. "You see, unless you convince your daughter to call off the wedding, I will make public the earl of Holingbrook's Irish Catholic lineage. He will lose everything. Your husband may also find it uncomfortable to explain his position to the King about his wife's deliberate ruse, parading herself as the late earl's totally English daughter when she knew it to be a lie."

"What makes you think Rosaleen will comply?"

Garnet made a disapproving sound. "That clever minx will see she has no choice. She posed as Black Ned easily enough."

"Oh, Your Grace, that is preposterous. All Kinsale knows the late Sean Kelly was Black Ned."

"Tripe. Copping a sheep was the extent of Kelly's abilities. You always love so blindly. Percy Bembridge and I know better, as does that besotted son of mine. If Rosaleen does not call off this wedding with my son, I shall make certain Percy goes back to Sir Jeremy with the truth that Black Ned is very much alive." Her look was smug. "And we both know Percy will do anything I ask."

"It is too late. Lucien would not be put off so easily."

"I have no doubt that black-eyed witch could humiliate Lucien with a grand performance of leaving him at the alter for some Irish tradesman's son. It is merely a question of whether you ask Rosaleen to do it. Of one thing I am certain. Your daughter, for all her headstrong ways, possesses an unwavering loyalty and protectiveness toward her family."

"Two virtues I see you were never burdened with" came the soft-spoken reply from the other side of the bar.

"My, you are showing an unusual display of spirit tonight." Under the guise of reaching into the slit at the side of her skirt, Garnet latched on to her jeweled dagger. All trace of equanimity departed. "Now, I will have your answer."

"My answer, Your Grace, is no. Further, tonight you will end your bent on revenge against my family. You have harmed us for the last time." Without hesitation, the woman took the pistol from the folds of her red cloak and pointed it at the duchess.

Garnet's unrestrained laughter echoed throughout the empty pub. "You homely twit. Did you think I'd forgotten? All Kinsale knows you never carry a loaded pistol. Fool," she scoffed, her slender finger encircling the handle of the knife. "Millicent, you were never a match for me, even when we were children." With practiced skill, Garnet quickly threw the jeweled stiletto at the tall figure.

Before the woman could jump out of harm's way, the lethal weapon plunged deep into her body, just below the left shoulder. The unexpected attack caused the woman's fingers to squeeze the trigger and the pistol fired at an angle.

Astonishment, then pain distorted Garnet's features. At first she could not believe the gun was loaded. Blood spewed from the wound at her breast, turning the ivory linen scarlet. She swayed then fell backward on the dirt floor of the Irish pub.

Rosaleen pushed back the red hood of her mother's cloak and jumped off the wooden crate she'd been standing on behind the bar. Gritting her teeth, she pulled the dagger from her flesh, trying to ignore the searing pain. Her cloak hid the beginning gush of blood that trickled across the front of her lilac gown. She tossed the knife to the floor, then walked over to stand above the prone figure of the duchess.

"You!" Garnet accused, recognizing the cold determination in the girl's dark eyes.

"My mother and I have the same voice, but I had

358

o find a way to disguise my shorter stature. You
are right, Your Grace," Rosaleen added without
emotion. "My mother is no match for you, but I
am, for I am also O'Rahilly's daughter."

"Bitch," the duchess tossed at the girl.

"My sentiments exactly," Rosaleen countered, as
she stared down at her vanquished enemy.

"No matter what. . . ." Garnet had to stop to
catch her breath. "No matter what I did, I am still
his mother. Lucien will never marry you now."

Rosaleen did not flinch. "I weighed the cost and
made my decision when I armed my pistol with ball
and powder tonight." It took all her effort to keep
the real anguish from her voice at the realization
Lucien was now lost to her forever.

"Rosaleen! Let us in. For God's sake open the
door!"

Rosaleen recognized her mother's outcry. Then
Lucien and Taggart's command, followed by more
pounding. "It is over, Garnet."

"You think so, do you?" Even in this state, the
fighting spirit was still with the duchess.

Using their shoulders, Lucien and Taggart, with
Liam behind, broke open the pub door.

Hiding her knife wound from the others, Rosaleen stepped out of the way into the shadows as Lucien and the others raced into the dimly lighted
tavern.

"I am fine," she lied, then clutched her mother's
red cloak about her. She pointed to Garnet on the
floor.

Lucien reached his mother first. He bent down
and took her upper body in his arms. "My God,"

he whispered. He saw the blood soaking the left side of her jacket. "Mother, I never wanted it to come to this," he said, a grim sadness engulfing him.

"I loved only two men in my life," she confessed. "I lost you both. Oh, I'm dying. Look at the mess that she-cat made of my silk blouse." The duchess recoiled in horror when Liam Collins came to kneel on the other side of her. "Get out. I don't want him here. Lucien, tell that Irishman to go away. A dying Englishwoman ought to be treated with more regard. I will not have any Irish vermin pawing at me."

"Garnet," Collins murmured softly, "please let me see if the ball lodged past your breast."

"No, you should never have come back here." She pulled away. "Lucien, don't let that man touch me."

Dr. Collins shook his head when Garnet slapped his hands away once more.

"All right, Mother. Dr. Collins will not see to you. However, you must allow me to arrange for someone skilled to tend to the wound. If the ball is in your lungs or heart—Mother, please let me help you."

"No, not yet. Not until I choose to go. I will rot right here on this dirt floor before I'll allow anyone to destroy all my efforts to protect us."

"Your Grace, I beg of you to tell your son his father's name."

"Go to hell," Garnet growled at the physician.

Dr. Collins focused his gray eyes on Lucien. "It was John Nolan's name your mother called out during her difficult labor, saying Nolan would never see his son."

"Damn you, shut up," Garnet cursed, then coughed, the effort to speak too much for her. She strangled for her next breath. "Lucien won't believe you," she added in a fevered voice. "Calvert was going to divorce me, so I poisoned him slowly with those mushrooms. I enjoyed telling that old goat just before he died that I had murdered him. Collins should have been hung for the murder; then the only other person who knew the truth would be dead. But that fool brother of mine had to ruin everything with his vicar's conscience."

Lady Millicent buried her face against her husband's coat at the woman's confession.

"Mother, how could you have let poor Nigel torture himself all these years, allowing him to believe he'd accidentally poisoned Calvert?"

"I had to protect your title as duke. I earned that money staying married to that wheezy old fool for years. I would not trust anyone finding out you were a bastard, son of an Irish squire. I had to protect our legacy. And now you want to throw it all away by marrying that Irish bitch. I'd rather see you dead."

Lucien felt sickened by the ugliness of it all.

Garnet fought to retain consciousness. "No," she growled, when Lucien tried to lift her, clearly intent on getting her back to Montrose Hall. "I'm not ready yet. I won't leave until it's finished." She clawed at the edge of Lucien's coat. "Promise me you will never marry Rosaleen. You owe me that. At least give me this one gift before I die. Yes, a dying woman's last request. A paltry thing, I know, but it would speed me to heaven with celestial choirs about me and—"

"Your Grace," Dr. Collins whispered, "since you are still with us, it is possible you will live, you know."

"Mind your own business," the duchess growled. "I know I'm dying. Look at the amount of blood that ruined my clothes. Probably isn't an ounce left in me. I feel quite faint as it is, so stop tormenting a defenseless woman." She turned back to Lucien, who still cradled her in his arms. "Please, you must promise me never to marry O'Rahilly's daughter."

Sadly, Lucien shook his head. "I love her, Mother. Father Michael Collins married us last week." His blue eyes filled with pity for this angry woman who had loved John Nolan and lost him.

Quietly, Rosaleen walked over to stand near them. She felt no anger toward this pathetic woman now. "Please, Your Grace, let us end this hatred between our families."

Lucien looked up sharply when blood spattered the back of his hand. In horror he took in the whiteness of Rosaleen's face, the wet, dark stain seeping through her cloak. Until now, no one realized she'd been wounded in this confrontation. "My God." Unable to desert his mother, the duke shouted, "Liam, see to Rosaleen; she is hurt!"

Instantly, the physician and Rosaleen's parents focused all their attentions on the wounded girl.

"Even if that priest did marry you, it does not matter," Garnet murmured, continuing to watch her son, who still held her upper body in his arms. The old Garnet returned. "I soaked the knife in poison.

362

Your bride is already dead." Her white-skinned throat curved to the right as she fell back in a faint, a serene smile of triumph on her rouged lips.

Lucien propped Garnet gently against the front of the wooden bar. A new horror gripped him, and he bounded to his feet and began a frantic search for the weapon his unconscious mother had used. He spotted the knife at the end of the bar. Bending down, he picked up the handle end with his pocket handkerchief. Suspicions engulfed him. "We have to get Rosaleen home immediately." He quickly told the others what Garnet had just confessed.

"Mother of God," Millicent cried, a frantic look at her daughter. "Taggart?"

"Easy now, sparrow. Lucien is right. We must get her home." Taggart looked over at the duke and Collins talking in low tones away from them.

Feeling strangely light-headed, Rosaleen could barely get her legs to move. Surely Lucien must hate her now, for she killed his mother. Yet, she admitted she would do it again to save her family. "You are free, Lucien," she said when he came closer to her. "English law will not recognize the marriage." She pushed his hand away when he reached out to steady her. "You are free," she mumbled again; then her legs went out from under her.

Lucien caught her before she fell to the floor.

Chapter Twenty

With all Garnet's complaints about her brother, Nigel's penchant to collect, catalog and study mushrooms, the woman had been shrewder than anyone suspected. Clearly, she had boiled down the poisonous mushrooms, then soaked the knife in the extracts.

Back at Fitzroy Hall, Lucien hovered over Rosaleen. A worried frown distorted his features. Taggart was trying to comfort his weeping wife. Millicent looked up to give Lucien a sad smile of understanding. He saw the doctor make ready to cauterize the still-bleeding wound.

Lucien removed his coat and prepared to assist Collins. "Perhaps it would be better, sir, if you took your wife downstairs," he suggested to Taggart.

Taggart saw the knife, thin animal intestine, and needle on the table and realized what needed to be done.

"Mr. O'Rahilly, if you agree," Lucien added, "it is my intent to stay here to look after Rosaleen throughout the night."

Taggart gave the Englishman a measured look, then nodded his approval. "Come, Millie, they will see to Ross. We are only in the way here. Lucien will call us if there is any change."

After they left, Lucien rolled up his sleeves, then scrubbed his hands with soap and water in a basin on a nearby table. He told the doctor what he surmised Garnet had used. "With such a small knife, it would not have the same effect as if Ross had ingested the poison over time as poor Calvert had."

Liam was bending over the fireplace, the edge of his knife in the flames. "But the poison has already entered her bloodstream. The point missed her heart, thank God; but it is a very deep gouge, and I cannot stop the bleeding. It will be close, Lucien."

"I know," said the duke, his face drawn with worry. "But she is a scrapper, Doctor. God help her, she is a scrapper."

"I dare not give her any more laudanum," Collins stated.

After cutting the material of the white nightgown away from her shoulder, Lucien sat next to her on the bed. Her eyes were closed, her breathing shallow. Her skin felt cold, and there was a grayness to her color. The Irishman stood next to him with the heated knife in his hand. Lucien placed his hands on either side of her arms to keep her from moving. He looked down at the deep cut on her shoulder and thought of this once soft, pale skin he'd adored with his lips. "All right. For God's sake do it quickly."

Liam placed the flat side of the knife against Rosaleen's skin. The searing sound and pungent odor of flesh burning assailed the two men.

Her scream tore at Lucien, but he held her still. He was almost undone by the look of shock, then betrayal as she stared up at him, as if he were the cause of this new torture.

"You . . . you hate me that much?" she asked, then fell back against the pillows.

"Thank God, she's fainted," Collins said, placing the knife in the earthenware jar of alcohol on the table set up with his wooden medical chest.

Lucien had a soothing poultice of healing herbs ready. With infinite care, he bandaged Rosaleen's shoulder, then pressed a cool cloth on her warm forehead. "When will we know?" he asked the doctor.

"I cannot tell for sure, but the next two days will give us our answer whether this small girl can fight the poison and loss of blood. You look exhausted, lad. Why not ask Taggart and the earl for a room down the hall?"

"No." Lucien's tone was adamant. "I will see to her tonight. She is my responsibility now."

Liam understood. He shoved down the sleeves of his shirt. "In truth, the ride from Cork wore me out." He tried to relieve some of the duke's anguish. "Imagine your mother's outrage when she comes to and her maid informs her old Dr. Murphy removed the ball in her breast? Good thing she had fainted. Murphy is a good physician, but he'd have little patience with Garnet's carrying on about 'Irish vermin' touching her."

"Then Garnet will recover?" Lucien doubted he could ever call her "Mother" again.

Liam began putting his medical supplies away. "She'll have an ugly scar on her left breast as a memento, but, yes, Lucien, she will live to create more trouble for us all here, I dare say."

"No, Liam, Garnet will not be back in Kinsale again," the duke stated. "As soon as she is well enough to travel, she will return to Paris."

The Irish physician read the cold determination in the younger man's face. "I'm getting too old for these intrigues. I will be next door if there is any change. All we can do is replace the bandages, hope no fever develops, and pray to God He spares this young woman's life."

A few hours later, Lucien was desolate to find Rosaleen covered with sweat. He sponged her fevered body throughout the night in an effort to lower her temperature. In her delirium, she kept mumbling things about the devil in a black cape.

"You cannot give up, Ross."

"Everything is lost," she sobbed.

"No, your family is safe," he whispered close to her ear, then wiped her forehead with the cool cloth once more.

"I'm a murderess. He's lost to me."

He did not understand most of her ravings. "Just rest."

Rosaleen felt so hot, yet her hands and feet were cold. Her shoulder burned and throbbed fearfully. "No, let me go."

"Shh, darling, you are safe. Just concentrate on getting well."

"I want to die," she cried, feeling her heart break over losing the duke.

"Stop that talk," Lucien ordered, for his sake as well as hers. "You have never run away from a battle in your life, Rosaleen. Don't be such a bloody little coward now."

Her glazed eyes opened, but she could not make out the angry man hovering over her. "I'm not a coward."

"Are you not? An Englishman is worth two of you any day. Faith, I believe you are turning out just like many of these Irish—quick to raise your fists but quicker still to turn and run when the odds stack against you."

Rosaleen attempted to sit up but found the effort too much. "Blast your eyes, take that back, English cur. Where's my sword? Someone hand me a sword!" she shouted.

Lucien could have hugged her close if he weren't afraid of causing more pain to her wounded shoulder. "Gently, virago." He eased her back against the pillows. "Rest now, there's my feisty little gypsy."

"Lucien?" she asked after a few moments. The tender, masculine voice was familiar. She tried to focus her gaze on the source of those words, but her lids felt too heavy.

It was afternoon of the following day before Rosaleen's eyes fluttered open without the fevered wildness. She felt too weak to speak, but she tried to make out the figure in the chair next to her bed. Clothes rumpled and stained, blond hair matted about his shoulders—never could she remember seeing the duke so unkempt. He seemed to stir from his uncomfortable sleep. When he peered at her, she noticed his eyes were puffy and bloodshot.

368

He touched her forehead; then a broad grin split his unshaven face. "The fever is broken." He quickly began loosening the clean bandage he'd changed a few hours earlier. "The bleeding has stopped, thank God."

"Oh, my. Stop that," Rosaleen protested, realizing he was in her room, and she was practically naked. "You will scandalize my relatives if you do not cease—"

"They already know Father Michael married us," he reminded her.

She tried to reach back into her fogged memory. "Before they go to bed, I must speak to Mama."

"Little one, you have been like this for a day and a half."

Lucien did appear as if he'd stayed with her the whole time. Automatically, she tried to get out of bed.

"Now, you just stay put." Gently but firmly, Lucien moved her back down. "Dr. Collins says you will be frail for at least another week. God, when I think I might have lost you, I—" He closed his eyes, realizing this was not the time for that discussion. He saw her squirm. "Here, I will help you. Do you need the chamber pot again?"

Again? She backed away from the hands that sought to assist her. A pink stain washed over her face. Suddenly, she was glad she did not remember all the details of the last day and a half. Still unaccustomed to his casual intimacy over such matters, she shook her head. "No, I am fine. Thank you." When he did not leave, she forced herself to meet his puzzled gaze. "Your Grace, I thank you for your care of me. However, I think I should tell you I meant what I said about your being free. It is best we leave things as they are."

He matched her cool formality. "Is that what you honestly wish, not to be my wife?"

She steeled her features, knowing it had to be this way. No matter how much he thought he loved her, time would never erase that she had murdered his mother. "Yes, it is what I wish. According to English law, there is no marriage. As an Anglican, you are not bound by that Catholic ceremony. I will deal with this in my own way."

"You do not love me, then?" Lucien studied her face but could only see the wall she'd erected between them.

It took her a moment to answer. "I thought I did, but it was more likely gratitude for rescuing me. What is more important, after what happened between your mother and me, I am quite certain if you and I stood before the vicar and married, eventually we would hate each other. It could never work, for there is too much bad blood between our families."

He felt heartsick, confused. He had tried wooing her, then cajoled her into marriage. All had failed? She did not love him. There seemed little else to say. "Then, I will send Liam to you. Good-bye, Ross." He headed to the door while he still had mastery of his aching heart.

"You are right, my boy, you must tell no one else about this, for both your and Rosaleen's sakes. Wretched business."

"Before coming to see you this morning, I sent a letter to Edwin," Lucien told the vicar. "He is in Naples with Rinaldo right now. I did not tell him what actually occurred, Uncle. After recovering from a sudden illness, I said, she was returning to Paris for her health."

"Quite right. Edwin always had a blind eye where Garnet was concerned. Suppose we all did." Sitting across from his nephew in his rectory office, the vicar stared down at the white tabs at his throat. "S-s-s-still can't believe she poisoned poor Calvert. I'll never understand how someone so beautiful could be s-s-so evil. Wicked woman," Nigel added, more pity than malice in his voice.

As Nigel walked Lucien out the door toward his waiting carriage, he took a deep breath, obviously attempting to shake off the morbid mood they both shared. "You know, I have been thinking about formally putting my sketches and notes on mushrooms in more order. Perhaps have them published."

He saw the light in his uncle's eyes, a spark that had not been there since first he thought he'd accidentally poisoned Calvert. The truth had transformed him. "That is a splendid idea," the duke agreed.

Nigel's full-bottomed wig moved as he turned to give his nephew a shrewd look. "She is a selfish, misguided woman, Lucien. I will not say I am sorry she has gone back to Paris for good, but we must learn to bury the past. You have a life ahead of you, too, you know."

Lucien could not tell his uncle the wedding was permanently off. Nigel seemed suddenly more full of life than he had been in years, and the duke could not mar his happiness today. "I would enjoy going out in the woods with you again to gather more mushroom samples for you, as I did in the old days."

"Nothing would please me more. Oh, and do give my best to Rosaleen. Tell her, though the wedding is delayed until after she is fully recovered, I shall look forward to performing the ceremony soon."

Lucien turned his face away for a moment. "Yes, of course."

During the next three weeks, Lucien stayed away from Fitzroy Hall as Rosaleen had requested. He spent his days working on his estate, seeing to his duties as the resident duke of Montrose. However, it was more a mechanical existence with no spirit, certainly no joy.

Early one morning, when he'd just sipped some tea and politely sent the cook's bountiful breakfast back to the kitchen, Brian Fogarty came to him.

"Pardon, Your Grace," the Irishman began, unusually formal, "there is a visitor to see you in the sitting room."

Was it Rosaleen? he wondered. Hope surged through him. He was out of his chair and racing toward the sitting room before Brian could say another word.

Opening the door, Lucien's smile vanished when he saw the man standing near the fireplace, his tricorn under his arm. "Mr. O'Rahilly. I trust your daughter is well?"

Taggart took a closer look at the young man. "The knife wound is healing right enough, but she is listless, eats little, sleeps poorly, and looks as bad as you do."

"Will you sit down? Perhaps some tea?" Lucien offered.

"Damnation, man, I don't want ta sit down, and I sure in hell didn't race over here ta sip tea." Irritation made Taggart's brogue thicker. "Rosaleen tells me she won't marry ya before the vicar and she's serious about ya bein' free from that ceremony before Father Mike. What I want ta know is, are ya goin' ta do anything about it?"

Lucien did not flinch from Taggart's challenge. "There is nothing more to be done. She does not love me. Indeed, the last few weeks have given me time to sort things out. I have begun to think she is right; there is too much bad blood between our families. You fought a duel and killed the man Mother loved, the man who was my father. Ross almost killed my mother—I know to protect her family, but there it is. How could we hope to build a proper marriage out of those ashes? Besides," he added, looking past the Irishman, "lately I have wondered if my blood may be tainted. From what I understand, the late squire, John Nolan, was a cold, ambitious man who did not shrink from murdering Lady Millicent's father, as well as arranging your own father's death by having him falsely accused of treason. My inherited blood does not make me the sort to welcome as a son-in-law."

Taggart let out a ragged breath. "I'll admit I wanted no part of ya at first. But then I started to

373

see how you helped your tenants, the patience you showed with my daughter, your caring ways. 'Tis the honor in ya that forced me ta see the truth. You've a chance ta do some good here."

"I am not Calvert's rightful heir," Lucien pointed out. "I am living a lie every time I place my seal on a document or when someone addresses me as 'Your Grace.' "

"Blarney. 'Tis what a man does with his life that counts, not the seed that started his growth in a woman's belly. You are Calvert's son, for it was that gentle old man who raised you, showed you how ta be a man of integrity."

Pain etched across Lucien's lean features. "It is because I honor Calvert's memory too much that I cannot steal what is not rightfully mine."

"I knew Calvert well. He loved you as only a father can love his son. He would want you ta be the next duke of Montrose, to help his tenants. Build something fine and lasting here in Ireland." Taggart's irritation rose as he watched the unyielding expression in the man before him. "Your mother wins even now if you let her. You are letting her win now with that stiff-rumped code of yours. Bend a little, Montrose. It is how we all survive the hard blows life deals us."

Hands clasped behind his burgundy coat, Lucien walked slowly over to the marble fireplace, pondering what Taggart had just told him. He tried to focus on what he felt, rather than viewing things through that logical slant.

When Taggart saw the tenseness leave Lucien's shoulders, he pressed his advantage. "Ross believes you hate her, for she keeps focusing on how close she came to killing your mother. She's talking about forming an underground group to see that money gets to the Irish who are secretly trying to overthrow English rule here. God's nightshirt, she goes from one scrape ta another. I can't handle her," Taggart admitted, running a flustered hand across his cheek.

Turning back, Lucien could not suppress a slight smile at the Irishman's words. He refrained from pointing out how Mr. O'Rahilly had indulged his rash daughter since childhood. Yet, a part of him did sympathize with her father. "Rosaleen does have a way of latching on to a cause."

"Sure and you speak the truth, Montrose. She's out right now riding with Henry Lorens. The earl is talking of marriage again. Says he'll have that Catholic service annulled by the Pope if he has to."

"By hell, she cannot marry Lorens. I am her husband, damn it!" A dormant spark suddenly ignited in the depths of Lucien's eyes. He walked over to a side table to compose himself for a second.

Taggart waited for him to speak, then grew more impatient when he did not seem in a hurry to go anywhere. Finally, he demanded, "Are you going ta just stand there philosophizing? By St. Patrick, have you no blood in your veins? Are you going to be that milksop she supposed when she first saw ya? Or are you the duke of Montrose? Sure and you probably don't deserve my daughter. That dunderheaded Henry will be just the sort of mouse she'll enjoy molding to her ways."

"It is a good thing you are my father-in-law or I

might bloody well punch you in the nose," the duke stated, only half in jest. "Where did you say Ross and Henry were riding?"

"Just past the grove of trees on Dunstan's lands." Taggart grinned. "Would you like me to come with you?"

"Thank you, no. I can handle Rosaleen myself."

Taggart heard the resolve in the duke's tone. "Yes, I believe you can, Montrose. My daughter will be lucky to have you as a husband. You know, I'm beginning to like you."

Lucien laughed outright. "My being half Irish probably pushed you over to my side, O'Rahilly." However, the duke was pleased by the Irishman's change of heart. His expression sobered for a second. "Thank you for coming here today, Taggart. I almost lost someone very dear to me."

After Lucien left, Taggart began whistling a Gaelic tune. He sauntered over to the side table and poured himself a generous glass of Lucien's brandy. The Irishman couldn't wait to see how Lucien fared when his firm proclamations on parenting collided with the reality of an adorable little girl with a mop of dark curls and impudent brown eyes. "To my first granddaughter," he toasted aloud, then took a sip of the amber liquor.

Rosaleen tried to keep her mind on what the earl of Dunsmore was saying. "Henry, could we not go faster? This pace is going to put me and Bradai to sleep."

Henry looked across indulgently at the small colonial dressed in a dark lilac riding outfit. "After that severe cold, I do not think you should take a fast canter. You might get too overheated."

"As you say, my lord." Though she liked Henry well enough and told him she would consider his marriage proposal, she had to admit staying a spinster appealed to her over a dull life with the earl.

The sound of a rider ahead made Rosaleen look up toward the hill. She felt something flutter inside at the sight of Lucien Huntington riding over the crest toward them. He was dressed in burgundy coat and breeches, pristine neckband, and high black riding boots. Why did he always have this power over her? She had to learn to look at him and not have her insides go to jelly or feel like bursting into tears because they could never be together. The healing wound at her shoulder began to throb once more, and she pressed her leather-gloved hand to it for a moment.

"Montrose," Henry greeted, then smiled. "Pru and I thought you were becoming a hermit sequestering yourself at the Hall. Worry over your dear mother, no doubt. They say in the village it was heart trouble."

"Yes," agreed the duke, a sudden coolness in his voice. "Mother has a bad heart."

"Well, we all adore the duchess and were relieved to learn that kind lady is well and back in her beloved France. Now you should cease fretting over her and return to your own life, too, old boy."

"Thank you, Henry. I agree. Today I thought I should get on with living." The blond-haired man focused his attention on Rosaleen. He was pleased to find her looking better, though he did not miss the faint shadows under her eyes. "It is good to see you again, Rosaleen."

So formal, she thought, her heart sinking. She forced the same politeness into her voice. "Your Grace." He looked splendid and healthy, a bit drawn in the face, but she could almost feel the strength of him. She would have to go back to Virginia with her parents, she told herself. Never could she remain in Ireland. Seeing him often, when she knew they could never be together, would be too painful.

"Henry," the duke requested, "would you mind if I have a few moments alone with Rosaleen? There are matters we need to discuss in private."

Henry looked at Rosaleen, clearly waiting for her to tell him what to do. "Well, I do not know. Ross?"

Warning lights went off, for Rosaleen read the determination in Lucien's casual request. "Stay right where you are, Henry. The duke is mistaken. We have nothing further to say to each other about anything."

Henry looked from Rosaleen's fiery expression to the duke's amused but suddenly menacing features. "You know, I really think you two might benefit from calmly sitting down to chat things out. I mean, Ross, you did run headlong into marrying him, even if it was only to a priest and does not count."

"It counts all right," Lucien snapped. "And the lady can vouch from our wedding night, she is not just my wife in name only."

Horrified dark eyes looked into arrogant blue ones. "How dare you imply such intimate matters in front of poor Henry."

"Imply?" Lucien repeated. "Damn me, I stated a fact. I might add, I would not change any of that passionate, wonderful night for anything, though you almost wore me out. You were warm and inquisitive, with all the fire a man could ever dream existed within one woman. No, I would never change anything about it, including," he added, deviltry in his eyes, "that bare-bottomed spanking you asked for to cap the evening off."

"Good God!" Henry blurted, appearing shocked. "I, ah. . . ." The earl gulped. Clearly uncomfortable, he looked back at Rosaleen. "It is evident my presence here is most awkward. Miss O'Rahilly, that is Rosaleen, I feel your nature . . . that is, your propensities are a bit too . . . too lively for my simpler tastes. Perhaps it would be best if you disregard what I spoke to you about yesterday. I . . . ahem." He doffed his hat to her. "I bid you good day." Then Henry turned his horse about and began charging away from the two of them.

When they were alone, Lucien allowed his humor to burst forth in a bellow of laughter. For the first time in weeks, he felt mirth envelop him.

"Oh, you unspeakable cad! Monster! Villain!" Rosaleen could hardly breathe she was so upset. "You deliberately painted such a lurid picture to Henry, I believe you scandalized him forever against females. How dare you distort everything to make it sound as if I—you know perfectly well I never asked you to . . . to strike me."

Enjoying himself, Lucien was not the least intimated by her temper. "You certainly did ask for that paddling when you punched me on the jaw for the third time. Actions, not words, are the measure of true feelings."

Her heart was broken and he dared make fun of her. Before tears stung her eyes, she pressed her knees against Bradai's flanks.

Rosaleen raced across the open meadow, trying to put as much distance between her and Lucien as possible. However, she could hear the pounding of Jasper's hooves just behind her. When she chanced a look over her shoulder, the dark-haired woman was amazed to see Lucien grinning, as if he was actually enjoying himself. What ever was the matter with him? she wondered. "Leave me alone, Lucifer. I told you, you're free."

Easily, Lucien brought Jasper up alongside her horse. He reached across and scooped Rosaleen up in his arms, placing her in front of him. "But I do not wish to be free, Rosaleen." Pulling back on the leather bands in his fingers, the duke slowed Jasper's pace. Bradai continued charging ahead toward the direction of the Fitzroy stables.

Rosaleen felt something lurch inside at the close proximity of Lucien's arms about her. Didn't he realize how painful it was for her to do the best for him, to leave Ireland? "Please, Your Grace, put me down."

His amusement changed to concern. "I am sorry, Ross. Did I hurt your shoulder?" He jumped down from Jasper and reached up to encircle her waist with his hands.

Worry etched across his handsome features as he lifted her carefully down to stand in front of him.

"No, you did not hurt my shoulder." When she saw his relief, she shook her head. "Lucien, I do not wish to see you again. I believe I made that clear weeks ago."

"It must be the Irish part of me," he said, reaching out for her, "but I find I do not believe you, nor am I prepared to let you go. I want you to be my wife, before a priest and an Anglican vicar."

"No," she said, trying to move away, but his gentle yet firm hands held her still. She looked up into the blue of his eyes, right now not able to ignore the longing and new resolve in his gaze. "But it is too late, Your Grace. We would only hurt each other in the end. What if I lost my temper with you? Words hurt worse than any blow. What if I said things about your mother, or you countered back that I'd . . . tried to kill her? The past could harm our marriage and hurt our children."

"Then, you do not love me?" he asked patiently. "The truth, sweet elf, no hedging this time, no excuses. Search inside and tell me what you feel."

The tenderness of his arms and his coaxing voice were her undoing. Tears misted her dark eyes as she looked away. "I do love you. That is why I must leave Ireland . . . and you."

"Why do you feel you must leave?"

Her tormented gaze met his. "Because I am afraid. So much has happened to drive a wedge between us, I fear our love is not strong enough to last. Would it be fair to burden our children with all the painful things that our families caused each other? Look how their past hurt us."

"Rosaleen, we must bury it and live our own lives now." He moved her slender body closer, encouraged when she did not pull away. "We have room for a few skeletons in our family closet."

"There is practically a regiment in there now. Yes, I can just hear us telling our curious children, 'Well, you see, your mother almost killed your grandmother with a pistol after Grandmama plunged a poisoned dagger in Mama's shoulder.' "

"I dare say we can find a more suitable way of telling them if they should ask later." He caressed her black curls with his fingers. Lowering his blond head, he kissed her cheek, then moved his lips near her ear. "I am not saying it will be easy, but I have learned to fight for what I want. You taught me that, sweet elf. Will you toss both our happiness away out of fear? Someone I am beginning to respect told me my mother wins even now if we let her." With maddening accuracy, the duke kissed her silken neck, then fondled the swell of her breasts through her riding jacket. "So desirable and warm," he murmured. His lips found hers in a long, searing kiss of passion and love.

Rosaleen felt sweetly vanquished as Lucien went on kissing her, molding her soft curves to the hardness of his body. She experienced that familiar fire in her blood. Catching herself, she pulled away before she lost complete control. "I . . . I do think it might be prudent to wait until Nigel marries us before we . . . continue this particular discussion."

The corners of his sensual mouth moved upward at her proper manner. "You know, Ross, I believe you are going to make a delightful duchess. However, I should not like you to change too much into a proper wife," he teased. "Gypsies do suit me."

She giggled at his outrageous remark. His boyish smile warmed her. "I have a distinct feeling, Lucifer, being married to you will never be dull, for lately you have begun to sound quite scandalous." The dimple at the corner of her mouth widened with mischief. "Of course, if I become bored, I can always take to the highways."

"I shall see that the children and I, along with our work to help our tenants, keep you too busy to think of ever resurrecting Black Ned's ghost. That, gypsy eyes, is a promise."

She was not intimidated by him this time. "Should we tell our children about Black Ned?"

"Only when they have grown children of their own," Lucifer replied, then took his impudent wife in his arms once more.

"I'll make two promises right now, *and I'll keep them both."*

When Kim tried to turn away, Jerry touched her chin, urging her to look at him fully. "First, I promise you that I am not your ex-fiancé, nor will I ever hurt you the way he did. My second promise..." he drew in a lungful of air "...is to watch over you and protect you. I will do whatever it takes to keep you safe."

Kim suddenly wanted to lighten the mood. "That's what guardian angels are for," she joked, fingering the gold pin on her blouse.

"That's exactly it!" he insisted proudly. "I'm your guardian angel." And before she could protest he pulled her into his arms.

Dear Reader,

Remember the magic of the film *It's a Wonderful Life*? The warmth and tender emotion of *Truly, Madly, Deeply*? The feel-good humor of *Heaven Can Wait*?

Well, we can't promise you Alan Rickman or Warren Beatty, but, starting in June in Harlequin Romance®, we are delighted to bring you a brand-new miniseries: **GUARDIAN ANGELS.** It will feature all of your favorite ingredients for a perfect novel: great heroes, feisty heroines, breathtaking romance, all with a celestial spin. Written by four of our star authors, this witty and wonderful series will feature four real-life angels—all of whom are perfect advertisements for heaven!

We'll be bringing you one **GUARDIAN ANGELS** romance every other month.

Titles in this series are:

June: THE BOSS, THE BABY AND THE BRIDE by Day Leclaire
August: HEAVENLY HUSBAND by Carolyn Greene
October: A GROOM FOR GWEN by Jeanne Allan
December: GABRIEL'S MISSION by Margaret Way

Have a heavenly read!

The Editors

Falling in love sometimes needs a little help from above!

GUARDIAN ANGELS
Carolyn Greene
Heavenly Husband

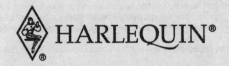

HARLEQUIN®

TORONTO • NEW YORK • LONDON
AMSTERDAM • PARIS • SYDNEY • HAMBURG
STOCKHOLM • ATHENS • TOKYO • MILAN • MADRID
PRAGUE • WARSAW • BUDAPEST • AUCKLAND

With many thanks to Kim Barnes for inspiring
me to write this book

ISBN 0-373-03516-0

HEAVENLY HUSBAND

First North American Publication 1998.

PROLOGUE

KIM had always imagined that when you broke up with someone there would be screaming involved…from at least one of the two parties. And maybe some china thrown for dramatic effect.

The real thing turned out to be nothing like that. Somehow, she just couldn't dredge up the energy to raise her voice. She felt dead inside, as dead as the love she'd once had for Gerald Kirkland. As for the china, she liked the blue-and-white pattern of the set that had once been her mother's—the set her father had given her in anticipation of her upcoming marriage to Gerald. The delicate pieces were too precious to be wasted on the likes of him.

As for her fiancé—*former* fiancé—he was taking the news in a manner that suggested she'd just told him there was a power failure and they'd have to eat out tonight.

Kim moved to the door and held it open for him. "If you've forgotten anything, I'll pack it up and send it to your apartment." The thought flitted through her mind that she could burn anything he left behind or get rid of it in a garage sale, but, for now, she hurt too much to let her thoughts linger on revenge. All she wanted was to get him out of here—out of her house, out of her life, out of her mind, and mostly out of her heart.

Gerald bent to pick up his briefcase, the movement causing his biceps to bunch under the starched white shirt. Then, in a gesture that came more from habit than from intent, he leaned toward Kim as if to drop a casual kiss on her cheek. When she drew back, he seemed to realize the foolishness of his action.

"This is a big mistake," he said. "You're jumping to conclusions. Why don't you be reasonable and forget about what you saw? Then everything will be the way it used to be."

He flashed her a smile that, just a few days ago, would have made her weak in the knees.

Kim's hand tightened around the doorknob. She considered herself a tolerant person. There was a lot she'd tolerate in others, but laziness and lying were two character traits she considered unforgivable. Not that there was a problem with Gerald's work habits. In fact, other than the way his custom-tailored suit fit—from his broad shoulders to his narrow waist and hips and down over his thick-muscled thighs—his ambition was what appealed most to her. She'd never known a man so willing to work so hard to get ahead. He had lofty dreams and expensive tastes, and he was prepared to do whatever it took to get what he wanted.

But the lying. That was another matter.

She'd had vague suspicions about what he'd been up to when he broke dates with her and claimed to be working late. Even so, she'd given him the benefit of the doubt when he did show up—late—smelling of a citrusy feminine perfume. Even yesterday, after Gerald had told her he'd be working straight through lunch, she had wanted to believe him. When she drove to pick up a sub sandwich a few blocks away, she'd been surprised to see Gerald's Lincoln a few cars ahead of her. She was even more surprised to see a woman seated beside him. Although the hat that shielded the passenger's face prevented Kim from identifying her, something about the woman seemed familiar. She reasoned Gerald had changed his mind and decided to take a co-worker after he couldn't reach her at her desk. Assuming he was also headed to the sub shop, Kim followed him, intending to join them for lunch. When he passed the popular meeting place, she continued to follow him, thinking he'd stop for a burger farther down the road.

Instead, he'd pulled into the parking lot of a small motel. Staying a discreet distance behind them, Kim had watched in horrified disbelief as the couple walked, arm around waist, into the building.

Now, leaning against the door—more to prop herself up than to prop it open—Kim looked up and saw that Gerald was waiting for her to "be reasonable" and make everything "the way it used to be."

She tried to take a deep breath of air, but her chest felt so tight that all she could manage were shallow pants. "All right," she said at last, her voice coming out in a pitiful squeak. "I'll be 'reasonable'." Searching his face, knowing the expression she saw there would be more honest than the words that would come out of his handsome mouth, she spoke slowly and deliberately. "Tell me truthfully why you and that woman were at the Kelawnee Motel."

His gaze darted briefly away before he met her eyes and held them. "I told you, we had some business to discuss, and we didn't want to be disturbed."

His large fingers opened and closed around the briefcase handle. When she took notice of the nervous gesture, he squeezed the handle until his knuckles turned white.

Her voice sounded flat, even to her own ears, giving the impression that there was no knot in her throat, no crushing tightness at the pit of her very being. "Then why did you sign in as Mr. and Mrs. Gerald Kirkland?"

She hadn't intended to let him know she'd stooped so low as to follow them inside. She hadn't wanted him to know she cared. For, if he knew how much she cared, he must surely know how much she was hurting. And her pride couldn't take it if pity prompted him to apologize or, worse, tell her he loved her.

He wouldn't meet her gaze...just kept glancing at his car in the driveway. By now he'd moved out onto the gray-painted slabs of the old farmhouse's broad front porch. He shifted the briefcase to his other hand and opened his mouth to speak.

Kim shook her head. She couldn't bear to hear any more lies.

Resolutely, he closed his mouth and gave her a grim-lipped nod.

"Drive carefully," she said. As she watched his car pull away for the last time, she realized how stupid that must have sounded. For, in her heart, she hoped she never saw him again.

Less than an hour later, the telephone rang. Thinking it might be Gerald trying to change her mind, she let her answering machine take the call.

After the beep, there was a slight hesitation before a woman's voice spoke.

"This is the emergency room at Memorial General Hospital. I'm calling about—"

Kim snatched the phone out of the cradle. "Yes. Yes, I'm here." She felt her heart pounding against her ribs. Her father's health had seemed better since his last operation. She dreaded hearing what must surely be bad news. Even worse, she couldn't bear to be away from her father if he was having a relapse. "What's the matter? Is he all right?"

The woman didn't answer her panicked questions, and Kim assumed the worst. "Are you Ms. Barnett?"

"Yes," she blurted. "Yes, I am."

"You're listed as the person to contact in case of an emergency."

"What's wrong? Is he badly off?"

The woman's voice softened. "You'd best come in, Ms. Barnett. He's not expected to make it through the night."

Kim felt her mouth go dry. She held the phone in stunned silence for several seconds before she spoke in a hoarse croak. "Was it his heart again?"

"I'm not aware of a heart problem," the woman said gently. "Mr. Kirkland was injured in a three-car accident."

CHAPTER ONE

TAKING a surreptitious glance at his fellow fenuki players, Jared reached into the billowing sleeve of his pristine white robe and withdrew a perfect gilded feather. Confident no one had witnessed his deft maneuver, he placed the coveted game piece on the table atop the plain white plumes placed by the other two players.

"Fenuki!" he shouted, proclaiming himself winner for the umpteenth time this century. Jared felt his halo slip to the left as if to herald to the others that this game—like many of the others—had come to him by sleight of hand.

As he counted his winnings, Mehrdad reached across and placed a quelling hand on his arm. Although his tone was gentle, his voice held a warning. "If Nahum thought that any of his staff wasn't one hundred percent virtuous, it would be quite difficult for that staff member to earn his wings, don't you think?"

Heedless of the implied threat, Jared laughed. "Would it matter? I now have almost enough fenuki feathers to make my own wings."

Mehrdad bristled and rose to his feet. The tension caused light to crackle through the air. *Heat lightning,* the humans down below would call it.

But before Mehrdad could argue further, the wispy covering of fog swirled about them. A moment later, the thin veils of white parted and settled around their knees and ankles. Asim stood before them.

"Nahum wishes to see you," the messenger told Jared. At his questioning glance, Asim added, "It is time for your performance appraisal."

With a taunting grin at his fenuki opponent, Jared tucked the last of the feathers into his robe pockets and rose to follow Asim to the supervisor.

After all these centuries, he knew it would take more than luck to improve his abysmal performance record. Maybe he just wasn't cut out for this kind of work. Workers in the Human Resources Department were expected to be reliable, dependable, and have an intimate understanding of the most fickle and confusing of all creatures…humans. As it happened, Jared possessed none of these qualities. Especially the last.

Nahum sat in beatific splendor upon his chair of gold-painted wicker. Jared knew it wouldn't be long before his supervisor would be trading in that humble chair for a throne in another department. Already, Nahum had moved up the ranks of wing size until he now sported a pair that was taller and wider than himself.

Jared would have been happy with a pair of dinky baby wings made of gray down. Considering his own track record, it would take him at least several millennia, if ever, to earn such a glorious pair as Nahum's. Jared tried to still his wayward thoughts. Wing envy was frowned upon up here.

But he had broad, strong shoulders that Nahum had told him gave him the potential to carry the weight of large wings. Although his supervisor had routinely given him low, yet honest, appraisals, he'd always encouraged

Jared to put aside his playful ways and set his mind to the tasks he was asked to perform.

But, somehow, Jared's attention would stray and he'd fail the assignment or have to turn it over to a worker with a better track record.

But this time was different. This time, he would do whatever Nahum asked, even if it meant safeguarding an accident-prone human. Jared grimaced as he remembered the last klutz he'd been assigned to watch over. After one too many mishaps while he'd let his mind wander, he'd been forced to let Mehrdad assume the responsibility of protecting President Ford.

Nahum nodded benevolently, his gaze falling upon Jared's bulging pockets. "When your time comes to meet with the Chairman of the Board, I doubt he'll think much of wings made out of fenuki feathers," he said softly.

Sheepish, Jared stuffed the telltale overflowing fluff back into his pockets.

"I've been going over your personnel file." The left-hand side of the folder held page after page of not-so-glowing reports. The right-hand side, reserved for commendations and accolades, sported only two thin sheets of parchment. "In addition to your lack of…shall we say, finesse…as a protectorate, there seems to be a couple of other problems holding you back."

Jared couldn't help being amazed by Nahum's statement. Only a *couple* of problems? He waited in respectful silence for his superior to continue.

"The first is your cavalier attitude. You take everything so lightly, as if this were all just a big game. This isn't the place for someone who chooses to act like such a...a..."

"Free spirit?"

"Exactly. We're a team here. You must learn to work *with* others."

"I'll try to do better."

Nahum crossed his arms over his chest, exposing the many rows of gold trim that weighted his sleeves. "You can start by referring to Mehrdad by his appointed name rather than 'Mehrdy'."

So his fenuki opponent had apparently been complaining.

"And it would be best if you discourage others from referring to you by a nickname. 'Jerry' sounds a bit too modern and casual for the serious nature of our work."

Jared reverently bowed his head. "Thy will be done. And the other problem?"

Casting a skeptical glance at him for his easy acquiescence, Nahum opened another folder and produced a sheet of lined parchment, which he handed to Jared. "Apparently, there has been an oversight. Your training is incomplete."

Glancing through the list at the many workshops and seminars written in elegant script, Jared was sure his elder had made a mistake. "But I've taken all the courses offered, and I passed them with flying colors."

"You haven't served your apprenticeship on Earth," Nahum explained. "You need hands-on experience before you can move on to the next level of protectorate."

Jared returned the parchment to his superior. "I've walked among humans—I've seen how they are."

"But you've never *been* one. In all your previous assignments, you've remained invisible to your protectees, which means you've never had to learn to interact with them—communicate on their level.''

Jared started to interrupt and explain that he had spoken to his human charges on a number of occasions when he'd whispered warnings to them, but Nahum stilled his protest with an upraised hand.

"It is impossible to truly comprehend them until you've experienced their challenges and limitations—such as their inability to become invisible or to transmogrify themselves through earthly barriers. But you will see what I mean once you take human form.''

"Oh, no, you don't! You're not going to send me down there to go through the poopy diaper stage and have parents who tell me what to do all the time. You know I don't handle restrictions on my freedom very well.''

"Which may have been why you were overlooked for apprenticeship all this time. There were no parents who deserved such a test.'' Nahum leaned back in his chair, the winged back obscuring his face from all but the one directly in front of him, and thoughtfully stroked his long brown beard. "There is an assignment I'd like for you to handle.''

Jared breathed a long sigh of relief, then regretted his action when he realized the disorder it might cause in the form of hurricanes and twisters down below. If Nahum was giving him an assignment, it meant he wouldn't be forcing him to go through the childbirth process and schooling and such.

"There is a young woman who needs your protection.''

Jared arched one eyebrow. He'd do his best, but if she was clumsy, she'd best stock up on bandages and ice packs. "Give me five minutes to put on a fresh robe, and I'll be ready."

"You won't be needing it," Nahum said. "You'll be working as a protectorate while also serving your apprenticeship in human form."

Jared's mouth opened. He wasn't being let off the hook after all. "How am I supposed to protect someone while I'm squalling for a baby bottle?"

Nahum steadied a look of infinite patience upon him before answering. "There is a soul whose hourglass is almost empty. You will inhabit his vessel when he leaves it."

Jared rubbed his ears as if he might have misheard his supervisor's words. "You mean...no spitting up and no fighting schoolyard bullies?"

"You will be a thirty-two-year-old male, living in Chesden, Illinois. That's the United States, of course." The supervisor added, almost as an afterthought, "Perhaps the only country that would put up with your unorthodox ways."

"What about the woman? How am I supposed to protect her?" If he went into this assignment with a firm idea of what to expect, perhaps he could be better prepared.

Nahum closed the folder in front of him. "I don't have all the details. You'll have to find them out once you get there. But I do know that the woman is in danger of leaving her earthly body approximately fifty or sixty years sooner than her scheduled departure. Your job is to make sure she comes to no harm."

Jared shook his head in amazement. "Only fifty years? What's the big to-do about? In the overall scheme of things, fifty years is just a blink of an eye."

Nahum gazed down at the worker before him. He'd grown accustomed to the oversize wings he wore, not to mention the golden braids on his sleeves that signified his exalted status. He was also counting on moving up to that big throne on the next level up. If this mission failed, he could be stripped of his hard-earned rank quicker than a thunderstorm in July.

On the other hand, if Jared could somehow manage to harness that creativity and energy of his, he—Nahum—might find the rewards well worth the risk.

"I believe your experience on Earth will change your mind about many such misconceptions."

By the time Kim reached the hospital's emergency room, Gerald's condition had worsened. Her mouth unaccountably dry, she stopped at the water fountain near the ER receptionist. The water tasted stale and lukewarm, but the hesitation had allowed Kim a brief moment to gather herself together. For some reason, her thoughts kept returning to the feeling she'd harbored as she had watched Gerald drive away: She'd hoped she would never see him again.

Guilt plucked at her heart. What he'd done was despicable, but no one deserved this.

In the emergency room, Kim passed several curtained cubicles, some of which stood empty. One revealed a mother standing beside a bed whose occupant must have been no more than two years old.

Walking faster, she came to the nurses' station where

the hall broke off into more passageways with still more curtained cubicles. She paused, unsure which curtain Gerald was behind.

A bespectacled nurse glanced up from the rack of charts she'd been looking through. "May I help you, miss?"

"I'm looking for Gerald Kirkland."

"You his wife, honey?"

Kim paused. Would she be allowed to see Gerald if she didn't have some sort of family tie to him? "Um, fiancée." It was only half a lie.

"Well, come on, then," the nurse said, stepping out from the station. "They're prepping him for surgery. Maybe you can see him for a moment before they take him in."

Gerald looked almost as pale as the bleached white sheet beneath him. Two plastic bags hung suspended above him, one dripping clear fluid into his veins and the other replacing the blood he'd lost. An airway tube made a hissing sound as it pumped oxygen into his lungs.

Kim caught her breath at the sight of him. Only when she began to feel slightly faint did she make a conscious effort to breathe normally. It wouldn't do him any good if she flaked out now.

"You okay, honey?" the nurse asked her.

Kim nodded. Another half lie.

She stepped closer, trying to ignore the various tubes and wires attached to Gerald's body. His was a large, strong frame accustomed to vigorous activity. His body was the first thing she'd noticed about him. The reason she'd first been attracted to him. And perhaps the reason that other woman had been attracted to him.

She tried not to think of that now. Instead, she concentrated her effort on offering emotional support. She took his hand in hers and gently squeezed his fingers. He did not squeeze back, and Kim began to realize with a horrified understanding that there was nothing she could do to help him. Her eyes filled with tears that spilled onto his hand.

"He's not able to respond," said a man in scrubs, "but it's possible he can hear you. It might help if you tell him how you feel about him."

Tell him how she felt about him? As in, I don't love you anymore, but I don't want you to die, either? No, she couldn't be so cruel.

When at last she spoke, her voice cracked. "Hang in there." She squeezed his fingers again, as if the gesture would impart all the sincerity she was unable to put into words.

Blip, blip, blip. The only response she got was the unsteady beep of the heart monitor. Another man in green scrubs entered the tiny cubicle, and a woman in white followed.

Releasing his hand, she stepped away from the gurney and started out the way she'd come. She went out into the tiled corridor, determined to wait on the hard bench until the surgery was over.

Amid the murmuring of voices, the blips wavered briefly, then fell into one long, flat beep. Kim had seen enough television to know this was not a good sign. Activity in the room increased, and she rushed to pull the curtain open. For several moments, she watched in horrified fascination, wishing there was something she could do to help and knowing she was powerless to stop the current course of events.

Kim had no idea how long she stood there, watching without seeing, as the medical team struggled to bring Gerald back from the brink.

Finally, one of the men stepped away and began removing his gloves. "We've lost him."

Please don't let him die!

The man stopped what he was doing and looked up at Kim. Until then, she hadn't realized she'd prayed out loud.

"Get her out of here," he demanded.

The woman in white came to her and took her arm to guide her out, but not before Kim saw them raise the sheet over Gerald's face.

Exhausted, she allowed herself to be led to the bench across the hall. The woman with her was uttering words of comfort, but Kim didn't hear them. Her ears were tuned to the room where Gerald's body lay.

When the woman suggested she call someone to drive her home, Kim realized she hadn't told her father or stepmother before rushing over to be with Gerald. She dug some coins out of her purse and rose from the bench.

Someone behind the closed curtain asked, "Did he just move? I could have sworn I saw that sheet move."

As if to confirm the statement, the monitor once again began blipping, this time stronger and steadier than before.

The woman in white ran back to Gerald's cubicle. Kim's legs felt powerless to support her, and she sank back onto the bench.

"Let me see," came the voice of the man who'd ordered her out.

A moment later, the blipping of the monitor became more rhythmic.

A woman's voice spoke in quiet awe. "It's a miracle."

Jared became aware of the sounds around him first. The noise was loud and cacophonous, unlike the soft, melodious sounds he'd become used to "on high." First he heard a deep male voice asking if he had a problem with hemorrhoids. Then a click and a woman complaining about tough, grimy stains. Another click and the sound of something hitting against a hard object, followed by uproarious laughter.

With effort, Jared opened his eyes, squinting against the harsh light that came from two long cylindrical strips in the ceiling. Laughter rang out again, and he turned his head to the source, a large box projecting from the wall, with images of miniature humans showing inside it. He'd heard that the Chairman of the Board had such a box, to watch the activities of those below, but something told him this wasn't the Big Guy's office. Something rustled beside him, and he turned toward it.

A lovely creature sat in a chair near him and pressed a button on a small black box every so often. Each time she did so, the noise and pictures emanating from the box on the wall abruptly changed.

A vision of femininity, she was so beautiful he didn't think she could possibly be human. But she wore no wings, and instead of the traditional white robe, she was garbed in two layers of loose-fitting upper clothing, neither of which had sleeves. Her lower limbs sported two dark blue casings that appeared to be held on the wearer by a series of buttons below her waist. And her feet were encased in a soft-looking white material. Like the sandals he was accustomed to, these were also tied, but instead of leather thongs, they were held together by white strips of fabric with clear, hard tips on the ends. Printed on the flap that protruded from the top of the foot covering was the word "Adidas."

His gaze was drawn upward to her face. The eyes, cinnamon brown framed by lashes of black, were trained upon the box on the wall. Her features were of a pleasing proportion, and the dark brows and sun-darkened complexion complemented the burnished brown locks that surrounded her face.

Jared felt a strange sensation in the pit of his being. She was more beautiful than any angel he'd ever seen.

His thoughts returned to the name printed on her foot covering. Adidas. He was familiar with Adonis, the Greek god, and had even beaten him at a hand of fenuki. Could this, perhaps, be a beautiful goddess, maybe even a heretofore unknown relation of her handsome male counterpart?

She turned in her chair and became aware of his steady perusal. "Oh, you're awake." Her eyes were filled with compassion and pity. But something else lurked there, as well. A wariness emanated from her, making her appear torn inside. "Maybe I should call the nurse."

"What are you doing here?"

She leaned forward and touched his arm, which was covered by a clean white blanket. "We almost lost you.

No matter what our differences, I couldn't leave you here alone, Gerald.''

"My name is Jared," he corrected her.

She tilted her head slightly and gave him a small frown. "Do you know my name?"

How could he *not* know it when it was emblazoned on her garments? "Of course."

The goddess appeared relieved for a spare moment, then leaned closer. "Tell me who I am."

Jared didn't know what sport she found in this game, but he decided to humor her. "You're Adidas."

His response appeared not to satisfy her. If she'd tell him the rules of the game, perhaps he'd be a more worthy opponent. Nothing seemed to make sense to him right now.

With a clatter to announce her entrance, a young woman entered the room pushing a cart laden with trays. "So, Sleeping Beauty finally decided to wake up, eh?" She positioned a narrow, wheeled table so that it reached across the bed where he lay, then placed one of the trays on top of it.

Jared didn't know what he'd done to earn such treatment. Here he was, lying upon a chaise of white, with a nubile young goddess beside him and a servant woman to feed him. But he didn't understand why there were no palm fronds to shade him from the harsh light and no clusters of grapes to be fed to him one by one. He would have to speak to Nahum and find out what was going on.

"Here's your lunch, honey." Turning to Adidas, she added, "I'll tell the nurse that he's come around."

Adidas thanked the servant woman and moved her chair closer to Jared's chaise. "Are you hungry?"

Was he hungry? He'd never experienced such a need in all his existence. Only humans wanted for physical sustenance.

Then realization dawned. He was now a human serving his earthly apprenticeship. He looked around him at his stark surroundings, taking in the painting that tried desperately to cheer up a wall filled with hoses and silver-colored fixtures. Taking in the clear, fluid-filled bag that hung over his bed—not his chaise—and that dripped liquid into a tube that disappeared under the blanket near his arm. Finally, his gaze fell on the goddess beside him. Could she be a mere human? If so, he wondered why he'd been so reluctant to complete this portion of his training.

She watched him expectantly, and he remembered she was waiting for his response.

"I don't know," he admitted.

She picked up a cream-colored box beside his pillow and pressed a button. The bed vibrated and moved upward until he was in a near sitting position. Then she took the cover off his tray of food. "Mmm, vegetable soup. Why don't you try to eat a little, even if you're not hungry? It'll help you get your strength back."

Jared tried to lift his arm to pick up the spoon, but the appendage was much heavier than he'd anticipated. And when he put more energy into his effort, his arm jerked upward and flopped heavily against the tray, spattering orange soup on the white blanket.

"It's okay," said Adidas. "I'll feed you." She turned her chair until she faced him and dipped the spoon into the soup. Scraping the bottom of the spoon against the bowl, she lifted it to his mouth.

Jared wasn't sure how to do this. He watched her as she opened her mouth slightly when the spoon approached his face. Copying her action, he parted his lips. Warm liquid and lumps of vegetables touched his tongue, and he found the sensation quite pleasing. Adidas withdrew the spoon, and the liquid dribbled out of his mouth and down his chin.

He sat open-mouthed as most of the soup made a drool path down to his neck.

"It's okay. I'll get it." The auburn-haired woman dabbed at his chin and neck until it was once again dry. "Maybe this time we should use a bib."

As she tucked a paper napkin under his chin, a terrifying thought occurred to Jared. It appeared Nahum had changed his mind and decided to make him serve his full apprenticeship, starting as a baby.

Judging from the equipment in the room and the sterile smell of it, he decided he must be in a hospital. Could it be that he was a newborn and this gorgeous woman was his *mother?* Mothers feed their babies, and she was certainly doing that. He couldn't remember the birthing experience, but then he'd heard that all humans forgot the events accompanying their emergence into the world.

The worst part would be going through life desiring his own mother. There was no way he could stop the strange urge that compelled him to stare at the beauty of her face, listen to the soft melody of her voice, or notice the gentle curves of her earthly form. How could Nahum do this to him!

But wait. Didn't babies drink from bottles? Or elsewhere? Jared tried to rein in his errant thoughts as he pictured himself suckling from Adidas's ample breast. No, if he were a baby, he wouldn't be having such thoughts.

In fact, if he were a baby, he wouldn't have been able to converse with her.

She pushed another spoonful of soup into his mouth, and this time he closed his lips around it, keeping the savory nourishment inside as she withdrew the spoon. It sat on his tongue as he wondered what to do with it.

This was quite different from on high. Up there, when they'd sipped wine or sampled grapes, it had been a symbolic procedure. The wine and grapes, having no dimension, had presented no problem, but this soup...

Reflex took over, and he swallowed. The chunks of vegetables lodged in his throat, bringing on a fit of coughing.

Adidas leaned forward and patted him on the back. Through a tear-filled haze, Jared was rewarded with a glimpse of the soft white flesh that filled out the front of her upper garments. Thoroughly distracted now, he ceased coughing. Strange, but this unexpected sight created even more pleasure than his first taste of vegetable soup.

"For goodness' sake, Gerald, you've got to chew your food before you swallow it."

"Chew?"

"Yes. You know, mash it between your teeth." She stared at him with a mixture of curiosity and exasperation.

For some unexplained reason, Jared didn't want her to be displeased with him. He wanted to see her smile, wanted her to lean close again so he could smell her sweet floral scent. And he wanted something else. It was a need that was so deep-rooted he couldn't put a finger on what it was. What he *did* know was that this need somehow involved Adidas.

"Who is Gerald?" he asked.

She frowned at him a long moment before answering. "You were involved in a car accident...at the Pike Creek Overpass." She waited a second as if she expected him to be familiar with this information. When he didn't reply, she continued, her tone slow and careful, as if she was afraid of upsetting him. "You came very close to leaving us." Her gaze dropped to her lap, and when she looked up again, her eyes glistened with moisture. "Your name is Gerald Kirkland. The doctors said you might suffer a temporary memory loss. But don't worry, it'll come back soon, I'm sure."

Then Jared recalled Nahum's words. *There is a soul whose hourglass is almost empty. You will inhabit his vessel when he leaves it.* So he had been placed in Gerald Kirkland's body. At first he felt a twinge of guilt for invading the man's physical casing. Then he remembered that the body would have died if he had not come into it.

He wondered if Adidas was the woman he was supposed to protect. And if so, how was he supposed to look out for her while confined to a hospital bed?

Jared lifted his right hand and was surprised to note how large it was. Dark hair covered the thick forearm. He reached for her, and she held his hand in her lap. Her skin was soft, even softer than a fenuki feather, and he relished the sensation of her fingers touching his.

"Tell me about your relationship with—" although he was inhabiting the man's body, he couldn't claim to *be* the former occupant "—Gerald."

If she thought his question was odd, she didn't show it. Instead, she seemed to be focusing on how best to word her reply. "We were..."

Hesitation. Wariness. There was something she obviously didn't want to tell him. And she didn't.

"We *are* friends. Just friends."

"That's it?"

"Your memory will come back gradually. Don't push it too fast, Gerald."

Jared squeezed her fingers. "Call me Jerry."

She sat up straight in her chair and seemed to be trying to ignore the pressure of his fingers against hers. "You hate it when people call you that."

"Not anymore." With conviction, he added, "I'm not the man you used to know."

CHAPTER TWO

KIM didn't know what to do. Jerry—as he now insisted on being called—was driving her nuts. He was turning her home from a sanctuary into a zoo.

She realized she should try to have more patience with him. But it had taken repeated corrections and finally a look at her driver's license to convince him her name was Kim, and not Adidas. He had seemed surprised to learn that she was only twenty-eight...in *human years,* as he'd put it. And patience ran thin after dealing with his endless questions about the mundane events and artifacts of everyday life. It was as if he were an alien from outer space and this was his first close-up look at life on Earth.

Kim stirred sliced bananas into the pancake batter, then poured out four round globs onto the hot griddle. And look at her now. Here she was, second vice president of Barnett's Bakery—a woman accustomed to delegating work and giving instructions to high-level employees—taking breakfast orders from her temporary tenant.

As if it wasn't bad enough that she was taking a couple weeks off from work to care for him when she most needed to be at the office, Jerry seemed to take delight in finding new ways to make her crazy.

First he'd gotten hooked on television. Daytime soaps, talk shows, cartoons, game shows and educational TV—

he loved it all. Especially commercials. And he wanted her to buy him everything from the sugary cereal with a prize in the box to almost every sports car he saw advertised.

Then there was the telephone. He'd started out by listening to the dial tone until the electronic voice advised him to hang up and try again. After he got the hang of dialing numbers, he placed a flurry of calls to various 900 numbers. If he'd been confused by the horoscope predictions, he was absolutely bewildered by the sex-talk line.

"Why would a woman I've never met want to tell me what she's wearing under her dress?" he'd asked.

Turning off the stove, Kim stacked the pancakes on plates, then poured two cups of coffee…black for him and cream and sugar for herself. A large tray accommodated the load, and she carried it to the den where she'd last seen Jerry sitting with his leg in that gaudy orange cast propped on the sofa.

He was nowhere to be found.

Kim set the tray on the coffee table and went to look for him. As she headed down the short hallway, she saw that the bathroom was empty, and the library, where she often caught him looking things up in the encyclopedia or dictionary, stood vacant.

Then she heard his deep voice coming from the guest bedroom. "Sure, I'd be glad to, but would you mind telling me what I should hold on to?"

She peeked in the open doorway and found him sitting on the bed with the phone to his ear.

Jerry looked up and smiled, the expression open and

warm. It was an endearing gesture, and Kim tried not to be affected by it.

He placed his hand over the mouthpiece. "This guy told me to hold on, and then he started playing music for me. It's really thoughtful of him, but I wish he'd stop for a moment and talk to me."

Kim crossed into the room and sat on the bed beside him. "Who's on the phone?"

"Besides me?"

Patience, the doctor had told her. Have patience. "Yes, besides you."

"The guy on television who wanted to give me more information about life insurance."

"But you have plenty of insurance as an employee benefit with my father's company."

"Oh, no, this is for you."

She stared at the man who suddenly seemed so concerned about her, but his attention was diverted by the salesperson who had come back on the line.

"Yeah, it's for my friend," Jerry said. "How much will it cost to ensure that she lives at least another fifty or sixty years?"

Kim continued staring as his face took on an expression of disbelief. He slowly hung up the phone, apparently stunned by what he'd heard.

"What did he say?" she asked.

"I don't know why anyone would want to," Jerry said, "but he told me to put the phone somewhere that I don't think it will fit."

"He must have thought you were joking," she offered in an effort to undo the effect of the salesman's harsh words. Unlike the pre-accident Gerald, Jerry was at a loss for dealing with various types of stress. If she'd been that salesman, she, too, would have thought Jerry was making a prank call.

When the doctor had told her he would suffer memory loss, she hadn't thought it would extend to such basic life knowledge. Jerry was certainly keeping her busy as she tried to teach him all the things he'd formerly known.

"Buying life insurance doesn't *ensure* that you'll continue to live," she explained. "It just means that when you die, the insurance company will give a predetermined amount of money to your survivors so they can pay your burial expenses."

He seemed genuinely surprised. "Then why don't they call it death insurance?"

Kim shrugged, then put the phone back on the nightstand. "Come on, breakfast is waiting for you in the den. I made banana pancakes just like you asked."

She stood and offered an arm to help him up, but he insisted on getting to his feet under his own steam. When he was balanced against his crutches, she led the way into the hall toward the adjoining room.

It wasn't until she heard the thud and crash that she realized he hadn't followed her out of the room. Dashing back to the bedroom, she found him lying in a heap on the floor, one crutch thrown to the side and the other balanced on his chest.

"Jerry, are you all right?" She ran and knelt beside him as he tried to struggle to a sitting position. "Don't move until we're sure you haven't broken anything else."

With a light touch, afraid that even a slight pressure

could cause further damage, she ran her hands gently over his arms, body and legs to check for possible broken bones.

"Does that hurt?" she asked.

He closed his eyes. "No, it feels great."

She jerked her hands away as if she'd been burned. It was enough that she was taking care of him these next couple of weeks. She certainly didn't want him to get the impression he could expect anything more than room and board.

Kim helped him to his feet. "What happened?"

He lowered his head and gave her a sheepish grin. "I tried to take a shortcut through the wall."

She felt her eyebrows draw together. "You can't go through walls."

"You're right," he agreed. "Not anymore, I can't."

"Huh?"

Jerry rubbed his head. "Human bodies can't transmogrify."

Again, Kim led the way to the hall, but this time she watched her charge to make sure he followed her. "I think you'd better lay off the cartoons for a while," she advised as he made his way to the den and lowered himself onto the sofa.

With his hands, Jerry moved his leg up onto the cushions and sniffed the air appreciatively. "Smells great," he said of the food on the coffee table.

"Thanks. I hope you like it." And she did. Despite the angry way in which they'd parted and the constant annoyances he caused her since he was released from the hospital, it was fun watching him get so excited over small things. Before the accident, it would have taken a drastic improvement in the stock market or the opportunity to travel abroad and do some skiing to elicit anything more than a benign, controlled smile from him.

Jerry dug into the breakfast she'd prepared for him, and Kim watched with delight as his expression changed from hopeful anticipation to pure ecstasy. It had taken some practice, and she was glad to see he'd finally mastered the use of a fork. His attitude changed after he sampled the coffee.

"No offense," he said, "but this is disgusting."

Kim put down her fork. "You always loved black coffee—said you couldn't make it through the day without at least three cups."

Jerry grew quiet. "I told you before...I'm a different man now." He looked at her with such silent intensity it seemed as though he was trying to convey some truth, some deep meaning along with the words.

The silence stretched out. Was he trying to win her back? Did he remember what he'd done to cause their breakup? For that matter, did he even remember their breakup? Was he telling her that the accident had made him a changed man and that he wouldn't cheat on her again?

No, she was convinced he remembered nothing from before the car crash. It was as if Gerald had received a personality transplant. Dr. Richmond had told her he may have suffered some brain injury, which would account for some unlikely behavior, but she'd never expected he'd be like a totally different person. Why, he even insisted on a different name for the new personality he'd become.

She could drive herself crazy if she tried to understand

it. Perhaps it would be best to gradually reintroduce him to familiar things that might help him recall his past. In the meantime, she'd let him stay here until his body and mind healed enough for him to move back to his condominium without further injuring himself or burning the place down. And if she enjoyed the company of the sweet, thoughtful man who complimented her and made her laugh, what would be the harm in that? Before long, he would regain his memory and resume his relationship with that woman he'd taken to the motel.

Her teeth clenched at the memory, but she pushed aside the hurt feelings that arose whenever she thought of that fateful day. "Here," she said, handing him her coffee mug. "Try mine. Maybe you'll like it better."

He sipped it, and she watched as he touched his lips to the rim of the mug and drank the sweetened beverage. After he sampled it, his handsome mouth turned downward at both corners. He handed it back to her. "No thanks."

She got up and went to the kitchen for a glass of orange juice. When she came back, he was staring at her once again in that odd, penetrating way of his.

She set the juice down in front of him, but he ignored it. "I'm sorry you're having to miss work on account of me."

At first she thought he was joking. The old Gerald would have expected as much as his due for merely existing. But when she saw how sincere he was, she gave a little shrug. "It's okay. I don't mind."

"Did Gerald...do I have any relatives? Maybe someone else I could stay with?"

She'd answered so many questions about mundane,

everyday things that she was surprised it had taken so long for him to get around to asking about his past. Perhaps what she told him would help jar his memory. And although anything she said to him at this point would be new information, she didn't want to shock or hurt him.

"Your parents are gone." At his questioning glance, she added, "Your father left when you were a baby, and your mother passed away when you were a teenager. Your only relative is your Aunt Rowena who lives in a nursing home." She didn't bother to mention that he would have had a wife if only he hadn't been such a jerk.

He twisted on the sofa, moving his leg to the cleared portion of the coffee table so he could face her. "What about you?"

"What about me?" Forgetting about the wobbly chair leg, she scooted back into the cushions, causing the furniture to resettle with a *thunk*.

Jerry moved forward as if to catch her in case she fell.

"I'm okay," she told him. "It's done this before."

"Why don't you sit over here?" Jerry said, patting the sofa cushion beside him. "I'd feel terrible if you got hurt."

Kim had to do a double take. It was hard to believe this was the same man who'd made a grid of dates and took bets from their co-workers on when the chair would finally collapse under her. When she saw that he wasn't joking, she took him up on his offer.

"This place could use a little work," he said once she'd settled beside him. "I noticed a loose step on the front porch, and last night when you went upstairs to your room, the banister swayed under your hand. If you'll show me where your tools are, I'll try to fix some of the stuff around here.''

He was right. There were quite a few things that needed fixing in this old farmhouse. But Gerald had never before offered to do any of the handiwork, partly because he considered it beneath him to do ''common labor'' and partly because he hated the big white farmhouse she'd bought outside the city. He kept insisting that they would buy a newer, bigger condominium to settle into once they were married. Gerald had considered it wasted effort to fix up a house he wouldn't ultimately live in. Although she'd agreed to their engagement, they'd never finished working out where they would live.

And now he was offering to roll up his sleeves and be her live-in handyman despite the encumbrance of a cast on his leg.

''There's no need,'' she said. Eventually, she would get around to doing the chores herself, or she would hire someone to do the work after she was finished with the big project she was working on at the office. ''I'll take care of it before long.''

But that wasn't soon enough to suit Jerry. He made her promise to show him where she kept her tools so he could start work after breakfast.

He shifted on the sofa so that he faced her. Once situated, he decided instead to pursue the line of questioning he'd started earlier. The more he knew about her, the easier it would be to protect her. And having her think he suffered from amnesia was a convenient tool for getting the information he needed. "We never finished talking about you. Tell me about your family."

As she told him about her father, Maxwell, her young stepmother, Carmen, and her own single-child status, Jerry soaked up the warmth of the room as well as the warmth in her voice.

The house and its furnishings reminded him of her. It was simple and unpretentious, but still classic and welcoming. The old white frame house was situated in the middle of forty acres, about half of which were cleared. A small lake behind the house invited quiet introspection and meditation at its edge, and a barn gave shelter to the assorted wild geese and ducks that congregated near the water.

It was the inside of the house that most clearly displayed Kim's personality. The blue overstuffed sofa and chair invited inhabitants to put their feet up, and the wood theme of floors and half-paneled walls gave an earthy feel. It was a house a man could feel comfortable in, but the ruffled curtains and thick blue-and-cream rug saved it from appearing masculine.

He knew from his forays into her library that she was an eclectic reader, sampling everything from the classics to science fiction, mystery and romance. He had been pleased to note that not only did a Bible sit among her collection, but it appeared by its worn condition to be well-read.

As she told him about her father's thriving bakery business whose distribution covered a three-state region, Jerry took in the assorted magazine pictures of horses adorning the walls. On the fireplace mantel sat a framed photo of a young girl perched atop a pony while a man stood nearby holding the reins and smiling down at his tiny charge.

When she finished describing their planned expansion of the company, he changed the subject. "Why don't you have any horses in the barn?"

She rolled her eyes and lolled back against the sofa. "That's one reason I bought this place...so I'd have a place to keep the horses I've always wanted. But the business expansion keeps me so busy I don't have time to care for an animal right now. Not even a cat."

"How long until you've finished the expansion?"

"As soon as six months or as long as two or even three years, depending on how things go."

He scratched his head. "I noticed a rosebush at the corner of the house. Do you ever take time to stop and smell the roses?"

Now it was Kim's turn to scratch her head. If this question had been asked before Gerald's accident, she would have known he was joking. But now...well, she just wasn't sure.

"*You* are lecturing *me* about stopping to smell the roses?"

He grinned, the action deepening the small dimple in his left cheek. His whiskery cheek. Kim had never seen him unshaven before, and she couldn't help noticing that the casual look on him was anything but casual. It made him look darker, more brooding, and more powerful than the clean-cut, three-piece-suited man she was accustomed to. Not even the gentle charm of his grin could lessen her gut-level response. In fact, the contrast actually emphasized the depth of his blue eyes and the sharp angle of his jaw.

"Does that surprise you?"

"Of course it does. You're the workaholic pot calling me a black kettle. *You* were the one who talked Daddy and me into the expansion in the first place."

Jerry frowned slightly as he took in what she was saying. "Did I work with you and your father at Barnett's Bakery?"

"Yes," she said gently, "and you worked just as hard or harder than both of us to get the merger started."

"I did?"

Kim nodded. Her bangs fell forward and tickled her eyebrows. She hadn't taken the time to mousse her hair this morning after her shower, and now her chin-length auburn hair swung softly around her face in free abandon.

"Then it's about time I changed my ways," he confessed.

"That'll be the day." The doctor hadn't said whether Jerry would remember his recovery period once he regained his previous memories. However, Kim felt sure that once he recalled the events and motivations that had led him to become the person he'd once been, he would most likely go back to being the old Gerald. As for right now, he probably felt vulnerable and lost, which accounted for this new attitude of his.

"No, I'm serious."

He touched her arm, and Kim shrank from the warmth of his touch. No matter how appealing he might be at the moment, she knew that, like a puppy that eventually outgrows its cuteness, Jerry would leave behind the innocence and charm that now warmed her heart. She expected he would probably also go back to the woman he'd been seeing. Her gesture didn't go unnoticed by Jerry, and he removed his hand from her arm.

"It's obvious that you and Gerald...uh, you and I...have our priorities mixed up. It's impossible to enjoy the good things we have when we're so busy working to acquire more."

Kim narrowed her eyes at him. Same face, same hair, same body, and same gestures. If she didn't know better, she'd think this was Gerald's twin. The *good* twin.

"So I think it would do us both good to attend church this Sunday," he continued. "You know, get in touch with our inner selves and make peace with the Big Guy for forgetting about all the good stuff He's done for us. I understand He gets really ticked when people ignore Him."

"Church?"

"Yeah. You know, the place with the steeple and the stained-glass windows," he said as if she was the one who needed her memory jogged. "Or temple, if that's your preference."

It had been a while since she'd last attended church. Ever since she'd become involved in the expansion plans, she had either worked on Sundays or been too tired to get up in time to go to the morning service, so she was certainly overdue. As for Jerry, it was possible that he was searching for something to fill a void in his soul. Perhaps if he found spiritual peace, it would stay with him even after he regained his memory. Although she herself didn't want to take another chance by becoming involved with him again, she hoped any such comfort he got from church would help make him a better person—both for himself and for the next woman in his life.

"Okay," she said. "We'll go to church this Sunday, but you have to shave first."

Sunday morning, Kim set out a can of shaving cream and a fresh razor on the bathroom counter. Then she went into the living room to read the paper before getting dressed for church.

A moment later, he announced, "This is a leg razor." A long pause followed. "A *pink* one."

"That's okay," she told him. "It'll still do the job."

"But the guy on TV said a man needs a swiveling head."

Kim stood up and fastened the robe tighter around her waist. Going to the bathroom, she reminded herself that he'd be returning to his own apartment in another week or two. Then she'd be able to pick up the pieces of her life.

As she entered the tiny room midway down the hall, he smiled and proceeded to make a long sweep with the razor that extended from his left ear, down to his chin, and back up to his right ear.

Kim gasped. "Good heavens, you look like you're trying to slit your throat. Give me that razor."

He did as he was told, and she reached up to blot the nick on his chin with a square of toilet paper.

"Here, I'll show you how to do it." He obligingly turned toward her as she lifted the razor to his face. "You have to take short, smooth strokes. Otherwise, you'll look like you shaved with a kitchen blender."

As she stood close to him, she was aware of just how

tall he was. Even stooping over the crutches, he was tall enough to make her arms ache as she reached up to him. Her hand quivered, and she drew back.

"Is something wrong?" he asked.

His brow furrowed, and Kim was hauntingly reminded of the strong physical attraction she'd felt the first time she saw Gerald. It had been lust at first sight, but even that didn't compare to the raw physical craving she was feeling right now. Sure, he looked the same, except for a healing red line above his eyebrow and a few lingering bruises sprinkled across his body. But there was something different about him. About the way he looked at her as if he was committing the tiniest details of her image to memory.

Kim gave herself a mental shake. He was probably just recognizing something familiar in her features and trying to use them to dredge up lost memories. If she wasn't careful, she might find herself falling for the temporary stranger in her bathroom.

"It's just awkward...standing here like this," she said at last. "My arms are getting tired."

"What if I sit here," he said, putting the lid down, "and you sit on the side of the tub?"

That would put them at about the same level. Perhaps if he wasn't towering over her, his closeness wouldn't have such a strange effect on her. She propped his crutches behind the door and took a seat next to him.

Once again, she lifted the razor to his face. As she stroked it over his skin, she thought of the many times she'd watched him shave after he'd spent the night at her place. A man of habit, Gerald had a particular procedure for almost everything he did. It was as if he turned something as basic as grooming into a science. It was hard to imagine that—after so many years of shaving in a certain fashion—it hadn't become second nature, something for which he didn't have to remember the steps in order to do it.

"Do like this," she said, and twisted her mouth to one side.

Jerry stared at her lips and followed suit as she moved the razor over his flattened cheek. For some reason, he couldn't seem to take his eyes off her mouth. Sometimes, he noticed, when she was dressed up, her lips were a deeper red. This morning, however, she hadn't done whatever she normally did to transform her appearance. Her eyelashes, though dark, weren't as black as usual, and her eyelids were free of the pale brown shadows that made her irises appear as dark as the devil's food cake he'd sampled last night. Up close like this, he could see the sprinkling of freckles across her nose that she usually managed to hide.

Fascinating as all that was, it was her lips that held his attention. Though the rest of her features were angular and sharply defined, her mouth was soft and full, reminding him of the tempting swells that rounded out the front of her upper garments. A tempting shade of pink, her lips somehow beckoned him.

She directed him to lift his chin so she could shave under his jaw. He did as told, his gaze never leaving her mouth as she removed the last of his whiskers.

Her lips tightened, and her tongue darted out. "Is something wrong?" she asked.

"No, everything's perfect." Knowing that, as all humans, she must have flaws, Jerry found it hard to believe she could seem so incredibly perfect.

"Oh, good. I was beginning to think I had egg on my face."

He couldn't picture her with that yellow food marring her appearance. However, he remembered watching her eat pancakes with syrup this morning. He wondered if a remnant of the sticky sweet stuff clung to her lips, and the thought made him want to taste them to find out.

Her tongue darted out again as she watched him watching her.

Instinct took over. Jerry impulsively leaned forward and touched his mouth to hers. Sure enough, a hint of maple offered itself to him as their lips pressed together.

It was wonderful...much better than pancakes. He tried without success to compare it to a sensation he may have experienced before. The closest he could come was being fed peeled grapes while reclining upon a pristine chaise, but even that was a mere shadow to what was happening here in this small room. Yet, for some inexplicable reason, the idea of combining this feeling with lying on the chaise made his pulse pound in his temples.

If he'd thought it was great before, Kim made it glorious when she returned the gesture and tasted him. His breathing quickened as Kim's hands went around his neck, urging him closer. Moving so that his bum leg stretched out to one side, he reached out to her, his hands gripping her sides as he pulled her to him and positioned her between his thighs.

With his hands lightly touching her ribs, he allowed his thumbs to explore the tender flesh that he'd admired since the first time she leaned over him at the hospital.

Although the white terry-cloth robe shielded her skin from him, he savored the softness and was surprised when the centers of the two hillocks hardened beneath his exploring fingers. This wasn't heaven, he knew, but it wasn't far from it.

Kim gasped, and Jerry could tell she was experiencing a similar quickening in her breathing. She squirmed in his arms, and just when he felt as though he might explode, she pulled back, breaking the contact of their lips. The look she gave him was one of fear and shame.

"Oh, my gosh," she said, standing abruptly, "I can't believe I just let that happen."

CHAPTER THREE

ORGAN music swelled around them as they settled themselves into a pew near the aisle of the historic church. Jerry laid the crutches under the pew in front of him and stretched out his right leg. The orange covering of his cast practically glowed neon where the severed pants seams didn't meet. Despite his less-than-immaculate appearance, Jerry seemed pleased with the way he looked in the three-piece suit.

"Cool," he'd said when he caught sight of himself in the mirror this morning. If the old Gerald's personality had returned, Kim was certain he would have insisted on waiting until his leg healed before going out in public like this.

He leaned toward her and whispered, "You tasted good."

Kim fidgeted beside him. If they were to get through these next couple of weeks, she would have to make sure he understood the ground rules. Otherwise, she'd be right back where she started...falling for a low-down, womanizing, arrogant—

She stopped herself from further mental tirades. Besides, it wasn't proper to think evil thoughts in church. Looking over at the man who sat so erectly beside her, she realized that he currently was none of the descriptions that had just played through her mind. But he wouldn't remain this way. Kim wanted his memory to return in order for his healing to be complete, but she couldn't help wishing he'd stay like this.

The doctor seemed confident his memories would eventually return. And when they did, she didn't want to be involved with a man who was a low-down, arrogant womanizer.

"You shouldn't have done that," she told him.

"Yeah, I suppose you're right." He looked down, his countenance thoughtful. "Next time, I'll make myself a pancake. But, you know, syrup just doesn't taste as good on a pancake as it does on you."

Kim stared at him as if he'd lost his mind. And then she remembered that, in a sense, he had. "I'm talking about kissing. I realize you've forgotten our past, just like you've forgotten everything else," she said gently. "But it's important that you know we've tried this before, and it just didn't work out."

"Kissing? You and Gerald have kissed before?"

If she didn't know better, she'd think he sounded not only surprised, but jealous, too.

"I thought you—we—were just friends," he said.

"Well, we…" How much should she tell him? If she told him too much, he might become possessive. On the other hand, if she told him too little, he might try to start anew. "We had a relationship."

He frowned, and Kim noticed a couple of whiskers she'd missed near his ear.

"Why didn't it work out?"

Good question, she thought. Was it because of some flaw in her for not being able to keep him interested, or because he was just a born jerk? Although she worried that the former may have been at least partly true, she was certain the latter was the biggest reason.

The music rose louder as the choir members filed into the loft.

"Someday we'll have a long talk about it," she promised. "But now isn't the time or place."

He touched her hand covering the Bible in her lap, his expression full of regret. "I'm sorry if he...if I hurt you."

She didn't know what to say. He looked sincere, and that simple fact touched her in a way that she knew she shouldn't allow it. It almost had her wishing they could try again. She resolutely pushed the thought to the back of her mind as she opened her hymnal to "Amazing Grace."

Kim loved this song and could sing some of it by heart. Gerald had hated attending church, considering it a waste of time, so she was surprised when the man she now called Jerry didn't bother to open to the proper page. She was further surprised when Jerry belted out the words in a clear, confident baritone.

By the time they reached the third verse, Kim had to resort to singing from the hymnal, but when she moved to share her book with Jerry, he politely declined. He continued through the fourth verse, not missing so much as a syllable of the lyrics.

When it was over and the congregation took their seats, Kim leaned closer to him and whispered, "How did you remember the words to that song when you never knew it before?"

Jerry hesitated, a puzzled look crossing his face. Then,

a bit sheepishly, as if he wasn't sure of the answer himself, he suggested, "Televangelism?"

Kim found that hard to believe, but the same thing happened with the rest of the songs throughout the service. He even knew the hymn that she was only vaguely familiar with, and that one had six verses.

The man was incredible. He had to be taught how to tie his shoes, use a fork, and shave, but he was intimately familiar with every song they sang and every Bible verse they read aloud together.

When the service was over, Jerry pointed out the depiction on the stained-glass window nearest their pew. Jesus, His sandy brown hair and beard grown long and His eyes full of kindness and love, sat with His arms outstretched as children and a lamb gathered around Him. Whenever the sermon was boring, Kim would stare at the likeness, noting the brilliant colors of the stained glass and the movement of the trees swaying in the breeze behind it. Apparently, it had caught Jerry's attention, as well.

"He doesn't look like that," he informed her.

"Yeah, some people say He probably had black hair and darker skin."

Jerry shook his head. "Actually, He looks more like—"

"Well, hello! I thought it was you sitting over here whispering during the service." Maxwell Barnett enveloped his daughter in a hug and then turned to Jerry to shake his hand. "It's a good thing you didn't get your knuckles rapped," he added teasingly.

Carmen moved from her husband's side to hug them both. "What a nice surprise to see you out and about."

Recognition dawned in Jerry's eyes as he fixed his gaze on Kim's father and his young wife. "I know you," he said.

Something gripped Kim's heart at the knowledge that his memory was returning. A mixture of relief and regret swept over her as she realized the Jerry whose company she had actually come to enjoy these past several days was going to transform back into the Gerald who had hurt her so deeply. "You do?"

"Sure, I'd know their voices anywhere," he declared, obviously pleased with himself. "They came to visit me while I was in the hospital."

Although she was only eight years his senior, Carmen gave Jerry a maternal smile and patted his arm. "You seemed pretty much out of it when we came by," she said, her smile dissolving as she slanted a meaningful look up at him. "Are you telling us you were only pretending?"

"No, I was asleep, but I could still hear you." He shifted the rubber pad of the crutch under his arm. "I thought I was still in heaven, and I heard your voices talking about a steering pin."

Carmen nodded knowingly, the action making it look as though she was humoring him.

"*Still* in heaven?" Kim asked. "Don't you mean you thought you'd *gone* to heaven?"

Jerry appeared confused for a moment, then nodded his agreement. "Uh, yeah. There was a long tunnel and a bright light. And I think there were some pearly gates, too."

"You actually saw pearly gates?" Kim's father asked.

"Yes, but I don't think St. Peter was on duty that day. He was probably off playing fenuki."

At her parents' quizzical expressions, Kim urged Jerry out into the aisle and followed him. "I think Jerry's getting tired," she explained. With the long line of people waiting to shake the preacher's hand on their way out, they could be standing here quite a while. "I think we'll leave by the side door."

After they said their goodbyes, Kim and Jerry made their way up the long, carpeted aisle toward the pulpit, nodding a greeting to all those they passed.

A few minutes later, when she drove past Burger Heaven, he insisted she turn around and go back. She glanced in the rearview mirror, taking note of the giant rotating hamburger perched above the roof of the restaurant. Behind it was a sign cut out and painted to look like fluffy clouds, but the silver-colored lining had long since chipped away. The halo that hung suspended above the burger sat in the same cockeyed position it had been knocked into during a storm back in the eighties.

"Why do you want to go there? It's a dive."

He shrugged.

Kim had misgivings about going into such a place, but it was the middle of the day on a Sunday. She supposed it would be all right and made a U-turn only to discover there were two large motorcycles parked outside the restaurant. "I think maybe we should go to Shoney's. It's only a couple of miles from here."

"No, this will be fine," he insisted. "I want to try their angel fries."

She glanced over at him. "They're just French fries

that are sliced extra thin.'' Her lackluster response did nothing to quell his enthusiasm.

After she pulled into the parking lot, she stayed close to Jerry in case he should lose his footing on the broken pavement. At least, that's what she told herself. Logically, she knew there was little a man on crutches could do to protect her, but for some reason she felt better when she was near him. Once inside, she decided not to explore the reasons for such feelings and, instead, diverted her thoughts by concentrating on the menu.

There were ''billowing clouds'' of mashed potatoes, ''lightning bolt'' hot wings and ''heavenly'' hamburgers. There was even ''reincarnation stew,'' a hodgepodge of leftovers from the past several days. Kim decided to forgo the stew and opted instead for a hamburger. Jerry got the angel fries and hot wings.

She stared at the fried chicken wings covered with red-pepper specks. ''Don't you think you should have ordered something a little milder?''

He grinned, the action creating a dimple beside his mouth. Kim averted her eyes from his mouth and tried not to think about the incredible things he'd done with it this morning. He'd never kissed her like that before, and she couldn't seem to get it out of her mind.

''I'll take my wings any way I can get 'em,'' he said as they made their way toward a table in the back.

''But it'll upset your stomach. And you didn't bring your ulcer medicine.''

''My stomach's fine,'' he said with a smile.

She shrugged and slid into the booth, then emptied the tray's contents onto the table. She pushed the plate with the hamburger on it toward Jerry. "Do you want to switch with me?"

"Heavens, no," he declared. "I'll say a prayer and take my chances." At that, he bowed his head and mumbled a few words. When he opened his eyes, he caught her staring. "What?"

"I...I've never seen you say grace before."

"You're telling me Gerald ate unblessed food?" He seemed appalled by the thought.

Kim toyed with her hamburger, hoping he wouldn't notice the missing bite. "Well, a lot of people don't say grace in public," she admitted. "I guess they don't want to draw attention to themselves."

He looked around the restaurant as if to verify her statement. His gaze fixed upon a young couple in their early twenties. Judging from their tattoos, denim jackets and tattered jeans, Kim wouldn't be surprised if they owned the Harleys parked outside. She cleared her throat, trying to drag Jerry's attention back to his own table, but the sound merely alerted the couple to the scrutiny they were undergoing.

"You got a problem?" the young man asked.

Unfazed by the hostility in the man's tone, Jerry merely smiled broadly and shook his head. "I was just looking."

The woman brightened and pushed a lock of straight brown hair behind her shoulder. The action didn't go unnoticed by her companion, who stood suddenly, knocking his chair to the floor with a crash. By now, everyone in the restaurant was watching to see what kind of drama might be unfolding.

Kim reached across the table and placed a restraining

hand on Jerry's arm. "Let's just mind our own business, Jerry, and let them eat in peace."

"I only wanted to see if they were going to say grace," he insisted.

"Jerry?" said the man in denim. "You must think you're a regular Jerry Lewis or something."

"No, I'm Jerry Kirkland," he said, standing up and offering his hand in greeting. "And you are…?"

By now, the other man was walking slowly toward him in the cautious, stiff-legged gait that dogs use when they're about to launch into a fight with hackles raised.

"Aw, Alex, leave him alone," said the woman at the other table. "Can't you see he's got a crip leg?"

He continued advancing toward Jerry, his jaw clenched and his whole expression menacing. Jerry was a good four inches taller than Alex and considerably heavier. If he wanted to, he could give better than he got, but Kim didn't want to see the situation degenerate to that point. Before the accident, Gerald would have prevented the incident before it started, using only his voice and a stern glare. But now, as Jerry, he seemed so…so innocent and unsuspecting.

The handshake not forthcoming, Jerry stuffed his right hand into his pocket and balanced himself against the back of the booth with the other. If Alex decided to throw a punch, Jerry would be an open target.

"If you so much as touch that dude," his girlfriend continued, "I'm gonna tell all your friends how you wimped on a guy with his leg in a cast."

Kim shuddered. If he was a member of a motorcycle gang, he might get his friends to come find them and finish off whatever was left of Jerry.

Fortunately, Alex hesitated and appeared to reconsider.

Kim took advantage of his indecision as she moved out from behind the booth. "Excuse me," she said, clutching her purse and moving past the angry young man. Reaching for Jerry, she made up a quick fib. "I bet you forgot all about going to visit your Aunt Rowena at the nursing home."

"I did?"

"Yes, and we'd better hurry up because she'll worry if we're late."

Jerry turned to follow her and then stopped abruptly. Moving past the surprised smaller man toward the table with the barely touched food, he grabbed his paper plate. "Forgot my hot wings."

"Goodbye," Alex's girlfriend called after them as they left.

Kim led Jerry quickly to the door in time to see a white-haired gentleman and another man young enough to be his son mounting the motorcycles she'd noticed earlier in the parking lot. She breathed a sigh of relief.

After they were back on the road, with some distance between them and the site of their near altercation, Kim whacked Jerry with her purse.

The hot wing he'd been gnawing fell to the floor. "What'd you do that for?"

Her face flushed hot with anger. It was all she could do to keep from taking him back to his apartment right now and leaving him there to fend for himself—broken leg or not. "Don't you realize you could have gotten yourself killed?"

He looked puzzled. "The hot wings weren't *that* hot, and besides, I don't think I have an ulcer anymore."

Kim felt her shoulders sag. "I'm talking about that guy in the restaurant. Couldn't you tell he wanted to break your other leg?"

"Alex? He was a little uptight, but I didn't sense any hostility."

"Then I suggest you stock up on bandages and ice packs, because you're going to need them if you keep blundering your way through life. And, if that's the case, I don't want to be in the line of fire when you get what's coming to you."

Jerry practically choked on his last hot wing. Bandages and ice packs. When Nahum had assigned him to be Kim's protectorate, Jerry had thought in jest that if she was clumsy she should stock up on those two items. And now she was echoing his own thoughts back to him.

Only it looked as though *he* was the klutz this time. With a sinking sense of dismay, he realized the episode at the restaurant could have ended much worse. Thank goodness Kim had been there to recognize the potential danger and get them out of it.

But that was his job. He was supposed to be taking care of her, not the other way around. Guilt nudged his conscience as he thought of how she'd been taking care of him since he left the hospital. And he'd reveled in it, asking her to make his meals and accepting the myriad thoughtful things she did for him each day.

She was constantly rescuing him from himself, he realized. The shave hadn't endangered her, but what if she'd hurt her back while helping him up from the floor after he'd attempted to transmogrify himself through the wall? Or, worse, what if the tense young man at the restaurant had been carrying a weapon? Not only could Jerry have gotten himself killed and left Kim vulnerable to whatever threatened an early emptying of her hour-glass, but he could have been the indirect cause of her premature departure.

He'd been so giddy about the idea of *getting* a pair of wings that he hadn't considered what he had to do to *earn* them.

He could have lost his human ward and, consequently, the wings he wanted so desperately. But the wings seemed insignificant when he considered that he could have lost Kim.

Jerry looked over at her, taking in the delicate beauty of her face. Impulsively, he placed his hand over hers, where it rested on the gearshift knob.

She glanced up, a hint of curiosity showing in her dark eyes, but she didn't pull away from his touch.

Jerry felt his heart fill with an unexplainable sensation when he realized the serious impact his carelessness could have had on Kim.

Kim, the woman who was more beautiful than a pure white dove. Whose lilting voice was more melodic than a finely tuned lyre. Whose heart was as pure as the streets of gold that awaited his return upon completion of his mission.

His mission…to spare her from an early demise. Until now, he'd been quite lax about seeing to his duties. Instead, he'd been focusing his attention on savoring many of the sensory pleasures that came with be-ing human.

He lifted her hand to his lap and traced his fingertips over her soft skin. With a shy smile, she turned her hand upward and laced her fingers with his.

Jerry vowed that, from this moment on, he would become the model protectorate for Kim. And that would mean forgoing sensory pleasures in order to put Kim's safety first. The vision came to mind of Kim in his arms as he stole maple-flavored kisses from her, and he regretted having to sacrifice that particular pleasure. Then again, she had already told him such activity was hereafter off-limits, so it was a moot point.

First thing tomorrow, he would examine the house with an eye for the slightest hazard and repair it lest an accident should befall her. "It won't happen again," he said, referring to that day's near catastrophe. "I'll do everything in my earthly power to keep you safe."

Reluctantly, he moved her hand back to the gearshift and busied himself with placing the remains of his lunch in the litterbag.

She slanted a questioning glance at him but kept silent as she focused her attention on the road.

"This is the way home," he observed.

"Your short-term memory is good. Now all you have to do is work on the long-term memory."

"But you said we were going to see Aunt Flo. She'll worry if we don't show up."

"Aunt Ro," Kim corrected.

"Yeah, right. That's what I meant."

"We don't really need to go today. She's not expecting to see you until the Fourth of July, when you usually go."

Jerry found a pencil on the dash of the car and stuck

the eraser end down into his cast to scratch an itch that would not cease. "Fourth of July? How often do I usually see her?"

"Easter, Fourth of July and Christmas."

"Yes, but how often each *week* do I see her?"

"That's it," Kim said, looking ill at ease. "Three times a year."

The pencil paused in midscratch. "That's all?"

Kim chewed a fingernail and added somewhat reluctantly, "You said the smell of the nursing home bothers you."

Jerry unclenched his teeth to ask, "If it's that bad, then why did Ger—" He caught himself. "Why did I allow her to stay there?"

Looking neither apologetic nor accusatory, she shook her head. Since she offered no excuses, Jerry assumed she felt the same as he did about Gerald's lack of attention to his only living relative.

"Let's go now. I bet she'd love to have some company."

"But you said you wanted to spend all afternoon reading the funnies and playing Nintendo."

"That can wait."

She looked at him as if she didn't know who he was. "Why are you so insistent on going today?"

"If we don't go, that would make you a liar," he said, referring to her reason for rushing out of the restaurant.

"And?"

"I've said it before, and you must believe me," he began.

Kim finished the statement for him. "You're not the man I used to know." She made a left onto High Street and headed back to town. "That's the understatement of the year."

When they walked into the nursing home, Jerry paid special attention to the smell of the place. It wasn't so bad. A little like antiseptic, but not much different from the hospital. It bothered him that Gerald would cling to such a weak excuse for not visiting his aunt.

They made their way to the activity room where men and women of various ages and abilities mingled. Some sat in wheelchairs doing crafts or chatting with friends, and a few roamed around aimlessly.

Kim pointed to the back of the room. "There she is."

A tall woman, big-boned like himself, stood watching the commotion around them. Her hair was dark like his, but the white roots clued Jerry in to her bottled youth. When she noticed him watching her, she smiled and flashed her perfect white dentures at him.

Leading the way toward her, Jerry propped his crutches against the wall and held his arms out wide. "Aunt Flo!"

The older woman's smile brightened, and she opened herself to his embrace. After a moment, Jerry released her and examined her at arm's length. "You haven't changed a bit."

Her powdered cheeks pinkened under his perusal. "It was so nice of you to come visit me."

He felt a tap on his shoulder and turned to find Kim wearing an amused grin.

"Aunt Rowena's over there," she said, pointing to a tiny, white-haired lady who seemed swallowed up in a thickly upholstered sofa. The woman stared out the window, apparently unaware of their presence.

Embarrassed, Jerry extricated himself from the wrong woman by promising to play a game of cards with her before they left.

Kim pulled up a chair for Jerry, then sat beside his elderly aunt. "Aunt Ro," she said quietly, gaining her attention, "it's me, Kim."

Rowena smiled, her eyes crinkling at the corners. "Of course it's you. Did you think I wouldn't know you?"

Kim pursed her lips, leading Jerry to understand there were days when Gerald's aunt was not quite so lucid. Even so, she didn't leave it to chance that she would remember him. "Then I'm sure you'll be glad to see your nephew. Gerald couldn't wait to come see you."

Aunt Ro peered at him, squinting her pale blue eyes. She frowned, then lifted the bifocals that hung on a chain around her neck. "That's not Gerald."

Jerry gulped.

"Of course it's Gerald," Kim insisted. "Just look at him. Same hair. Same face. The only thing that's different is the cast on his leg."

Rowena let her bifocals drop back to her ample chest. "He may only visit me three times a year, but I know my own nephew when I see him. And this is *not* Gerald."

CHAPTER FOUR

JERRY cleared his throat. "Of course it's me, Aunt Ro. In the flesh!"

Kim leaned Jerry's way and whispered, "Maybe she's not as clear today as I thought."

Rowena harrumphed and tilted her nose upward. "I may be a little forgetful sometimes," she said, angling a glare at Kim, "but my hearing is perfectly fine."

Kim bit her lip, making it clear she regretted having possibly hurt the older woman's feelings by her careless comment.

A movement near the front of the room caught Jerry's eye. A young woman in a pink uniform had entered carrying a tray with a pitcher and paper cups. Putting on his most endearing smile, he fixed it on Kim. "Looks like it's juice time. Would you mind getting us some?"

"Make mine prune juice," Rowena said.

When Kim was gone, Jerry turned back to Aunt Ro. "You're making me look bad," he told her.

"Who are you?"

"Kim already told you. I'm Gerald."

"Don't give me that hooey. I'm old, but I'm not stupid. Now, what's your real name?"

He took a deep breath and let it out slowly. She was onto him, and he could tell she wouldn't let it rest until he told her the truth. "Jared, but I prefer to be called Jerry," he said at long last. He took her hand in his and

62

stroked her pale, thin skin. "Go along with me on this. Please?"

Obviously skeptical, she looked down at the hand he held but didn't make any attempt to withdraw it. "What's in it for me?"

He thought a moment. "I'll come visit you more often than Gerald did."

Her eyebrows lifted a margin. "More than three times a year?" she asked hopefully.

Jerry cringed. Of course he'd come more than that. "Twice a week?" he suggested.

Rowena smiled and placed her other hand over his. "Once a week is enough, but bring me some butterscotch when you come."

"It's a deal."

The elderly woman hesitated as she narrowed her eyes and peered at him through her thick glasses. "One more thing."

For being so frail-looking, the old lady sure drove a hard bargain. He raised his eyebrows, wondering what she had on her mind.

"Are you a good witch or a bad witch?"

Jerry grimaced and glanced around them to see if anyone might be eavesdropping. The coast was clear, and Kim had gotten sidetracked by a man with a cane who was showing her a scar on his bony ankle.

"Neither. I'm a protectorate."

"A proctologist?" She shifted on the sofa. "I've been having this problem that even bran won't help—"

"I'm not a doctor," Jerry hastily interrupted. "I'm a guardian angel." Then, lest she get the wrong idea about that, he added, "*Kim's* guardian angel."

Her mouth puckered into a wrinkled O. "You're from the Great Beyond?" She sank back against the sofa cushion, and her expression relaxed. "I'm looking forward to crossing the River Jordan someday. Put in a good word for me, will you?"

Jerry hadn't been in direct contact with Nahum—much less the Chairman of the Board—since his arrival here in Chesden, but he nodded his assent nevertheless. He made a mental note to bring it up immediately after he was sized for his new wings.

Kim returned with three cups of juice balanced in her hands. He took two of the cups from her, handing one to Aunt Ro.

Kim settled on the sofa next to the octogenarian. No matter what her arguments with Gerald had been, she was pleased to see him spending time with his aunt. "Aunt Ro, the nurse's aide was telling me this is the most talkative you've been in weeks. You must be happy to see your nephew."

Rowena took a sip from her cup and leaned toward Kim. "He's an angel," she whispered.

Jerry smiled sheepishly and raised his shoulders.

"I don't know about that," Kim countered with a teasing grin, "but he has been very sweet since the accident."

Aunt Ro's gnarled hand covered hers. "You don't have to worry about accidents anymore. Jerry is going to watch out for you and keep you safe from all harm."

Right, Kim thought, and who would keep her safe from *Jerry?* Despite her firm resolve to the contrary, she found her heart going out to her former fiancé. Seeing this new side of his personality had made her closer to him and more vulnerable than she'd ever been before. And it frightened her. Who, she wondered, would protect her heart from being crushed when this new, sweet Jerry regained his memory and returned to being the Gerald she'd broken up with prior to the car crash?

Rowena drank the last of her juice and set the paper cup on the table beside her. The thin puffs of white hair that framed her face shone faintly blue in the afternoon sunlight filling the activity room. She patted her pale lips with a napkin, then laid her hands in her lap and folded and refolded the lipstick-marked paper. When she was done with her little ritual, she turned back to Kim.

"Are you still going to marry him, even though he's not Gerald anymore?"

Kim almost choked on her orange juice. She broke into a fit of coughing and couldn't stop until her eyes filled with tears and her face felt red with heat and embarrassment. Creating even more of a spectacle, Jerry had leaped from his chair and proceeded to pound her on the back.

She raised her hand to wave him off. "I'm okay."

"Are you sure? Because I know first aid."

"You do?"

He looked down at the floor. "Well, I'm sure I could fake it pretty well."

"Isn't it wonderful to have your own guardian angel?" Rowena declared, the pride evident in her voice.

Kim gave a sigh and wiped the moisture from her eyes.

Jerry sat down beside her on the sofa, sandwiching her between him and his aunt. His elbow propped on the sofa back, he stared intently at Kim. "You were going to marry Ger...er, me?" He paused and appeared to absorb the impact of his words. "When's the big day? And why didn't you tell me about it?"

Kim felt trapped as both pairs of eyes bore down upon her. She hadn't wanted to tell him about their relationship yet, and she certainly didn't want to go into it in front of Rowena, who hadn't heard about their breakup.

"We, um, broke up shortly before your accident."

He seemed taken aback by all this new information, and Kim could tell by the way the gears were turning in his head that he would be asking more questions about their former relationship—if not now, then certainly later.

"Gerald let you go?" Rowena demanded. "What an idiot." She leaned across Kim to speak to Jerry. "Comes from his father's side of the family."

Kim stared in amazement at the elderly woman who was speaking of Gerald as if he wasn't even in the room. True, he was going by a nickname now, and he had forgotten everything about his past, but he was still the same person. Wasn't he?

She chastised herself for allowing a disoriented old woman to confuse her. Of course he was the same person. He just didn't remember it yet.

And Kim wanted to make sure that he recovered his memory and returned to his own apartment before he worked his way any deeper under her skin.

They stayed and visited a short while longer with Aunt Ro before she became tired and returned to her room for a nap. After a rousing game of gin with Mrs. Duffy, the woman Jerry had first thought was his aunt, they drove back home.

Kim had just taken the key out of the ignition when they heard a commotion from the lake behind her house. Jerry maneuvered himself out of the car and leaned against his crutches.

"It sounds like the Neidermeyers' dog got loose again, and he's after the geese."

She started toward the noise, but Jerry stopped her with a hand on her arm. "No, it's too dangerous." Then, ignoring his own advice, he hobbled toward the back of the house. "Go inside where it's safe," he called to her over his shoulder.

"Jerry, don't get in the middle of it. You'll only get hurt."

Although the geese were wild, they stuck around for the grain she scattered for them each day and bedded down in the relative safety of the barn. She knew from experience that a nip from a powerful beak could be quite painful. A dog's fangs could certainly inflict much more damage.

Heedless of her warning, Jerry continued down the hill. It was clear he intended to break up the fracas bare-handed. After all he'd gone through to survive the car crash, she couldn't let him endanger himself unnecessarily. Remembering the handgun Gerald had given her for protection out here in what he referred to as "the boondocks," she opened the side door to go in the house and returned a moment later with the heavy weapon.

By the time she made it down to the lake, there were feathers everywhere. The stout-chested dog—inappropriately named Muffin by the Neidermeyers who had bought him to guard their home—clung to a wildly flapping brown goose. The bird's terrified shrieks pierced Kim's heart.

Lifting the pistol, she fired a shot into the air, but the noise only seemed to intensify the dog's attack on the hapless goose. This time, she held the weapon with both hands and drew a bead. Jerry stood squarely in the middle of her sights.

"Get out of the way," Kim cried.

She wasn't the best shot, she knew, but even if she only grazed the dog, maybe it would be enough to frighten him away. And if she missed and hit the goose, a quick death would still be preferable to the painful one Muffin surely had in store for it.

The problem was, Jerry refused to move out of the line of fire. Ignoring her request, he hobbled closer to the action.

Kim squeezed her eyes shut. Helpless to stop him and certain that the rampaging dog would turn on him, she could not watch what was sure to follow. She could go call the emergency number for help, she realized, but they wouldn't get here in time to prevent the disaster that was imminent. They could, however, rescue what was left of him.

When she opened her eyes a mere second later, Jerry was threading his belt through the dog's collar. Muffin sat obediently at his feet, tail thumping apologetically on the ground. The goose had broken free and taken refuge under the forsythia bush by the barn.

Easing closer—cautiously, for fear of agitating the dog again—she picked up Jerry's crutches and handed them to him. In return, he passed the makeshift leash to her.

"If you'll take him next door, I'll have a look at the bird's wing to see how badly it's injured."

Stunned, Kim stared down at the complacent dog at her feet, then back up at her former fiancé.

"It's okay," Jerry assured her. "He won't hurt you."

"How did you do that?"

Adjusting the crutches under his arms, Jerry gave her a smile that looked almost beatific. "I have a way with animals."

"You didn't like animals before. You said they were a nuisance."

Forgoing a reply, he merely shrugged.

He was right, Kim realized as she led Muffin back to his yard. In many ways, Jerry wasn't the man she used to know. She paused and turned to watch as he limped toward the trusting goose.

It wasn't natural, she decided. Even though she'd been feeding the wild birds since she moved here two years ago, she'd never been able to get closer than five or six feet from them. And now here was Jerry, fetching the docile creature out from under the bush and examining its wing.

The goose must be in shock. Yes, that was it. In its dazed condition, the bird was too foggy brained to remember its fear of man.

That might explain the bird, she thought, but what of the dog? As they passed the gate that led to the neighbor's backyard, she saw the loosened fence rail that had been pushed aside, allowing Muffin to squeeze through to freedom. How had Jerry managed to calm the animal that, only seconds before, had been thirsty for blood?

By the time she had spoken to Mrs. Neidermeyer—

who graciously offered to pay any veterinary fees—and returned home, Jerry was coming back from the barn.

He shook his head. "The wing isn't broken," he said as he entered the house behind her, "but it's going to take some time to heal. I'll check on him later tonight and again in the morning."

His suit pants were muddy and flecks of blood dotted his shirt, but he was otherwise unscathed by the incident. As he wiped his shoes on the mat by the kitchen door, Kim was hit by the realization that it could have been *his* blood on the shirt. And, much more than she would have liked, the thought that he could have been seriously hurt unsettled her.

Oddly, her fear for his well-being was different from the feeling she'd had when he was in the hospital. Then, she'd been responding out of a universal love for a fellow man. But this unease in the pit of her being told her that her reaction was out of a specific love for this particular man.

Kim crossed the kitchen to the sink and ran some water into a glass. Her hand was shaking as she lifted it to her lips.

She couldn't allow herself to feel this type of concern for him or indulge in the warm, sensual dreams that came to her at night. He'd already hurt her once, far more than she'd ever been hurt by anyone before, and she could not stand there like a bowling pin waiting to be knocked down again.

She had to get him out of the house. It wasn't a conscious choice. Rather, it was a decision made of instinct, much as a mouse instinctively fears a hawk. Only, in her case, it was a matter of survival of the heart.

Setting her glass in the sink, Kim knew what she had to do. If Jerry was well enough to go chasing down to the lake to break up a fight between dog and goose, then he was well enough to stay by himself while she went back to work. Hopefully, not long after that he'd be well enough to return to his own apartment. She placed her hands on the sink's edge to steady herself. If only she could calm her shaking nerves.

Thumping across the vinyl-covered floor, Jerry stopped behind the woman he'd been assigned to protect. She stood with her back to him, and though it appeared that she tried to hide it, he could tell she was trembling.

Reaching out, he touched her small shoulder. She flinched but did not move away.

"Are you all right?"

She turned to face him, her eyes red and misty and her mouth tight with tension. "Just scared," she said, trying to shrug away the incident.

Propping himself on his crutches, he opened his arms to her. After a second's hesitation, she came to him and pressed her cheek against his chest.

Of course. He should have known. She had been frightened by the attack on the goose...perhaps even frightened for her own safety.

Then it occurred to him. If he hadn't been there to break up the fight, she could have been seriously injured. He may have even saved her life. Jerry wondered if he should stand away from her in case he was suddenly called home to collect his reward of a brand new pair of wings. He stroked her hair and thought how, even though he'd only known her a short time, he would miss her.

Looking heavenward, he waited for a sign that he had successfully completed his mission. Instead, all he saw was that a spider had spun a web in the corner of the ceiling.

No lightning bolt struck, and he didn't vaporize and drift upward out of Gerald's body.

Bummer.

Kim straightened and pulled away from him, breaking the pleasant human experience of having their bodies touch.

Double bummer.

"I'm going back to work tomorrow." She turned toward the refrigerator and started pulling out ground beef, tomatoes, green peppers and onions. "Judging by the way you handled Muffin and the goose, I think you're capable of staying by yourself for a few hours during the day. I'll make plenty of spaghetti tonight so you can reheat the leftovers for lunch tomorrow."

All afternoon he'd been wanting to ask her more about the subject Aunt Rowena had inadvertently opened. But he could tell Kim must have anticipated his curiosity about her engagement to Gerald and was steering the conversation to safer territory.

Jerry backed out of her way as she headed to the pantry for spices. She didn't look at him as she moved methodically around the kitchen, and he got the feeling her brusqueness was intended to put emotional distance between them.

That feeling was still there the following morning as she prepared to go to work.

When he heard her moving around, he got up and joined her for breakfast. This morning they had frozen waffles, but they didn't get a chance to repeat yesterday's kisses. At the speed she was moving, it was impossible even to carry on a conversation with her. All Jerry could do was sit and feel the breeze she created as she ran around gathering briefcase, purse and keys.

She was calling goodbye as she ran out the front door. A moment later, the door opened again, and she left a slip of paper on the coffee table. "Here's my number at work. Call me if you need anything."

And then she was gone. It was the longest day Jerry had experienced since he'd taken on this assignment.

First he busied himself by washing the breakfast dishes in the liquid detergent he'd seen advertised on television. When he was done, he examined his hands to see if they were any softer than when he'd started. Rubbing the fingers of his left hand over the back of his right, Jerry couldn't discern any difference. Compared to Kim's skin, they seemed rough. Hmm, maybe it would take more than one dishwashing session for the change to be noticed.

After all that time, he decided it must surely be lunchtime. He glanced at the digital clock on the microwave. Eight-seventeen a.m. He tried to recall the hour when they usually had their midday meal, but he knew eight was wrong.

Let's see. It was a holy number, if he remembered correctly. Three, maybe? For the Holy Trinity? No, that didn't seem right. How about seven, for the number of days it took to create the earth and to rest afterward? No, that would have been an hour ago.

Then it must be twelve, for the number of disciples. Yes, that was it! Jerry smiled, immensely pleased with

himself for getting it right. Then he sat down to wait for
the microwave to change to the numbers that would in-
dicate it was finally lunch o'clock.

While he was watching, he wondered why he had received no sign from Nahum since saving Kim's life yesterday. Hadn't he done his job by putting her safety first?
He was extremely proud of himself for staying alert to
his protectee's needs. So why hadn't his superior ac-
knowledged his success?

Jerry puzzled over Nahum's silence on the matter,
watching the clock until 8:21. Lunchtime was taking too
long this way. Perhaps he could do something else while
the electronic numerals blinked their way toward noon
and, ultimately, Kim's return home.

Remembering his promise to check on the goose's
recovery, he made his way out to the barn, picking up
feathers and stuffing them down his shirt as he went.
Inside the barn, the goose had bedded down on a shelf
near the tin of grain.

Jerry opened the can and offered the bird a handful
of kernels. The goose's healthy appetite was a good indicator that he would make it through the ordeal.

"I thought for sure you were a goner," he told the
trusting bird as he inspected its bedraggled wing.
"Lucky for you, Lazarus, you managed to defy death
this time."

If he wasn't in this human body, he would be able to
pass some of his energy to the bird to heal it. Deciding
it was worth a try, he took a quick glance around him
to see if anyone was watching before he moved his
palms slowly over the wing. When he was done, he took
another look.

Same as before.

Jerry sighed, frustrated by his inability to perform even to his former inadequate standards. If he'd been lacking as a protectorate, how was he supposed to take care of a bird—much less Kim, while in human form? It would be impossible to carry out his assignment if he had to work with such severe limitations.

Maybe that was part of his test. If he could—by wit or whatever—fulfill his obligation despite the flesh-and-blood equipment he'd been given to work with, perhaps he could bypass the starter-wing set and go straight to the intermediate pair.

As a protectorate, he'd often seen—and wondered why—humans overlook their best source of strength. With their ability to communicate directly with the Chairman of the Board, they could accomplish so much more if they would only tap into the power of prayer.

Well, he wouldn't make that mistake. He bowed his head and said a quick one, asking for help in keeping Kim safe. Not wishing to leave the goose out, he added, "And Lazarus, too."

Then, leaving another handful of grain on the rough board in front of the bird, he went outside and scattered more for the ducks and geese at the edge of the lake.

Back inside, he dumped the loose feathers he'd collected into a pillowcase and set it beside his bed. He didn't know what he would do with the feathers, but he hated to see them go to waste.

The microwave clock showed that it was only 8:52. Since the last thirty-one minutes had ticked by faster than the four he'd watched, he decided to turn his attention to some of the potential dangers he'd noted around the house.

After locating some tools in the utility room, Jerry spent the rest of the morning tightening the stair banister, fixing the uneven porch step, and shoring up the loose leg on Kim's favorite chair. The workmanship wasn't the best, but at least his efforts would reduce the risk to Kim's well-being.

That done, he ate his leftover spaghetti in front of the television. Today, Dirk and Andrea were conniving to send their rich aunt to an early demise so they could collect a fat inheritance.

Jerry snorted in disgust. It was people like this who made the job of protectorate so difficult. He punched the TV zapper until he came to an attractive woman extolling the qualities of washable wall paint. A telephone number was displayed at the bottom of the screen, and she was urging him to get his credit card now.

He didn't own a credit card—at least, he didn't *think* he did—but Kim had one in her desk. When he'd asked her what it was, she'd explained that a person could buy stuff with it and that she kept hers at home so she wouldn't be tempted to use it.

Well, this would be his good deed for the day. By using the credit card for her, he'd be sparing her the temptation. Jerry gave himself a congratulatory pat on the back for being so virtuous. He hoped he'd get bonus points in his performance folder for this.

Before the day was over, he'd ordered the paint, sheepskin seat covers for the car, a set of limited-edition prints depicting various kinds of horses, an all-purpose kitchen utensil, a year's supply of chewable vitamins, a copper bracelet for Kim and a picture of Elvis in neon colors on black velvet.

He smiled as he returned the credit card to her desk drawer. Kim would be so pleased when she found out what he'd done.

except his reflection in Kim and a picture of them in love in a bottle on the bureau.

He started to remind the employees of his best days with a smile. Then gritted, as he had looked at what he'd made.

CHAPTER FIVE

BY THE end of the week, Kim was ready to kick off her shoes and put her feet up in the chair Jerry had fixed for her. What with all the work that had piled up while she'd been pulling nurse duty, not to mention the merger deal that was finally getting under way, she hadn't taken the time to eat lunch today.

Her stomach growled as she pulled into the driveway, reminding her that Jerry may have started dinner again. This week, he'd attempted some simple microwave recipes, all of which had turned out fairly well. She'd asked him not to try using the stove yet since this old farmhouse would go up like a torch if he made a mistake.

As she got out of the car, a brown van pulled up behind her, and a man in a matching brown uniform handed her a small package.

Kim frowned down at the box in her hands. "Who's this from?" she asked. "I wasn't expecting anything."

He shrugged and turned to get back in his delivery van. "Probably something else for Jerry." With a smile, he added, "Tell him my wife wants that microwave cake recipe. I'll pick it up when I see him next week." And then he was gone.

Jerry met her at the door. "Oh, good, it came."

He started to take the package from her, then seemed to reconsider.

"Go ahead and open it. I know you're going to love it."

Kim looked down at his legs that, except for the orange cast, were bare from the knee down. "What happened to your good slacks?"

"They're shorts now." He looked as proud as if he'd sewn them himself. "Everybody on TV is wearing them, so I thought I'd try it, too. I'm just having a little trouble getting them to sag."

The custom-tailored pants had been chopped off at the knees and pushed down at the waist to expose the white elastic band of his skivvies.

He hooked a thumb under the waistband of his plain white briefs and gave a tug. "And these whitey-tighties aren't cool anymore," he said, using the teen slang he'd heard on television. "But I should be getting some new boxers any day now."

Kim closed the door and sank into the overstuffed chair. Out of habit, she braced herself for the inevitable jolt. Then she remembered that Jerry had fixed the chair earlier this week. She'd been trying to hold on to such positive thoughts when faced with the surprises he'd sprung upon her return home each day. She sank back into the chair again and covered her eyes with her hand.

"Is something the matter?" he asked in all innocence.

Innocence. It helped to keep in mind that he wasn't *intentionally* driving her crazy. "You'd think so if you remembered how much those slacks originally cost you."

He looked down at the abomination with an expression of disdain. "I thought they were hand-me-downs.

Didn't imagine anyone would purposely buy clothes like these.''

"You may as well get used to them. The closet at your apartment is filled with that style of clothes."

Jerry—correction, Gerald, as he was known before the accident—had always insisted on buying the best brand-name clothes from the most exclusive shops. He never wore jeans and always prided himself on his crisp, tailored appearance.

Kim found it amusing that these clothes clashed with the new, casual side of his personality that had emerged since the accident. She'd tried to get Gerald to loosen up in his attire, at least when he wasn't at work, but he'd refused. "If you want, we can go shopping for new stuff this weekend."

His demeanor brightened visibly. Apparently remembering the package she'd carried in, he pushed it toward her. "Aren't you going to open it?"

He perched on the edge of her chair while she tugged at the filament tape that held the parcel shut. Kim tried not to notice the strong, muscled thigh that crowded her or the light furring of hair that covered the exposed part of his leg. When he balanced himself by propping one hand against the back of her chair, it was all she could do to keep from leaning back into him.

It was too bad that the men with heavenly bodies couldn't also have personalities to match. Of course, since the accident, Jerry had been sweeter and more personable, but she knew it wouldn't last. As soon as his memory returned, he'd go back to being the same hard-driving, goal-oriented, me-first kind of person he'd always been.

Maybe she should keep her eyes peeled for the ugliest, most wimp-bodied man in Chesden and ask him for a date. If she couldn't have both looks and personality, she'd opt for the man on the inside.

She sneaked a glance up at Jerry, who was urging her to be quicker about opening the package. Dark eyebrows that matched his short-cropped hair in color hooded the shimmery blue of his eyes. His well-defined nose, cheekbones and chin offered a classically masculine profile. And his lips, which she'd grown accustomed to seeing pulled in a thin, straight line over his white teeth, were now turned upward in a most endearing smile. The gesture created a small, vertical dimple in his cheek that tempted her to touch it.

What a shame all of that was wasted on him.

As she pulled away the bubble wrap that surrounded the contents of the box, something mooed.

Jerry laughed. Unable to wait any longer, he withdrew two colorful plastic figures, one a cartoonish cow wearing an apron and the other a pig in overalls. "Aren't they great?" He pointed to the holes on the tops of their heads. "They're salt and pepper shakers. Watch this."

He turned them upside down and shook them as if he were seasoning his food, and each made its respective barnyard sound.

"I'll bet you've never seen anything like this before."

"There's a reason for that," she said dryly. Even so, she couldn't resist shaking the tacky things.

Before the accident, he would have insisted on nothing less than Waterford lead crystal, a style that would have been even more at odds in her rustic farmhouse than these childish gadgets.

"How much?" she asked.

"Fourteen ninety-five." He paused. "Plus shipping and handling."

Kim sighed. "Well, that's still less than Waterford."

Jerry swiveled on the arm of the chair to face her. "You don't have to worry about the cost," he assured her. "I used your credit card."

"You what?"

"When I called the number on television, the person who answered asked for the numbers from a credit card. And since you didn't want to use it yourself, I spared you the temptation." He beamed, apparently proud of his industriousness. "You know, those people were so nice. They said that because of all the stuff I ordered, I am now a *preferred* customer."

"You mean there's more?"

"Sure. Do you want to see it?"

As she followed him to his room, her gaze was drawn downward. How could a man with such a cute butt have such a thick head?

If she'd been surprised by the salt and pepper shakers, then she was flabbergasted by the rest of the junk that littered the guest room. "Why did you buy all this stuff?"

"I didn't buy it," he insisted. "I just gave them the numbers on your credit card and they sent it to me."

She was going to have to block all but the Disney channel if he kept this up. "It's got to go back. All of it."

When Jerry started to argue, she shook her head. Why was she being tested like this? She picked up a bottle of vitamins shaped like Jerry's favorite cartoon characters. Beside the carton of vitamins lay a copper bracelet.

"What did you intend to do with all this stuff?" she asked.

"Most of it's for you." He slid the bracelet onto her wrist. "This is to ward off bad luck, and the vitamins are to keep you healthy. I want you to live at least into your eighties."

He seemed so sincere that Kim hated to disappoint him. But there was no way she could afford all this. Briefly, she explained how credit-card purchases work, and his surprised reaction proved he hadn't even considered the possibility that she would eventually have to pay for them.

By the time they went through it all, they'd decided to keep the paint because the kitchen could use a fresh coat, the horse prints because Jerry convinced her they'd look better than the magazine pictures that currently adorned the den, and the salt and pepper shakers because...well, she hadn't figured that one out yet.

The only thing still unboxed for return was the Elvis-on-velvet picture. "You're not thinking of keeping that, are you?"

"Of course." He thoughtfully ran a finger over the black velvet. "I met him once."

Kim couldn't hold back a snicker. "Before or after he died?"

"After, of course. We played fenuki." He looked up, his sky blue eyes capturing her gaze. "I would've won if he hadn't cheated more than I did."

Kim hadn't the vaguest notion what he was talking

about. "We'll have to talk to the doctor about these hallucinations of yours."

"That reminds me," he said, holding a finger aloft. "The doctor's secretary called today. I have a follow-up appointment scheduled for Tuesday."

Great. Maybe the doctor would give him a clean bill of health so he could return to his own apartment. Maybe if she didn't see him every day, she wouldn't be tormented by traitorous thoughts of reconciling with him.

Then again, maybe fairies lived in the woods beyond the lake.

"Tell me what you see."

Jerry sat on the edge of the flower box that the previous owner had built at the base of the mulberry tree. Reaching a hand up, he tugged at her wrist until she joined him.

Once she was seated, Kim leaned wearily against him. Turning to her, Jerry draped an arm around her shoulders and couldn't help noticing the twin pillows of white that peeked out from the scoop neck of her shirt. He experienced an immediate physical reaction to the breathtaking sight.

"I see a lake, a barn, and a patch of woods behind them both. Now, if you don't mind—" she moved to get up, but Jerry held her tight "—I have work to do."

"What's so important about your work that it won't wait until the sun finishes showing off for us?"

As if to punctuate his statement, the pink-and-orange ball slipped lower over the lake, its image reflecting on the water's surface and blending with the sky in watercolor shades of pink, purple, orange and yellow. The ducks, shaking their feathers as they came out of the lake, seemed unaware of the magnificent display behind them.

She didn't answer his question, but she made no move to leave, either. Finally, she admitted, "It *is* beautiful. I've lived here two years, and this is the first time I've watched the sun set."

They sat in companionable silence until the sun had submerged itself behind the trees, leaving a fading canvas in its wake.

"Here," he said, handing her a small blossom plucked from the rosebush beside the house. "Smell this."

She accepted the flower and gave it an appreciative sniff.

"You work too hard," he said solemnly. "You need to learn to enjoy the many blessings you receive every day."

She touched the rose to his cheek, noting the coarse whiskers that had sprouted since this morning. A month ago, even if she and Gerald had bothered to walk down here to the lake, their conversation would have been filled with details about the pending merger. This corporate change had been high on Gerald's priority list. Now, if it was on his mind at all, it was pushed far to the back.

"Maybe I can slow down after this business transaction is completed," she suggested.

"Maybe?"

"You're starting to sound like my father."

"And you're starting to sound like a workaholic."

"Well, you're a fine one to talk." She didn't mean

for her tone to sound so snippy, but it irritated her that he was the one who had insisted on the merger and now he was chiding her for picking up the ball he'd dropped. When she spoke again, her voice was softer. "You were the one who initiated the merger," she reminded him. "You said this would be a good way to increase our profits."

He looked thoughtful for a moment. "Is your father's company in financial trouble without the merger?"

Kim gave a little laugh. "No, Barnett's Bakery has never been stronger."

Giving a nod of understanding, he turned to face her. "So, merging will help reduce your workload."

She looked down at the ground and followed the progress of a beetle through the grass. "Actually, it'll mean *increased* responsibilities."

"Then why are you going through with it?"

Bless his heart, he looked as though he really cared about how this change would affect her. Last month, he'd been more concerned with how the new promotion opportunities would affect *him*.

"Because of you," she said honestly. "It was something that meant a lot to you. Dad doesn't care whether he expands the business this late in his life, and I have enough work and income to keep me happy. But since you were so gung ho about the possibility, we were willing to support it." She stretched her foot out to block the beetle's path, and the bug did an about-face. "When Carmen suggested that you be given a position on the subsidiary company's board of directors, Dad said it was the least we could do to keep his future son-in-law happy."

As soon as she said it, she realized her mistake. By bringing up their former relationship, she was certain she'd opened a can of worms. She glanced over at him to see if he would bite at the bait she had inadvertently dangled in front of him.

He did.

"Why didn't it work out?"

Kim took a deep breath. It was a question she'd asked herself many times. Rather than bring up the incident that had sealed his fate with her—and risk a second humiliation—she summed it up as simply as she could. "You weren't ready to settle down."

Leaning back against the tree trunk, he idly stroked his hands over the cheerful mix of spring flowers that grew at its base. "What besides work did you and Gerald have in common?"

By now it seemed natural to refer to Jerry's previous persona as a separate being, for the man she talked with tonight was nothing like the man she'd been engaged to marry. Her lack of an answer told him what he wanted to know.

"Then what attracted you to him?"

Kim couldn't help grinning as she recalled the first time she'd seen the new executive her father had hired. Gerald was bending over the water cooler, his crisp, tailored slacks pleated to perfection and providing an outstanding showcase for what was one of his best features.

"His butt," she said without hesitation. "He had the cutest derriere that was neither too tight nor too round. It was all I could do to keep from pinching it." If she'd thought Gerald was impressive from behind, she had been stunned into speechlessness when he had straightened from the water cooler and given her a glimpse of the broad shoulders, firm chest and thick upper arms that filled out his white dress shirt. "Talk about body chemistry…my gosh, I practically went into heat just looking—"

She stopped, suddenly embarrassingly aware that she was talking about *Jerry*. It was bad enough that she had let him know what power he held over her body; it was worse that he may have wrongly interpreted her remarks to mean she was still interested in him.

"I—I'm sorry. I don't know why I blurted that out." She stood, trying to distance herself from the man who had managed to wring her emotions inside out. "Let's just forget I ever said anything."

He didn't move from his seat. Didn't try to gloat or laugh it off. Just sat there, staring at her as she shoved her hands into her jeans pockets and paced in front of him.

"Do you know what I first noticed about you?" he said gently.

Kim stopped pacing, her back to him. She wanted to end the conversation and go back to the easy friendship that had grown between them in the weeks since the accident. But, even more, she wanted to hear what he had to say. Needed to hear that there was something he'd found attractive about her…that is, before he'd noticed something even more tempting in that other woman.

He didn't wait for her response but just plunged right in. "I noticed that you had kind eyes. Eyes that had seen pain but still looked with compassion on a fellow human in his time of need."

Of course. She should have realized he was talking

about the first time he'd seen her at the hospital. It was stupid to wish he'd felt the same physical pull, the same rush of adrenaline....

"Kind eyes. That's what someone might say about a cocker spaniel." She turned in time to see his handsome face redden.

"Well, there was one other thing—two, actually—but I wasn't sure it would be gentlemanly to mention how pretty you looked in that tank top."

This time, it was Kim's turn to blush.

Jerry stood and joined her. Thinking he was ready to go inside, Kim handed him his crutches, but he propped them against the tree and reached for her instead. Her emotions swung crazily between a strong physical thrill at being held closely in his arms and a sense of foreboding that told her not to let her heart get too attached to this temporary man in her life.

She looked up at him, noting his expression of concern. The sky glowed eerily behind him, and she could have sworn she saw a hazy ring encircling his head.

"What's the matter?" he asked.

"It's the strangest thing. From this angle, the colors in the sky make it look like there's a halo around your head."

He looked away from her and fidgeted a moment before answering. "Must be that new shampoo I ordered from TV. It's for hard-to-manage hair. Heavenly Hair shampoo is guaranteed to make it behave like an angel." With a grin, he added, "Must be working."

Jerry turned so that his back was no longer to the setting sun. To distract her from what she'd just seen, he steered the conversation back to the subject of work.

"I think you should forget about the merger."

"That's crazy. The wheels are already set in motion."

"Can't you stop it?"

"I suppose. But why should I?"

She tried to step out of his reach, but when Jerry pretended he needed her support to help him balance, she remained in his arms.

"Because you need to lighten your burden. Because Barnett's Bakery is doing just fine as a family business. Because—" he ran a hand through his hair "—if the merger takes place, what will you do besides work yourself into an early grave?"

And ruin his chance of getting his first-ever pair of wings. Humans could be so exasperating sometimes.

"You have more to contribute than that. There's so much more in life for you to experience than just work."

She appeared to consider his words. "As soon as you get over your amnesia, you'll want to start the acquisition again."

"No, I won't," he said sincerely. To prove himself, he would have to convince her that he'd already recovered his memory. So he started reciting some facts he'd memorized from the papers in Gerald's wallet. "My name is Gerald Everett Kirkland. I live at 305 Downing Street in the city. I'm thirty-two years old, and my blood type is O positive. See, I have my memory back and I still want to forget about the merger."

She looked skeptical. "What's your secretary's name?"

Fortunately, there had been a note tucked in the wallet reminding him of an appointment that had been scheduled for the Monday after the accident. He took a chance that the person who'd signed the note was his secretary. "Donna?"

Surprise flickered in her eyes, but she quickly recovered. "How many fish are in the tank in your office?"

Jerry frowned down at her. She was making his job more difficult than it needed to be. He'd been fortunate so far, and he hoped his luck would continue to hold. Remembering the miracle about feeding thousands with five loaves of bread and two fishes, he ventured a guess. "Two?" Even as he spoke, the number seemed too low.

"Hah! You don't have any fish!"

"They died?"

"No, you *lied* about getting your memory back."

She pushed at his chest, but Jerry couldn't bring himself to let her go.

"What difference does it make?" he asked. "The important thing is that I care about you, and I want what's best for you."

What scared him almost as much as the thought of her working so hard was the fact that he was starting to care for her...too much, perhaps. That hadn't been part of the plan when he took this assignment. Although there had been occasions when he'd grown fond of the clients he watched over, they'd been nothing like this. If he wanted to do his job well, he would have to keep his mind—and not his heart—focused on Kim.

Even so, he couldn't resist one last kiss.

At the mall the following day, Kim found that Jerry couldn't resist striking up conversations with total strangers. At first, his behavior embarrassed her, but when she saw how some of them—older ladies, especially—took a shine to him, she stopped worrying.

"Hey, where'd you get those sandals?" he asked a preteen boy who was coming out of the candy shop.

The shaggy-haired kid popped a gummy candy into his mouth and hitched a finger over his shoulder toward the discount shoe store. Jerry saluted his thanks to the boy and started off in that direction.

"Are you sure you want to go in here?" Kim asked. "You always used to prefer the *quality* shops." She grimaced at the obnoxious way Gerald's pet phrase sounded coming out of her mouth.

Jerry paused outside the store. "Quality's good. Do you suppose they sell shoes like that boy is wearing?"

She shrugged. "I doubt it."

Using one of his crutches as a pointer, he waved her in ahead of him. "Then this place is fine."

Inside, she pulled a box from an overstacked shelf and handed it to Jerry, who had taken a seat nearby. "All they have in your size is this black-and-brown pair."

He made a face. Obviously, he would have preferred neon-bright rainbow colors. Nevertheless, he tried them on. His broad foot fit perfectly in the confines of the wide nylon straps, and the odd mix of masculine colors looked better on him than it did in the box.

"Not bad," she said.

But he was more interested in the Velcro closure. "Look at this," he declared in a hushed tone of amazement. "You don't have to wrap the ends around your ankle and tie them on. They fasten all by themselves!"

The repeated ripping sound of Velcro being pulled apart filled the store. A toddler, distracted by the sound, pulled away from her mother to get a closer look. The little girl stood there and giggled until her mother dragged her back to their bench where she'd been trying on pink sneakers.

Feeling a kinship with the parent of the distractible child, Kim stood and handed Jerry the shoe he'd worn into the store. He had only tried on the one sandal since the cast covered part of his right foot. She picked up the box. "Are you going to get these?"

"Of course."

From the back of the long, narrow store, they would have to dodge children squirming on the floor, adults standing in the aisles, and boxes and their contents scattered helter-skelter. Kim walked in front of Jerry so she could clear a path for him and his crutches.

When they were halfway to the cash register, she came upon two boys horsing around in the center aisle. She wasn't sure of their age, but their large size was an indicator they were old enough to know better. Rather than risk having them bump into Jerry and knock him off balance, she stepped to the left aisle where the going was clear except for a couple of shoe boxes that someone hadn't bothered to return to the shelf.

She paused, waiting for the *thump-thump* of Jerry's crutches to catch up with her. The boys' laughter in the next aisle abruptly stopped, and one of them told the other, "Quit it!" The other child mimicked the first, and sounds of scuffling followed. Kim wondered why the children's parents didn't intervene and put a stop to the unruly behavior.

When Jerry had caught up with her, she turned to lead the way once again. From the other side of the shelves, she heard the sound of a fist hitting flesh. Angry words were exchanged, and what had started as horseplay now turned into an all-out fight.

In the next instant, the shelves beside her shook with the force of a hundred-pound kid being thrown against it. Above her, teetering boxes of men's hiking boots were thrown loose from their precarious position.

From that point on, it seemed as though things happened in slow motion. But, despite the fact that she could see what was happening and her mind was registering the danger of the situation, she couldn't bring her body to react.

A strong hand gripped her upper arm, and with a split second to spare, Kim was pulled backward, away from the hurtling boxes.

She felt herself crash against Jerry's chest. The momentum sent them both tumbling downward. His arms encircled her, and she felt his body twist so that he hit the thin carpet first. Unable to prevent it, she fell against him, knocking the wind out of them both.

As she tried to regain her breath, she saw that the heavy wooden shelf in front of her had been thrown forward—its contents in a disheveled heap on the floor—its descent stopped only by the wall of shoes to her left.

If Jerry hadn't pulled her back when he did, she would have been bombarded with the plummeting boxes and then hit by the falling shelf. Her breathing easier, she leaned on one elbow to look at the man who had saved her from serious harm.

His eyes were shut. She leaned closer, her breasts

touching his hard chest, and stroked his dark hair away from his forehead. "Are you all right?"

Jerry opened his eyes, displaying light blue irises that now looked paler than she'd ever seen before.

He sucked in a deep breath, noting with pleasure the soft pressure of her breasts against his sore ribs. She pursed her full lips, concern evident in her every feature. He looked down the length of her body. Except for her mussed hair, she seemed to be unhurt.

The leaning shelf beyond them and the boxes scattered at their feet gave testimony to their near miss. Jerry's heart raced when he saw how close she'd come to serious injury. Looking up at the heavy shelf, he knew that if she had been caught in its path, she could have been crushed against the wall.

She could have been killed. Fear for her coiled through his body. He raised his hand to her face to assure himself that she was, indeed, safe from harm.

Then realization dawned. He had saved her life. Unlike the dog-and-goose fight, there was no doubt that his intervention had protected her.

His mission now complete, he prepared for the return trip home where he would be presented with his first pair of wings. A sadness filled his being as he thought of not seeing her again for at least fifty years.

Of course, fifty years would pass in the blink of an eye back home. But now that he'd come to know Kim and care for her, an eye blink was too long to wait. He reached up and slid his hand behind her neck. Since he wasn't sure which method Nahum would use to transport him back, or even *when* his supervisor would do so, he would have to say his goodbyes quickly.

"My time here on Earth is over. I'm going to miss you," he told her, "but we'll meet again in Heaven."

With that said, he pulled her to him and kissed her as he'd never done before. This would be her last memory of him, and he wanted it to be special. And, selfishly, he wanted a memory of his own to treasure as he awaited their reunion on high.

It was a passionate kiss, full of unfulfilled hopes and dreams...full of the sweet sadness of what would never be.

CHAPTER SIX

HER lips were full and soft, and she willingly responded to his kiss, returning it with a passion that matched his own. He slipped his arms around her and was rewarded with a sensation of light-headedness.

After a long moment that surpassed anything he'd ever experienced in paradise, Kim pulled away, her soft brown eyes watching him carefully. Her lips, red and swollen from their kiss, lifted in a gentle smile.

"You're not going to die, Jerry."

"Perhaps not as *you* know it, but I'll be leaving you soon."

Apparently unconvinced, she smiled wider and shook her head. She got to her feet, and Jerry reluctantly clambered up after her.

What with all the confusion, it took a while for them to make their way to the front and pay for the shoes. By the time they exited the store, Jerry was beginning to wonder if Nahum had failed to notice his extraordinary deed.

Just his luck. He'd finally kept his attention on his assignment long enough to make the save of his career, and nobody noticed.

They stopped near a bookstore. Kim faced him and touched his arm. For some unexplained reason, he wanted to flex his muscles for her. Instead, he just leaned more heavily on that crutch. He was rewarded for his effort when she idly traced her finger along his raised triceps.

"Thanks for what you did in there. You saved my neck."

He'd saved her *life,* actually, but he resisted the urge to correct her. No sense bragging...he was just doing his job.

At that moment, a bearded man in a rope-banded headpiece and flowing white robe came around the bend toward them. Jerry stared, transfixed, as the image came toward him. Nahum's messenger appeared so clear, so lifelike, that he wondered if Kim was aware of his presence.

"Is something wrong?" she asked.

Without thinking, he automatically said what was on his mind. "He's coming to take me away."

She followed the direction of his gaze and gave a laugh. "No, that would be a man in a white *coat.*"

Jerry frowned at her. Humans said the strangest things sometimes. He noticed that her eyes were following the messenger who was approaching them. Maybe she could see him after all.

Seemingly unaware of their presence, the messenger looked as though he might walk right past them. Jerry moved into the walkway, effectively blocking his path.

"I am prepared to go now," Jerry announced in his most formal tone. Then, quickly, he added, "No, wait a minute."

Reaching for Kim, he gave her one last, quick kiss. She looked confused by his action. Not surprising, since humans weren't familiar with the workings of the Human Resources Department.

"Of all the people I've been assigned to protect," he told her, "you are the most special." The messenger was getting fidgety…trying to continue his walk down the corridor. He'd have to make this quick. "We *will* meet again," he told her sincerely.

And he'd be waiting for her. It took a great deal of courage for him to walk away from this particular human. Steeling his resolve, he turned to the one who would accompany him back.

Jerry supposed they'd just start walking down the corridor and then do the fade-out thing. He got in step beside him. "I'm ready when you are."

The messenger's eyebrows drew together, calling attention to the mole in the center of his forehead. When he spoke, it was with a lilting accent. "I beg your pardon?"

He felt Kim's hand on his arm. "Jerry, leave the man alone. Come on, let's go get lunch, and I'll buy you an ice cream for dessert."

For the first time, it occurred to him that this might not be someone from Human Resources. The man watched him cautiously, and Kim seemed more confused by Jerry than usual.

He felt himself grow warm. Apparently, Kim had been right when she'd thanked him for saving her neck rather than her life. It looked as though his job here wasn't finished after all. Embarrassed at having made such a glaring error, he tried to cover his tracks. "Uh, I was wondering if you could tell me where you bought your robe?"

The man scowled a moment, then answered, "Mecca."

Jerry stepped aside to let him pass. "Thanks. That's all I wanted to know."

The stranger walked away, glancing over his shoulder a couple of times, possibly to make sure he wasn't being followed.

When Jerry turned back to Kim, he saw that she had her hands on her hips. He was learning to read her moods, and this wasn't one of the better ones.

"Awesome outfit, huh?"

"If you bother anyone else today—including me— I'm going home." Her brown eyes darkened perceptibly. "With or without you."

Kim glanced at the confusing man sitting beside her on the mall bench. After that incident with the Arab man, Jerry cleaned up his act and refrained from initiating conversations with strangers. In fact, the rest of their shopping trip had actually been fun. His observations of people and situations were fresh and held a childlike sense of discovery. Because of his unique insights, she had been forced to examine the small, interesting tidbits of everyday life that she normally didn't pause to notice.

Why couldn't Gerald have been more like this before the accident? Sure, he was exasperating at times now, but at least he was fun and he made her laugh. And at least he wasn't two-timing her with another woman.

Where was that woman anyway? she wondered. Why hadn't she come forward after the accident and been there for him during his recovery? Obviously, she was a user who only wanted him when she could get something from him. And now that he needed help, she must have turned to another good-time Charlie.

Kim shook away the crazy sense of indignation that overwhelmed her. As the two-timed party, she should be feeling indignant for herself rather than for Jerry. But, for some reason, she couldn't work up any anger toward him. And that scared her.

She stood and gathered some of the bags that littered the bench and floor around them. "It looks like it's going to rain. Maybe we should leave now before the skies open up."

Jerry flashed her a heart-stopping smile and followed her lead, picking up shopping bags filled with new clothes. He had abandoned his former starchy style and settled instead on classic casual pants and shirts.

They had just stepped outside when he spoke to a passerby. Oh, jeez, he was doing it again!

Jerry stepped forward and shook the older gentleman's hand. Mr. Sikes? Settles? Sizemore—yes, that was it! It had been at least forty Earth years since he'd seen his former protectee, but he could recognize those distinctive eyes anywhere.

"Mr. Sizemore," he said, "it's so good to see you after all this time. How have you been? I take it you recovered from your football injury?"

The man peered at him through smudged bifocals while Kim and the young dark-skinned woman who gripped his elbow watched in curiosity.

Jerry had been temporarily assigned to watch over Walt Sizemore, who had been a college athlete at the time. The young man had so much going for him—a scholarship, a job offer pending graduation, a pretty girlfriend he was planning to marry, and an overall bright future.

And then disaster struck. It was the football game prior to the homecoming dance. Walt, as star quarterback, had led the game in points scored. Then, in the last quarter, he made the mistake of taking his mind off the game for a split second while he glanced over at his girlfriend who was shaking her pompons on the sidelines.

As protectorate, all Jerry had to do was whisper in Walt's ear to snap him back to attention before he got beaned with that football and layered with players from the opposing team. Unfortunately, Jerry had also been distracted by the cheerleaders. By the time he realized what was happening, it was too late. Walt ended up in the hospital with a broken back, and Jerry was pulled from the assignment before his charge had made a full recovery.

He'd always wondered what became of the personable young man, and now was his opportunity to find out.

"Recovered from my football injury?" Mr. Sizemore repeated. "Not hardly. To this day, I still have back pain."

Hunched over as he was, he looked older than his sixty-some years.

Jerry was sincerely sorry to hear that his protectee had suffered lingering effects from it. Guilt stabbed at his conscience. "Well, I trust you've done well in other areas of your life," he suggested, as much to console himself as to help Mr. Sizemore focus on the positive.

"Not hardly." The older man raised his voice as he described the circumstances that followed the mishap on the football field. "While I was laid up in the hospital, my girlfriend went to the homecoming dance with another guy. Eventually married him, she did, and I'm still a bachelor to this day. I lost my football scholarship. And since I couldn't finish my senior year of college, the bigwig company that was holding a job for me withdrew their offer.''

The young woman at his side intervened. "Mr. Sizemore, you're going to make your blood pressure go up again."

He turned to her, patted her hand affectionately and then belligerently raised his voice another octave. "And if it wasn't for this sweet angel from church who drives me around on my errands once a week, I don't know what I'd do."

Kim touched Jerry's arm. The gentleman was obviously agitated, and it appeared as though his unfortunate situation had affected Jerry, as well. "I think it's time to say goodbye."

The young woman with Mr. Sizemore apparently agreed. She flashed Kim a smile of thanks, and the two couples went their separate ways.

As they moved apart, Kim heard the young woman say, "Who was that?"

The older man cleared his throat. "Heck if I know."

Colorful yarn overflowed the bulging tote bag that sat beside Kim's feet. A strand of burgundy snaked out of the tangled mass as she gave it a tug and resumed the clicking of her knitting needles. Jerry was tempted to forage in the bag for some scraps with which to make the God's-eye charm he'd seen demonstrated on a TV crafting show, but he resisted the urge and studied the purl stitch that slipped off her needle.

Kim had once told him that needlework served as a stress reducer for her. If that was the case, then she must be catatonic by now. She'd been knitting furiously ever since they got home from the mall on Saturday. She'd even taken it with her to the doctor's office when Jerry went for his follow-up appointment earlier that afternoon. He wondered if she could sense that her Grand Exit loomed near.

Since Nahum hadn't called him back after he'd rescued Kim from the shoe-store incident, he could only surmise that was not what he'd been sent here to protect her from. Maybe it had been a warning of sorts. A warning designed to prepare Kim for the true threat, as well as to remind Jerry to stay alert to hazards that existed around them.

He had learned—the hard way—the importance of keeping his mind focused on the person he was supposed to be watching over. It ate at his conscience to know that he was responsible for poor Mr. Sizemore's troubled life.

There was no way he could make it up to the older gentleman, but he could prevent such an unfortunate occurrence from happening to Kim. Bowing his head and closing his eyes, Jerry rededicated himself to the task of protecting Kim from all harm. He would remain alert to all danger, regardless of how many fun distractions the world had to offer. And he would stay by her side day and night if he had to. Whatever it took to keep her safe.

"Jerry?"

He opened his eyes and lifted his head. She had placed in her lap the burgundy-and-cream afghan she'd been making for the back of the sofa and now watched him with a mixture of concern and curiosity.

"You look bored. Why don't you get those feathers you've been collecting, and maybe we can think of something to make out of them."

Great idea! Maybe he could make a pair of wings while waiting for the real ones that would be his upon completion of this assignment. He could practice wearing the homemade pair so he could get used to the extra appendages on his back.

Jerry stood, noting with satisfaction how light his leg felt since having the cast taken off this afternoon. He started toward his room to retrieve the pillowcase stuffed full of feathers.

But then he remembered his recent recommitment to his job as protectorate. Turning his back on the tempting project, he returned to his seat beside Kim, pulling one foot up on the sofa so that he sat perpendicular to her. She gave him a quizzical glance after his abrupt change of mind but continued with her knitting. From this vantage point, he could watch her to his heart's content.

"Quit it," she said, shifting against the overstuffed cushion.

"Quit what?"

"Staring at me like that. You're giving me the heebie-jeebies."

He'd never had that complaint when he was invisible to his protectees. Jerry sighed and turned away from her. His peripheral vision allowed him to watch her while he studied the cross-stitch sampler on the wall near the kitchen.

An apple a day keeps the doctor away.

Kim was all out of apples. He'd have to make sure they got some on their next trip out of the house. No sense taking any chances.

"This afternoon, I heard you tell Dr. Richmond you'd started to regain your memory. Why didn't you tell him the truth?"

"It's coming back," Jerry hastened to assure her. He had thought that, perhaps, if he could get a clean bill of health and prove that he was the same old Gerald she used to know, Kim would stop trying to keep him at an emotional distance and let him do his job. As it was now, every time he made a bit of headway and she started to open up to him with details of her life, she seemed to think better of it and clammed right up. "Just the other day, I remembered my full name and my address."

But Kim wasn't as easily fooled as the doctor had been. He noticed her shaking her head now.

Still dressed in a blue silk blouse and tan skirt from her morning at the office, she looked prettier than he'd ever seen her before. Her hair, though short, was fluffed around her face, making her appear softer and more feminine. Jerry found himself wanting to kiss her until...well, he wasn't sure what. But he somehow knew that a kiss from Kim could lead him to pleasures even more wondrous than anything he'd experienced during his brief time living in Gerald's body.

Under his intense scrutiny, Kim shyly lowered her gaze and focused on the freckles that dotted her right forearm. When the silence dragged on, she sought to turn their attention back to the subject they'd been discussing before he began looking at her with a desire that made her blood run hot in her veins.

"The doctor said your recovery is like nothing he's ever seen before," she said. "In fact, you're healing so fast it's as if you never had the lacerations or cracked ribs. And there's no sign of your ever having an ulcer."

Jerry smiled his pleasure at the excellent health report he'd been given. Then, as if she could have forgotten, he proudly reminded her, "He also said I'm able to manage on my own now."

But Kim knew better. What Dr. Richmond had actually said was that Jerry could manage just fine at home. *His* home. It was what she'd been wishing for, but Kim wasn't sure she actually wanted him to leave now. She'd become accustomed to his bright outlook and quirky sense of humor.

A glance in his direction showed that he remembered the doctor's exact words and was as uncertain about this change as she was. It was probably for the best, though. She was becoming far too attached to this man who had the power to hurt her all over again.

Kim wrapped the yarn around the needle and tried to think of a gentle way to ask the question that had been nagging at her since their excursion to the mall. She had dropped a bug in Dr. Richmond's ear this afternoon but hadn't heard any more about the subject.

"When you left the examining room to have your leg x-rayed, did the doctor happen to ask you about your, uh...?" At a loss for words, she paused in her knitting and twirled a finger around her ear. As incomprehension drew his eyebrows upward, she added, "Lately you've been saying some crazy things."

Jerry crossed his arms across his chest and flashed her an indignant expression.

"Well, you have."

"Such as?" he prompted huffily.

"For one thing, you seem to think you're going to die soon."

He stilled the clicking needles by covering her hands with his own. Kim tried unsuccessfully to ignore the solid pressure of his warm palm against her skin.

"He said it wasn't so unusual for someone who came as close to leaving this world as Gerald—er, I—did."

"But you keep walking up to strangers and acting like you know them, and they don't know you," she persisted.

"Perhaps my memory is better than you think."

"But you weren't even *born* when Mr. Sizemore played college football!"

He didn't bother to explain but merely stated, "Kim, my reasoning ability is intact."

He was right. And she'd heard the doctor say that if Jerry was interested in going back to a more independent lifestyle, there was no reason to stop him.

Maybe Jerry thought she was being overly apprehensive or maybe a bit too maternal. But she couldn't help it if she was concerned about the possibility of his setting fire to his condo or, perhaps, striking up a conversation with the wrong stranger…someone who would cause bodily harm or, at the least, take advantage of his good nature.

"Now, about work," Jerry said. "I'd like to go back to the office tomorrow."

Dropping the half-finished afghan in the tote bag, Kim got up and paced the room.

"Work! How are you supposed to get there? How are

you supposed to remember the office procedures?'' And, most of all, how was she supposed to keep an emotional distance from him if she couldn't manage to get some physical distance?

Why was it that all of a sudden the room felt so small and he felt so close? Too close. But that didn't stop him from interrupting her pacing by blocking her path with his body.

She stood stock-still, squared off in front of him as if he were a jungle cat ready to pounce. Her heart pounded, but she suspected it was more from exhilaration than fear. There was something quite heady about the way he leveled his unflinching gaze at her. Indeed, he looked as hungry as a wild animal. As if to confirm her thought, he licked his lips expectantly.

Yes, it was clear to see that, like a lion ready to spring, he wanted flesh. Her flesh. Although her mind screamed for her to stay away from him—that he was nothing but trouble and heartache—her body cried out, *Here, kitty, kitty.*

When he spoke, his voice was husky and low. ''If I want something badly enough,'' he said at last, ''I'll find a way.''

It wasn't until much later that she realized he'd been answering her questions about work.

Jerry had thought he would continue staying with Kim, at least until he got the hang of things at work. But shortly after their conversation, she'd said something about his needing to regain his independence...and her needing to regain her personal space.

''I really can't go to the apartment right now,'' he

insisted as she opened the dresser drawer and started stacking his clothes in a box. "I need to be here with you."

"I'm sure you'll get along fine." She never slowed her efficient movements.

"It's not me I'm worried about...it's you. I want to stay here and protect you."

She laughed softly, and Jerry memorized the melodious sound so he could replay it in his mind later.

"Believe me, I'll be better protected with you living at your condo in town."

He couldn't imagine what she may have meant by that, but he knew he had to change her mind fast. Once his belongings were loaded into her car, that would be the end of his usefulness as a protectorate.

During the past few weeks, he'd grown very fond of her. Since he'd never experienced romantic love before, he couldn't say for sure that's what he felt for Kim. He'd never known anything to feel so good and so bad, all at the same time.

It was wonderful to be around her and feel the tingly sensations she sparked inside him. And it was awful to be leaving her, knowing the only time he would spend with her after today would be at the office. He couldn't imagine that a corporate meeting room would be very conducive to personal chats...or tender kisses and warm hugs.

He reached out and took her arm, causing her to cease packing for the moment. "I'm going to miss you," he said sincerely.

She hesitated, then gave a slight nod. "I'm going to

miss you, too," she said at last. "Having you here has been a lot different than I expected."

"What did you expect?"

"I'm not sure, but I didn't think it would be this exasperating." She paused a second, then added, "Or this much fun."

It sounded as though she was experiencing the same mixed feelings that plagued him.

Her wide-set eyes watched him, and he found himself drawn into their pale brown depths. In them, he saw uncertainty and perhaps a little bit of fear...the same emotions he felt for her.

Breaking the mesmeric pull of her gaze, he lowered his eyes, taking in the small, straight nose, full lips that bowed upward in the center, and delicate chin that came to a gentle point. Noticing that a link in her gold necklace had twisted, he reached up to straighten it.

Her skin seemed to sear him where he touched her, and he blazed a path along her collarbone with one finger. She didn't move, didn't seem afraid as she sometimes had in the past when they'd stood in close proximity.

He allowed his finger to trail downward, brushing against the blue silk blouse that came to a vee precisely where the intriguing valley between her breasts began. A pearl-glazed button stopped his exploring descent.

"I'm going to miss kissing you," he said, touching his mouth to hers.

Her response was a groan deep in her throat. She kissed him back, her lips softening beneath his. As they moved closer, his hand was trapped between them, and the soft white flesh beneath her blouse molded itself to him.

Without thinking what he was doing, he unfastened the first pearl button. Then the next. When he was done, he pushed the garment off her shoulders and toyed with the smooth, soft skin that now lay bare to him. He followed the white lace straps back down to the cleft and grazed the heels of his hands across the tempting peaks.

Kim was the first to break their kiss. But, to Jerry's surprise and unexplainable pleasure, she deftly opened his shirt and slipped her arms around his waist.

He could discern the topography of her body's curves...from her cheek resting against his chest, to the fullness of her breasts, down to the hollow of her waist, and to her slim thighs that pressed against his own legs.

His legs suddenly felt weak, though he doubted it had anything to do with having had the cast removed. He backed up—still holding her close—until he touched the edge of the bed, then allowed himself to collapse onto it.

Kim followed him down until they were both horizontal, she on her back, and he propped on one elbow beside her. Continuing the kiss where they'd left off, Jerry marveled at how right it felt being with her this way. She made it feel even more right when she slipped her arms around his neck.

"Oh, Jerry," she murmured in his ear, "I must have lost my mind to be doing this." But she made no effort to break contact with him.

Instinctively, he moved his leg to trap her body beneath him. As he did so, he became aware of a need he'd never known before. Resting his full weight on her, he felt compelled to ease the situation by moving closer to her. Kim's response was to curl against him.

He could feel his pulse pounding in his ears, and her breath came in warm, ragged puffs against his neck.

Surprisingly, his need worsened as he sought closer contact with Kim, but at the same time the sensation pleased him beyond words. It was as if she was, at once, the cause and the cure for his affliction.

Undoubtedly, Kim was the prettiest creature he'd seen in his entire life...or before. And she'd been at the center of his thoughts every time his body had responded so powerfully.

As realization dawned, it took all of Jerry's willpower to pull away from her. Wasn't this one of the no-no's listed on the tablets Moses brought down from Mount Sinai?

She opened her eyes and watched him with a large measure of curiosity. "What's the matter?"

"I'm not sure yet. Give me a moment."

He was ticking down a finger for each of the Thou Shalt Nots when something on the nightstand distracted her.

Her ardor doused by the delay and her curiosity piqued further by the unexpected sight, Kim moved forward and propped herself on her elbows. It was another package, probably from that home shopping channel. Technically, the contents of the package were none of her business, but considering the spendathon Jerry had conducted previously, she figured she had a right to ask.

"What's that?"

He smiled and, leaning across her, retrieved the box. When he handed it to her, she pondered what useless, overpriced item Jerry might have ordered this time. He practically radiated his enthusiasm as he waited for her to open it. "I know you didn't want me to buy anything else I saw on TV, but I couldn't resist this."

She didn't want to burst his bubble, but she also didn't want him to continue his foolish spending habits. "It's addressed to me," she said suspiciously. "You didn't use my credit card again, did you?"

"Nope, bought it with my own money. When they asked me who it was for, I gave them your name." With one arm still draped across her midsection, he idly stroked her bare stomach. "I guess they must've wanted to know whom to ship it to," he said sheepishly.

Raising herself up, she leaned her back against the pillow, putting a scant few more inches between them. Turning the small box in her hands, she hesitated a moment, then tried to hand it back to him. Suddenly, it felt as though all the air had been sucked out of the room. She didn't know what the package contained, but something—her survival instinct, perhaps—told her not to open it. "I don't think I should accept this."

"Why not?" Jerry sounded offended by the very thought. "Maybe it's a birthday present for you. Besides, I think it's something we'll both appreciate."

She slanted a look of disbelief at him. "Or maybe it's full of sea monkeys," she guessed, and studied the box more closely. "Judging from the plain wrapping and the post office box number as a return address—" not to mention his timing or his unbridled enthusiasm, she thought "—it's probably more of a present for *you*."

A sex toy, most likely. If so, it appeared as though he'd intended all along to weasel his way into bed with her. How conniving and sneaky could a person get? She had thought their spontaneous—though perhaps foolhardy—encounter just now had been their natural response to the attraction that had grown between them these past several weeks. She would never have believed he could be so underhanded as to deliberately seduce her. Maybe Gerald hadn't changed that much after all.

She pushed the package back at him. "Mark it Refused By Addressee—Return To Sender."

Jerry took the box. It appeared as though he was about to open it for her. If he did, someone would have to pay to return the unwanted item.

Quickly rising from the bed, Kim donned her blouse. If she'd been unthinking a few moments ago for allowing him to initiate a physical relationship, she'd have to be insane to continue it now. She grabbed the parcel away from him.

Kim bolted, but he chased her across the room, cornering her near the closet before he reclaimed the so-called gift. Jerry blocked her escape with his large body, making it impossible for her to ignore the rise and fall of his lightly furred chest or the heat that seemed to warm and melt her resistance.

"Send it back." Her statement would have been a command if it hadn't sounded so breathy.

"We'll keep it."

"No, we won't." She was ready to clobber her soon-to-be-ex houseguest. Lunging toward him, she tried to take the package away, but he caught her around the waist and pulled her close.

She could feel his body stiffen as she wriggled within his arms. When she realized how she might be making matters worse for both of them, Kim ceased trying to escape. Instead, she struggled to maintain her composure.

Taking a deep breath as if to fortify himself, Jerry turned his attention to the box and a moment later lifted out a small, shiny object for her to see.

It was a miniature angel with gold filigree wings and a tiny halo perched above her head. Kim let out a breath she hadn't realized she'd been holding. "Oh, Jerry, it's beautiful."

"Not half as beautiful as you," he said, surprising her with the depth of conviction in his voice. "This, of course, is no substitute for the real thing, but after your recent near disasters with Muffin and then with the shoe rack, I wanted to give you a little reminder that you don't walk alone."

She flinched when he touched her. As he pinned the brooch to her pocket, his knuckles grazed her breast. Kim gave herself a mental scolding for enjoying the sensations he aroused in her.

"I'm here for you, Kim, and I will do whatever is in my power to keep you from getting hurt." Then he lowered his head to seal his promise with a kiss.

As she gave in to the tender gesture, she felt tears of self-reproach sting her eyes. What about the disaster area that was her heart? How was she to keep it safe?

All too soon, the kiss ended. Kim could see the concern in Jerry's eyes as he watched a tear spill over, leaving a salty trail as it slid down her cheek.

But the dam was broken, and she couldn't hold the water back. It was obvious she was making Jerry even more concerned, but she couldn't turn off the flow. It seemed as though the stress of the past few weeks and the foolishness of the feelings that were growing inside her for Jerry had finally taken their toll.

"Did I stick you with the pin?" he asked. "Tell me what hurts, honey."

She rested her cheek against his chest. His voice was soothing and his arms comforting, but they only served to feed the self-pity that came over her.

But what could she say to his question?

My heart hurts?

I want you no matter how wrong you are for me?

Instead, she hiccuped loudly. Jerry squeezed her closer to his chest, and she tried not to notice the scent of him.

If she didn't get him out of this house soon, she would give him not only her body but her heart, too. And once that happened, she would never get it back.

CHAPTER SEVEN

JERRY paced the condominium that had once been Gerald's. He'd tried to persuade Kim to let him stay at her place, but she seemed convinced that he needed to regain his independence and that she'd be safer with him gone. Then she'd muttered something about her heart being safer, too.

Maybe she had a heart condition. He would have to ask her when he saw her at work the next day. Even so, he doubted that's what threatened the early emptying of her hourglass. Heart attacks were almost always a part of the Master Plan. Whatever was threatening to shorten her time here on Earth was an external force.

He would have to approach this in a more organized manner to find the source of her problem. He couldn't continue leaving her safety to chance. By skimming the surface and looking only for obvious dangers, he could be putting her in more jeopardy.

Jerry sat on the plush white sofa. At Kim's place, he would have put his feet up. But not here. He liked the mostly white color scheme of Gerald's apartment, but the rest of the stark glass-and-brass decor was too formal for his taste.

Unable to sit still, he got up and paced some more. A public service announcement he'd heard on television popped into his mind. *Knowledge is power.*

Perhaps the more he knew about Kim, the better he'd

be able to protect her. And if Gerald had once been engaged to her, there might be some mementos or other clues about her in his apartment.

He went into the kitchen and began opening cabinets and pulling out drawers. After finding nothing other than a note to "buy some champagne to celebrate," he tucked it into his pants pocket and made a sweep through the dining and living rooms.

Celebrate what? he wondered as he picked up a photo of Gerald and Kim kissing. Wiping the crystal frame over the front of his shirt, he dusted the photo and studied it.

Even though it looked posed—as if both Kim and Gerald were self-conscious about kissing for the camera—the permanently frozen gesture tormented him with its suggestion of intimacy. They were his own lips that touched hers in the photo, but it was Gerald she was kissing.

When Jerry had kissed her today, had she been thinking of the man in this photo, or had she been responding to Jerry himself? She had told him that their engagement was called off because Gerald wasn't ready to get married. Had Gerald broken things off, leaving her pining for the man she couldn't have?

No, if that were the case, she wouldn't have tried so hard to resist Jerry's advances. He could tell she liked touching him as much as he enjoyed touching her. It was as if, after a few moments of heady forgetfulness, she would suddenly remember her former relationship with Gerald and call a halt to their caresses. Maybe she thought she was doing the honorable thing by waiting until Gerald's "memory" returned before becoming involved with him again. He would have to keep searching the apartment in the hope of finding the answers he needed.

The bedroom didn't turn up anything of interest. Just some stock reports and information about the company Barnett's Bakery was trying to acquire. And another photo of Gerald and Kim, this time posing with her father and stepmother.

It wasn't until he got to the spare-bedroom-turned-office that he hit pay dirt. The problem was, most of the notes and scraps of paper didn't appear to mean much.

A pile of unopened mail sat in the center of the desk. Mostly advertisements, but there were also a few bills and a bank statement.

He skimmed through the file detailing the proposed merger, hoping to familiarize himself with the situation before going to work tomorrow. At the back of the folder was a handwritten note in neat script reminding him to call Mr. Hoskins, the comptroller at Goode Foods. He tucked that into his pocket, too, and made a mental note to contact him tomorrow. Perhaps Mr. Hoskins would be a good source of merger information, thereby freeing up more time for Jerry to keep an eye on Kim.

In the bottom desk drawer he found Gerald's checkbook and credit-card statements. Van Claude Clothiers apparently was a favorite. Jerry let out a low whistle at the exorbitant sums. And judging by the grocery-to-restaurant ratio, Gerald obviously preferred eating out. At expensive restaurants, no less.

Scanning the papers, he was surprised to see a number of charges to an inexpensive in-town motel. Hmm, maybe he stayed there on the nights he worked late.

No, that didn't make sense. Kim had told him the condo was no more than a twenty-minute drive from the office. He could drive home more quickly and easily than checking into a motel. And with his expensive tastes, why would he stay at such a cheap place?

He had hoped to find some answers at work the next day but, to his chagrin, more questions were raised than resolved.

Kim had given him a ride to the office since his car had been totaled in the accident and she wasn't sure whether he'd understand the bus schedule. But if he'd thought her generosity would extend to letting him loiter near her desk, he was mistaken.

"Your office is on the next floor down," she said when he tried to make himself comfortable on the couch in her office.

"Couldn't I move my desk up here?" He ran a hand over the polished teak paneling. "I wouldn't mind working on this floor."

She slanted him a cautious gaze. "Maybe you haven't changed as much as I thought," she said. "For the three years you've worked here, you've had your eye on the senior vice presidency."

"Oh, I don't care about that. I just want to be near you."

She looked like she didn't quite believe him. He considered telling her why he needed to stay close, but decided against it when her assistant interrupted by placing a heavy accordion file folder on Kim's desk. "Here's the information you asked Donna for."

"Donna?" Jerry asked Kim after the other woman had left. "My secretary?"

Kim nodded. "When I asked for this yesterday, I didn't realize you'd be back at work so soon. Since we're nearing the point where we need to make an offer or pull out altogether, I thought I'd start wrapping up your loose ends."

"I vote to forget about the whole deal."

Her eyebrows formed perfect arches above deep-set brown eyes. There was no mistaking her opinion on the matter. Even so, it was all Jerry could do to keep from reaching out to run a thumb over one dark brow or brush back the fringe of bangs that fell over it. Instead, he busied himself by picking up the thick file stuffed with a computer printout that appeared to be a duplicate of the one at Gerald's condo.

"I'll take this. There's no sense in you working yourself to death."

She tried to argue with him, but Jerry refused to return the papers. On his way to the elevator, he stopped in to say hello to Maxwell Barnett.

A few minutes later, on his own floor, he paused at the water cooler for a drink. When he straightened up and wiped a hand across his mouth, an older man in a wrinkled shirt stood beside him.

"It's all yours," Jerry said, gesturing toward the cooler.

The man made no move, either to take a drink or to get out of Jerry's way. "You think you can go around doing whatever you please, however you please." His eye twitched as he tried to stare Jerry down. "Well, you're not so high-and-mighty. I'm onto you, so don't assume you can go around making up your own rules."

With that dour expression, the fellow reminded him

of Mehrdad, who was a stickler for following procedures. Jerry guessed this guy must work in accounting.

He scanned the wall behind the cooler, checking for
a ticket dispenser before addressing the stranger.
"What? Was I supposed to take a number or something?"

The peculiar man merely wagged a warning finger at
him and left without another word.

Jerry brushed off the incident and turned his attention
to finding his office. Kim had told him it was on the east
side of the building. But when she had started talking
specifics, he had tuned everything out as he focused on
the sweet, floral scent of her. Hers wasn't a single
flower's fragrance, but it seemed more like a delicate
bouquet of assorted wildflowers. As she talked, he had
moved closer, taking in not only her fresh smell, but the
beauty of her large brown eyes, the smoothness of her
skin, and the rise and fall of her soft voice. When she
had finished and asked him if he understood her directions, he didn't have the heart to ask her to repeat them.

So now he stood here, facing the east wall of the
building, wondering which of the three women stationed
in the reception area might be Donna. Since the staff
hadn't been told about his so-called amnesia, he couldn't
very well ask one of them the way to his office. Kim
had feared that some of the employees might mistakenly
equate his "amnesia" with mental instability. He found
it touching that she didn't want such feelings to under-
mine their confidence in his ability to perform his job.

Buying a little time, he started flipping through the
Goode Foods printout. After a moment during which he

found himself engrossed in the columns of figures, a fourth woman walked up to him.

Dressed in a crisp beige skirt and jacket, she appeared to be a little older than Kim. Thirty, possibly. Her blond hair, though worn down, was carefully turned under at the ends and sprayed so efficiently that he was certain not one hair dared leave its assigned position.

"Welcome back, Gerald. I was beginning to wonder if you had decided to quit your job and become a househusband."

"A househusband?" He tucked the printout back into its folder. "Why would I want to marry a house?"

She laughed and quickly settled down to business. "I have a stack of letters awaiting your signature. What do you want me to do with them?"

Perfect opening. "I have my hands full right now. Why don't you put them on my desk?"

She nodded, and he followed her to Gerald's office. Although it looked different from the condo, Jerry could tell the room had been inhabited by the same man. Rich brown leather covered the sofa and desk chair, the desk sported a smoked-glass top, and all around on the desk, credenza and bookshelves were brass lamps, brass picture frames and various other brass accessories.

"This place needs a fish tank."

Donna cast him a curious glance as she set the papers on his desk. "You used to say they're for daydreamers and that you were too busy to sit and stare at fish swimming in circles. Did the accident make you have a change of heart?"

"Oh, no," he assured her, thumping his chest for emphasis. "It's the same heart that's always been in this body."

She laughed again. "Sounds like the time off did you good. I'll be back in a few minutes to get those letters."

After she left, Jerry quickly signed the letters. One was a memo reminding employees of the company picnic in two weeks. "All right!" he declared, and marked the date and time on his calendar.

Then he proceeded to snoop through the desk and credenza drawers. Most of what he found appeared to be files of supporting data for projects already completed. In the top desk drawer sat a stack of non-urgent business to take care of as time permitted. The bottom drawer, however, refused to open.

Jerry fished through his pants pockets for the ring of keys that had been among Gerald's possessions at the hospital. The first two he tried didn't work, but the third one turned with a satisfying click.

The drawer opened to reveal a small bottle of mouthwash, a spare shirt and tie, a bottle of aspirin and a package of condoms.

The first few items could very well be work related, he deduced. But the last? He tried not to think about Kim being with Gerald in that way. It had been bad enough finding that picture of them kissing.

But if they were for intimate moments with Kim, why did he keep them locked in his desk drawer? Wouldn't it have been simpler to keep them at her house or his condo?

Then Jerry remembered the motel receipts. Perhaps she met him for midday trysts? Personally, he didn't think that sounded like Kim's style. And even if it was, why wouldn't Gerald just stash his supplies in his wallet like most other men did?

His eye caught a glimpse of white. Looking closer into the drawer, he saw a corner of paper protruding from the folds of the shirt. Figuring it must have fallen from the drawer above, he retrieved the envelope and withdrew the contents: a lone check from Gerald's personal account, already processed and canceled.

The payee was an Otto Hoskins, and the signature—composed of sharp, bold pen strokes—read Gerald E. Kirkland. The sum written on the check could have bought a lot of goodies from the television shopping channel.

Hoskins, Hoskins…where had he heard that name before? And why had Gerald paid him so much money? If it had been anyone other than Gerald, Jerry might have concluded he'd bought a used car from Otto Hoskins. But Gerald Kirkland was not the type to buy someone else's castoffs.

Jerry returned the check to the drawer. Perhaps if he collected enough puzzle pieces, he'd be able to put them together in time to spare Kim an untimely ending.

More and more, the focus of this assignment was shifting from merely earning a pair of wings to being deeply concerned about his charge's welfare. In all his other jobs, he'd been able to keep a safe emotional distance while performing his duties. Sure, he'd become rather fond of many of his protectees, but never had he experienced anything like what he felt for Kim. And now, he was worried that his concern for her might hinder his effectiveness as her protectorate.

The printout sat on the desk in front of him, reminding

him of his work obligation. But what was he supposed to do with these figures anyway? They didn't make sense, especially since none of the column totals matched the printout he'd studied last night at Gerald's condo.

He locked the desk drawer and dropped the key ring into his pocket. His fingers touched the scrap of paper that he'd transferred to his pants earlier that morning. He pulled it out and read the note again. "Call Mr. Hoskins, comptroller. Goode Foods." It was dated a couple of weeks prior to Gerald's accident.

"Oh, good, they're all signed." Donna came in and swooped up the pile of memos and letters from his desk. "I'll just get these out of your way."

"Uh, Donna?" When she paused in her whirlwind activity, he laid the note on the desk and flattened it with his hand. "Do you remember why I was supposed to call Mr. Hoskins?"

Her penciled eyebrows drew together, creating a vertical crease that was the only flaw on her painstakingly painted face. She twisted her mouth to one side and chewed the inside of her lip as she silently pondered his question.

"Sorry," she said at last. "I've never heard of Mr. Hoskins."

"Otto Hoskins?" Jerry hinted.

She shook her head. "Nope."

This time, Jerry felt his eyebrows pulling together in a line of concentration. "Didn't you write this note?"

Donna leaned closer. "It looks like a woman's handwriting all right, but it isn't mine." She started toward the door once again and then halted herself. "Speaking of handwriting—'' she glanced down at the top paper on the stack of letters ''—what's with the new signature?''

It was then that Jerry recalled the bold slashes of black ink on the check. Gerald must have been a firm believer in making an impression with everything he did, wore or owned. Obviously, he wanted to be seen as aggressive and powerful.

Jerry's own signature, however, was simple and straightforward. Strong, in its own way, but also unassuming.

He grinned at Donna, who was flipping through the stack of papers. ''I guess you caught me in a mellow mood.''

She handed one of the sheets back to him and tilted her head as she fixed a look of concern on him. ''You don't seem to be yourself lately. Did you realize you signed this letter 'Jared Kirkland'?''

Jerry didn't know what to say, and when he didn't respond, she gave a shrug and tried to laugh it off as she headed back to her desk.

''That bump on your head must have been quite a doozy.''

After waiting for the elevator that never came, Jerry walked up the single flight of stairs to Kim's office. Donna had offered to order lunch for him, but he had declined, hoping instead to spend his break with Kim.

He bypassed Kim's assistant, walking into the office and making himself comfortable in the visitor's chair.

Her head was bent over a yellow pad, and she appeared deep in concentration. Jerry might have even believed it if her mouth hadn't tensed into a straight line. He'd seen that expression often enough, mostly when she was trying to avoid being close to him. He wondered what Gerald had done to make her try to keep him at arm's length.

Or was it *him?* He reached forward and touched her hand that gripped the pen with forceful determination.

Kim jumped at his touch. Why did he have this effect on her? Why couldn't she just wash her hands of him and get on with her life...the way it had been before she ever met Gerald? Why did he have to keep reminding her with his presence how sweet and cute and sexy he was?

The physical cravings he stirred within her were stronger than any she'd ever known before...even stronger since the time she'd spent with him during his recuperation. It wasn't fair that someone who was ultimately so wrong for her could make her feel so good inside.

"You startled me," she said, blaming her reaction on surprise rather than barely restrained passion.

"Sorry." It was clear that he knew the truth, but he didn't call her bluff. "It's lunch o'clock. Wanna go out to eat?"

"Oh, um..." She paused, wondering how she could avoid being near him and thus avoid feeding the craving in her soul.

Luck intervened with the arrival of her stepmother. Carmen popped in, also uninvited but definitely welcome. "The elevator never came, and I had to walk up all twelve flights," she said, her breath coming out in a whoosh. "Are you ready to go, dear? Your father wants to try that new Italian place over on Fourteenth Street."

Jerry was all smiles. "Hey, that sounds great. I love Italian food."

The truth was, he loved any kind of food. But Kim wouldn't get into that now. She felt her brain spin as she tried to come up with a polite way to put the nix on his self-invitation. "But you have to stay here and—"

"He needs to eat," Carmen said, interrupting Kim's feeble excuse. Then, fixing her blue eyes on Jerry, she added, "We'll be glad to have you join us."

She adjusted the purse strap over her shoulder and lifted the bag in a little wave to them.

"Why don't you two try to get an elevator while I drag Maxwell away from his desk? We'll meet you there in a moment."

Kim glanced over at Jerry, who had already stood and was now offering a hand to her. Not wishing to compound her former rudeness by ignoring the gesture, she lifted her fingers to his and felt the strength and warmth in his hand.

Why, oh why, did she have to fall for the wrong man? Even crazier was the fact that she loved him more now than when they were engaged. She must have some sort of self-destructive tendencies that led her to fall more deeply in love with a man after learning of his infidelity. There was no other rational explanation for her absurd change of heart.

His fingers closed over hers as he curled her hand through the crook of his arm. His palms, though formerly smooth, were covered with fresh calluses that lightly chafed her skin. The first blisters had come after a day spent clearing out the barn so that the wild ducks and geese would have a safe refuge from predators. After that, he'd added more calluses during his work transforming the area near the lake into a tiny park where she could relax and reflect. He'd even ordered—with his own credit card this time—a wrought-iron bench for her and had promised he would move it to a shady spot and secure it once it was delivered.

These were things Gerald never would have done before his accident. Such a small thing, but the calluses drove home to her just how much he'd changed since their breakup. They were changes that she liked and could easily get used to having in her life. But breaking up with him the first time had hurt so much. How much more it would hurt to watch him turn back into the smooth-skinned, smooth talker who had brought her all that anguish.

She paused at the threshold. "Gerald...I mean, Jerry?"

He smiled down at her, his face radiant and kind. His dark eyebrows, classic nose and firm chin were all the same. However, there was a difference in the set of his mouth and even in the way he brushed his hair. No longer did he comb it severely and precisely, with each hair standing in regimented order. It was still neat and brushed to one side, but the wash-and-go look made him appear somehow more approachable and friendly.

There was something else, too. Another difference...one she couldn't put a finger on. She'd heard of patients becoming gentler and more easygoing after a head trauma, but the change in him seemed to go beyond mere forgetfulness...beyond all outward changes in appearance and behavior. Dr. Richmond had remarked that, other than the amnesia, he showed no other physical symptoms of the brain injury that was suspected to have brought on his failed memory. So what was it about him that made her respond in a way she'd never felt before?

She wasn't going to find the answer by staring into his questioning eyes. Trying to ignore the dark rim of lashes that surrounded pale blue irises, she found herself struggling with a memory loss of her own as she fought to remember what she had started to say to him.

"Your parents are probably waiting for us," he prompted.

Yes, that was it. She cleared her throat. "I, uh, haven't told Carmen or Dad that our engagement is off. With Dad's history of heart problems, I didn't think he should have to deal with the stress of our breakup on top of worrying about you."

He considered that for a moment. "So you want me to act like a fiancé? Maybe give you a kiss in front of them?"

Did she detect a note of hopefulness in his voice? Worse, did she feel her heart do a back flip in her chest?

"I just meant that I'd rather you didn't mention it to them." She supposed she should get her own emotions straight before having to contend with the disappointment that was sure to come from her father and step-mother.

"Sure, on one condition." He removed her hand from his elbow and pushed the door shut. Pressing his fist casually against the door frame, he blocked her exit. The posture served as a visual reminder of how large and powerful he was, just in case she took the notion to push past him. Then he leveled those mountain-sky eyes at her. "Tell me what caused your...our breakup."

When he looked at her with such intensity, Kim felt as though he could read every thought and feel every sensation she'd ever known. If she tried to brush off his question as she'd done the first time he asked—or, worse, lied—he would certainly know it. She hadn't wanted to get into this subject with him until his memory returned and he could answer a few questions of hers. And she especially didn't want to delve into the matter while her father tapped his foot at the elevator. But, seeing the determination in Jerry's expression, she knew there would be no further stalling.

"There was someone else. Someone who came between us." She looked down at the floor, focusing on the vacuum mark the cleaning crew had left on the plush carpet. "I don't really understand how it happened to us...whether it was a matter of falling out of love or maybe not being in love in the first place."

He looked crestfallen. Taking his hand off the door frame, he slumped his body against it instead. When he looked at her again, she could see the pain and disappointment in his eyes.

"You *cheated* on your fiancé?" He shook his head as if trying to clear his mind of the horrible thought. "If it was anyone else—the president, or the pope even—I could see it as a common human failing. But you...I thought you were different."

Suddenly, Kim found herself in the bizarre position, not so much of defending her reputation, but of trying to ease the suffering that the confusion was putting Jerry through.

"No, no, you have it all wrong." Kim didn't bother to point out that the pope would never be in a position to do such a thing, or even that more than one president had strayed from his promise to love, honor and cherish. She wanted him to know the truth, but she didn't want to slap him in the face with it. She used care in phrasing her next words. "There was a woman..."

She didn't have to say any more, for she could see his awareness grow as the gritty truth sank in.

Kim snapped off a dead leaf from the ficus tree that stood beside the door. She tossed the casualty back into the planter. It would serve as fodder for the next generation of leaves, just as her experience with Gerald would serve as a caution not to make the same mistakes with the next man who came into her life. "I think it would be better if we put what's happened in the past behind us."

"Better for whom?" he asked, stepping closer.

So close that Kim had difficulty breathing. She *had* to stop letting him do this to her. She turned aside, throwing a barrier between herself and the man who had already turned her world upside down and who now threatened to set it spinning in reverse. "We have to go."

"Why are you afraid of me?" He started to reach out to her, then seemed to think better of it and let his hands drop to his sides. "All I want to do is take care of you."

She raised her chin and squared her shoulders. He still towered over her, but that didn't keep her from putting up a good front. "I'm not afraid of anyone."

"Then you must be afraid of some*thing*." This time when he reached out to her, he brushed a hand along her arm and gently squeezed her elbow. When he spoke again, his voice was husky. "Whatever it is, I'm here to help."

Help do what? Complicate her life and confuse her until she couldn't remember from one minute to the next why she had given back his ring? Help fill her dreams with visions of a handsome, smiling man who wore her heart like a souvenir around his neck? If so, he was doing a good job of it.

Yes, she was afraid of something. She was afraid of acknowledging the chaotic emotions that he set bubbling in her spirit, and even more afraid of letting them out of the recesses of her heart. For she was sure that once she did, her life would never be the same again.

She sidestepped him, taking care to avoid contact with his steadfast gaze, and pulled open the door. "Dad and Carmen must be wondering what happened to us."

Without waiting for a response, she stepped out into the reception area and crossed to the tiled floor where, sure enough, her father's foot tapped a steady rhythm on the polished surface. She was aware of Jerry joining them, but she didn't acknowledge his presence.

"Still no elevator," Carmen said, setting to rest Kim's concern that Maxwell's impatience was caused by their dawdling. Carmen rummaged through her purse a moment before turning to her husband. "Max, honey, I can't find my contact-lens solution, and my eyes are burning like a California forest fire. I think I left the drops in your office."

A bell chimed, and the light on the Down button went out.

"You two go ahead," her father said, gesturing toward the tardy elevator. "We'll meet you at the restaurant in a few minutes."

The double doors slid open behind her. With her mind focused on the possibility that Jerry might be breaking through her fragile defenses, she continued watching her father accompany Carmen back to his office.

As Kim absentmindedly edged back toward the elevator, she was aware of Jerry's expression changing to one of alarm as he reached for her. Instinctively, she sought to keep distance between her and the man who wreaked havoc on her emotions with his slightest touch. In the space of a split second, she saw his alarm grow. Immediately, she felt herself begin to keel backward as her foot touched nothingness.

Startled, she opened her mouth to scream. Like a slow-motion moment in a movie, her arms went up and she seemed to hover for a second in midair. The next second followed with a blur of action when Jerry clasped her wrist in an iron-hard grip and gave a yank so hard it felt like he'd pulled her arm out of the socket.

Kim lurched forward and slammed into the brick wall that was Jerry's chest. She clutched desperately at his shirt, and his fingers dug into her back.

Her mouth was swollen from the impact with his ribs, and the scream she had gathered in her lungs was squeezed out in a muffled "Urmph!"

Sobs of relief and hysteria shortly followed. Jerry comforted her by refusing to loosen his hold on her, a hold that would no doubt leave bruises on her battered but grateful body. She felt his lips on her hair and heard him murmur soothing words as she pressed her face against the crisp white fabric of his shirt.

When Kim's heartbeat finally slowed to a fast gallop, she lifted her head to look at her rescuer. Her mascara and tears had smeared his shirt, and as she balanced precariously on her one remaining shoe, she could see that he was trembling.

Kim became aware of a crowd gathering, but neither of them made a move to break their awkward embrace. It was Carmen's high-pitched voice that pierced through the fog of excited voices around them.

"Somebody call maintenance. There's nothing here but an empty elevator shaft!"

CHAPTER EIGHT

"I WANT to move back in with you."

Kim looked up from the flat "stones" they were making by pouring dyed concrete into a mold. When the project was finished, the artificial stones would form a quaint footpath down to the miniature park Jerry had designed by her lake. He had been right about Mother Nature's ability to wipe the day's stresses from her body and mind.

But he wasn't right about his reason for wanting to move in with her.

"I think you're taking a couple of simple, understandable accidents and blowing them all out of proportion."

Jerry pulled a handkerchief from his pocket and wiped the perspiration from his forehead. "Okay, maybe the falling shoe rack was a mere accident. But what about the elevator?"

She sighed. They'd been over this a thousand times since the elevator incident two weeks ago, but he refused to see the situation for what it was.

"The maintenance man said it was a simple malfunction. Once he isolated the problem, he had it fixed in a matter of minutes."

"A *simple* malfunction." He snorted. "And you could have been *simply* dead."

"But I'm not dead." She touched his arm. "And I have you to thank for that."

Jerry dumped the last of the cement into the mold and

walked over to the new park bench they had placed there earlier that evening.

He sat down on the new lawn furniture and crossed an ankle over his knee. Now that his cast had been taken off, he didn't even show a hint of a limp. Except for not remembering anything before the accident, he showed no signs of his former injuries.

Kim held a brief mental debate about whether she wanted him to recover completely or to remain as he was now: sweet, gentle, funny, and without a trace of his former memories and personality. She was ashamed of her selfishness in wishing for the latter.

"Don't thank me yet," he said morosely. "I have a feeling there's going to be a next time."

"Well, aren't you the harbinger of gloom." She sat down on the bench beside him. "Usually, you're more upbeat company than this."

He'd certainly been the life of the party at the nursing home when they visited Aunt Rowena last weekend. He'd entertained them all by tossing butterscotch candies into the air and catching them in his mouth, telling jokes, and teaching her and the elderly folks an odd game in which they dealt feathers rather than playing cards. Kim had never heard so much laughter or seen the residents so active in all her previous visits.

He ignored her not-so-subtle hint to lighten up. As he turned toward her, a frown marred his handsome face. "This farmhouse is old, and the wiring needs to be replaced. What if a fire is set and I'm not here to protect you?"

"Chill, Jerry. No one's going to set a fire. And even if there was a fire, the smoke detectors would warn me in plenty of time. As I recall, you installed at least two on each floor, just to be sure.'' She chuckled as an irony occurred to her. ''Besides, I worried more about the house burning down when you were here cooking. With you out of here and in your own condo, I should be safe.''

A long silence passed between them. Good grief, he was making her feel guilty, and she hadn't even done anything wrong.

''Would it make you feel better if I hired an electrician to rewire the house?''

He shrugged. ''It would help.''

A female wood duck ambled over and checked the ground for anything edible. Ever the softy, Jerry reached for the heels of bread he'd brought for just this purpose. He handed one to Kim, and together they tossed crumbs to the feathered crowd that gathered around them. Even Lazarus, who had healed from the wounds inflicted by the neighbor's dog, showed up for the handout. The goose accepted Kim's tossed offerings but wouldn't come close. With Jerry, however, it ate out of his hand.

He leaned forward to entice a shy duck that had missed out on bread crusts to its faster and more aggressive counterparts. Surprisingly, the timid creature waddled forward and grabbed for the treat.

As Jerry sat beside Kim, the sun once again threw a golden cast about his head. She decided then that she ought to either get her eyes checked for glaucoma or start using his brand of shampoo.

When the crumbs were gone, he set both feet on the ground and rested his elbows on his blue-jeaned knees. ''I've been thinking about what you said about that other woman coming between you and…Gerald.''

He paused for such a long time that Kim began to

think his mind had drifted to another topic. It was probably just as well, since she wasn't in a mood to hear excuses.

"There's no excuse for cheating."

At first, she thought she'd misunderstood what he said. Then, when she realized she'd heard correctly, she experienced a moment of hopefulness...that Jerry now remembered the affair and was remorseful and, better, that he truly had changed his ways.

But talk was cheap. "Right," she said with a hollow laugh. "This, coming from the man who cheated on his own aunt in that finky feather game."

"Fenuki," he corrected.

"No harm done," he'd said with a mischievous grin when she confronted him about it later. He was just "bending the rules."

"Just like you cheated during our engagement."

"That wasn't me," he said, standing and pacing in front of her. "I'm not Gerald, and I never have been."

"If you're suggesting we start over, you can forget it. As soon as you get your memory back, you'll forget we ever had this conversation and you'll go back to your old ways." Suddenly, the little park-by-the-lake lost its magic for dissolving stress. Kim folded her arms over her chest.

Jerry stopped his pacing. "Is that what you think?"

She nodded. What else *could* she think?

He reached for her hands and pulled her to her feet. Without letting go, he forced her to face him as he continued. "Kim, there is no more Gerald. He's gone." He made a sweeping motion toward the sky. Then, gently, "Gerald is dead, honey. What you see before you is exactly what I am. And this is exactly the way I'm going to stay, for as long as I'm on this earth."

She pursed her lips. "How do I know that? How do I know the old Gerald won't come back tomorrow, or the day after that, or the month after that?" He was sincere, no doubt about it. She met his gaze. She was sincere, too. "Don't make promises you can't keep."

His fingers closed more tightly around hers. "I'll make two promises to you and I'll keep them both." When she tried to turn away, he touched her chin, urging her to look at him fully. "First, I promise you that I am not Gerald, nor will I ever hurt you the way he did."

"That's irrelevant since we're no longer engaged."

He overlooked her sarcasm and went on to his next point. "My second promise—" his chest expanded under his knit shirt as he slowly drew in a lungful of air "—is to watch over you and protect you. I will do whatever it takes to keep you safe."

The tone of their conversation had suddenly grown very somber, making Kim want to lighten the mood. "That's what guardian angels are for," she joked, fingering the gold pin on her blouse.

Shrugging loose from his grasp, she walked toward the lake, sending ducks and geese charging into the water. Too bad she couldn't get rid of her ex-fiancé as easily.

He followed her to the water's edge. "That's exactly it!" he insisted proudly. "I'm your guardian angel. Only, up yonder we're referred to as protectorates."

She was going to have to mention this to his doctor. It didn't take a psychologist to see that he was becoming delusional.

"You know," he added, "it would make my job a lot

easier if you would just let me move back in and follow you around wherever you go.''

''Look, Jerry, just because you happened to be there at the right place at the right time and you reacted quickly when I almost fell down the elevator shaft, that doesn't make you my personal...protectorate!''

''And the shoe store,'' he reminded her. ''Don't forget the falling shoe rack.''

His expression was so serious, it convinced her he was either very delusional or a very good actor. ''And what about the Burger Heaven restaurant, where I saved you from getting pulverized by that guy who thought you were flirting with his girlfriend?'' she countered. ''I suppose that qualifies me as *your* guardian angel.''

''Actually, no. First, you'd have to go through extensive training—''

''Oh, gee, next thing I know, you'll be pretending you're Richard Dreyfuss in that movie, *Always,* or Warren Beatty in *Heaven Can Wait.*''

He shook his head. ''No, those movies aren't realistic.''

''Jerry, quit pulling my leg. Of course they're unrealistic—it's all make-believe.''

His hands gripped her shoulders. ''There is nothing make-believe about my wanting to protect you.''

Before she could utter a word of protest, he pulled her to him. And once she felt how the softness of his knit shirt flowed over the sharply curved muscles of his chest, she couldn't summon the energy or the desire to pull away. She relaxed into him, resting her cheek against his shoulder. He stroked her hair, letting his fingers brush against her ear and trail down to the pulse spot in her neck. When he spoke, she enjoyed feeling the warm rumble of his voice.

"You don't have any idea how important your safety is to me. And it's not just for the wings, either."

Reluctantly, she lifted her head. "What?"

"Kim, what I'm telling you is true. If you try to believe it with your head, you'll start analyzing and trying to make it fit your rules of logic." Jerry kissed her lightly on the cheek. "Sometimes you just have to listen to your own spirit and accept the truth that it speaks." He tapped a forefinger lightly to her heart. "You have to believe from here. With faith."

At the company picnic that weekend, Jerry tried to stay close to Kim in case she should get stung by a bee or hit by a softball. Unfortunately, she kept giving him the slip.

He hadn't been successful in trying to move back into her house, either. Picking up a hot dog from the concession booth, he loaded it with relish and mustard and took a large bite. Another few bites and it was gone.

If only he could make whatever was threatening Kim's safety disappear as easily. He glanced around the private club grounds that Kim's father had rented for the event. A few employees, and especially their children, had opted for a cooling dip in the pool. Some had organized a ball game. Still others—like himself—milled around, either socializing or trying to look like they were enjoying themselves. Jerry fell into the latter category.

He had crossed paths with his secretary earlier, and they had engaged in a few moments of polite chitchat. The thought had entered his mind that Donna might be the one Gerald had been seeing on the side. But she'd never shown anything other than a professional interest in him. Playing it safe, perhaps?

No, she seemed more interested in tracking down the senior executives than spending time with him. Yep, she was definitely on the fast track up the secretarial ladder. Then again, if Gerald and Donna *had* been having an affair, maybe he was just another rung on that ladder.

Having worked for such a short time at Barnett's Bakery, Jerry hadn't become familiar with many of his co-workers. And although they knew him—knew Gerald, to be exact—there didn't seem to be any true friendships among them. Gerald must have been an extreme loner, or perhaps just incredibly off-putting to others.

A short, stocky man was walking in his direction. There was something familiar about him, and, deciding it would be more interesting to talk to someone than stand here wondering what to do, Jerry stepped into his path.

The man looked up and scowled, causing Jerry to remember where they'd run into each other before. It was the water cooler guy. "I don't believe we've been introduced," he said, hoping this wasn't a longtime acquaintance of Gerald's.

"And why should we have been? Before now, you never had a reason to talk to me. But now that I have the goods on you, you're suddenly realizing that we have more in common than appears on the surface."

The fellow was a regular sourpuss. But Jerry wasn't going to let that deter him from his plan for the day. The picnic provided the perfect opportunity to meet a variety of people, ask a few key questions, and make some sense out of Gerald's activities. He stuck out his hand. "I'm Jerry Kirkland."

"I know who you are." Instead of returning Jerry's courtesy, the man shoved his hands into his pants pockets. The action pushed his breeches down only an inch or so, but it was enough to allow his rounded belly to lop over his belt. "You're the guy who thinks he can get away with anything you want just because you're engaged to marry the boss's daughter."

Jerry withdrew his hand and swept it through his hair. "If you're still peeved about my cutting in front of you at the water cooler—"

"I'm peeved about your putting the company—and my *job!*—in jeopardy."

The little man's voice had risen, calling attention from the group of women who'd stood chatting in the shade of a nearby tree.

Jerry nodded to a more private spot on the far side of the clubhouse. A dirt path led to a wooded trail beyond it. The man followed him past the corner of the building before continuing.

"I've worked in the accounting department at Barnett's Bakery for thirty-six years, starting as a clerical assistant and eventually moving up to manager of the department. I'm fifty-four years old, Mr. Kirkland, too old to find a new job if you go through with your foolhardy plan."

So he'd been right about the fellow working in the accounting department. Jerry gave himself a pat on the back for his insight into human personality types. He hoped Nahum was taking notes. "What did you say your name was?"

"I didn't, but it's Tackett. Pete Tackett." He fidgeted

and glanced around them. "I've probably already put my job on the line by confronting you over this, but if I'm going to lose it anyway, I'd rather go down fighting."

"I don't understand. What makes you think you're going to lose your job, and why did you say the company is in jeopardy?"

The earlier animosity faded. Tackett studied him for a full minute and apparently decided that Jerry's question had been sincere. "You mean you really don't know about the loophole in your merger plan?"

Frowning, Jerry rested a hand against the rough brick building. "What loophole?"

The little man moved closer and lowered his voice. "If the merger is handled as planned, it will open Barnett's Bakery to a corporate takeover. And whenever something like that happens, the top level of management is often immediately replaced." And in case Jerry hadn't caught the implication, he poked a thumb at his own chest and added, "That means me."

Suddenly, Jerry didn't feel very well, and he didn't think it had anything to do with standing in the bright summer sun. Had Gerald known the merger arrangements would leave the company vulnerable? When Jerry thought back to the two different sets of printouts, he had a sinking feeling there was something more sinister in production than a simple oversight.

Fortunately, here was someone who knew more about the situation than he did and who had a strong reason to want to clear things up. Even better, Tackett now believed that the situation was merely the result of a careless mistake. The smart thing would be to enlist his aid in rooting out whatever was amiss. And he could start by having the accounting manager interpret the confusing figures on those printouts.

"Look, would you come to my office Monday morning? I'd like to go over a few documents with you."

Tackett's spirits lifted noticeably. "Sure. I'll be there first thing."

"Having fun?"

Kim turned to find Jerry holding out a bright yellow helium balloon to her. She accepted, then wrapped the string around her fingers. "These were supposed to be for the children."

He grinned. "I told the lady I was ten, and she believed me."

She took in the formfitting white tank top that showed off his tan and his broad, bulky shoulders. The memo announcing the picnic had advised employees to dress casually, and he had followed it to the letter, finishing off his summer look with jean shorts and Birkenstock sandals. His calves—even on the leg that had been broken—were firm knots of muscle.

Yes, ten was a number that suited him very well, but not with regard to his age. She lifted her hair off her neck. Was it her, or did the sun suddenly feel warmer?

"Kim, there you are." Her stepmother approached them and gave her a brief hug. "Your car is blocking Phyllis Fletcher in, and she's about to have a fit because she's already running behind on her To Do list for today."

Kim was familiar with Phyllis's list. A fixture with the company since it was a modest-size bakery with a small but enthusiastic niche of customers in the city, the woman had to be close to seventy, but she showed no sign of retiring anytime soon. She ran her life, and tried to run everyone else's, the way she tackled her work...with a list written in ink that absolutely, positively must have everything crossed off by the end of the day. And God help anyone who interfered with her list crossing.

She checked her watch. Almost five o'clock. Obviously, Phyllis didn't want to be late for the amateur wrestling match on television. The older woman's love for the sport was almost as well-known as her list compulsion.

"I'll go move it." Kim dug in her pocket for the car keys, but the balloon string got tangled in the ring.

"Don't bother, I'll do it," Carmen said. She reached for the keys, and in the next moment the yellow balloon sailed heavenward. "Oops, sorry. You just go ahead and visit with your fiancé. This won't take but a minute."

With a little wave to them both, her stepmother headed off to the parking lot.

When Kim turned her attention back to Jerry, she found him staring forlornly at the diminishing balloon. "I'm sorry," she said, wondering why it felt like such a big deal.

"It's okay. Whenever that happens, it breaks up the monotony up there in the Great Beyond." He gave her a warm smile. "You wouldn't believe how everyone scrambles to be first to pop the balloon."

Hooking her thumbs through the belt loops on her jeans, Kim gazed up at the man who, except for one major flaw, seemed perfect for her in every way. She was beginning to think—irrationally, perhaps—that Jerry was right. Maybe he wasn't going to turn back into the person who'd shattered her trust. Maybe she should take a chance that Gerald's old ways had died and that Jerry's new ways would remain. Come to think of it, she rather liked the new sense of humor that Jerry had developed. His teasing good humor was a refreshing change from his former grim, type A personality. "Still pulling my leg, huh?"

"Oh, no, I wouldn't do that. Especially not in public."

He was so serious, Kim had to laugh. "Oh, so you only like to tease me when we're alone? Smart move. No witnesses."

Jerry moved closer, as if to tell a secret, so she leaned toward him to hear.

"If we were alone," he said, "I would love to tease you. But it wouldn't be with words."

Her pulse quickened at the thought.

He licked his lips and continued. "I would start with your mouth and kiss it until all your words of protest turn into moans begging for more. And then I would kiss you right here."

He touched a finger to the hollow under her chin, and Kim wished his lips were touching her there instead.

"And then I would hold you—" he dropped his finger to the button between her breasts and held it there as if he was contemplating plucking it open "—in my hands and in my mouth."

She should say something, should stop his words of sweet torment, but she felt powerless to do anything other than listen to the low rumble of his voice and picture the delicious vision that he painted for her.

"And before you got tired of that, I would pull you into my arms and—"

"Car's all moved. Here are your keys." Carmen

tossed the ring at her, causing her to crash back to reality as she quickly moved to catch them. "The band should be arriving soon, and your father wants to know where they should set up their equipment."

Effectively doused with the cold-water reminder of her duties, Kim chanced a quick look at Jerry. His eyes were slightly foggy, as if he was still thinking about the scenario he'd whispered to her a moment before.

"I, uh, I'd better go help Dad get things straight for the entertainment."

When she was gone, Carmen smiled and tilted her face toward Jerry. "Maxwell tells me you've given some pretty impressive arguments for dropping the merger deal."

"I really can't take full credit for that. Most of what I said is just commonsense stuff about not taking on more than he can reasonably expect to handle." Jerry waved a gnat away from his face. "Next, I'm going to see about getting him to discontinue the devil's food cakes."

Her smile vanished and was replaced by a look of utter incredulity. "That's insane!"

"You're right. They do taste great, and they sell well, too." He rubbed at the hairs that were tickling his chest. "Maybe we could just rename them. You know, something a bit more sacrosanct."

"I'm not talking about that. What's insane is your attempt to unravel everything we've managed to put together during this merger effort. Are you crazy?"

"No, a lot of people think that, but I just don't remember a lot of stuff since the accident."

She eyed him cautiously. "Okay, I'll play along," she

told him, "but I think you're taking this amnesia act a bit far."

"What do you mean?"

She shook her head, making the soft reddish curls bounce around her face. "I saw you making eyes at her. Leading her on."

He wasn't ashamed of having flirted with Kim, but he hadn't meant for anyone else to notice. She kept stressing the importance of maintaining a businesslike relationship at the office. He only hoped that no one else had noticed. In an attempt to downplay the incident for Kim's sake, he casually said, "Well, we *are* engaged."

"You can drop the amnesia act with me," she said, placing her hands resolutely on her hips. "I know what a two-timing toad you are."

Jerry hesitated. Obviously, Gerald's indiscretion hadn't been much of a secret. And Kim had been trying so hard to keep it from her parents. "How did you know?"

"I told you, there's no need to be coy." She pointed to the path that led into the woods. "That hamburger I ate is sitting like lead in my stomach. Come with me while I walk it off."

Imperiously, she looped her arm through his and headed off on her walk. Jerry glanced back, wondering if Kim would need his help. But when Carmen urged him on, he decided to take advantage of the opportunity to find out what else she knew about Gerald. So far, nothing irreversible had happened to Kim in the weeks since he'd been assigned to protect her. He could only pray that she would continue to stay safe for the few minutes that he would be gone.

When they had gone a short distance down the forest

path, Carmen stepped behind a tree. When he had followed her there, she turned to face him. "So, did you call Otto?"

Jerry halted abruptly to avoid colliding with her. "Otto Hoskins?"

"Of course Otto Hoskins. I gave you the note weeks ago. Don't tell me you haven't done it yet."

Well, that answered one question, but it didn't explain what he was supposed to discuss with him or why Carmen was involved. "I've, uh, been sort of busy."

"Yeah, I know, recuperating and all that. But we don't have any time to waste if we're going to get everything in place before the deal is signed." She paced back and forth for a moment, one hand cupping her elbow and the other on her chin. Then, wagging a finger at him the way a schoolteacher would scold a child, she added, "Meanwhile, you've got to keep your mouth shut and stop filling Maxwell's head with stupid ideas about keeping the company smaller so he can take it easy."

"It wasn't a stupid idea. He agreed my suggestions made plenty of sense."

"Gerald, *think,* dear." She tapped his temple with a delicately tapered nail. "This merger is possibly the only opportunity we'll ever have to acquire controlling interest of the company."

Jerry felt his mouth open, then quickly snapped it shut. The situation was getting stickier by the minute. Carmen's revelation didn't explain all the puzzle pieces he'd collected, but it did convince him that the proposed business merger—or something related to it—was the reason he had been sent here to protect Kim.

"Just think, Gerald, about all the designer suits you can buy and all the ski trips you can go on when the cookie business is ours. Perhaps I'll even buy a villa, and we can live there part of the year.''

He felt the muscle in his jaw contract as he flatly summarized her plan. ''We'll be rolling in the dough.''

She laughed. Considering what he'd just learned, he would have expected a witch's cackle, but the sound was deceptively pretty. Like the rest of her.

''My, my, it sounds as though you've grown a sense of humor, my dear Gerald.'' Carmen closed the distance between them, and Jerry detected a faint acrid scent. Like oranges.

''I'm not Gerald,'' he said, capturing her hand as she reached to tug the tank top loose from his waistband. ''My name is Jerry.''

''That amnesia act has got to go.'' She looped her free arm around his neck. ''Maybe this will jar your memory.''

He should have seen it coming and somehow evaded the kiss she planted on his mouth as she pressed her body against him. Perhaps if he'd had more experience as a human, he would have. But, since he was still reeling from her surprise disclosure, he got caught flatfooted.

The kiss was nothing at all like the one he had experienced with Kim. Although it only lasted a second or two before he could gather his wits enough to push her away, the ugly details assaulted his senses. From her full, groping lips to her tangy perfume, and even to the soft grunting noise she made as she tried to encourage him to respond, everything about her repelled him.

Nearby, leaves rustled, and a twig cracked.

The kiss Carmen had inflicted on him far surpassed the offensive taste of coffee, his only other negative sensory experience since coming into Gerald's body. With effort, he backed away and disengaged her arm from around his neck.

"Jerry? Is that you? Dad wants to know if—" Kim stopped short on the wooded path, taking in the horrible scene.

Jerry wiped his mouth with the back of his hand. The yuck factor ran high, and it was all he could do to keep from gagging.

He watched helplessly as Kim's smile collapsed, along with whatever trust he'd managed to build with her these past weeks. Her look of surprise...her complete disbelief and disappointment...would stay with him for tens of thousands of years. And even then, he knew it would hurt no less.

CHAPTER NINE

THE next day, Kim skipped church, and she didn't go with Jerry to visit Rowena as had become their weekly habit. At this point, she couldn't tolerate hearing more excuses.

Opening the storage closet under the stairs, she stuffed the vacuum cleaner inside and withdrew a cloth and bottle of furniture polish. She had to do something to burn off the energy that raged within her.

"Be reasonable," Gerald had told her the first time she'd caught him philandering. If she would just forget about what she saw, he'd said, everything would go back to "the way it used to be."

Right. And if she were gullibly naive, he could go on eating his cake and having it, too.

This time was worse, though. Far, far worse. This time, she'd known he couldn't be trusted, but she'd foolishly begun to think that he had changed. She had allowed herself to fall deeply and irrevocably in love with him.

And then there was Carmen. Not only had her stepmother and Jerry betrayed Kim, but they'd deceived her father, as well. And, because Kim would not tell him about it and thus risk bringing on another heart attack, she was now drawn into their web of deceit.

She swished the rag over the coffee table where Jerry had often rested his feet. If her departed mother could see Kim now, she'd be horrified to find her only child performing housework on a Sunday. Kim buffed the furniture to a shine. Better this sin than breaking the Sixth Commandment.

Thou shalt not kill. Right now, she was tempted to finish off what Gerald's car accident had failed to do.

A knock sounded at the front door. Glancing out the window, she saw a taxicab pull away from her driveway. She wondered who it could be. Taxis didn't usually come this far out of the city.

A look through the peephole showed her dark-haired nemesis on the broad front porch, his hands shoved contritely in his pockets.

Going back into the den, she cleared the lamp and lace doily from the end table and proceeded to polish the piece with a vigor it had never seen before.

Another knock. She ignored it.

"I know you're in there. If you don't open up, I'm going to go next door and sweet-talk the spare house key out of Mrs. Neidermeyer."

Kim threw the rag on the floor, stalked back to the door and flung it open. "Whatever you want from me, the answer is no."

She started to close the door, but Jerry blocked the movement with his body. Against her obvious wishes to the contrary, he let himself in.

Dressed in his Sunday finery, he was enough to turn any woman's head. Kim looked away from him, not wanting to see how his tie had been tugged loose and the soft hairs on his chest sprang from the loosened top button of the dress shirt. Not wanting to see how much,

despite all that had happened, she was still attracted to
him.

He towered over her. His hand touched her face, and
she steeled herself to his charm and the smooth words
that were sure to follow. At the pressure of his thumb
against her chin, she turned back toward him, but she
did not look up at his face. Her gaze fell on his chest.

"Nice red tie," she remarked with a false lightness.
"Couldn't find a letter *A* to wear instead?"

"You're jumping to conclusions. Kim, this is all just
a huge misunderstanding."

That got her attention. This time, she met his eyes and
glowered fiercely up into the shadowed blue depths.
"What is that, a *script?* The least you could do is try to
be original for a change." She put her hand on the doorknob, replaying the scene that had taken place here just
before his car crash. "You know how much I hate re-
runs, Gerald."

He covered her hand with his own, holding it captive.
"I told you before. I am not Gerald."

"Oh, yeah, that's right—you're supposed to be my
protectorate. Some guardian angel you are. What I'd like
to know is, who's supposed to be protecting me from
you?"

"If you would just let me explain—"

"If I would just let you explain," she interrupted,
"you'd probably tell me another cockamamy story. Only
this time, it would be about how you're a secret agent
and you were only kissing my stepmother to protect the
security of our country."

He wouldn't, of course. But even that would be preferable to whatever lies he might tell about the insignif-

icance of his relationship with Carmen and how much he still loved Kim.

The worst part was that she would *want* to believe the lies.

He pried loose her grip on the doorknob and wordlessly led her to the den. When they were seated on the sofa, facing each other and knees bumping, he took her hands in his warm ones.

"Kim, I hate to be the bearer of bad news, but there's some very unpleasant stuff going on."

"You can say that again."

"Please, let me finish." He waited for her nod of consent before continuing. "I don't know how to say this gently, so I'm going to just spit it right out. Your stepmother has been involved with Gerald in some very reprehensible activities."

"Duh!"

"Well, there's the obvious, of course," he admitted, "but there's something else, and it involves the proposed merger with Goode Foods."

"If you're trying to confuse the issue, it's not going to work." She pulled her hands away from his and placed them, fists clenched, in her lap.

"No, really, she told me so herself. I haven't figured out all the particulars yet, but I know that the merger is the vehicle for Carmen taking controlling interest of the company."

Kim shot to her feet, almost overturning the coffee table. The book she'd left there earlier thumped to the floor. "That's the most ridiculous thing I have ever heard."

"No, it's the truth."

He stood up, too, and tugged at the knot of his tie until the loop resembled a noose. As far as she was concerned, he was indeed hanging himself with his words. She didn't know what he'd hoped to accomplish with this crazy story, but all thoughts of an amiable parting had now fled from her mind.

"You've got to believe me, Kim. Your stepmother told me all about how she wants to be rich and buy a vacation home where she can live part of the year."

When Kim spoke, it was through gritted teeth. "She's already rich. If Carmen wanted a vacation home, all she'd have to do is buy it herself or put it on her Christmas wish list." Her hands went to her hips. "She was just as wrong as you are for what happened. If you ask me, it seems rather cowardly to try to shift the blame for your own misdeeds onto someone else."

"You don't understand. Something sinister is going on, and you are at the center of it."

"No, *you* are at the center of it," she said, poking a finger at his chest. "I've heard more than enough of your nonsense."

"Let me stay here with you tonight," he implored. "Something bad is going to happen, and I don't want you to be alone."

If he stayed here a minute longer, she could vow that something bad would happen. From what she'd heard, she wouldn't be responsible for her actions in a crime of passion.

"Please go now."

He sighed, obviously disappointed that she didn't capitulate to his charm and good looks. "I can't."

She stared at him, wondering what perverse pleasure he was getting out of torturing her.

He shrugged and pulled at his tie again. "I don't have a ride. Can you give me a lift?"

The nerve of the man! "Even if I wanted to—which I *don't*—I can't." He seemed to be expecting more of an explanation, so she added, "The car is acting funny. I don't want to drive it any more than necessary before I take it to the repair shop."

Nudging him with a hand to his elbow, she guided him back to the foyer.

"So I would suggest that you leave the way you came."

Evicted from the house, Jerry sat on the porch step for an hour before the cab came to take him home.

It took less than an hour for Pete Tackett to determine the reason the computer printout figures had been so confusing to Jerry.

"There you go," the older man said, sitting back in the guest chair, a satisfied smile crossing his rounded features. "This first set of calculations—" he tapped the file Jerry had brought from the condo "—incorporated the complete data. But the second set is missing this small column of information. Probably nothing more than an oversight."

Sure. An "oversight" for which the receipt was locked in Gerald's bottom desk drawer. Naturally, he would let Tackett continue to think it was an innocent mistake.

"By going into the deal with the wrong results, you're leaving some areas of negotiation unaccounted for in the merger contract. Next thing you know, some wise guy learns about our Achilles' heel and..." Tackett made a spiraling motion in the air. "Poof! We're ripe for a corporate takeover, and I'm out of a job."

And Gerald and Carmen were the ones who stood to gain from that Achilles' heel.

Jerry recalled the photo of Gerald, Kim and her parents at the condo. It had probably pleased Kim to think that he cared enough to display a picture of her family. But it was probably the only way Gerald could have a snapshot of Carmen without raising suspicion.

The motel and restaurant receipts, as well as the package of condoms gave evidence of their secret outings. As for the note to buy champagne, it must have been in preparation to celebrate the success of their collusion.

And at the picnic on Saturday, when Carmen had asked if he'd contacted Otto Hoskins, she'd been checking to see if Gerald had arranged for the falsified printout.

All this was interesting, but it didn't explain how or why Kim's life was in danger. But one thing was sure: he needed her cooperation in order to protect her. And to gain it, he must first show her the evidence he'd collected and then convince her that the tenuous merger situation had come by design rather than accident...even if it meant implicating himself.

Jerry stood and extended his hand to the man who'd helped bring all this to light. "Pete, you don't know how much I appreciate your pointing out this problem."

"And you don't know how much I appreciate the opportunity to hold on to my job and retirement benefits."

When he was gone, Jerry fortified himself with a deep

breath. Grabbing up the file folders and incriminating receipts, he bypassed the elevator and took the stairs two at a time to Kim's office.

Upon hearing him enter, Kim swiveled her chair toward him and cast him a curious glance.

He took that as an invitation and pulled the guest chair around to her side of the desk, dumping his evidence in front of her. "Maybe this will convince you that what I tried to tell you last night is the truth."

She rested her forehead against the palm of her hand. "Jerry, I'm very busy right now."

"All I'm asking you to do is take a moment to look at the facts. The proof, if you will."

He waited as indecision wrinkled her forehead. When she finally nodded that she would hear him out, he launched into the pieces of evidence he'd found. She listened, a grim determination pulling at the corners of her pretty mouth. Her composure faltered only at the mention of Gerald and Carmen's furtive meetings at expensive restaurants and the in-town motel.

"The sneaking-around part I believe, and I'm glad you're finally admitting it," she said at last. Her tone was deadly flat. "But I don't understand why you are now trying to paint her as a criminal. I never imagined you to be so vindictive."

"It wasn't just Carmen." Jerry swallowed before telling her the rest. If Kim thought he was a heel now, just wait until she heard that Gerald had bought falsified documents.

The only fortunate part of this whole mess was that Kim would not have him fired. Because she didn't dare tell her father about the affair for fear the knowledge would adversely affect his health, Jerry would still be able to work near her every day and keep a watchful eye out for her. Of course, that still left her vulnerable on nights and weekends.

She took the news better than he expected. But he could see that she felt overwhelmed by it.

"I'd be lying if I said I wasn't shocked by this." She leaned back in her chair and closed her eyes. She opened them a moment later and fixed the brown spheres on him. "I appreciate your owning up to your part in this...complicity. But I fail to understand why."

"Why Gerald did it?"

"No. Why you're telling me about it at all. It's possible you both could have gone undetected, at least until you took what you wanted and fled the country. Why are you spoiling your own well-laid plan? Unless..."

She leaned forward and tapped a pencil on the desk blotter. After she'd pondered a second or two, biting her lip as she did so, she pointed the writing instrument at him.

"Unless you and Carmen had a falling-out and you're acting out of vengeance. In which case, you're willing to take the heat right along with her, just to watch her suffer."

"No, I don't take heat well," he said, thinking of the Place of Torment. "That's why I work for the good guys."

That look crossed her face again...the one mixed with confusion and surprise. "What are you talking about?"

"I'm talking about the reason I'm here—to keep you safe from harm."

She shook her head and pushed the papers to the corner of her desk. "Please. Don't start that craziness again."

"Kim, I'm not sure how you figure into the scenario," he said, touching a hand to her arm. She flinched but didn't move away. "But I am sure that your life is somehow in danger. Let me move back in with you so that I can protect you." Ever so sincerely, and with his heart feeling even more fragile than the elder Barnett's, he whispered, "I don't want you to die."

Kim hung up the phone and sank back into her chair. This just wasn't her day. She had still been reeling from Saturday's events when Jerry came to tell her about the potentially illegal scheme he and Carmen had been plotting. And now the person at the repair shop had topped things off by saying they couldn't look at her car until tomorrow morning.

It was odd, but the corporate situation Jerry had brought to her attention affected her less than when she'd seen him and her stepmother kissing. It hadn't been this tough on her when she'd broken their engagement.

She recalled the emotional numbness that had paralyzed her when she'd confronted Gerald about his trip to the motel with that woman. With Carmen.

How she wished now for that same numbness. For that would be better than this awful searing pain that sliced through her. Not wishing to acknowledge that her feelings for Jerry had grown since his first betrayal, she told herself the relentless ache came out of concern for her father, who would be devastated by his young wife's infidelity. Or that the overtime she'd been working had left her tired and on edge.

Kim pushed away from her desk. It was late. She couldn't think anymore today. Tomorrow she would decide how to break the news—both personal and professional—to her father.

Tonight, however, she would try to escape from both issues. Read a novel, perhaps. Something deep and dark and depressing. Something that would exceed her own foul mood, thereby making her feel better by knowing that at least a fictional character had it worse than she did. Anything but a romance, with its guaranteed happy ending.

She fished the keys out of her purse and went home, leaving behind the documents Jerry had given her and— she hoped—leaving behind the anguish he had brought her.

Cornering Fourteenth Street, she passed the Italian restaurant where she, Jerry and her parents had planned to eat the day the elevator malfunctioned. Its brightly lit sign pierced the quickly falling darkness. Carmen had recommended this place. Had she and Jerry met there before?

The traffic light turned red, and Kim pressed the brake harder than necessary. The pedal slipped a fraction before bringing the car to a jerky stop. Gerald had always insisted on trading in his car for a new model every two or three years, while she had argued that doing so was costly and wasteful. Maybe she should have listened to him on this. The rest of the way home, she drove more cautiously than usual.

Unfortunately, the silence that filled the long trip to

the country gave her ample opportunity to replay painful scenes and scraps of conversations in her mind. She reached over and cranked the radio up as loud as her ears could tolerate. Maybe the noise would drown out the unwanted thoughts that bombarded her brain.

The country songs were all about love gone wrong. Annoyed, she switched to a popular rock station. These songs were all about love gone right.

The rap station was even worse. The singer, in a chant that reminded her of the songs she'd jumped rope to in her youth, advised her to lie down in front of an oncoming train. "Ain't no lookin' back, when your essence leaves that track."

Click. Silence once again filled the small sedan. Things might be bad, and Kim certainly wondered how she would make it through each day, but nothing could be so terrible as to warrant that kind of "solution."

Besides, Jerry had already killed a tiny but vital part of her. Remembering an educational television program she'd seen, she recalled that if cells in a certain part of the brain were destroyed, a neighboring section would soon develop the ability to handle that function.

Perhaps, if she waited it out, she would learn to live life without her heart.

Kim pulled into the driveway, gunning the engine to give it enough gas to climb the shallow rise. When she reached the crest where she always parked, she touched the brake. The pedal held briefly, then buckled under her foot, stopping only when it touched the floorboard.

The car continued over the rise. Kim pumped the brake furiously, to no avail. Now the headlights showed that she was headed downhill toward the barn. With only a split second to react, she veered away from the building, bumping over the stone path she and Jerry had built. The left front fender narrowly missed the bench. Seeing several ducks directly in her path, she blew the horn long and hard.

The blaring vehicle bounced over the grassy incline, sending birds flying in all directions. As the car approached the water, Kim crazily thought how unnecessary train tracks would be right now. Surely she would die by drowning.

Kim closed her eyes against the impact and felt the air bag explode in her face. Next she felt herself plunging into the lake, sinking deeper and deeper. The night grew murky as the body of water swallowed the headlights.

Taking a full breath, she held it, knowing it could be her last, and fumbled to unfasten the seat belt. Cold water surged around her ankles, rose quickly to her knees and then to her waist as the car filled.

She had to get out. Now!

Gathering her courage and another full breath of air, she reached for the window knob to roll it down. Prepared to swim to the surface, she was surprised when there was no inflow rushing over the top of the glass.

Her hand tightly gripping the knob, she continued turning…slowly and steadily. It wasn't until the window was almost fully lowered that the cold liquid gushed forward onto her arm.

The car wasn't completely submerged after all! At this point, the water was only waist-deep.

Relieved, Kim moved to pull the door handle. With effort, she pushed it open and eased herself out.

Although the sun had been warm earlier that day, the night air had turned chilly.

Kim hugged herself and slogged through the muddy mess that sucked at her feet. Lazarus swam by in front of her, honking his displeasure at having his quiet evening disturbed. With only the pale gleam of the quarter moon to light her way, she walked up the hill to the relative safety of the house.

The sodden silk skirt clung to her legs, making them feel heavy and clumsy. When she reached the side door, she remembered that her purse and keys were still in the car.

Fetching the spare from beneath the flowerpot that adorned the window ledge, she let herself in. She picked up the phone and dialed, heedless of the puddle forming around her on the kitchen's vinyl floor.

"Hello, Jerry? Is your offer still open to come stay with me?"

CHAPTER TEN

KIM didn't know why, but having Jerry here made her feel better.

After they had called the tow truck to pull her car out of the lake, he had insisted she take a warm bath and dress for bed. While she did that, he dealt with the tow-truck driver and then slipped over to the Neidermeyers' to borrow their spare car for her.

Later, when they sat together in the den, they talked about this latest in her series of mishaps. Unlike his usual preference, this time he didn't prop his feet on the coffee table. Instead, he sat on the edge of the sofa, leaning his elbows on his knees.

"Yes, I know it's odd for a person to have so many accidents," she said after her nerves had calmed and they'd had a chance to talk about it, "but I don't think it's anything more than just a string of bad luck."

He waited for her to stop pacing the floor before responding. Kim sat down beside him on the sofa and tried to still her fidgeting.

"Then why did you call me?" he asked at last. "Why were you afraid to stay here by yourself tonight?"

"I'm not afraid."

Her words and tone of voice reminded her of the time her father had taken her on her first roller-coaster ride. She'd been terrified.

She sank back into the sofa. "Okay, I admit I got a

bit rattled for a while, but don't you think we're making a mountain out of a molehill?

He folded down a finger for each disaster she'd narrowly escaped. "The shoe rack. The elevator shaft. And now your car in the lake. That's three strikes, Kim. The next time you won't be so lucky."

She sat forward, twinning him as she perched on the edge of the sofa. "And what makes you so sure of that? How is it that all of a sudden you're such a whiz at looking into the future?"

Jerry looked down at his hands. "I told you before, but I don't think you believed me."

"Oh, no, not that guardian angel stuff again."

He stared at her for a full minute. Under his scrutiny, Kim reacted oddly...she felt negative and mean-spirited for doubting his crazy story.

When he spoke, his voice was soft. "You read the Scriptures, don't you?"

She nodded.

"And you believe what you read there?"

"Of course."

He left the room a moment and came back with a black book, which he handed to her. "Then you must believe Hebrews 13:2."

She opened to the verse and read aloud as he hovered over her. "'Be not forgetful to entertain strangers: for thereby some have entertained angels unawares.'"

She didn't agree, but she didn't disagree, either.

"Angels don't kiss the stepmothers of their ex-fiancées."

He sat down heavily beside her. Taking the book from her hands, he closed it and placed it on the coffee table.

Then he held her hand in his. Kim tried to ignore the warmth that flared between them.

"I didn't kiss her, Kim."

He seemed so sincere as he explained what happened that day that she wanted to believe him. Wanted to believe Carmen had initiated the kiss and that Jerry had been taken by surprise. One thing was certain—he was clearly repulsed as he recalled the unfortunate incident.

"I would never do anything to hurt you."

She felt her heart soften. Maybe she was a fool, but she knew he was telling her the truth. The Gerald she knew before the accident would lie to her and, perhaps, so would the Gerald who would return along with all his original memories and personality traits.

But the Jerry who sat in her living room—the man who had captured her heart despite his wicked past— truly was incapable of lying...and especially of doing it so convincingly.

When she had come across Jerry and her stepmother near the wooded path, her first and understandably natural reaction had been to assume that he had recovered his lost memory and was picking up where he'd left off with Carmen.

However, if that was the case, why would he have exposed the shady dealings he and Carmen had cooked up? The old Gerald, who would do anything to better his situation in life, would have explained away the printout discrepancy as a mere oversight. On someone else's part, of course. Not his. And not even for revenge would he be willing to forgo the bounty he stood to gain from the dishonest transaction.

Some might call her a fool for believing Jerry had not

willingly received Carmen's kiss. Something in her gut told her she was right about him. But she drew the line at this angel story of his.

Recalling the first part of the verse she'd read, Kim said, "You're not a stranger."

"Am I not?" He smiled at her, and a small dimple formed in his cheek. "Am I the same person who inhabited this body before the fatal car crash?"

"It wasn't fatal! You're living proof of that."

He shook his head. "Gerald died in the emergency room. When he left, I was sent to abide in his body and protect you from harm."

Kim's thoughts veered back to the night she'd rushed to be with Gerald as he clung to life. The heart monitor had stopped beeping and registered a long, flat tone. The medical staff had done everything they could, administering electric shock and a powerful drug to get his heart started again. Eventually, they had given up and pulled the sheet over his face.

A moment later, the monitor started beeping again—stronger than before—and the nurse declared it a miracle.

Could it be...?

No, that notion was nothing short of lunacy.

Jerry must have seen the confusion on her face. "Normally, I don't give clients the details of my assignments. Then again, my clients don't usually know I'm around."

For the next twenty minutes, he relayed a long, involved tale about a performance review, a supervisor called Nahum, a pair of wings, and serving his apprenticeship as a human.

She stopped him with an upraised hand. "Okay, I

think I get everything but the poopy diaper part. But what does this have to do with me?''

"I was assigned to your case because your hourglass is in danger of emptying fifty or sixty years too soon."

Kim stared at him, stunned by how seriously he spoke about something so far-fetched.

"I know it's a lot to take in, but I could use your cooperation." He must have noticed her hesitation, for he added, "This is only until I save your life, then I'm outta here."

"Jerry, how can you ask me to believe this, much less go around with you being my bodyguard?"

"Protectorate," he corrected. "Just look at the evidence. You've already admitted I'm not the same person Gerald was."

"Yeah, but—"

"Did Gerald know all the words to the songs at church?"

"No, but—"

"And what about how quickly the injuries healed? Even the doctor said it wasn't humanly possible."

"True, but—"

This time, she interrupted herself. He was right about all the things he had cited. And he hadn't mentioned the ease with which he'd broken up the dog-and-goose fight, or even the halo she'd seen shining around his hair when they were down by the lake. But...

"I'm sure all these things have a logical explanation."

"How do you explain my knowing Mr. Sizemore?"

Jerry had clearly been familiar with the older gentleman he'd seen at the mall. And Mr. Sizemore had seemed baffled as to who he might be.

"I failed him," he said, regret filling his voice. "My mind wandered, and because of that momentary lapse, a nice college boy suffered a hard life and became a bitter old man."

He released her hand and rubbed his palms against the knees of his jeans. He seemed agitated, and Kim worried that he might be going over the edge.

"Believe me, Kim, I won't fail you. This time, I'm going to do whatever it takes to get my job done right."

"Because you want your wings," she prompted, humoring him.

He leaned toward her. "You still don't believe me, do you?"

Before she knew what was happening, he was kissing her. It was a long, impassioned kiss, full of feeling and promises. Kim found herself returning the sentiment with matching enthusiasm.

When he finally broke the embrace, he continued to hold her face in his large hand. "You're so beautiful," he told her. "It's against regulations, but I've fallen head over heels in love with you." Brushing his thumb against the corner of her lips, he asked, "Do you know how I know?"

She didn't, but she wondered if he had the same sick, scary feeling in the pit of his stomach that she had in hers.

"When I set aside all the facts and all the shoulds, and I listen to the quiet voice that's speaking to me from deep down inside, I know."

As she watched, his eyes seemed to deepen until they were almost green in color.

"Listen carefully to your spirit as it speaks to you,"

he said, "and you'll know that all I've told you is true. You'll know that the man who has just professed his love to you, and who wants to keep you safe, is not Gerald."

She tried to speak, tried to tell him that this whole conversation was an overreaction to the car plunging into the lake. But he wouldn't heed her words.

"When you hear it," he emphasized, "you will know."

Kim didn't know why she had let him talk her into coming to the office tonight. She supposed she must have been hearing voices after all. What other explanation could there be for rummaging through desk drawers and files, searching for clues that could help Jerry prevent the early "emptying" of her "hourglass"?

Besides, it was hard trying to concentrate on the task at hand when her thoughts kept going back to his profession of love. Idly, she allowed her fingers to trace the outline of the tiny gold angel pin she'd fastened above her heart earlier when she'd changed into the simple cotton top. His words were sweet and sincere, and they carried far more impact than Gerald's meaningless declarations that had been accompanied by wine, roses or chocolates.

"Maybe we should just go home," she suggested. They weren't having any luck, so they might as well get some sleep.

Jerry took one last look around and nodded his agreement.

After they'd locked up and gone back to the Neidermeyers' station wagon, Jerry turned suddenly toward her. "What about the factory?" he proposed. "Maybe we'll find something there."

Kim slumped wearily over the steering wheel. "It's the middle of the night. Besides, no one's there for us to question. We don't run a midnight shift anymore."

She didn't bother to mention that the merger plans called for a return to twenty-four-hour production.

"All the better." Jerry smiled. "We can look around to our hearts' content without having to explain our presence to anyone."

She sighed heavily and steered the car down deserted Broadnax Street, leaving the city's tall buildings behind as she headed for the sprawling factory-and-warehouse district that lay on the other side of the river. After parking beside the curb in front of the Barnett's Bakery factory, she unlocked the main door and let them in.

Jerry switched on lights as they made their way through the empty building to the shift manager's office. The utilitarian metal desk that stood in the center of the cluttered office was covered with papers that seemed to be stacked in some sort of order. He started flipping through the papers, taking care not to get them out of sequence. "Nothing but job orders here."

"Jerry, I feel funny about searching an employee's office."

"I won't look at anything personal," he promised. Then he flipped through the desk calendar, but appeared not to find anything of interest. Next were the desk drawers: a box of Barnett's doughnuts in the top, which he ignored, and a girlie magazine in the bottom. He extracted the magazine and riffled through the pages. It fell open to the centerfold.

His eyebrows shot up and his jaw dropped. As he snapped it shut, he quickly laid one hand over the picture and shut the pages with the other.

"Heavens!" he declared, and dropped the magazine in the trash can beside the desk.

Kim laughed out loud at his response. "Maybe we should go now."

Jerry was wiping his hands on his pants legs, as if to rid himself of whatever contamination he may have picked up. "No, let's take a look at the factory first."

She started to argue. Since she had the car keys, it would have taken nothing more than a threat to leave by herself to make him come with her.

He shivered as if he'd seen a ghost. "Something is telling me your time is very near."

"We're both being silly," Kim said. "Now we're scaring ourselves with all this cloak-and-dagger stuff."

He shook his head sadly. "I wish you were right, but there's no mistaking this feeling. We have to find our answers *tonight.*"

Reluctantly, she went along, following him to a large room filled with vats and mixers. Maybe a quick look would convince him there was nothing to be found here. At least, she hoped so.

It was eerily quiet. When in operation, the machines rumbled loudly, filling the room with their noise and vibrations. Tonight, they sat ominously silent, dwarfing Jerry and Kim with their massive size.

Kim thought she heard a noise. Although she knew it was probably nothing more than the usual creaking associated with old buildings, she felt the tiny hairs rise on her arms.

"Jerry, nothing here is going to answer the questions we have. I'm going home. Now."

Another click. Only this time it was right behind her. Jerry heard it, too, and he turned with her at the sound.

Carmen blocked their exit from between the dough vats. Both hands firmly gripped a large handgun, which was pointed straight at them.

Kim didn't know much about guns, but it certainly looked deadly to her. Although she knew Carmen's motives probably weren't so innocent, she pretended to misunderstand. "It's just us," she said as lightly as she could manage under the circumstances. "You can put that away now."

The gun barrel didn't waver. Nor did Carmen's steely glare. "You have questions? Try asking me."

Kim's heart pounded against her ribs, and she felt Jerry tense beside her.

"You can forget about trying to do the hero thing," Carmen told him as she directed the gun at Kim's chest. "If you make me nervous, I might just *accidentally* shoot her."

Jerry didn't move, but his voice was hard when he spoke. "You're the one who tried to kill Kim."

"And you're the one who kept her from getting 'the shaft,'" Carmen sneered. "I thought for sure the elevator trick would do the job."

"And since it didn't," Jerry prodded, "you decided that tampering with her brakes would finish her off."

"I don't understand," Kim said, breaking through the fear that had paralyzed her a moment earlier.

"It's quite simple, really," Carmen said as casually

as if they were having a conversation at dinner. "I wanted to own the company."

Now Kim was really confused. "But you're already part owner, by virtue of being married to my father."

"I wanted more," her stepmother said sincerely. "And I got tired of waiting around for the old coot to die of natural causes. Besides, if he went first, you would become the majority owner in the company, and I'd be no better off than I am now. Probably worse." She jabbed the gun toward Kim. "But with you neatly out of the way before he croaks, I'll get everything...lock, stock and barrel."

Carmen laughed at her own joke.

Kim felt Jerry touch her arm reassuringly. "But that doesn't explain why you and Gerald monkeyed with the merger process."

"My first choice was to achieve my goal without getting my hands dirty with your blood. The original plan was to arrange the deal so that I could become majority owner and maybe eventually the sole owner. Just as I instructed, Gerald set the paperwork in action, having been promised a fair reward for his assistance. The problem was—" she turned to scowl at him "—I recently discovered he got greedy and tried to cut himself in and me out."

Carmen's hands shook, and for the first time Kim realized her stepmother was not as calm as she pretended to be.

"Which is why I loosened the steering pin in his car. But that failed, too. So now—" she alternately pointed the gun at Kim, then Jerry. "—it looks like I'm going to have to get my hands dirty after all. When the shift manager opens up in a couple of hours, he'll find your bodies here and the petty cash missing. Naturally, the police will assume it's a homicide motivated by robbery.''

Jerry stepped forward, but the muzzle of the gun stopped him in his tracks.

''You may have survived the car crash,'' Carmen told him, ''but you won't be so lucky this time. After I dispatch my stepdaughter, the next bullet is for you.''

''No!''

Stunned, Kim watched the crazed woman move the gun back toward her. Her stepmother's finger tightened against the trigger, and Kim knew she was a goner.

A shot was fired, but before Kim could react, Jerry leaped toward her, pushing her out of the way. Pain flared up her arm as she fell against the concrete floor. When she looked up, she saw Jerry facing off with Carmen.

Blood stained the center of his shirt, but he seemed unaware of anything other than removing the gun from Carmen's deadly grasp. He lunged at her, struggling with her as his strength quickly waned, trying to keep her from firing again.

Despite the pain in her arm, Kim rose to her feet, determined to help Jerry subdue her stepmother. But she was too late.

The gun went off again, this time seriously wounding Carmen. Dropping the weapon, Carmen clutched her bleeding side and stumbled out of the building.

Jerry fell to the floor, and Kim felt her heart sink. She knelt beside him, taking care not to cause him more pain as she cradled his head in her lap. His breathing came with difficulty.

She started to move, but he reached up and gripped her hand with amazing strength. "I won't leave you," she promised, "but I have to call for an ambulance for you and Carmen."

His grip remained firm. "Right about now, she should be meeting with a fatal accident." Jerry looked up at her, his eyes filled with a pain that came from more than his wound. "Her hourglass is almost empty. I could feel it just before the gun went off the second time."

Just the way he had felt that Kim's hours were limited? "But I have to get help for you," she insisted.

Tires screeched outside, lending credence to his words. And although Carmen had shown herself to be a horrible, self-centered person driven by greed, Kim couldn't help feeling sorry about her demise. Most of all, she hurt for the loss her father would feel upon learning of his wife's death. She prayed that his frail heart would be able to withstand the shock.

"No," Jerry said, stopping her with the urgency in his tone. "My mission is complete. I'm being called back home."

Kim's eyes filled with tears, blurring her vision.

"Don't cry for me," he said softly. "For I am the one who has been enriched by the time I've spent with you. I love you, Kim."

She felt his fingers loosen their hold on her hand, and she gripped them tightly, as if the gesture was enough to keep him from leaving her. "Please," she begged, her voice tight with emotion. "Please don't go."

Her fingers touched the gold pin above her breast, and

she recalled what he'd told her about his desire to protect her.

It might have been crazy and it might have been illogical, but somewhere deep down inside, something spoke to her. It was as if a tiny voice was assuring her he had been telling the truth all along. And, for the first time, she believed.

But why couldn't she have heard this inner voice sooner? Why couldn't she have spent the short time she'd had with him more meaningfully? She had come to love him deeply. How could she *not* have loved him? To have him torn away from her now, when she had just recognized how much he meant in her life, seemed so needlessly cruel.

But she was being selfish, thinking of her own loss at a time like this. She wiped the tears from her cheeks and noticed Jerry's eyelids slowly close.

"You finally earned your wings." And Kim was certain he would wear them well.

His eyes fluttered open again, and he fixed his clouded gaze on her. "I'd trade them in a second for one more day with you."

When he closed his eyes again, his body went limp in her arms. Kim's tears flowed harder as the anguish of her loss filled her soul.

In the next instant, the room filled with an eerie glow that rose from his body and lingered for a second near the ceiling before disappearing.

A knowledge filled her being, reminding her that she would see him again in fifty or more years, and she knew in the recesses of her heart that this knowledge was a message from Jerry. But, sadly, it was of little comfort to her now.

Kim's cry came out in a scream of despair.

"Congratulations, Jared." Nahum lifted himself and his massive wings from his ivy-covered chair and extended a hand. "You have reason to be proud."

Jerry returned the gesture, but he wasn't as enthused as he had anticipated. His victory felt empty and meaningless when he thought of going on without Kim. He remembered his earlier comment about fifty years passing in the blink of an eye, and he realized even that would be too long to wait to see her again.

"However," Nahum continued, "you were only supposed to save her, not sacrifice yourself for her."

Jerry didn't respond. His mind—and heart—were elsewhere.

"Never mind that," his superior said magnanimously. "I suggest you go straightaway to be fitted for your wings. Because of your dedication to your mission, the promotion committee and I decided that you have earned the right to bypass the beginner stage. You are hereby officially an intermediate-level protectorate."

Nahum beamed broadly.

He should have thanked him. Should have been more excited about this fantastic upturn in his career. He knew that if Nahum was disappointed by his poor response to the good news, then he would certainly be shocked by Jerry's request.

"I'd like to trade my wings for fifty more years with Kim," he announced.

"Your protectee?" Just as he'd expected, Nahum was

clearly stunned by the unexpected change in Jerry's attitude. "This is highly irregular," he insisted. "In fact, it's against the rules."

Jerry was respectful but firm when he countered, "You know I've never been one for following rules."

An anguished wail reached their ears. Nahum walked over to a large box and clicked it on.

"Hey, I thought only the Chairman of the Board had one of those," Jerry said.

"When He received the report of your assignment," Nahum explained, "He insisted that I get one to monitor your activities."

The picture showed a lovely dark-haired woman weeping over the body Jerry had formerly inhabited. She lifted her face, reddened and streaked with tears, and Jerry felt her grief as well as his own.

"Please don't take him from me," Kim pleaded as she aimlessly rocked the lifeless body in her arms. "I love him."

If it were within his ability, Jerry would be back with her that instant. But he was powerless to go to her or even to communicate with her. Restlessly, he paced the floor.

Her quiet, plaintive voice once again emanated from the viewing box. "Please don't do this to us."

Nahum, clearly affected by the display of heartrending emotion, snapped the picture off. After he had composed himself, the supervisor commented, "As you said before you left for your assignment, fifty years will pass in the blink of an eye." With a wink, he added, "Surely you won't be missed for such a short time."

Startled, Jerry searched his supervisor's face. When

Jerry had suggested trading the wings for more time with Kim, he knew such a thing had never been done before. Even so, he knew he had to try. Nahum wasn't inclined to joke, and he hoped he hadn't chosen now to start. If this was for real, Jerry knew the price of a pair of wings was minor compared to what he'd gain from spending the next five decades with the woman he had come to love.

"There's no need to give up your wings," Nahum decreed. "You earned them, Jared, and you should have them."

As the supervisor clasped his hands together, they disappeared beneath his billowing white sleeves. Jerry noticed a new row of gold braid adorning the robe. The risk Nahum had taken in handing Jerry this assignment had been rewarded by a promotion.

"Your new wings can be put in storage while you return to Earth to finish the life you began in Gerald's body."

This was even better than he had imagined possible. He wanted to whoop with joy and throw his arms around his stodgy-but-kindly boss. But an unfinished piece of business—a promise he had made—momentarily stilled his rejoicing. "Before I forget," Jerry said, "I'd like to put in a good word for Gerald's aunt, Rowena."

Nahum nodded solemnly. "It will be noted in her record."

Before Jerry could thank him or offer to polish Nahum's sandals for granting him extra time to spend with Kim, Jerry was sent into a whirling vortex that blurred time and space.

He awoke at the touch of a droplet on his cheek.

When he opened his eyes, he saw the face of his beloved. Although her eyes were puffy and red, she was the most beautiful creature he had ever seen.

"Oh, Jerry," she cried, hugging him to her breast. "I thought you had left me for good."

He reached up, cupping her delicate face in his hands. She leaned into his touch and kissed the palm of his hand.

Jerry urged her closer. Heedless of the searing pain in his midsection, he raised up to touch his lips to hers. The kiss was tender and sincere, and through it he sought to let her know that he would never leave her again.

When they parted and he relaxed back against her lap, he told her, "Believe me, Kim, I will be with you until the end of time."

"I believe you," she said, her voice catching in her throat.

And he knew she did. This time, they would be free to love each other without the shadow of Gerald hanging over them.

"I love you," he told her, "and if I have to, I will spend the next fifty years trying to persuade you to marry me."

Kim smiled down at him, and she looked absolutely luminous as she kissed him again.

Then, with a small shake of her head, she asked, "Who am I to argue about a marriage made in heaven?"

Remember the magic of the film
It's a Wonderful Life?
The warmth and tender emotion of
Truly, Madly, Deeply?
The feel-good humor of *Heaven Can Wait?*

Well, even if we can't promise you angels that look like
Alan Rickman or Warren Beatty, starting in June in
Harlequin Romance®, we can promise a brand-new
miniseries: GUARDIAN ANGELS. Featuring all of your
favorite ingredients for a perfect novel: great heroes,
feisty heroines and a breathtaking romance—all with a
celestial spin.

Look for Guardian Angels in:

June 1998: THE BOSS, THE BABY AND THE BRIDE (#3508)
by Day Leclaire

August 1998: HEAVENLY HUSBAND (#3516)
by Carolyn Greene

October 1998: A GROOM FOR GWEN (#3524)
by Jeanne Allan

December 1998: GABRIEL'S MISSION (#3532)
by Margaret Way

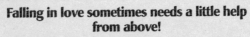

**Falling in love sometimes needs a little help
from above!**

Available wherever Harlequin books are sold.

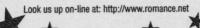

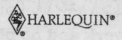

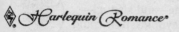

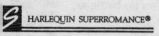

MEN at WORK

All work and no play?
Not these men!

July 1998

MACKENZIE'S LADY by Dallas Schulze

Undercover agent Mackenzie Donahue's
lazy smile and deep blue eyes were his best
weapons. But after rescuing—and kissing!—
damsel in distress Holly Reynolds, how could
he betray her by spying on her brother?

August 1998

MISS LIZ'S PASSION by Sherryl Woods

Todd Lewis could put up a building with ease,
but quailed at the sight of a classroom! Still,
Liz Gentry, his son's teacher, was no battle-ax,
and soon Todd started planning some
extracurricular activities of his own....

September 1998

A CLASSIC ENCOUNTER
by Emilie Richards

Doctor Chris Matthews was intelligent, sexy
and *very* good with his hands—which made
him all the more dangerous to single mom
Lizette St. Hilaire. So how long could she
resist Chris's special brand of TLC?

Available at your favorite retail outlet!

MEN AT WORK™

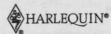 

Look us up on-line at: http://www.romance.net

PMAW2

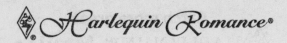
Harlequin Romance®

Get ready to meet the world's most eligible bachelors: they're sexy, successful and, best of all, they're all yours!

BACHELOR TERRITORY

Look out for these next two books:

September 1998:
WANTED: A PERFECT WIFE (#3521)
by Barbara McMahon

November 1998:
MY GIRL (#3529)
by Lucy Gordon

There are two sides to every relationship— and now it's his turn!

Available wherever Harlequin books are sold.

HARLEQUIN®
Makes any time special ™